THE FOUR BUBBAS OF THE APOCALYPSE:

FLATULENCE, HALITOSIS, INCEST, AND... NED

Edited by Selina Rosen

Second Edition ISBN-13: 978-1-945-941-02-3
The Four Bubbas of the Apocalypse: Flatulence, Halitosis, Incest, and... Ned, First Edition Copyright © 2003 by Yard Dog Press
Individual copyrights to authors of these new, original works as
      follows:
    "Foreword," © 2003 by Selina Rosen.
    "The Psycho Pigs Meet the Yumbie Bitch from Hell," © 2003 by Bill D. Allen.
    "The Ultimate Weapon," © 2003 by M.H. Bonham.
    "Savin' Ned," © 2003 Robert D. Brown.
    "Lefric Lights A Fart," © 2003 by James K. Burk.
    "Bubba and the Amazing Technicolor Dream Fart," © 2003 by James S.
        Dorr.
    "Bringing Home the Sauce," © 2003 by Linda J. Dunn.
    "A Rose By Any Other Name," © 2003 by Melanie Fletcher.
    "Bubba-Rap," © 2003 by Bennie Grezlik.
    "Yuppie Zombie Baby Farts," © 2003 by Matt Howl.
    "Bubba In A Blue Dress," © 2003 by Gary Jonas.
    "Mr. Ned and Dr. Ted," © 2003 by Andrew Zimmerman Jones.
    "Gas," © 2003 by John M. Lance.
    "83 Best Monkeys," © 2003 by Lee W. Lindsay, Jr.
    "Widder Liggett and the Breath O' God," © 2003 by Lee Martindale.
    "Attack of the Godless Undead Zombies," © 2003 by Tracy S. Morris.
    "The Bubbas of Troy County," © 2003 by Gloria Oliver.
    "Home Baked Air Biscuits," © 2003 by Garrett Peck.
    "Hal's Crossroads," © 2003 by Robert Pickering.
    "A Crazy Tasty Love Story," © 2003 by Mark Shepherd.
    "Raven's Back In Town," © 2003 by Bradley H. Sinor.
    "Sweet Meat," © 2003 by Glenn R. Sixbury.
    "The Siege and Investiture of the Athens BilMart," © 2003 by Mark W.
        Tiedemann.
    "The Boys From Brownsville," © 2003 by Jeff Turner.
    "Why A Good Man Nowadays Is Hard To Find," © 2003 by Laura J.
        Underwood.
    "1001 Alabama Nights," © 2003 by Billy Vincent.
    "Flatulence, Halitosis, Incest, and... Ned," © 2003 by Selina A. Rosen.
    "Ned and the Cookie Girls," © 2003 by Julia Blackshear Kosatka.
    "Flatulence," "Halitosis," "Incest," and "Ned," four poems © 2003 by Paul D.
        "Ajax" Hocker.

All rights reserved, including the right to reproduce this book or portions thereof in any form, including electronic format, except for purposes of review.
Yard Dog Press
710 W. Redbud Lane
Alma, AR 72921-7247
http://www.yarddogpress.com

Edited by Selina Rosen
Copy Editor Leonard R. Bishop
Technical Editor Lynn Stranathan
Cover art by Keith Berdak.
First Edition December 1, 2003.
Second Edition October, 2016
Printed in the United States of America
0 9 8 7 6 5 4 3 2 1

TABLE OF CONTENTS

FOREWORD

If y'all has read Bubbas of the Apocalypse, then ya kin jus' go on ahead an read the first story. If not... What kind of a commie pinko, pervert are ya! Get yer cheap ass up an' go buy ya a copy right now! What ya tryin' ta do, break us? Christ on a crutch! How ya 'spect us ta buy our chew an' make the trailer house payments?

Case ya didn't guess from the title, this here book's jus' about the same as that first one, 'cept in this one all the writers had to use one of the four Bubbas of the Apocalypse, Flatulence, Halitosis, Incest or Ned.

In case ya is still refusin' to buy the first book or ya jus' need a reminder, here's the background...

In the year 2025 the worst happened. A deadly virus known only as Yuppie 25 escaped from a secret government lab (it is believed that it was tracked out on a piece of toilet paper stuck to the bottom of a scientist's shoe). The air borne virus spread quickly through out the fifty states, and thanks to unusually low airfares that year within weeks the entire world was infected. Scientists worked day and night to try to find a cure, but most of them were already infected and succumbed to the Yuppie madness before they could find an antidote.

One scientist, Hector Von Trap, noticed that certain people of a certain class and lifestyle seemed to be completely immune to the bug. Upon testing several of these subjects he found an unusual enzyme in their blood.

Further testing linked the strange enzyme to a cheap preservative used in generic barbecue sauce, which apparently mutated when it was grilled. He learned that individuals who had consumed large amounts of the barbecue sauce on grilled meats over their life times had built up a natural immunity to Yuppie 25. Hector was well on his way to perfecting the cure when he succumbed to Yuppie madness and choked to death trying to eat his PC.

There was rioting on a global scale, as leaders died leaving countries with no leadership and no laws. The sick and dying filled with the Yuppie madness went on killing rampages, while those yet uninfected fought for their lives and searched for food. The cities and suburbs were the first to go up in smoke.

Within in a few months most of the population of the earth was dead. Only Bubbas and their families survived untouched.

In some business professionals who had spent their entire lives in front of PC's, Yuppie 25 mutated and they live on as crazed deranged Yuppies. They have cocktail parties and still go into the office and try to maintain an upper middle class lifestyle. They also eat human flesh.

While all of these Yuppie-zombies, sometimes called Yumbies, consume human flesh, mutations differ from one locale to another. Some are groaning, hardly moving imbeciles while other are fully mobile, you might even say upwardly mobile, and while they are completely out of their minds don't smell of rotting flesh and can even pass themselves off as normal for short periods of time. While the actual cause for the variations of zombie subculture is not completely known (cause ah all them scientists dyin' off fore they could figger it out) it is believed by most that the level of the severity of a Yumbie's zombieness can be weighed in exact correlation to the amount of Brie he consumed in his lifetime.

Many Bubbas were out hunting or fishing when the virus hit, or were in trailer parks where no one was affected, so they had no idea that civilization was crumbling all around them. Especially since they never did pay any attention to that gol-danged CNN.

Bubbas are now our last best hope for humanity.
GOD HELP US ALL!!!

Yep, if ya done read *Bubbas of the Apocalypse*, 'bout now yer sayin'. "Shiiit that's almos' t'azaclly the same as the openin' ah the first book!"

Well yeah, dumb ass, I done told ya that. Now stop yer belly achin' an read yerself this fine collection of stories 'bout fartin', bad breath, sleepin' with yer kinfolk, and our old buddy Ned. Yep, this sure nuff is some classy stuff.

FLATULENCE, HALITOSIS, INCEST AND NED

Selina Rosen

Everythin' had been perfect for us till that bastard showed up.

Let me explain. See for us over in Justin Holler, Arkansas, the Plague weren' the end ah the world – t'was the beginnin'. Till then none of us had ever had more than two cents ta rub together. We was always jus' minutes from havin' ta beat the shit outah some poor repo guy – who was jus doin' his job – in order ta keep a trailer house roof over our heads and four beat up pickup truck wheels under our asses.

We was always hittin' each other up for five bucks to tide us over till payday. Hell, there was one five bucks I was sure traded hands between me, Jim Bob, Roger and Ned for 'bout three years. One of us always a'owin' it ta one of the others.

Cops was always comin' to the trailer park haulin' someone off for one bogus charge or 'nother. Sellin' beer out of a fridge on the front porch in a dry county had landed nearly every male body in the trailer park ta jail at one time or nother. Not payin' child support. Failure to pay some ticket or other. Hell, Cousin Merv got towed off fer sleepin' with cousin Yerlin. Never did understand why she didn' have ta go ta jail, too. Jim Bob said it had somethin' ta do with her bein' sixteen an' underage.

Till then I didn' know there was an age limit on sleepin' with yer cousin.

Then there was all the freakin' preachers. Our women folk would grab all them screamin' brats an' haul 'em on down ta church ever so often jus' so as they wouldn' come out like us. They'd come home all "filled with the spirit," an it was a sure bet we wouldn' be gettin' us no pussy till they come down off their religious high horses. My woman was always given some stupid pud wackin' preacher my beer an' Skoal money, so I hated those fat polyester wearin' bastards even more than I hated the cops. After all, if ya was careful ya could sneak around an keep the cops off yer back, but them damn preachers was everywhere an they turned our women folk inta spies and enforcers of God's law.

Cops and preachers were both 'bout doin' the same thing – makin' sure that no normal feller got out of their place. Yuppies liked havin' someone to look down on, an' they couldn' very well do that if we was doin' as good as them, so way I figured it cops an preachers were workin' for the yuppies ta make sure we jus' flat couldn' ever get ahead.

Anyways, all that persecution come to a screechin' halt when the plague hit.

Me an Ned was off fishin' – an' jus gettin' away from the women an' our kids fer a few days – so we didn' even know nothin' was wrong till we got home an' my old lady was a yellin'. Started tellin' me that one of our brats had done been et by a zombie in a fancy business suit carryin' a brief case. I asked if she was sure he hadn' jus been carried off by some fuller brush man, an' she said no it was a zombie fer sure. I asked how she knowed it was a zombie since none of us had seen one afore, an' she said it was cause of he et little Alfie junior.

Don' get choked up none on junior's account. My name ain't Alfie, an' that little bastard weren' one ah mine. He was the spawn of Mary Jean's first husband, Alfred Simmons, who had been incarcerated for cookin' meth.

Alfie junior was a retarded, booger eatin' little shit. Mary Jean said she figured he et some of them meth ingredients when he was a toddler, an' hadn' been right in the head ever since. Any way, he weren' no great loss in my book, an' I never will understand why Mary Jean was makin' such a fuss. It weren' like the zombie got any ah the good kids. Any way, nothin' would do but that me an' Ned went right after this zombie dude.

Hell, we couldah jus' sat there on the porch an' drunk us a couple of beers. By the time Ned an' I caught up, the rest of the fellers had tracked him down, had him hangin' in a tree by his ankles an was jus' havin' some fun playin' with him. Sort of like a cat plays with a mouse 'for he eats it.

That was the beginnin' of what we all like to call the Time of Good an' Plenty.

Folks everywhere was droppin' like flies from the Yuppie 25. There weren' many of them zombie things out our way, and they weren' that hard ta kill. Course we'd been ready for some sort of popacolypse for as long as I could remember and we had us enough fire power to fight a small war.

The power went off after awhile, so did the water an' the gas, but we was all used to it bein' turned off on a fairly regular basis anyhow, so it was really like nothin' had changed. 'Cept none of us had ta go to work, an' the power wasn' gonna come back on again when we paid the bill.

Yep, we was livin' the high life.

That was up till we started to run low on the essentials of life, like charcoal briquettes, beer, pork rinds, an' moon pies.

That was when it dawned on me. The whole world was basically ours for the pickin'! All those fancy houses were just sittin' there in Little Rock, with their fancy SUVs sittin' in them garages bigger than most of our trailers, an' weren' none of it bein' used. There were plenty of grocery, liquor stores and Wal-Mart's filled to the gunnels with stuff jus' sittin' an' waitin' fer someone to use it – an' it might as well be us.

Well, we moved right on in and took over the city. Oh, we had to kill a few of them there zombie things, but there weren' that many in Little Rock, and the few fellers that had lived through the plague and hadn' turned into them zombies, well, they was good ole boys an gals jus' like us. Go figger.

Well, we didn' stay there too long cause one day as Ned, Jim Bob, Roger and me was jus' sittin' on the bank of the river fishin' an drinkin' beer, ole Roger – he always was one smart sonofahbitch – gets this real thoughtful look on his face an says, "Disney World."

"Disney World?" I asks.

"I read where they had switched everythin' over ta run on solar power a few years back, an'... well... I sure do miss TV an' stuff. They got plenty ah power there, an' I was jus' thinkin' what's ta stop us from movin' inta Disney World?"

Well, weren' a damn thing, so we did. We loaded up our new SUV's an' weeniebegoes with grub an' beer, grabbed the battery operated pump we used to get gas, an' headed for Floredee.

There was a shit pct load of them zombies at Disney World, but that was sort've a good thing, cause they had done et up most ah them dead bodies 'fore we got there. Sides, we made short work of them things – stuck them an' the rest ah the bodies in a huge freezer. We thaw one out every few days an' throw it to the lions. There was some stuff what needed fixin', but we had us plenty of duct tape an' bailin' wire, an' sooner then you could say jeecoozee we were livin' in the lap oh luxury. We rode the monorails from one park to another, an' in an' out of the hotels. There was food an' booze of every kind, everywhere, an' we lived in the hotel rooms, an' when one got dirty we didn' clean it – we just moved.

An' talk about huntin' an fishin'! Well boy, howdy! That Animal Kingdom was jus' full oh hungry animals. We kilt an' et the weak ones first, then the ones that annoyed us. Aardvark tasted perty funny, too much damn nose, an' no matter how much barbeque sauce you slather on it, I jus' cain't eat it. Monkey ain't too bad, an' neither is parrot. Kangaroos ain't nothin' but grizzle an' bone, like chewin' on a rubber tire.

Old man Hanks'd, had him a farm 'fore he lost all his money playin' bingo an' had to sell out to a land developer. He said he reckoned on how antelopes an' Gerafies weren' that much different than goats an' sheep. An zebras weren' nothin' in the world but striped horses. He learned us how to take care of the animals over in the Safari, an now whenever we want ta have us a barbeque we go out on Safari an bag us somethin'.

If we really want some fun, we let one of them lions out with the other animals an' then try to shoot it with one of them tranc darts – found boxes of those suckers there. One day a bunch of us hit one ah them poor bastard all at once. Took ole Leo 'bout a week to wake up. He's mostly all right now, though occasionally he falls over for no apparent reason what so ever.

As for fishin'... Well, ain't one single body oh water in this place ain't stocked to the gunnels with them pretty colored carp, an' let me tell ya they ain't bad eatin'.

Yep, we had it all, an' best of all weren' no one to tell us what we could an' couldn' do. All the old rules had been torn down, an' we were truly the kings of all we surveyed. Hell, we even had us a castle!

If we wanted to fart an' belch at the dinner table, we did. We bathed when we felt like bathin' an' brushed our teeth when an' if we felt like it. If some guy wanted to sleep with his cousin, no one said nothin' bout it. Everyone minded their own damn business.

We were livin' in Walt Disney's dream world. We weren'

hurtin' no one, an no one was hurtin' us, cause if they tried we kilt em.

Some other people came to join us from time to time and if they weren' the brain eattin' undead we welcomed them with open arms. We weren' greedy or selfish; there was enough to go round.

But like they say, no good deed goes unpunished, an' it was bein' so damn friendly that got us saddled with "that" ass hole.

He'd come drivin' right up to Cinderella's castle in a big ole white Cadillac, and we should ah known the minute he stepped out in his green and brown checked polyester suit with his hair as tall as his face was wide, an' his belly so big it hid his belt buckle, that he was gonna ta be trouble. I guess that if me an' the boys had gotten' ta him first we would ah gotten rid ah him 'fore he could start his shit. But it weren' us but the women folk what greeted him, an' that was very nearly the beginnin' of the end of our uruptia.

"Gather round, gather round!" he yelled out, an' already I knowed I wasn' gonna like him. See he hadn' been there ten minutes an' he was already tellin' us what ta do.

"My name is Reverend Gerald K. Rowdy, an' I have come here today to give you the one thing you are sorely missing."

"Far as I knew we ain't missin' nothin'," Ned said. "An ifin somethin' goes missin' I think we know whose ass ta kick."

Why that rude bastard ignored Ned like he hadn' said shit, an' he didn't know Ned like we did, so there weren' no cause for that.

"I have come to bring you the word of the almighty God."

"A preacher!" the woman all said at once, an' from the look of them an' the sound of their combined voices, ya would ah thought Elvis his own self had just arrived.

Well, as soon as we heard, we boys knew it was goin' to be bad. See preachers... Well, like I told ya, they ain't never meant nothin' but trouble fer normal folks. Spent most of their time taking money from our stupid women folk an makin' up rules that them same women folk 'spected us ta live up to while all the time that preacher man is a breakin' those rules as fast as he can make em up.

That very night as I was sittin' in my shorts in the middle of the king-sized bed finishin' up the rest of the nuts from the little fridge there was in everyone of them rooms, my woman Mary come into the room a'screamin' an' a'hollerin' like she'd gotten a tick on her snatch.

"Ya has got ta clean yerself up, ya smell like death!"

I looked at her like she was crazy. Hell, I'd just took me a bath not two days before.

"Yer a bad example fer the kids," she said.

I frowned some confused. "Which kids?" I asked.

"Our kids. Suzy, Billy Bob and little Elmore."

Elmore *is* my name.

"Hell, woman, we hardly even see them damn kids no more. They sleep in the next room over and spend all their time on Space Mountain."

"I think we should spend more time with the kids, honey," she said, and that was when I knowd fer sure she had done been brain washed.

'Bout a week later as Ned an' I were goin' to the Pirates of the Carapeein, jus' 'cause we hadn' been in a day or two, we saw the women folk an' the kids all dressed up an' freshly bathed, standin' in line outside the Small World ride.

"That's jus' wrong," Ned said. An' I knew exactly what he meant. No one in their right mind wanted to hear those stupid dolls singin'. It was a shit ride.

"What the hell's goin' on?" I asked.

"Reverend Rowdy is a holdin' a revival," several women said at once.

"Well fuck that shit!" I shouted out loud.

"Elmore Jacobs, you watch yer mouth," Mary Jean ordered, and I knew from the tone in her voice I wasn' gonna get me no lovin' fer a couple ah days. Least ways not from her.

"I cain't wait ta hear his sermon," cousin Yerlen said. "Right here in the Church of It's A Small World."

"Wouldn' hurt you or your stupid friend none to come hear the good word," Mary Jean said.

I cringed, then grabbed Ned's arm – figurin' he was the stupid friend she was referrin' to – an' drug him aside. "Maybe we should go."

"Ain't no piece ah pussy, no matter how sweet, worth listen ta no preacher scream an holler fer two, three hours," Ned said.

"It ain't fer the pussy, dumb ass," I said, slappin' him upside the head with my good John Deer cap. "That feller there's the enemy, an' we might ought to know what he's a feedin' our women folk." I could see Ned still weren' convinced, so I said, "Look at them poor kids, Ned, they look like sheep bein' lead ta the slaughter. Someone's gottah save them. We don' want our kids growin' up like that fat bastard, do we?"

Ned said he reckoned on how he could go through the torment seein' as it was ta save the kids an' all.

We all filed onto those little boats an' rode down towards the main chamber. He had programmed them dolls to sing a different song but it had the same tune. I don' remember the song exactly, but it went somethin' like this;

> "It's a world of evil, a world of sin
> It's a world of beer and too much gin
> Things would be really great if you'd all cooperate
> It's a filthy, dirty world.
> There is too much farting and Halitosis
> Sleeping with your cousin
> You won't get any rest.
> You will all burn in hell if you don't learn to floss
> It's a bad, bad evil world.
> It's an evil world after all
> It's an evil..."

Ah hell, you get the gist I'm sure.

I took my gun out of its holster an' shot me a couple ah them dolls 'bout the third time those stupid things sang. Would ah shot them all with Ned laughin' the whole time ifin Mary didn' start screamin' again.

"Elmore Jacobs, ya stop shootin' God's little plastic disciples right this minute! I swear, yer headed straight fer hell!"

I sighed and holstered my gun. That guy was goin' to ruin everythin' unless we could find some way to get rid of him. I muttered as much to Ned, who nodded in agreement. We finally made it to the main chamber where the little boats stopped, an' we all filed out to stand in amongst the dolls. By this time I was holdin' my hands over my ears to keep out the sound of those demented little plastic shits singing their stupid little song, an' it was obvious that the women folks was all in a trance of sorts.

Yep, this guy was some sort of genius.

I kicked one ah them dolls jus fer spite, an' when my old

lady glared at me I acted like it was a accident.

"Brothers and sisters," Reverend Rowdy started with a fine preacher rumble. "I'm glad so many of you were able to come. I had a vision last night of the future, a vision of all the evils of this new world, and I saw as I looked out across the land that there was nothing left but smoldering ash, and an angel of the Lord came unto me, and I asked, 'What happened here,' and this is what the servant of the Most High said unto me his lowly servant. 'See ye how the world lays in waste?' and I said 'Yes, that's what I was asking about.' And he said, 'This is what will become of the world if things are allowed to continue as they have. When all those people died it should have been a time of great rejoicing, for the Lord had brought judgment against all of the evil-doers of the world, but too soon God's chosen did turn away from all which God had given them. They squandered their bounty, and they turned away from God's will. Flatulence, halitosis, and incest became as a way of life for them, and stupidity was treated as a virtue."

An' I swear that bastard looked right at Ned when he said that last bit. Course Ned proved he deserved it when he lent over and whispered, "Ya suppose God really said that bout fartin' an stuff?"

I wrapped him in the head with my knuckles. "God didn' talk ta him ya knumbnuts," I said in an' angry whisper.

"Ouch! Elmore, that hurt," Ned said rubbin' his head.

"It was spossed to, ya dumb ass."

Reverend Rowdy had stopped talkin' and was lookin' right at us. All the women folk was lookin' at us too, an' they let out a huge communal *shsh!* liked ta knock the caps right off our heads.

Reverend Rowdy continued. "And I said to the angel of God, 'How can I stop them from destroying the world?' and he said, 'Tell them to repent, to learn some manners and keep themselves and their space clean. To turn away from sleeping with their kin and to brush regularly twice daily, also tell them to keep their flatulence pent insideth themselves till they goeth to the bathroom, then let it blow forth as a mighty wind, but not until then. For all the destruction you see before you was caused by a large communal pooney.'"

That's right. He called a fart a *pooney*. Yep, he was sure nuff a pretty talker.

Me an' Ned didn' listen no more, we'd done heard enough.

We walked back up the service path and called us our own meetin'.

All us men was gathered there in the Bear Country restaurant – an' newly appointed bar — when I called the meetin' to order in the usual fashion.

"Hey ya dumb asses shut up for a minute this here's important."

"What's up?" Roger asked, "More Zombies?"

"You wish, it's that damned preacher," I said, then I told them all of what that dumb fuck had said to our women an' the kids.

"Well we gottah kill him." Jim Bob said without a second thought.

"No," Roger waved his hands in the air all excited like. "We cain't jus' kill him. Then our old ladies will turn on us bigger than shit. They'll be sure he was right 'bout everythin' and that we done went an' shot the servant ah God. We'll have ta do our own cookin' an' warshin'. We'll have ta do *everythin'* ourselves, if ya know what I mean."

An' of course we all did cept Ned. Fortunately he was pickin' his nose an' not really listenin' so we didn' have to waste time 'splainin' it to him.

"Roger's right," I said. "We'll have ta kill him right quiet like an' then feed him ta the lions late at night."

"No... That'd be worse. They'd think God had done took him up cause ah him bein' so righteous and all. No. We has to decredit him," Roger said.

I said it before, an' I'm sayin' it again, that Roger is one smart sonofahbitch.

We worked on our problem an' a keg of beer fer most of the evenin' an' came up with one hell of a plan.

"Why's it got ta be me?" Ned asked.

"Cause ya volunteered, Ned," I said.

"I don' think I did," Ned insisted. He didn't, but he didn't know it.

"Sure ya did," Roger assured him.

"All right then, but make it quick." Ned stood up tall an' gritted his teeth. Jim Bob raked his fingernails down Ned's face, leaving bloody marks. Ned yelped like a schoolgirl.

"Christ on a crutch!" Ned protested.

"Now bite his shoulder," I ordered Jim Bob, who turned to

me makin' a face.

"You sure *I* volunteered?" he asked.

"Sure ya did," I said. Hell, he didn't remember, either. That's what he gets for hoggin' the beer.

"Ya could ah bathed, Ned." Jim Bob made a face then moved forward an' bit Ned's shoulder.

"Christ, that's enough!" Ned yelled in pain. Good thing the rooms are mostly soundproof, or he'd have brought people runnin' in way before we wanted them to.

It wasn' bleeding, but it was good enough. I poked my finger into the blood drippin' down Ned's face an' smeared it around the bite mark to make it look worse. We'd already ripped up a shirt for Ned to wear, an he put it on.

Weren' too long after that ole Reverend Rowdy opens the door an' walks in his motel room, like he don' have a care in the world. He knowed he was wrong 'bout that as soon as he seen us.

"What the hell?" he yelped.

"We come for a little spiritual healin' Preacher man," I said pointin' my gun at him even as Roger and Jim Bob did the same.

He smiled then. I guess he figured he could smooth talk us. "Now what are you boys up to?" he asked.

"Go on, Ned," I ordered, an' Ned opened the door an' ran from the room screamin' like a banchie.

"Zombie! Zombie! The preacher's a Zombie!" he yelled.

Ole Rowdy must have realized he was screwed then, because he looked at us an' said, "All I wanted to do was bring the good Lord's word to you folks."

"Nah. Ya was jus' tryin' to make yerself God, jus' like preachers always do," I said. We all took a turn killin' him, an' then before any of the women folk could get there we smeared his own blood all over his mouth.

Every woman in Disney World was there in a matter of minutes, an' I 'splaned things to them.

"Ned came here to talk to the preacher cause he felt powerful bad bout sleepin' with his cousin after hearin' the preacher's sermon. He starts pourin' out his soul, an' that guy tried ta *eat* him! Good thing we happened along when we did. Turns out he was a zombie." I carefully showed them all the damnin' evidence we had "found"—the mini fridge filled with brie, bottled water, an' wine coolers. The copies of GQ magazine, the polo shirts an' khakis hidden under his polyester suits. "You women thought ya was lettin' God in, an all ya was doin' was openin' the doors an' given' yer children up ta the devil his own self."

We went right that minute an' burnt the Small World to the ground just on principle.

Well, all them women folk they felt plum sorry 'bout what they'd done an' how they'd been actin'. I don' think we'll have ta worry 'bout them lettin' no damn preacher move in again soon, and if they do we'll know jus' how ta get rid of him.

In the meantime we've once again made the world safe for flatulence, halitosis, incest, and Ned.

THE END

Selina Rosen is the kind of asshole that would edit an anthology, give her story the coveted first spot, then basically shuffle all the other stories and just stick them in haphazardly and pretend like they were placed where they were for a reason.

Check out her website at www.selinarosen.com.

FLATULENCE
Ajax

Big Cecil was speedin' on his way out of town
From the Baptist church chili feed which now was shut
down
Nearly twenty-four gallons was cooked for the feed
And barely three quarts were left over for seed
Big Cecil was sweatin' and so was Darlene
And the kids in the truck bed was soundin' obscene
With the groanin' and squeelin' of gas on the go
Darlene knew Cecil was ready to blow
He was turned an odd color, and his bug eyes were tellin'
His size forty-eight jeans were unbuttoned for swellin'
He had held on too long and now the full berth
Was unleashed in sick glory on an innocent Earth
The belching had ended; and now came the worst
Darlene leaned out the window, and then Cecil burst
The truck lurched to the left, bark stripped off the trees
A lot full of hogs were dropped to their knees
The chillun's were gagging, Darlene was flushed white
The blast set sleeping folks bolt upright
A whole flock of sparrows lay dead on the clay
A chunk of the truck seat was burned clean away
Cecil wiped away tears to clear up his sight
As a tentative peace settled over the night.

BUBBA AND THE AMAZING TECHNICOLOR DREAM FART

James S. Dorr

Cast Into the Desert

Bubba Joe was abandoned, sold into slavery – or worse! – to the Yumbies. Well, maybe not that, not sold exactly, but he *had* been kicked out of the trailer village by the village chief himself, and here he was, easy prey for anyone who came along.

Bubba Joe was no fool. He knew well enough that where he had been left anyone who came along would be a Yumbie, a slavering, slobbering, long-pig-eating Yuppie. Moreover, Bubbas had been disappearing. Fourteen in all had gone out of the village on various errands over the last months and not one had come back – except, of course, for the ones like those who had left him, who had taken the precaution of safety in numbers.

And all he had done was diddle Cindy Lou, the village chief's daughter. Well, maybe not diddle exactly, but he and she, despite the fact that she had a bad cold, had gotten through *most* of the preliminaries.

That was when her father had caught them.

Bubba Joe had been quick. His pants still in his hand, he had risen and smiled. "Hello, sir," he said. "As I'll bet you may have already guessed, me and your daughter love each other very much. In fact" – he thought quickly – "I'd like to marry her."

"Oooh!" Cindy Lou squealed.

Cindy Lou's father, however, was not impressed.

"She is of age," the village chief said. "It's time she be married, but not to you, Bubba Joe. You're too uncouth for her."

"Wh-what do you mean?" Bubba Joe said, aghast. The thought had come to him; he really did love her. Even enough that he *wanted* to get hitched. "Before, when we was dating, you know how other fellas just come up the trailer and whistle a gal out. But I always walked up to the screen door and knocked, didn't I, just like a gentleman?"

"That's true," the chief said.

"And I never come empty handed either, but I always brought her flowers or something, what I picked myself, didn't I?"

"You did," the chief said.

"And I always call you 'sir,' and your missus 'ma'am,' don't I?"

"You do," the chief said.

"Then what's this 'uncouth' shit?"

The village chief told Cindy Lou to get dressed and go help her mother, then turned back to Bubba Joe. "It's like this," he said, "you know how you get when you've had a couple beers?"

"So I get a little gassy, so what?"

"A *little gassy!* You stink up the whole goldarned trailer park, Bubba Joe, from front to back and top to bottom. You lay a brown cloud down what nothing can live in, hardly, but what we've been drinking beer too and laying our own farts. But even then what you cut's in its own class, rising high and outward, like one of them toadstool clouds, all poison-like an' double obnoxious – well, shucks, even Cindy Lou would tell you, weren't for the cold she has stuffing her nose all up."

"B-but -" Bubba Joe started.

"I ain't the first one to complain 'bout this either," the village chief said, and that had been it. Kaput. Finished and done for.

The village council had even voted, and Bubba Joe was out, wandering the wilderness. Cast out alone in the desert – or, maybe not the desert exactly, but a sort of wilderness anyway, of scrub pine and brushwood. And sometimes clearings, and maybe a stream or two.

Bubba and Potfer's Wife

Bubba Joe had been searching for one of those streams, because the sun was out and burning hot and the no 'count kind of woods he was in didn't offer much shade, and so he was thirsty. Instead of a stream, though, he came to a clearing, one all kind of mossy and grassy and with a great big flat rock dab in its center.

A woman sat on the rock, her legs crossed demurely, the way a real *lady* might cross her legs.

Bubba Joe crouched and gawked.

Part of Bubba Joe's reptile brain warned him: *This is a Yumbie female. Beware.* But another part answered, *She's beautiful, Joe! Almost as pretty as your Cindy Lou. Ain't wearing much clothes either!*

Bubba Joe strode from the brush he'd been crouched in, a smile on his face. "Name's Joe," he began.

"My name's Mrs. Potfer," the woman purred, placing a slight emphasis on the "Mrs." She inclined her head toward the large, armed man who had just emerged from behind a tree, then looked again at Bubba Joe. "You know why they call me that?"

Bubba Joe stopped. His eyes lingered over her tight-fitting shorts and her gold lame halter-top, then moved beyond to the large muscular man who had begun to scowl.

He thought real hard. "I, uh, guess 'cause your husband's a pretty rich guy," he finally said. "Like he got a lot more than just a *pot fer* to piss in."

"You know," Mrs. Potfer said, scowling herself now, "for a Bubba you're a pretty smart guy yourself. I think we'll take you to our Yuppie Leader."

She turned again to her male companion who had by now grabbed Bubba Joe by the shoulder. "What do you think, honey?"

The large man smiled. "I think that'll do just fine." He chuckled, gnashing his teeth together, a sound-combination that did not improve Bubba Joe's confidence – especially when Mrs. Potfer joined in too. "Our Leader *likes* smart guys."

Bubba Interprets the Dream of Pharaoh Pete

Bubba Joe was ushered into a throne room, its dark walls covered with pictures of things like birds and snakes and women with vulture wings, and maybe more snakes too, and faced a huge man in a gray pinstriped loin cloth wearing a funny hat.

"I am the Yuppie Leader," the man intoned, blowing smoke from his cigar through his nostrils. "My subjects call me Pharaoh Pete because I originally come from Memphis – well, not exactly the one in Egypt, but you know, in Tennessee. My wife's lady in waiting, Mrs. Potfer, tells me that you're a pretty smart Bubba." The huge man leaned real close. "She tells me your name's Joe."

"Er, yessir, it is, sir," Bubba Joe answered.

"So, you smart like she says you are?"

Bubba Joe nodded – he lowered his eyes to look at the stain spreading over his trousers. He had just then noticed Pharaoh Pete's sharpened teeth. How his eyes looked hungry, how his nose quivered.   He remembered the Potfers's gnashing chuckles.

The pharaoh again blew smoke out of his nostrils. "Then I've got a question. Suppose that I had... well, suppose that I had this *dream*. In this, uh, dream my hunters had brought these Bubbas to me, just like you, and put them all in this pen. Now, when I went to inspect the pen, I found that there were seven fat Bubbas and seven lean Bubbas. Now what's that dream mean?"

Bubba Joe thought hard. "You and your subjects, you fixing to *eat* those Bubbas?" he asked.

Pharaoh Pete snorted. "I'm fixing to eat *you* if you don't give me a good answer. What I'm worried about, you see, is that maybe it's a sign that we'll be catching lots of you Bubbas for, say, the next seven years, but then there might not be that many of you left for seven years after that. So what should I do?"

Bubba Joe scratched his head. "If I was you, I'd fatten those seven skinny ones up then. That way you'd end up having all fourteen fat ones."

This time Pharaoh Pete paused, as if *he* were thinking. "It might be worth a try," he finally said, his voice somewhat dubious. "How do you suggest we should go about doing that?"

Bubba Joe, recalling his thirst, had a ready answer. "Beer'll do it," he said. "In fact, if you got a can or two handy, I'll show you how myself."

Pharaoh Pete clapped his hands, summoning all his attendants to him. "Bring Bubba Joe beer," he ordered, "and not just cans, but a whole keg. Ice it down good and bring him a mug, too, right here in the palace. I wish to see this with my very own eyes."

Bowing, the well-trained Yumbies complied, including the

Potfers, until all were once again assembled to watch Bubba Joe drink. He drank first one mug full, and then another, starting off slow to build a good base in his lower belly. He blew foam off a third mug – no sense drinking just air – and quaffed it down more quickly, working into a long term stride by his fourth and fifth and sixth. Sipping, chugging, by his eighth or ninth mug he felt a small rumbling somewhere in his bowels. No big deal yet, just a small *poot! poot!* kind of thing. Clearing pipes as it were.

Then by his fourteenth or fifteenth mug, he felt more of a thundering, a major intestinal shaking and shuddering – a building of pressure in his colon. He held it in, straining to keep sphincter muscles closed. No use wasting beer, even in gaseous form. But then by his twentieth or maybe twenty-first muscles could hold no more.

Acquiescing to fate he rolled on one cheek, spreading his hams wide.

Bubba Joe let fly!

Roaring and screeching, tornadic winds rushed forth, roiling in brown clouds, in siennas and burnt umbers, all good earth-tone colors, to fill the throne room, the palace, the city. This was no mere fart, no mere big poot or demi-blat. Nor was it even a fabled ring-tailed snorter, but more than that, more than all fart-kinds combined. All classifications.

This was an *earthquake*-fart, a gaseous volcano erupting and bubbling for ten minutes and longer. Now greens, now yellow fogs mixed with the swirling browns. Stenches of sewers, of toilets and outhouses mixed with the sights and sounds, until one could not tell one from the other.

Yuppies fled, gagging, those few who survived the initial blast.

Finally, relaxing, Bubba Joe took a nap, belching and bubbling both from top and bottom now. These were only echoes, though, like tiny aftershocks, almost drowned out by his well-earned snores.

The Rescue Of Bubba's Lost Trailer Park Brethren

When Bubba Joe woke, he found out that the keg had somehow tipped over. The beer was all spilled. Having no reason, therefore, to linger, he left the palace by its rear door, going out through the kitchen.

In the back yard, behind the pantry, he found a chain-link, razor wire-topped enclosure. Above its locked gate there was a sign: EXPERIMENTAL BUBBA FARM PROGRAM, HOLDING PEN #1.

He recognized the figures inside, the fourteen missing Bubbas from his own village!

He thought of pharaoh's dream. "Some dream!" he muttered.

He found some wire clippers and opened the pen's gate. He called them out to him, the fat and the lean ones. Seven of each, he saw, more or less anyway.

"You guys okay?" he asked.

One of them shook his head. "Funny thing you should ask. Last night there was some kind of explosion. I don't know what it was, but, whooey, what a stench it made. Like as 'ud killed us, if we hadn't all fainted."

"Yeah," said another one. This was a female that Bubba Joe recognized. Maisy was her name and he had dated her, briefly, before he had set his heart for Cindy Lou. In fact, she had dumped him.

"Yeah," she repeated. "It was something awful. Like – like that time you and I went out, Joe, do you remember? That smell like the skunk works and glue factory combined? It was like that, this noxious brown cloud, glowing from the middle, like some kind of science fiction movie or something. Then we started gagging and coughing something awful." She stopped and looked around, first at Bubba Joe, then at the others. "You got any idea what it might have been?" she asked.

Bubba Joe shook his head. Then someone else added: "You know, I can still smell a little of it now. Eeeeew, boy it was sickening!"

Someone else nodded, this one an old hunting buddy of Bubba Joe's, back before whatever it was that happened, that turned the Yuppies all into cannibals. Back when they could come and go from their village without danger.

Someone else nodded, too. "Anyway it seems to have chased off the Yumbies. Maybe we should leave' too."

Maisy chimed in again. "Yeah, 'fore they come back. That is, if they come back. Eeeeew, you can still smell it, soaked in the dirt and stuff! Better we burn our clothes, too, when we get home."

The Bubbas' Migration Back To the Village

Upon their return, the Bubbas did just that. They made a huge bonfire and celebration, tossing their stench-ridden britches and tops in – having first, of course, gotten new clothes to put on from their home trailers.

Or maybe they didn't quite get them themselves, because by the time they got back to the village, it being downwind, a certain, well, aura of Bubba Joe's feat had already preceded them. Nevertheless, the village chief himself came out to greet them, albeit from some distance and with a clothespin perched firmly on his nose, but, insofar as Cindy Lou still suffered from her cold, he let the saved Bubbas tell *her* what they needed.

She fetched and she carried and helped them select bushes suitable for changing behind, then carried their discards herself to the fire. Everyone joined in the celebration, even Bubba Joe, eating barbecue and drinking beer, Bubba Joe having promised, however, to at least move downwind when the, as one might say, *spirit* came on him.

The village chief finally stood up to make a speech. "Bubba Joe," he announced, he having had his own share of beer as well by then, "you have returned us our fellow Bubbas safe from the wilderness. For this, in my official capacity as trailer village chief, I offer you any reward you might ask for."

Bubba Joe thought hard. He gazed at Cindy Lou.

Cindy Lou gazed back.

"Excepting, that is," the chief said, "for my daughter."

THE END

James S. Dorr's collection, *Strange Mistresses: Tales of Wonder and Romance*, was released as a trade paperback in November 2001 by Dark Regions Press (http://darkregions.hypermart.net/). Florida-born Dorr is an active member of SFWA and HWA, a past Anthony (mystery) and Darrell (fiction set in the US Mid-South) finalist, winner of the Best of the Web 1998 award, a Pushcart Prize nominee, and has had work listed in *The Year's Best Fantasy and Horror* ten of the last twelve years. Prior publications include *Alfred Hitchcock's Mystery Magazine, New Mystery, Tomorrow, Gothic.Net, Aboriginal Science Fiction, Future Orbits, Terminal Fright, Fantastic Stories, Dark Angel Rising* (UK), *Faeries* (France), and such anthologies as *Gothic Ghosts, Darkside: Horror for the Next Millennium, The Best of Cemetery Dance, The Crow: Shattered Lives and Broken Dreams, Strange Attraction, Children of Cthulhu, The Darker Side: Generations of Horror,* and the original *Bubbas of the Apocalypse.*

SAVIN' NED

Robert D. Brown

I looked across the table at my cousin Twist, and wondered what to do next.

Twist was one of those types that was hard to figure, a two-headed monstrosity on a body as big as a double-wide trailer house, kind of like Jack and Jill came down the hill shaken, not stirred. Not the sort of person to get into a staring contest with. You'd be outnumbered two-to-one.

I wouldn't have them any other way.

I gulped the last swallow of my beer, looked at my cards one more time, and tried to decide if I should go down and out this hand or just draw two from the bone pile and hope for the best. Twist just sat there, smiling that weird double grin of theirs, the one that always makes me nervous.

"We don't have all day, Hal. / C'mon an' play already," they said.

I knew they was eggin' me on, but my hand was already headin' for the bone pile when the front door busted wide open and cousin Stinky fell inside.

"They got Ned!" he cried, gasping for air.

"Dammit, Stinky! What the hell are you jabberin' about this time? Who's got Ned?"

"The yumbies!"

When the news finally sank in it was like I'd been clobbered by a two-by-four.

"Now hang on a minute, Hal! / Maybe it's not so bad," urged Twist.

I looked across the table at the twins and wondered if they had gone insane.

"Not so bad? Not so BAD? We're talking about out idiot cousin Ned, remember? Just how bad do you think it's not gonna get?" I roared.

Stinky caught his breath enough to shamble over to the fridge and open the door. When the light came on he froze like a statue, staring inside like some stupid deer in the headlights.

I was about to throw my beer mug at him when he suddenly stood bolt upright and ripped a stitch that sent a green vapor sliding across the kitchen floor which made the curtains smolder.

"Son of a bitch," I choked, "How many times do I gotta tell you don't do that crap in here? I'm gettin' sick an' tired of drinkin' buttermilk, and my collard greens keep wilting! You hear what I'm saying?"

"Aw, shoot," moaned Stinky as he carefully rubbed his backside, "That's the third pair of jeans this week!"

"Ah, hell, go on and get a spare from the closet," I sighed, "but next time you feel the need you take that shit outside, understand?"

Stinky waved back at me as he walked the length of the trailer toward the bedroom, mumbling something as he left. I shook my head in dismay as I turned and saw Twist was smiling like the Cheshire cat.

"What?" I demanded.

"They'll eat Ned. / The yumbies are vicious animals," they croaked, then in unison, "What are we going to do?"

Ever since the Virus let loose and wiped out most everybody, me and my cousins got stuck up here in this old run down trailer house, and we've been fighting these damn yumbies ever since. Everybody calls them yumbies 'cause they was smart once upon a time, like computer geeks and technicians and programmers and all manner of yuppie types. But then there was us bubbas, hidin' out in the dirt street towns and back woods and way up into the hills. Damn if I know what kept us alive. Some say it was Providence, others said is was the barbeque sauce that gave us the Immunity.

Those that weren't neither, well... they just died.

You see, we was all at Aunt Dorothy's after-church picnic when the Virus hit. I was just a boy, but I remember. We was having a fine chicken dinner that afternoon, corn on the cob with sweet cream butter, mashed potatoes, beans and rice, cole slaw by the tubfuls, and naturally gallons and gallons of that rancid barbeque sauce uncle Lester always favored. It must've been some really tainted sauce 'cause it changed me an' my three cousins – or is it four – forever.

I was the oldest of the boys, you know, so my change was the most subtle. Afterwards I just started getting these urges, like get mad all the time. Sometimes I'd get so worked up I'd just let loose with the raunchiest mouthful of vulgarities you ever heard. Folks used to kid me about cussin' a blue streak until old man McGregor's mule up and kicked me in the leg. I cussed that poor beast so hard it finally ruptured something, vomited its intestines on the ground at my feet and choked to death.

Stinky used to be named Simon. Now we call him Stinky every day 'cept Sunday. His change was not nearly as suttle. He came down with the gawd-awfulest case of gas you ever did see. He could smoke out an entire town in one afternoon. I know that for a fact 'cause he accidentally poisoned a whole town full of yumbies two seasons back after eating an extra big helping of squirrel-meat burritos and cabbage smothered thick in the sauce. Damned near choked everybody else for a league in every direction.

Cousin Twist is the youngest of us, and is certainly the weirdest of the lot. See, Aunt Dorothy was heavy with twins the day of the picnic, a boy and a girl, but it was still early yet, so when the Virus got to her and mixed with that awful barbeque sauce it changed the twins before they was even born. Doc Chesley told us they fused together somehow, he never could figure out how exactly, the boy on one side and the girl on the other. Those kids didn't talk a whole lot, but they could sing a duet by themselves, and they grew up smart, really smart. You could always just look at them and see they was working things out.

As for Ned, he was the dumbest thing on two legs as long as I could remember, but after that bad sauce did its work he got a lot worse. Nobody likes being around him 'cept us, and I'm not sure why we put up with him. I had a sneaking suspicion I probably ought to let the yumbies keep the raggedy bastard, for all the good he was, but he was family even though he was such a pain in the ass.

"Oh, alright, let's go get him back," I agreed.

Twist's smiles broadened into full-fledged grins as they raised their massive bulk off the bench opposite the kitchen table and crossed the room to wait at the front door. Stinky's hollering echoed throughout the trailer house as he half-ran back up the hall bouncing on one foot while heaving my best pair of britches up to his beer gut, which insisted on lapping over no matter how hard he tugged.

Together we piled into Stinky's ramshackle pickup truck

and drove over some of the most ill-begotten dirt roads you ever saw. Down, down the hill we bounced, once hard enough to make Twist's heads ricochet off each other with a crack. When Ash Grove came into view I knew we'd hit smooth ground soon enough, which thankfully we did just as Stinky pulled to a stop at the edge of town and fired off another noxious round.

"Oh you've got to be kiddin'," I wailed as we all botched a reverse Chinese fire drill to get out of that truck before we choked.

"I ought to strangle you," I said, "those are the only good pants I got."

"Sorry, Hal," he said, "I couldn't help it."

"Look out everyone. / Folks are coming," said Twist, and as I looked up I saw a couple dozen men, normals by the look of them, coming toward us with clubs and hoes and iron pipes held high. A scrawny, red-haired trouble-maker named Gus McDougle led the pack with an old shotgun held menacingly toward us.

"Stay back," Gus hollered, and the others behind him murmured agreement. "You stay right where you is at, and state your intentions."

"Now, Gus, you knows who we are," said Stinky, and I could tell by the sudden wrinkling of their noses the good townsfolk of Ash Grove remembered us all too well.

"Yeah, I do," growled Gus, "We all knows the likes of you..."

"Yeah, yeah," I interrupted bitterly, "the Four Bubbas of the Apocalypse. Very funny. We're so sick of hearing it we could puke."

"It's true!" one shouted. "Wherever you go good folks git killed!"

"Just turn around an' leave," warned Gus, "We don't want any trouble."

"We're not after you. / We're looking for yumbies," Twist offered.

I could tell from their faces they all got the creeps when Twist talked, just like I do.

"Well you just turn around and leave," one said.

"You're after.. yumbies?"

That last question came as a crookbacked old man appeared from behind the others, brandishing the big end of a pool stick. He had a splotchy half-bald head, one lazy eye, and not more than half-a-dozen teeth left, but I recognized him just the same.

"Yeah, Grandpa Frank," I said, and he glared at me sideways with his one good eye. "Cross my heart, we're just after yumbies," I added quickly.

"I don' believe it!" the old man scowled, grasping the pool stick tightly. "Last time you boys barreled through town you wuz drunk an' raisin' all sorts of hell! I lost your poor grandmother Tana 'cause of you, boy," pointing threateningly at Stinky. "God rest her soul."

Stinky's shoulders stooped a little, and was looking awful sheepish.

"Sorry, Grandpa Frank," he whined.

"What the hell brings you back to town," growled the old man, "after we had the good sense to throw you out the last time?"

"Well, you see, uh, it's like, you know...," I stammered.

"The yumbies took cousin Ned. / They'll kill him if we don't find him in time," said Twist calmly. I could see old Frank flinch a little, but not as bad as the others. Until then he'd deliberately been avoiding his two-headed granddaughter/grandson, but when he looked up at them his good eye was wide with surprise.

"The yumbies... captured... Ned?"

Stinky stepped a little closer to Grandpa Frank and told him of how he had seen his cousin carried off in the back of a minivan, wailing his brains out, what little he had. The yumbie had been dressed all in white, something he had never seen before, and the door of the van had a sign on it shaped like a triangle.

"You certain of that, boy?" asked Frank, and Stinky shook his head enthusiastically.

"You got a real tough road ahead of you," moaned the old man.

"Why is that?" I asked.

"Those weren't just any old yumbies," he said. "Those were Guardians."

"They were what?" asked Stinky.

"Back when I was a young feller," Frank started, "the yumbies got smart. Started figuring things out. The Bubba Uprisings went a long way toward putting a dent in their style, but it didn't get rid of them all. The one's you're looking for are bad, real bad. Went back to the old ways. Learned some of the ancient rituals. They holed themselves up east of here, over the Big River, in a ruined city with a pyramid of broken glass. If your cousin is still alive that's where he'll be. There's one bridge left, and no doubt it'll be watched, so take care crossing over."

They thanked Grandpa Frank for his advice and busied themselves with gathering some provisions for the trip. They pulled out of the camp reasonably well stocked with some ancient MREs, camping gear, and one sawed-off shotgun and a box of shells. Twist was an awful shot with anything. They always squinted with one eye, meaning there were three others squeezed shut, so they would lose their balance and fall flat on their butt. Grandpa Frank insisted they protect themselves, though, so gave Twist the aluminum baseball bat that he had played with as a kid.

On a good day, like the morning after enchilada night, Stinky was so eruptive that he would set his own hair on fire every time he popped off a round from his squirrel gun, so he couldn't be trusted with anything better than an old hunting bow that was stored neatly in the bed of the truck. That left me, and I gladly kept the shotgun in my lap.

Sure enough, after an hour's drive the dark steel arches of the old bridge came into view. A relic of an age so far distant nobody could remember it any more, the old bridge had weathered time and the elements fairly well, though in places it had been weakened by runaway barges hitting the foundations. We stood at the west end of the bridge regarding it for quite some time, then as if on cue gathered our supplies and began walking over the treacherous span.

We managed to walk almost all the way to the glass pyramid before we caught sight of anyone. Ashen-skinned yumbies were wandering the streets as if they were anticipating some big parade right through the middle of town. They seemed excited about something, that was clear, and it was only when we were hiding within sight of the mirror-glass edifice that we understood why.

They were having a party, and a helluva big one by the looks of it.

Hundreds of the ugly brutes were milling about, dressed in white robes with flowing hoods drawn back, stopping occasionally to speak to one another, or buy snacks from a street vendor that looked suspiciously like rats on a stick, smothered in mustard. Stinky muttered something about trying one with barbeque sauce, but Twist quickly nudged him to shut up.

"How're we gonna get inside?" I asked.

"I don't know. / Maybe we need a diversion," said Twist.

"Or a disguise," added Stinky.

"Hey, that's a good idea," I said. "Now where are we going to come up with a good disguise?"

"We ought to just clobber a couple of yumbies and steal their clothes."

As if on cue three of the ugliest yumbies we had ever seen walked right past where we were hiding. With an understanding look we snuck up behind the cloaked figures and clobbered them on their misshapen heads and drug them roughly behind an abandoned station wagon. In just a couple of minutes we had changed clothes, hidden our belongings, and were walking out in the open toward the entrance of the pyramid. Me and Stinky looked fairly normal in our get-up, but Twist was going to be a little hard to explain if we were discovered. The twins agreed to keep their hood pulled up and not say anything.

We passed several yumbies as we approached the entrance, exchanged mumbles and continued walking.

"What if they figure us out?" asked Stinky.

"What if you have to pass gas, you moron. Shut up and keep walking."

At the entrance a pair of hulking brutes with pointed teeth greeted us with growling sneers that made Stinky almost wet his britches.

"We're just here for the festivities," I squeaked uncertainly.

"Y-, y-, y-es, we... we're here for the party," agreed Stinky.

"Yews awlmust lait," growled one of the brutes, and the other one grunted in agreement.

"Itz ahlmozt time. Go find yer seatz."

The three of us scrambled timidly past the bouncer boys and wandered through the building trying not to draw attention to ourselves. There was a sense of upcoming spectacle all around us, as each of the yumbies we passed was hissing about this and that and seemed very excited. Some of them were waiting in a remote part of the building. It looked like they were practicing some kind of ritual that involved some really wicked looking swords. The sight made us gulp.

Robert D. Brown

"They're going to eat him," I croaked.

"Look at those swords... / ...They look like really big butcher knives," Twist whispered.

"I'm sc-scared, y'all. Let's get outta here," said Stinky.

"You big coward," I grumbled, and poked him hard in the side.

"Ow!"

"You two better cut it out. / You're gonna draw their attention," hissed the twins. "C'mon, you idiots. We need to find Ned."

"Yeah, but where's he likely to be?"

Just then a procession of yumbies dressed in oversized kitchen aprons shambled past carrying a huge black kettle and chanting a wicked sounding eating song.

If we ever get hungry,
We'll know where to go,
The man-flesh is yummy
When ya cook in the know!

The procession pushed its way through several tangles of the unholy party animals and disappeared through a big set of push doors at the end of the aisle.

"That must be the kitchens," I muttered, "so if Ned is still alive..."

"... he's probably in there," finished Stinky. He was beginning to squirm.

"Right. We need a way inside."

"Oh no you don't, we're staying right here until we find Ned."

"Uh, I need to go, Hal. Please?"

"Don't bother me, I'm trying to figure this out."

"But Hal, I need to go!"

"Oh, no, please not here. / You'll get us discovered," gasped Twist.

"Hey, that gives me an idea. C'mon, follow me."

"Where you takin' us, Hal?"

"You're taking us to the kitchen, aren't you? / Are you crazy?"

"You just never mind, I got an idea."

I led the others past the tangles of yumbies and toward the big double doors. As soon as we walked inside we knew it was the nastiest kitchen there ever was.

"Yech," scowled Stinky, "It's even nastier than our trailer,

Hal."

"Oh shut up and put on these aprons."

"Aprons? What do you have in mind?"

"Wearing these we can snoop around until we find Ned. When we do you can lay down a smoke screen, Stinky, and we can get outta here."

"Oh, I don't know. / That sounds awfully risky."

"You got a better idea then let's hear it. Here, put this on."

We replaced our robes with the oversized aprons and started wandering through the kitchens. The yumbies were certainly a wretched pack of animals, I thought.

"Place looks like a torture chamber," whispered Stinky.

"Shhh," I warned him.

"Here youz go," called a rotten-sounding voice from behind us. We turned to see a yumbie waving the gawd-awfullest meat cleaver I'd ever seen with one hand, and offering what looked like part of a leg with the other.

"Take thiz und chop it up for da stew," the yumbie said, it's yellow teeth showing in a crooked smile.

"Uh, ah, yeah, chop it up. Right."

When the yumbie walked away we examined the hunk of meat carefully.

"Is that Ned?" asked Stinky.

"I don't know. / Might be a woman," guessed Twist.

"Let's get outta here before we run into any more of them."

We turned to leave and ran smack into one of the huge guards from the front entrance.

"Yews lawst, arent yews?" the hulk grumbled.

We turned in unison only to collide with the second of the guards.

"The Grand Duknob will be wantin' to see yewz," sneered the second as he popped ten huge knuckles in hands as big as baseball mitts.

The what?

"Yah," croaked the first, "it's time fer ya to join in da fun."

"We're gonna get it. / What do we do?"

"Oh no no no... Hal?" squirmed Stinky.

"Let 'er rip, cousin!" I hollered.

Suddenly Stinky stood still as a tree, bent a little bit sideways, and with a slight grimace squeezed out an avocado-green fart that broadcast quickly through the kitchen. The two guards doubled over clutching their throats and gasping for clean air, while the rest of the staff turned purple-blue in the face and collapsed to the floor.

We ran from the kitchen, through several storage rooms, down a hall and turned toward what looked like the correct door. We ran into the room beyond and closed the door behind us.

"Where are we? / I'm lost, Hal." said Twist.

"We must've made a wrong turn back there somewhere, we'll have to go back. What the hell is wrong with you?"

The look on Stinky's face was one of pure pleasure.

"That felt g-o-o-o-d..." he sighed.

"You did good, Stinky, but we don't have time for.."

Just then the door burst open and several hulking yumbies burst into the room and surrounded us.

"Hit 'em with another blast, Stinky!"

"I can't! I'm all out. It's been too long since I ate. I told you I was hungry."

"What are we going to do?" asked the twins in unison.

The yumbies were drooling as they leered at us. One, a particularly lanky beast with greasy yellow hair, took a step closer and bowed slightly.

"The Grand Duknob wishes your presence at the evening's meal."

"Th-, the grand... what?" asked Stinky.

"The Grand Duknob," the yumbie repeated. "You are to be his... special guest at the evening's festivities." The yumbie glared at us, sniggering to himself, as the others crowded in and grabbed us roughly.

We were hauled out of the room, past the kitchens which still reeked of Stinky's gas attack, down two sets of stairs and into a locker room that looked like it hadn't been cleaned in a hundred years. They shoved us into the tiled shower stalls where, to our great surprise, we were treated to a shower of fairly clean water that was chilly but not cold. A minute later they hauled us back up the stairs again, soaking wet.

We were paraded around the entire circumference of the structure, it seemed, until at last we stopped at a large opening in the wall covered with what looked like very old tapestries. Beyond, the festivities were obviously under way, with weird music blaring and echoing from everywhere, mixed with the sounds of screaming and dancing and what sounded like wild mantras wailing through the din. The whole effect made me shiver uncontrollably in my shoes, and Twist grabbed themselves tightly in a truly awkward fashion.

One look at the unnaturally large puddle on the floor told me that Stinky had simply peed himself.

The lanky yumbie with yellow hair appeared again, and began speaking to other yumbies close by in a language I did not understand. When he finished he faced us once again.

"The... preparations... have been completed. The Grand Duknob awaits."

"Ohhh, this don't sound good, Hal."

"Shaddup, willya, and lemme think."

The tapestries were drawn aside to reveal a huge indoor arena. Seating extended up the walls in every direction, and it was a packed house. In the middle of the cavernous area a dais had been erected using what looked like scrap lumber and parts from junk pickup trucks. Several yumbies, both male and female, were dancing and singing ecstatically about the platform in step to music that confounded the senses.

We were led roughly toward the center of the arena, the brutes in their seats leering and taunting us. The room reeked of their odor, a mix of rotten buffalo meat and Dr. Pepper. The steps to the dais were rickety. Me and Stinky managed the ascent easily but Twist, with their added bulk, had to be pushed up the stair by a couple of yumbies that looked liked they were trying to get a minivan out of the mud.

A dozen more yumbies were waiting for us at the top. They grasped and tugged at us as they danced on the stage, playfully whirling us from one partner to the other until we were all dizzy. In the midst of a do-se-do in the center of the stage Twist's hood finally managed to fly back revealing their double-header annoyance to everyone's shock. It didn't take long for the noise of the party to die down until only the muffled murmuring of the audience could be heard.

"What do we do now?" squeaked Stinky.

"Twist, if we ever needed a bright idea now's the time," I said.

"I'm thinking, Hal. / It doesn't look good," intoned the twins.

Just then there was a loud clanging that sounded like someone beating the crap out of a hubcap with a cat, and when we turned in the direction of the noise we witnessed great bunches of yumbies falling to their knees in silence for the procession that was approaching the dais. The troop marched two abreast toward the stage, ascending the stair. These yumbies were dressed differently, with sky-blue robes and odd-looking jewelry. The group was knotted closely around yet another, somewhat different figure.

"Maybe that's their leader," I guessed.

"Could be their preacher man," Stinky suggested.

"Whoever it is seems important. / Sonofabitch, would you look at that?" said Twist.

One of the yumbies produced a microphone and drew it up to its mouth. "The Grand Duknob," it announced, and a roar of appreciation reverberated through the auditorium.

Me and Stinky turned to look in the direction Twist was facing. I couldn't remember the last time the twins uttered a cross word about anything. The procession had stopped immediately in front of us, and all but one of the group had dropped to their knees.

Standing before us, with a greasy chicken wing in one hand and a beer can in the other, was our dumbass cousin, Ned.

"Howdy, y'all! Come to join the party?"

"Party?" I asked indignantly, "we thought you were their dinner."

"Say what? Naw, I've 'splained everything to 'em, an' we're having ourselves a little party, instead! Here ya go, have yourself a wing, y'all. Tastes a little different but it ain't bad jus' the same." Ned waved the greasy meat at the cousins.

"Are you sure that's a chicken wing?" I asked.

"Nyaa-aaa-aaa," whined Stinky, "let's get outta here. Oh, man... I gotta go, y'all."

"Gotta admit it tastes a bit off, but hey! C'mon, y'all, there's plenty o' beer, too!"

The yumbies were closing on us, leering and slavering and moaning all at once.

"We need a plan, Twist, how're we going to get out of this?"

Their heads swiveled quickly in different directions, then turned to me.

"Grab the microphone, Hal. / Cover him, Stinky," they said, then pulled back the folds of their robe and drew Grandpa Frank's aluminum baseball bat like a samurai sword. They swung wildly, bouncing the old bat off the heads of the advancing yumbies with a satisfying thoingk! sound, sending them reeling backwards and off the edge of the dais.

I grabbed for the microphone, wrestling it away from the yumbie, and kicked him off the side of the platform.

"What am I s'posed to do with this," I shouted, but Twist was too busy bouncing the bat off yumbie heads to answer.

"Well, I know what to do," said Stinky. He winked at me, turned around and in one smooth motion bent over as he dropped his drawers and let go a gas blast that made half the yumbies on the stage gag and fall back.

"Oh, damn, Stinky!" yelled Ned, "Take that shit out-SIDE!" and with a flourish waved wildly behind him, tripped and fell, smacked a yumbie upside the head, and sent it reeling straight into my face. I took the full force of the impact and fell right on my ass.

I guess I lost hold of my senses just then because I let fly with a chorus of profanities that made the yumbies eyes swell and explode with a sickening pop. Twist, who witnessed the beast's gruesome demise, quickly dispatched another yumbie coming up the rickety stair, then turned one head back toward me. The voice was smooth, calm, and decidedly female, and commanded so much authority that there was no choice but to listen.

"Hal," she said indicating the pop-eyed yumbie, "Give-Them-Hell!"

It took a few seconds for the meaning to sink in but when it did I felt energized. While Twist went back to head bashing and Stinky gave the surrounding yumbies the full moon treatment, I gripped the microphone tightly, took a deep breath, and addressed the crowd.

It took me a minute, but I worked myself into a fine lather. I cussed, and cursed, and swore, and blasphemed, and said all manner of foul and loathsome filth into that microphone, and my voice filled the auditorium with a reverberating drone that made the skin of every yumbie present blister and peel. I went on and on, hardly stopping to catch my breath. The tension in the air increased quickly, building like the inside of a pressure cooker. Soon the yumbies were totally immobilized, clenching their ears and their heads as if in terrible pain. Many were wailing openly, many more were joining them. Eventually even my cousins, who were normally immune to my power began clutching at their ears and yelling from the pain, and still I did not relent.

Then, as if on cue, the yumbies just collapsed, hemorrhaging around the eyes and ears. I stopped cold, my breath coming ragged into my lungs, and I waited as the echo of my voice remained in the air for an unnaturally long time. Stinky hauled up his pants with a great sigh of relief. He had succeeded in creating a deadly glowing vapor that clung to the floor more than a foot thick in places, the bodies of dead yumbies scattered in knots everywhere. Twist was in tears from intense pain, because even though two heads are better than one for some things, it's simply not possible to clamp one pair of hands over two pairs of ears.

Still breathing with difficulty, partly from my own effort and partly from the poison gas attack graciously provided by cousin Stinky, I hauled up Ned's limp form, balancing his body expertly across my shoulders.

"Let's get out of here," I groaned.

We limped down the steps of the dais and stepped carefully around the tangled bodies, winding our way through the glass and steel building until we found the doors we had originally entered. When we stepped out into the late afternoon sun we saw more yumbie bodies lying about the streets in various states of disintegration.

We walked back to the bridge in the open, unchallenged, as there wasn't a single yumbie left standing as far as we could see. We said nothing as we crossed the bridge, not really noticing the Big River underneath, and piled everything back into Stinky's ramshackle pickup truck, and drove back home.

This time I made Stinky ride in the back. Heroes or not, we wanted no more Chinese fire drills that day.

THE END

Robert D. Brown works full time selling material handling equipment. In his spare time he enjoys reading, watching movies, hanging out on the Internet and, of course, writing. He got his first taste of sci-fi in college when a friend gave him a copy of *Nine Princes In Amber* by Roger Zelazny, and he's been hooked ever since. Now, twenty-plus years later, Robert remains active in fandom, and is webmaster for the local fan club and convention.

83 BEST MONKEYS

Lee W. Lindsay, Jr.

Joe glanced at the rotting, burned-out shack that stood across the corner from the hardware store as he pulled into the store's parking lot. The faded sign was smoked and the wording barely legible; he could just make out the 'Heavenly Java Shoppe' that used to be in such bold letters. It gave him a warm feeling to know that there weren't any more of those yuppie, fancy-pants, corner drive-through, coffee shops anymore. Now, the lines may be longer at the Clover Mart, but people were drinking real coffee, black and thick as mud, just the way it should be. Joe shut off his pickup. He left the keys in the ignition and patted Shemp, his shaggy, German Shepard-and-who-the-hell-knows-what dog. Shemp whimpered as Joe stepped out of the pickup. *Got to remember to get the new latch for the back yard gate,* he thought as he stepped into the store, *and check out that new power saw I heard about.*

"That's odd." he muttered as the door swooped closed behind him.

No sound came from anywhere in the store, except the slight echo of the door closing. Joe sniffed and waved his hand in front of his face as he looked around. The store looked empty, no one at the cash register or near the door. Joe wondered if he ought to check out the register, but thought better of it. He moved further into the store, down the main aisle past the checkout stand, looking down the nail and fastener aisle. The smell seemed to be getting worse, almost as bad as when he took a dump after eating tuna fish and jalapenos. Joe thought he heard something just as he passed the second aisle with the plumbing fittings. Then he heard the sound of someone passing gas, accompanied by another and another, more and more anuses joined in, some high pitched and one deep bass. It seemed almost musical in sound, then the scent reached Joe's nose. He gagged and backed up.

A head popped out from behind Aisle Four and Joe's eyes went wide. God almighty, no, thought Joe, it can't be him! I thought we got him out of town permanently; why would he come back?

"Hello, Joe. How's ya' doing?" said Ned. "What did ya' think of that? *Home on the Range* played by eighty-three monkeys and me. Pretty good, huh?"

"Ned! What are you doing back in town? I thought you had gone off to Seattle to teach them how to defend themselves against the wild Yuppie zombie." Joe backed toward the door. No wonder the place had been empty. "Maybe I ought to let you and your monkeys practice some more." The smell continued to get worse and Joe was sure he saw the shelving sagging as though melting.

"Hell, Joe, I never made it to Seattle. I got lost." Ned belched and scratched his crotch. "Why don't you stay? We could use your help."

The chattering of several voices came over the tops of the aisle. Joe looked up to see a wave of brown fur move and bounce over the tops of the shelves. The chattering became louder, punctuated by more gas. Joe groped for the door as the small, brown furred, human-like creatures headed toward him.

"Hey, Joe, you know how to sing," called Ned as he and the monkeys followed Joe to the door. "You sing pretty good in church. I'd like you to help us with our music." Ned smiled a dark brown smile and Joe wondered how a person's breath could be worse than eighty-four farts. "You'll help us, won't you?"

"Ned, I don't think..." Joe stopped. He felt a small hand on his back, then something tugging on his shirt as it climbed up his back. He turned to his right as a small monkey stepped on his right ear and let loose with another batch of gas. Joe's vision swam and he became light as a feather being lifted to heaven as his knees buckled.

Joe opened his eyes and looked at the sun shining through a small hole in the clouds that looked remarkably like a monkey's butt. Why was he lying in the parking lot? He felt Shemp licking his left cheek and he turned to his right and saw Ned sitting next to him. Oh, yeah. Did he drag himself out of the building or did Shemp pull a Lassie and drag him out into the fresh air? Joe opened his mouth to tell Ned there was no way he could stand to be around him or his monkeys long enough to teach them to fart *Twinkle, Twinkle Little Star*, let alone anything else, when he heard a familiar voice screaming in the distance. Joe got up and looked down Yakima Avenue. He saw Caleb running down the street, without a cap or shirt, his scrawny ribs heaving to support his running and shouting.

"Run! Run!" screamed Caleb, "Run, the zombies are coming!"

Joe jumped out into the street and looked around. Shemp barked and danced around, carefully avoiding Ned and the monkeys. Joe didn't see anything so he reached out and grabbed Caleb as he went flying by, swinging him around in circles until he slowed to a stop.

"Where are the zombies?" asked Joe.

"Ellensburg, they just took Ellensburg." Caleb waved his arms wildly, making Joe duck.

"Then what's all the fuss about? They won't be here anytime soon," said Joe, turning back to tell Ned to shove his monkeys and blow them over the Cascade Mountains.

"They have travel mugs," whispered Caleb.

Joe's stomach dropped. Anyone with a single brain cell more than Ned had, knew that travel mugs meant trouble. With travel mugs, zombies wouldn't stop until the weather was cold enough to freeze their cappuccinos, and today was April 15th.

"Zombies are coming!" Joe and Caleb screamed, running down the street with Shemp barking behind them as they turned down First Avenue and headed toward Union Gap. "Zombies! Run!"

Ned and the monkeys followed the two screaming men and dog, yelling and hooting and tooting. They raised a clatter and stench that cleared the road around them.

Joe was nearing the Union Gap barrier when he tripped. He fell, face down and felt one hundred and seventy feet tromp over him, each pair passing gas like a diesel truck exhaust. Joe felt his head swimming as he lay in the cloud of poisonous fumes. Maybe, thought Joe, it would be better to be zombiefied and have to drink cappuccinos than getting farted to death. Joe looked up and saw Caleb puffing while Ned and the monkeys danced around doing a halfway decent rendition of *Riders on the Storm.*

"You know, Caleb, " said Joe as he climbed to his feet, "when those zombies hit the gap from Selah, we're going to have a real mess here. They'll be tearing down the town looking for fancy coffee. I don't suppose you know of anyone with a stash of *French Roast* or *Mocha Java*, do you?"

"Damn it, Joe, you know I would never touch the stuff or hang out with anyone that would drink it!" Caleb gave Joe an ugly look. "You think I'm zombie fodder, that I drink that sissy piss instead of real coffee?"

"No, no. Sorry, I'm just rattled and hoped we could find a stash of stuff to get the zombies to head away from here."

"Say, Joe, why's Ned here and what are those things jumping around with him? It sounds like they're farting *Home on the Range,* now."

"They are and they're putting out enough gas to clear out the town for a year," gagged Joe, then he gasped as an idea hit him.

Joe woke up two minutes later with Caleb fanning him with his own cap. Shemp was wagging his tail over Joe's head, which might have helped, except that Shemp was farting as well. Joe waved both of them away as he sat up.

"Joe, you know you shouldn't take a deep breath around Ned. What the hell were you thinking?"

"I just had an idea." Joe smiled. "I know how to get rid of those zombies and make the monkeys happy." Joe grabbed Caleb and shook him. "Go get your guitar and stop by my place and get mine. Meet us at the gap into Selah as quick as you can."

Joe slowly stood up, breathing shallowly. He waved to get Ned's attention. "Ok, Ned, we're going to teach you guys a new song, but we need to move out of town a ways. Let's get back to my pickup and we'll go out toward Selah and practice your new song."

"Great, great." yelled Ned, jumping up and down.

The monkey's jumped up and down as well and the stench became worse and worse. Joe turned and walked quickly down the street, trying to stay ahead of the smell.

An hour later, Joe met Caleb at the overpass where Highway 12 goes into Selah. It took him twenty minutes to get the monkeys and Ned facing away from Yakima and toward Selah.

Then he and Caleb started to play their guitars.

"Thank God the wind is blowing toward Selah." said Caleb.

"Yeah." said Joe as he played a riff from *Dueling Guitars*.

"Doesn't your mother-in-law live in Selah?"

"Yeah," said Joe with a big smile.

"Oh." Caleb looked over at Ned who was grunting with a look of extreme concentration on his face. "Say, Ned, where did you get these monkeys?"

"What? Oh, I found them up north of here near Hanford. Some little town. Noticed how they all look alike, probably related, despite the fact that they boff each other like crazy. Probably a close knit family." Ned pushed out a loud D flat at just the wrong time, earning a disapproving look from the monkeys. "The whole place was glowing, just like Hanford does. Wasn't nobody else there and these little guys were running around looking hungry. Some of them looked like they thought I would make a good snack, so I let them have a couple a bags of jellybeans that I had on me. They've been following me every since."

The monkeys had actually become very good at the song that Joe dubbed *Dueling Butts*. Several bushes and trees in the area were beginning to look wilted, but the monkeys still tooted and hooted with gusto. Shemp howled a counter point. Ned was giving it his best shot, but was starting to look worn down. Joe started to think that they might need to take a break, when he saw the zombies.

It was bad enough that many of the citified people in the area had been turned to zombies, but they also lost all modicum of taste. The zombies all wore suits with loud, flashy, Rush-power-ties, even the females. It was horrible to see.

Joe watched as the zombies moved closer, funneling onto the bridge. He waited until the first bunch of zombies reached the center of the bridge, then he started the monkeys from the beginning of the song again. The toots and the hoots quickly drowned out the sound of Caleb's and Joe's guitars. Joe watched as the zombies moved closer, then the first one hit the cloud of gas and stumbled. The rest pressed forward and they stumbled as well. Soon the crowd of zombies were on their knees or staggering around. Joe smiled and set down his guitar then pulled out his pack of Camels, tapped one out. He pulled out a match and lit it up. He sucked in the smoke and flipped the match over the nearest monkey as he turned to Caleb. "Well, it looks like the gas..."

The explosion leveled half of Selah and the flame from the monkeys' butts melted the asphalt on the Selah Bridge. It was hard for anyone to get any kind of coherent answer from Joe after that, he's deaf and bald from the explosion. Poor Shemp disappeared and Caleb left Yakima shortly after recovering from his injuries. He's taken the job as manager of *Ned and the 83 Best Monkeys*. Last time they were heard from, they were clearing Seattle of zombies.

THE END

Lee W. Lindsay, Jr. now lives in Harrah, Washington, and should have grown up to be a bubba, after being born in Idaho and raised in Montana and Idaho. But somewhere along the way, he went from being a farm boy to getting a college degree and learning to like mochas, microbrew ales and jazz music. Go figure.

BRINGING HOME THE SAUCE
Linda J. Dunn

Posting on internet, December 23, 2024: The Crane Army Ammunition Activity (CAAA) is located 35 miles southwest of Bloomington, Indiana. It includes 3,000 buildings, 400 miles of roads and trails, 170 miles of railroad, and an 800 acre lake....

Added April 22, 2025: Y25 survivors are invited to seek refuge at Crane   We have the resources to rebuild and we'll welcome you with open arms.

Bubba pulled the duct tape and plastic loose from the window frame slowly, trying to be as quiet as possible and fumbling for a good grip in the dark. He could hear his folks buzzing and snorting in the next room and if Ma woke up and found him taking off with Ned again – after all that trouble they'd gotten into last night – she'd rip him a new one.

Tonight, they were gonna get themselves out of trouble. Ned had heard that Crane used to keep a big stockpile of food before Y25K killed off most people. Everyone was scared to go anywhere near Crane; so that meant the barbeque sauce was still there, ready for him and Ned to load it up and haul it home.

No chance of getting into trouble there. They'd be heroes when they got back.

Bubba pulled the last of the plastic off the window frame and was just fixing to climb out when Ned showed up. He honked the horn real loud before jumping out of the truck; then he threw open the trailer's front door with a loud bang against the siding and shouted, "Yo, Bubba! You ready?"

Bubba stood shock still for a moment, listening to the sound of grunts and snorts coming from the next room. Good. Somehow, they'd slept through that.

He ran to the front part of the trailer, where Ned was standing, grabbed him by the back of his shirt, and hauled his sorry ass back outside and up against the truck.

"Shhhh!"

"Hey, Bubba! What you shhhing me for?" Ned's voice could wake the dead. It had last summer.

Bubba pressed his hand tight against Ned's mouth and said, "Shut up, get in the truck, and drive before you wake up half the county. If Mama catches us, she'll nail both our hides to the tool shed."

Bubba let go of Ned and stepped back.

"But Bubba, the shed's metal. How's she gonna nail –?"

"Never mind. Just get in the goddamn truck and drive."

Damn! There were times when Bubba wished Ned would learn when the hell to shut up. Like *last summer*, when those Indiana University students had wandered through Owensburg.

Except it turned out there wasn't a college anymore or even a basketball team. They was all dead. Zombies. And all this time, he'd thought zombies were just some fairytale Ma had made up to scare him. Sort of like the boogey man, gremlins, and Santa Claus. Wasn't nothing scarier than that old man in the red suit and here those students had all been dressed in red shirts with white lettering.

If Ned had just kept his big mouth shut, those zombies would have kept on going and they'd still have a barn today.

Bubba pulled the truck door closed as softly as he could and whispered. "Drive."

Ned hit the gas pedal and the truck lurched forward into the tool shed.

"Reverse, Ned. Throw the damn thing into reverse."

Ned hit the gas hard – in reverse this time – and spewed gravel everywhere. Bubba squirmed in his seat and reached under his ass for the beer bottle that he'd sat on. The bottle was full, but he'd learned long ago not to trust Ned.

"This booze?"

"It was. I got thirsty on the way over."

"You're only a mile away!" Bubba tossed the bottle out the window.

"Hey! That was a good bottle."

"There ain't no shortage of bottles. Hey! Why the hell are you pulling a trailer?"

"Guess I forgot to unhitch it after Sally drove it home this afternoon and told the folks she was moving into it. Said she preferred the leavings of live pigs to the likes of us. Want me to stop and unhitch it now?"

"Hell, no! Wait a minute... is Sally in it?"

"Reckon so. I didn't think to look and Sally... well, you know how Sally is."

Everyone knew how Sally was. She was a full fourteen years old – just three years younger than him and Ned – and she still hadn't gotten herself even one kid yet. Last time he'd offered to help her make one, Sally'd knocked him halfway across the barn.

The truck hit the top of the hill and soared for a few seconds. "I expect Sally's awake now," Ned yelled.

Bubba felt around the floorboard. "You don't have anything to drink in here?"

"Nothing that I've not already drunk."

"You're a piss poor buddy, drinking all the booze before picking me up."

"Wasn't my idea to sneak out to Crane in the middle of the night."

"No, you were gonna go in broad daylight, when your daddy would've beat your ass to a bloody stump if you'd so much as looked at his truck. Still, good idea about the barbeque sauce, though."

"Yeah." Ned said. "Best damn idea I've had since setting the barn on fire.

Bubba braced his hands against the dashboard as the truck went flying over another hill. "If you'd kept your trap shut, those zombies never would have found us and you wouldn't have needed to set that fire. Dad's still sorer than hell about the barn."

Ned slowed down when they reached a gate that hung open. It looked odd. No rust. Nothing broken. A bit further down the road, they drove into a woods that just plain looked wrong. No weeds. Short grass. Then the woods turned into a small town that was nothing like Owensburg.

Chills ran up and down Bubba's spine and he swallowed hard. Damn, but he needed booze to wet his throat after seeing this.

No trailers, just houses. No plastic over the windows. No grass growing in the gutters.

This place was clean!

"Bubba! Are those graves?" Ned stopped the car just past

the town and Bubba leaned forward to see what Ned was looking at. Mounds. Big, mother-fucking mounds that were way too huge for humans.

Giants?

Those graves had some kind of doors leading into them like they expected the dead to walk in and out.

Giant zombies?

Something banged on the side of his door and Bubba screamed before looking out, half-expecting to go nose-to-nose with another damn zombie again. It was Sally.

"So what do you two imbeciles think you're staring at?" she asked.

"Graves," Bubba answered. "Must be some kind of giants."

"Munitions, you moron." Sally's voice had that damn know-it-all smugness to it again that Bubba hated. "I can read and your headlights are shining on the signs. You're looking at where they store the munitions."

"What's munitions?" Ned asked.

"Ammo munitions," Bubba said. So Sally could read. Big deal. Show-off!

"What do you two think you're doing, anyway?" Sally asked. "You know we're not supposed to go anywhere near here."

"We're raiding their food pile. Ned figures they're bound to have barbeque sauce, and you know how nobody can find any good sauce anymore."

"Looking to get yourselves out of trouble?" She shook her head. "Morons. Both of you. Did it ever occur to either of you that maybe we're not supposed to come here because there might be survivors? Government survivors? Maybe zombies?"

"What's a government?" Ned asked.

Sally opened her mouth, but before she could say anything, the place lit up like the sun'd come up early and a voice behind them said, "We're the government."

Bubba looked in the rear view mirror. There must have been a dozen folks standing there with rifles pointed at the truck.

One of them smiled and asked, "How can we help you boys?" He turned to Sally and his smile widened. "And you, Miss? Or is it Mrs.?"

Sally stared at him for a moment before asking about food. "What's Pie?"

"Three point one four one five nine two six –"

"Yes!" Sally leaped into the air like she'd just been offered their best moonshine. "You and Ned get the hell out of here. I'm staying."

"I'm afraid that we cannot allow your Neanderthal friends to leave," one of the rifle-holding men said. "Out of the truck, boys."

One of the women moved closer and gave Bubba a good once over. Bubba sucked in his stomach and grinned. The woman grinned back and he started feeling pretty good about things until she said, "Fresh DNA. I hope this time it's not just more of the same. They're terribly inbred."

Bubba leaned towards Ned and whispered, "What's DNA?" Ned shrugged.

"It's deoxyribonucleic acid," Sally said. "A double-stranded helix of nucleotides, which carries the genetic information of a cell. In simple terms for you morons, it's what determines the color of your eyes and how tall you'll grow."

"Intelligence!" one of the men shouted! "From one of them!"

"Are you adopted?" one of the women asked.

"We'll need to find a special place for this one," someone else said.

Everyone nodded and made a big fuss over Sally. Bubba couldn't for the life of him see why.

"This is wonderful." One of the men said. "It indicates some genetic variation at long last. We've been aggressively studying our own DNA and that of every survivor who's arrived, hoping to find the solution to the problem. All of our babies have turned into zombies. We need to learn why."

"Maybe you ought to try our women," Ned said. "None of them have any zombies."

Sally punched Ned hard enough to knock him into Bubba and they both fell. "Sometimes, Ned, I don't think you have two brain cells capable of thinking."

"I think all the time," Ned said. "Right now, I think I'm hungry. You folks got any food?"

They laughed and most of them lowered their rifles. "Come on, boys," one of the women said. "Follow us to the cafeteria and we'll feed you."

"What've you got?" Ned asked. "Chicken? Pork fritters? Catfish?"

"Barbequed baby back ribs," one of the women said. "We eat it every Wednesday. Helps to keep our immunity up."

"Huh?" Bubba scratched his head, trying to make sense of what she was saying.

"Cheap barbeque sauce provides immunity against the Y25 virus," the woman said. "The government always bought everything from the lowest bidder, so everyone working here who ate regularly in the cafeteria was immune when Y25 hit. We still haven't been able to isolate the vector, so we just keep eating the sauce."

"You got much of it left?" Ned asked. "Can you spare a few jars?"

The woman beside her laughed. "We exhausted the last of that sauce long ago. Fortunately, we were able to replicate the formula."

"Could I see the kitchen?" Sally asked.

"You can see anything you like," one of the men answered. "It's obvious you're not one of them. Did you say you were adopted?"

"No," she replied, "I just chose to use my brain and they didn't."

"Here's the cafeteria." One of them opened the door and Bubba stared into a room that was about the size of the abandoned school gym back in Owensburg. This room, however, still had a floor. No one had pulled up the wood for kindling.

Two of the women walked off with Sally to the kitchen and one of them said, "We'll be back shortly with some food."

Bubba sat down at the table and noticed the corked barbeque sauce bottle on the table. He picked it up and handed it to Ned. "Here. You taste it."

Ned hesitated a moment before uncorking it and sticking his finger inside. He sniffed his finger and took a small lick, then a longer lick, and then he stuffed his finger into his mouth and stuck it back into the bottle again.

"Hey! This tastes just like the good stuff."

Bubba grabbed the bottle from Ned and stuck his own finger inside.

Perfect sauce. Tangy, with that bitter flavor that he hadn't tasted since the good stuff ran out six months ago.

"That's it, all right." Bubba nodded at the people crowded around him.

"Tastes like ketchup watered down with urine to me," one of them said. "But it's good for us. Wait until you taste the ribs. We've got our own little farm out here."

"Here's the food for our new farmhands." The women returned from the kitchen, with Sally not far behind them.

They placed two plates of baby back ribs in front of them, and Bubba didn't wait for the food to get cold. Damn, but those ribs tasted good!

"What do you mean by 'farmhands'?" Sally asked.

"After we get the DNA samples," one of them said, "we'll tag the boys and put them to work inside the fenced-in farm section. They'll be with their own kind there and happy."

"Work?" Bubba dropped his ribs.

"Don't worry boys, you'll enjoy it," the old man grinned a little too widely. "Alice here has something special so you'll never want to leave."

Bubba glanced back at Alice. She didn't look any more special than any other woman he'd ever seen.

"Best moonshine you've ever drank and no hangover.'

Now that might be worth putting in an hour or so a day.

"You drug them and make them *slaves*?" Sally's voice had that high-pitched whine to it that usually came right before her first swing, if you weren't careful in your answer.

"They're not slaves," Alice said. "They're members of our community. It's just that we're busy with our research and have little time for physical labor. They, on the other hand, are unsuited to anything else."

"Of course. It's not like they're human." Sally sounded riled and that didn't make sense. These folks were just saying what Sally said to him and Ned all the time.

"Exactly," Alice said. "It must have been difficult for you, living among them. However did you educate yourself?"

"Ma taught me," she said. "Their seemingly low intelligence is nurture, not nature."

She patted Sally on the shoulder. "How sweet and innocent you are. I notice your brother didn't benefit from the same learning opportunities."

Alice turned her back on Sally and Bubba was torn between the desire to sink his teeth back into those ribs and his fear that he was gonna miss seeing Sally pick up a chair and hit Alice across the back with it. Didn't nobody have a fierier temper than Sally around these parts and didn't nobody fight better than Sally.

Weirdest damn thing! Sally just stood there getting redder

and redder and clinching her fists tight. Finally, she said, "Are you planning to turn me into a farmhand, too?"

"Of course not," Alice said. "You're our best hope for the future."

"How? As a new member of your breeding program?"

Bubba grabbed his plate and moved under the table. This was gonna be one helluva fight.

"We prefer to think of it as our futures program," Alice said.

Bubba stuck his head up, wondering why he hadn't heard any furniture breaking yet.

Sally stood there, smiling while her eyes burned like she was ready to strangle someone, and said, "I think I'm a little hungry after all. Would you mind if I got myself some food?"

"Of course not."

Sally was gone so long that he and Ned were licking their fingers clean by the time she came back. Her plate only had two puny little ribs on it.

The government folks went on talking like nobody else was there, making big plans for how they were gonna start a new nation and populate it with Sally's help. Sally's face got redder and redder and she barely touched her ribs.

"You gonna eat that?" Bubba whispered before Ned could say a word. Sally gave him the plate and he gnawed on the ribs until there wasn't any meat left.

"Before you show us to our new home," Sally said, "could I get some of my belongings out of the truck?"

They hesitated and shook their heads. "I'm sorry, but–"

"I need them!" Sally's voice took on that plaintive whine that Bubba hated. "It's *that* time of the month."

The women and men exchanged a look that Bubba couldn't figure out and then the head guy shrugged and said, "All right. But we'll go with you."

Once they'd gotten outside, Sally grabbed Bubba and Ned and said. "I'm gonna create a diversion."

"What's a diversion?" Ned asked.

"Never mind. When I say, 'Now!' I want you and Bubba to head for the truck, jump in, and drive like your lives depend upon it, because they will."

About ten feet from the hog trailer, she whispered, "Now!" and Bubba ran for the truck. He heard Ned behind him shout, "Now what?"

"Run, you idiot!" Sally screamed.

Bubba heard a shot and felt a bullet breeze past his right ear. He also heard a whoosh and a loud boom. That was enough to get him into the truck at lightning speed.

Ned was only a few seconds behind him, huffing and puffing. He started the truck and they took off. A moment later, Bubba heard something hit the door and when he looked, Sally was hanging onto the truck and trying to climb through the window.

She landed in his lap. "Floor it!" she screamed.

Ned did and they damn near flew down that road. Behind them, they heard a couple more loud booms.

"What's going on back there?" Bubba asked.

"They should have maintained the storage a little better," Sally said. "Those doors must have rusted enough for the fire to reach them. I put together a nice little explosive from some supplies in the kitchen, smuggled it and some matches outside, lit the fuse, and tossed it towards one of those mounds. Looks like it did more than I'd dared hope. That'll teach them to use slave labor! Call my brother inhuman, will they!"

"Wow!" Ned looked in the rear view mirror. "That's got to be the biggest fire I've ever seen. Even bigger than the barn fire."

Sally slid off Bubba to sit between the two of them and grinned ear-to-ear.

"Don't you feel a little bad about leaving your kind behind?" Bubba rubbed his legs, trying to get the blood moving in them again.

He didn't see Sally's fist coming until it caught him in the jaw. The blow sent him sprawling sideways against the door and he cracked his head on the broken window crank.

"Don't you dare call those people 'my kind'," Sally screamed at Bubba. "They might have been smart, but they were nothing like me. Nothing! Damn slave owners. Probably would have kept me barefoot and pregnant all the time, too."

Bubba rubbed his jaw and tried to sit up. He didn't know what she was so mad about, but he knew when not to rile her.

"What's wrong with that?" Ned asked.

"If you weren't my brother and if you weren't driving, I'd toss you out of this truck. I've got better plans."

"Yeah? Like what?" Bubba asked.

"I'm going to start a school. It's the first step towards

civilization."

Bubba burst out laughing and Ned laughed so damn hard that he drove off the road. Sally leaned forward, shifted the truck into park, and shoved Ned out the window. When she turned to Bubba, he jumped out before she could hit him again.

"What good's reading and writing?" Bubba shouted. "It don't do nothing for you."

"Oh, no?" Sally drove the truck back onto the road and leaned out the window to yell at them. "I found their recipe for barbeque sauce in the kitchen. I read it. I memorized it. When I get home and tell the folks, I'm going to be a heroine. You two slobs are going to walk home to another whipping."

She rove off, pelting them with gravel from the road.

"What do you think, Bubba?" Ned asked. "Is my sister nuts or what?"

"Nutty enough to be squirrel bait. Start a school!"

The two fell on one another, laughing until their sides hurt so bad that they couldn't laugh any more.

"You know Bubba," Ned said, "if we're gonna get whupped, we might as well do something to get whupped for."

"What've you got in mind?"

"The best damn fun we've had yet. Trust me."

THE END

Linda J. Dunn is a computer specialist for a DoD agency, and while she admits to some geek tendencies, she claims these are off-set by three years of trailer living and twenty years of eating lowest-bidder food.

Linda's short stories have appeared in various anthologies and print magazines, including *Analog*. Her most recent publication is *Blackbird Fly!*, published in *Women Writing Science Fiction as Men*, edited by Mike Resnick and published by DAW.

Her web site is at http://www.lindajdunn.com.

WIDDER LIGGETT AND THE BREATH O' GOD
Lee Martindale

"GaDAMN, George! What you figure done that?"

George and his brother were what you might call "local experts" on the subject of converting live Yumbies - if you could call such creatures "live" - into dead Yumbies. Their daddy had taught them proper, and they took it as gospel that your average walking-around-Yumbie wasn't pretty and your average moved-for-the-last-time one was even less so.

But the three creatures tangled together at the bottom of the gully were so far beyond "not pretty" that George turned his head and spewed the remains of his lunch into the grass before wiping his mouth and replying. "Hell if I know, Clifford. Whatever it was, it got the job done."

Now the boys had heard rumors about Yumbies being different in different parts of the country. But in and around Rocky Mount, North Carolina, your average Yumbie was a tough mother to convert from the walking-around sort to the moved-for-the-last-time sort. George was of the opinion it was somehow tied up with the ruins of that Weslyan College out on Hwy 301 toward Battleboro. Whatever the reason, unless you got a clean 12-gauge headshot or managed to separate the head from the body with something sharp, that Yumbie was going to turn you into supper, beginning with your face.

Which made the three formerly-upwardly-mobile carcasses in the gully even more of a puzzle. None of them had been decapitated, and the blast from a 12-gauge rarely left anything recognizably cranial above the shoulders. "If I didn't know better," Clifford mused as he examined the remains from the edge, "I'd say their heads collapsed from the inside out."

George reached out and popped his younger brother on the side of the head. "You *don't* know better, so stop makin' like you do." Then he slid down the bank for a closer inspection. "Okay, maybe you do," he called up after a time. "Gotta look close to see it, but they all still got faces that all look like they kinda melted in on themselves." He scrambled back up, shaking his head in puzzlement. "Makes me think somebody's come up with a new anti-Yumbie weapon, and I would surely like to know what that is."

Now every individual has his or her own special talent, and Clifford's was tracking. Daddy Franklin had often said that Clifford could read month-old sign from a flea crossing hardpack and trying to cover his trail, and he'd only been exaggerating a little. It didn't appear that anyone had tried to cover the trail that led away from the edge of the gully. "Looks like somebody with small feet, wearing work boots, used a mule to drag those three here - see those trails of black ooze? – and dump 'em over the side. Then jumped up on the mule – here – and rode it back the way he'd come."

"Let's go find out where that is and make his acquaintance."

A little more than a mile later, they were at the edge of a cornfield where the headed-to-the-gully track and the headed-back-from-the-gully track parted company. Clifford and George followed the latter through the corn, until it broke cover at the edge of a rail-fence paddock where dozed an aging jenny. Beyond lay a farmhouse and assorted outbuildings, all of which had seen better, more maintenance-intensive days. "Looks like somebody's home," Clifford observed quietly, nodding toward the house and the smoke that curled gently out of the battered brick chimney. With the kind of unspoken agreement often found between brothers and hunting partners, both checked their weapons before stepping out into the open.

Some say that what constituted good manners in the matter of strangers approaching a secluded farm had come into being with the Coming of the Yumbies, but that's not true. There were refinements tailored to allowing the *approachees* to determine, from a safe distance, that the *approachers* weren't the kind of folks to be cannibalistically inclined. But the basics had developed long before Yuppie 25 escaped the lab, back in the days of holler-hidden copper contraptions and proto-NASCAR driving techniques. And both Clifford and George had been raised to good manners, not to mention maintaining the watertight integrity of their skins.

The boys moved slowly toward the house, keeping themselves out in the open, their weapons out in plain sight. As soon as they heard a dog start barking, they stopped. And as soon as they saw the front door open and a figure move onto the porch, they carefully laid their weapons on the ground in front of them and began peeling out of their shirts. In due time they heard an ancient voice call, "You boys come on up to the house", to which they answered respectfully, "Yes, ma'am." before donning their clothes and picking up their weapons.

At the foot of the cinderblock-and-board steps, they stopped again. "Afternoon, ma'am," said George, touching the bill of his vintage Southern States gimme cap.   He introduced himself and his brother as he cast practiced eyes for telltale signs that something wasn't quite right.

"Any kin to Josephus Franklin over near Canetoe?"

"Our granddaddy, ma'am."

"Well,well," the tiny woman cackled, "that's just dandy. Knew your grandpa back when we were both young and comely. He courted me for a while before your grandma set the hook. I'm Lucretia Liggett... Widder Liggett they'd call me if there was anyone around these parts inclined to call me anything."

"Pleased to make your acquaintance, Miz Liggett," said George.

"Why don't you boys come on up and rest yourselves. I just made a pitcher of tea." Without waiting for them to accept the invitation, Lucretia turned around and scurried into the house. The young men did as instructed, taking careful seats in two rickety-looking rocking chairs and making friends with the hound-mix bitch that was giving them the nasal once-over.

"When was the last time you saw somebody come out to investigate visitors without a weapon in hand?" Clifford queried quietly as his eyes continued to scan the surroundings.

"Does kinda make you wonder how she's managed to stay alive all this time."

Presently she was back, apologizing for the lack of ice and pouring reddish liquid into glasses and handing them out. The brothers thanked her and took cautious sips, then grinned and swallowed with enthusiasm. People boiled a lot of things and called it tea, but what their hostess had boiled was sassafras root, and she'd sweetened the cooling liquid with wild honey. It had been a long time since they'd tasted anything as good.

The next little while was spent covering traditional topics: the health and welfare of the Franklin clan and who had become related to whom by marriage and such, a brief summary of

Lucretia's life and entry into the state of widderhood, and similar subjects considered, in that place and time, small-talk. With the offering of refills on their glasses, the boys took the opening to broach the reason for their "visit". "Miz Liggett," George began, "I don't mean to upset you, but we'd like to ask you a couple of questions about something we found." He told her about backtracking three Yumbies to her property.

"Oh my, yes," Lucretia chirped. "We're having to go farther and farther to find places to dump those nasty things. Beulah and I - Beulah's my mule - are both getting too old to traipse around the countryside like that, but you can't just drag 'em into the field and leave 'em. Ain't good for the grazing or the corn."

"Yes, ma'am," Clifford interjected, "but what we were wondering was, and please don't take this the wrong way, but...how come they're dead and you're...well...not?"

"Because," came the reply as a look of beatific bliss crossed the aged face, "I am Protected."

"Say what? I mean, excuse me?"

"I am Pro-tected. Sheltered by The Breath o' God, which smites the soulless and lays waste to the creatures of evil that seek to harm me and mine."

Clifford and George exchanged a look that clearly indicated they were sharing the same thought regarding the Widder Liggett's grasp on sanity. George was drawing breath, to either ask for further explanation or to mention a pressing previous appointment, when the dog growled low in her throat.

They say that timing is everything, and that a demonstration is worth a thousand theoretical abstracts. The figures that suddenly appeared out of the growing dusk, shambling toward the steps without regard for good manners or anything else but the potential for supper, were about to provide same.

As Clifford and George jumped to their feet, racking shells into the chambers of their shotguns, Lucretia also rose, clasping her hands tightly in front of her bosom. Before either man could fire, she'd moved to the top of the steps and, in a voice meant to carry to Heaven and the next county, begun praying for the swift dispatch of the wicked. The aforementioned "creatures of evil" reacted to the sound as if it were a dinner bell and began converging on it.

George yelled for the old woman to get out of his line of fire, but to no avail. She just kept praying. He yelled again, and when she didn't move, he shrugged and shouldered his Remington in anticipation of the shot he'd get when the Yumbies took her down. Clifford uttered a single-word curse of the kind one didn't normally use in the presence of ladies, and levered himself one-handed over the porch railing, hitting the ground running. Which is how both men had front-row seats to what came next.

The first creature to reach Lucretia - a female, dressed in the tattered remnants of high-dollar business casual and wearing a circular hood ornament on a chain around her neck - grabbed the old woman by the shoulders. She lunged, teeth bared in anticipation of a nose appetizer, at exactly the moment that Lucretia raised her voice even louder on the phrase "PRAISE TO GOD!" The Yumbie's head snapped back as if she'd run into plexiglas; she blinked, released her hold on Lucretia's shoulders, and backed into the body behind her. She was raising one foot, as if preparing to move forward again, when both taloned hands went to her face and a shriek of agony peeled from behind them.

The body into which the first Yumbie had bumped had apparently once belonged to a middle-aged Internet day-trader, based on vestigial nervous ticks and twitches and the fact his facial expression shifted rapidly from gloating joy to abject despair. A spark of his former aggressive style came to the fore as he swept his screaming colleague aside and grabbed for Lucretia. Another loud "PRAISE TO GOD!" caught him full in the face, sending him reeling backwards and tumbling off the steps.

The third member of the pack - a young male who'd apparently been into playing computer games if the remains of jeans and what was left of a t-shirt advertising "Body Count: The Game" on what was left of his chest were any indication, caught movement out of the corner of his eye and turned toward it. The blast from Clifford's Winchester caught him just under the chin.

The last Yumbie standing wasn't; she'd been knocked to her hands and knees, on which she was crawling toward Lucretia. In full view of both brothers, Lucretia went to meet her, leaning down until she and the Yumbie, dressed only in a cell phone ear bug, were face to face. "Lord, let the unholy know the power of THE BREATH O' GOD!" prayed Lucretia in triple-digit decibels.

It was at this point in the proceedings that time slowed for both Clifford and George. They saw the darkness begin to spread on either side of the Yumbie's nose, saw it turn black and take on a shape they'd seen in old magazine ads for allergy medication, saw the face fold in on itself as what kept it face-shaped apparently dissolved.

Time speeded up again and George found himself staring open-mouthed at the last casualty. He could hear Lucretia giving voice to her thankful attitude, still at impressive volume, and Clifford trying to get her attention to find out if she'd been harmed in any way. Then he heard Clifford gasp, then gag.

He looked up in time to see his younger brother staggering back, tripping over Yumbie bodies and landing on his back. He turned and ran toward Lucretia, drawing his machete as he went. Then he, too, got a noseful of what had caused Clifford distress. And, like Clifford, began gagging and trying to put distance between himself and the foulest stench he'd ever encountered. Which, considering the business the Franklin brothers were in, said volumes about the odor.

In an instant, Lucretia went from evangelical loudspeaker to Southern solicitude. "Are you boys alright?" she asked as she tried to approach first one, then the other, and render aid. Both frantically waved her off, protesting as quickly and convincingly as they could that they'd be fine in a minute, all they needed was a little fresh air, *please* don't trouble yourself, ma'am. "Then let me go in the house and get you some water to rinse your mouths."

Clifford, partially recovered, managed to make it to George's side. "That has got to be," opined Clifford, "the absolute worst case of hal-ee-o-toosis walking the face of the earth."

"Amen, brother. But you gotta admit, where Yumbies are concerned, it really *is* The Breath o' God."

THE END

Lee Martindale was a genteel lass, innocent of the way of Bubbadom, until the dastardly Bradley H. Sinor led her astray and into co-writing "Doin' The Drive-in" in *Bubbas of the Apocalypse*. Okay, that's not entirely true. Lee was born and raised in Kentucky, lives in Texas, and is married to a guy from North Carolina. But it's *still* all Brad's fault!

Lee's short fiction has appeared in numerous magazine and anthologies, three collections from Yard Dog Press, and online at *Bookface.Com* and *Elysian Fiction*. She edited Meisha Merlin's first original anthology, *Such A Pretty Face*, and has a story in its second, Lee & Miller's *Low Port*. Her story "Combat Shopping" is slated for Esther Friesner's *Turn The Other Chick*, #5 in the popular *Chicks in Chainmail* anthology series. Lee and her husband George live in Plano, TX, where she keeps friends and fans in the loop at http://www.HarpHaven.net

YUPPIE ZOMBIE BABY FARTS

(Dedicated to the late, great Johnny PayCheck.)
Matt Howl

Act One: Upon which our heroes deliberate on *foie gras*,
Yuppie cannibalism, their sexual identities, how we all secretly
enjoy the smell of our "own brand," and the fucking French.

Brrrappffffft ...pt..pt..pt..pt... Bphooo.

"Ooh, now that was a wet one. Warm, too. Feels like I
plopped down bare-assed Richard Gere-style on a freshly baked
hot fudge nutty brownie!" Johnny smirked at his cousin Dick
through a yellowish haze.

"Dammit, Johnny! I tole you to step out the car if you got
to break wind."

Johnny gently waved his right hand beneath his nose. "It
do singe the nostrils, don't it? To tell the truth, I'd be surprised
if we got any nose hair left. Or if I still got my ass hair for that
matter."

Johnny jokingly made fake gagging noises.

Dick made real ones.

"Damn, boy!" Dick whelped. "It's like trying to use the
outhouse behind grammy's farm after she just spent 40
minutes doing her dirty, dirty business. And she'd been eatin'
prunes."

Johnny, clearly enjoying his piquant attack, cupped a
handful of sour air and thrust it under Dick's nose. "Take a
snort, cousin. I feel Zestfully clean!"

"That's enough, Johnny! Jee-zis! We got to finish cleaning
out the valuables from this Saab so's we can bring 'em back to
camp. And if we ain't back by sundown, them fellars ain't
gonna hold up dinner on our account. They'll be getting back
from their own day of huntin' around and be fixin' to eat our
share and leave us with no beer."

Dick and Johnny had recently joined a survivalist
encampment, the members of which spent most days roaming
the Blue Ridge Mountain lowlands looking for food, gas, and
Skoal.

"Okay, okay, I'll roll down a window your majesty. Wouldn't want to offend your delicate senses. You know, you always was a mite particular, especially for someone in our fambly."

Johnny, sitting in the passenger side of the smashed-up car they found along Route 23/25, turned away from Dick to look at the door. He quickly adopted his normal expression of general bewilderment. As his eyebrows went up, he turned back to Dick. "Where the hell are the got-damn rollers? You mean to tell me for all the money them Yups used to pay for these piece of fuck Saabs, the Swiss couldn't never figure out a way to make windows what roll down?"

Dick looked at his cousin Johnny with disgust. "First of all, dipshit, this ain't no Swiss car. It's Norwegian." Dick shook his head. "And second, it's got bought out by GM so these's practically American anyway. Now see them little knobs in the door armrest where you been wipin' your boogers when you thought I warn't looking? They's automatic window openers. And if the car battery wasn't dead, we'd push on 'em to make the windows go down."

"How'd you learn about that?"

"Boy, what I know that you don't couldn't fit into Sally Anne Cavanaugh's dump truck ass-crack without calling in a Mack Semi fulla Pam."

"Sheeeet. You just think you're smart cuz you was in the Army."

"Wait just a minute, now. Everybody knows the Army is very selective. Very. It's ain't my fault you're the only one I ever heard of who they took one look at and told to skedaddle. Now me, they knew 100% prime beef soldier when they saw it. Even gave me $229 for junior college. That's free money! And I got to see the world. Well, Columbus, Georgia anyway. Till they kicked me out after I got caught with that faig. I still don't know how his dirty wang ended up in my mouth."

"Yeah, you know, that story never did quite make no sense to me. How did..."

"I said, I don't know." A deep red began spreading up Dick's neck and face as he turned away from Johnny. Speaking to his own door handle pretending to reexamine those fascinating devices called automatic window openers, he said, "Now are we gonna finish stripping this car or not?"

"Okay, okay. Sorry I asked."

Without warning, Johnny and Dick simultaneously jumped

at the sound of sloppy chomping and high-pitched giggles from the rear seat.

Dick looked gravely at Johnny and nodded his head towards the back of the car. Johnny shook his head from side to side and jerked it right back at Dick. Dick frowned and gestured more sternly towards the rear seat. Grimacing, Johnny slowly raised his Mossberg Persuader shotgun above the seat and peeked over the edge. Dick instinctively leaned back into the steering wheel and raised a Browning Buckmark pistol. "What is it?" Dick whispered.

"I don't see nothin'." Johnny put down the Persuader and surveyed the rear of the car. Nothing. Then he leaned over a little more to check out the back seat foot space. There he saw a Yuppie baby noshing on what appeared to be, given the soccer mom haircut covering the uneaten half of her head, its own dead mother. The baby looked up and smiled through blood-red baby teeth and bodily juices running down its chin. Johnny jerked back. "It's a baby zombie!"

Dick cocked his head to one side. "Now how in the fuck can there be a baby zombie?"

Johnny shrugged his shoulders. "I dunno. Maybe she was pregnant when she turned into a Yumbie?"

Dick laughed harshly. "Yeah, she probably couldn't even take time out from her job sittin' all day at some computer to give birth to her own kid. Hell, they probably just cut a hole in her chair so's she could drop the baby without missin' a single email."

"What's a email?"

Then both men heard a high-pitched, sweet voice say, "Orh raynes."

Dick licked his lips, swallowed hard, and forced himself to speak. "What did he say?"

"It sounded like, 'Orh raynes.'"

"I know that you idiot, but what the fuck does it mean?"

"I think he's saying, 'more brains.'" [1]

Dick tilted his head at Johnny. "Well anyway, he's obviously a Yumbie now. So fucking shoot the little bastard."

"How come I always got to be the one who shoots 'em?"

"Cuz you got the shotgun. It's better for this close-range killin'. Now get!"

---

1 Author's Note: Insert groan here.

"Aw man, but it's just a baby. I don't want to kill no baby. If we just let him be, he'll eventually starve to death anyway."

"And you think that's humanitarian? Come on, Johnny, I know you ain't that dumb. How come we been killin' and eatin' all them deer and turkeys and pheasants since even before the plague?"

"Cuz our McDonald's hired a black guy, and you was afraid he'd spit on your hamburger?"

"Well, sure that's part of it. But also if'n we don't keep a watch on these Yuppies, they start getting outta hand. I'm talking about simple population control. Just look back at what happened the first time around. If we'd done our job and thinned out them overfed, too-good-for-us, walled-in-community-livin' jerkoffs, they wouldn't have gotten so outta wack. But folks like you and me sat around on our lazy asses shoveling down teevee dinners with Sporks drowning ourselves in Boone's Farm and Judge Robo-Wapnar while them Yups went plumb loco. They got to the point they was makin' up bullshit innernet companies worth a billion dollars on Monday and goin' broke on Tuesday. Then they'd fire hundreds o' thousands of good ol' boy workers just to keep stock prices high. Hell, they even invented a $4 cup of coffee. Now what the fuck is that all about? So do the humanitarian thing and kill that Yuppie!"

Johnny leaned over the backseat and pointed the Persuader at the baby. The small Yup looked back up at Johnny and smiled again. "Aww...but, Dick..."

Then to their surprise, Sssssss...bpprapt!

The baby farted. A sulfuric green fog began rising from the rear seat.

"That can't be good."

"No shit, Shitlock. What the fuck is that? Lookee, that stuff's so thick you can see big fart particles. You shoulda killed it first! And you know how bad them baby farts smell."

"Yeah, plus this one's a mutherfucking zombie baby eatin' it's own mama!" Covering his nose and mouth, Johnny turned to his car door in a panic and started to punch at the dead automatic window openers.

"We got to get out the car and away from that smoke, Dick. My cousin Merlene's baby farted next to me one time, and I smelled it on my Wranglers for weeks!"

Thinking Johnny would've solved that problem if he had

just washed his jeans once in a while, Dick leaned towards the back seat with a quizzical look on his face. Like a budding scientist, he used his left hand to waft the thick green vapor back towards his nostrils and inhaled deeply. "Settle down beavis, we're gonna be okay. I never smelled anything so sweet in all my life. Slide over and take you a whiff. This baby farts manna."

"Fuck that. You must be as loony as a Yuppie if you want me to..." Snort! "Hey, that ain't bad. No sir. T'ain't bad at all. Smells kinda fragrant. Them big ol' mites o' fart dust kinda tickle my nose, but this might smell even better than back when I was plowin' down my best gal Mary Jane Moldjama's granny undies!"

"Yeah, you and everybody else..." Dick mumbled under his breath as he leaned into the deliciously thick plume of baby fart to suck in the sweet, dense air. He started to feel lightheaded as he drew in the fumes and their oversized particles.

Johnny angrily sat back outside the fart cloud and stopped inhaling gas. He snarled, "What'd you say, mutherfucker?"

Feeling high and mighty from the baby's methane mist, Dick said, "You wasn't even close to the only one puttin' your mouth on Mary Jane's 'moldy munchables.' Didn't you know she had every man in the county over 'to eat?' Way I heard, she even had over some o' their wives."

Johnny's head jerked around and spittle sprayed from the corners of his mouth as he snapped, "That don't mean nothing, son, 'cept that I've had me some pussy more recent than you. Hell, the last time you even talked to a girl, she told you to finish your Cap'n Crunch or you couldn't wear your KISS costume on Halloween. You call her 'Mommy.'"

"Well then you done went and dated her!"

"What do you care? Your Ma was separated from Grandpa Herdy at the time."

"That don't matter. I was only two trailers away. Didn't you think I'd see you sneakin' in every night? Your problem is all you ever think about is 'getting some!'"

"And you never seem to think about it at all! In fact, you're the only dude I know who ain't gummed up by the lack o' women round here. Maybe your little thing in the Army wasn't really no accident. Could be you and this Stephen or Bruce or whoever he was were..."

Johnny quit talking and twirled around to face the backseat.

"Mutherfucker!" he screamed. The Persuader jumped in his hands.

BLAM!

SPLOOSH!

Baby guts everywhere.

After a moment of stunned silence, Dick started screeching. "Got-Dammit! I got 'em all over me. You shot it, and I got yuppie zombie baby guts in my mouth and I do-oh-oh-on't like it." Dick spat out baby chunks while big frightened tears rolled down his cheeks.

"I'm sorry," Johnny bawled back. "I felt his Little Smokies fingers touchin' me on the back of my neck, and I knew he was going in for the kill. I shot 'im on instinct!"

Sniffing back tears, Dick snorted, "This tastes completely foul. I'd rather be licking that nasty, old Mary Jane's twat even after a bunch o' hunky guys already laid their sweet mouths down there..."

"What?" Johnny wiped away the greasy guts that had oozed into his eyes. "What did you say, you sumbitch?" Homosexuality took priority over yuppie zombie baby guts in the grand redneck scheme of things to fear and destroy.

"Um, nothing." Dick knew he had to regain composure quickly. Also more important than yuppie zombie baby guts was making sure your cousin didn't think you were a "damn homo." "I said I'd rather lick me some fine, fragrant pussy instead of eating a baby. Why? You got a problem with that?"

"Course not. I just thought I heard you say something about guys bein,' uh..."hunky?"

"What? Are you coming on to me?! I'm serious here. I'm serious as a fuckin' heart attack! Our standin' as 'cousins' depends on this, mutherfucker! I said 'funky.' Not 'hunky.' But if you're thinking about a man bein' a hunk or some shit..."

"Not me. I thought you was. I mean, I... Aw, forget it. I knew you wasn't thinking of naked men."

"Course not." Thinking of naked men, Dick shifted his Browning Buckmark over the rising tent in his pants. "We, uh, we gotta get the fuck outta here anyway. You know, is your neck okay? Let me see it."

Johnny rubbed the back of his neck. "Shit no, it ain't

okay. I got baby slime all over it. Damn! I can still feel those stubby little fingers grabbin' at me."

"Sorry, Johnny. Here, let me rub it a little. I kin try to work out some of the kinks in your shoulders, too."

Giving him a funny look, Johnny began wiping off the guts as best he could. "Nah, why don't you just look in the back and let me know if there's anything worth taking from the rear." [2]

Dick leaned over into the back seat and grabbed the only thing he saw besides dead Yuppies. It was a picnic basket lying on the floor.

"This is it. Guess mommy was taking her kid for a bite." [3]

Johnny started to inspect under the red-checkered cloth covering the top of the expensive looking hamper.

"So what's in there?" Dick asked.

"Let's see... there's a couple of books about being a momma. Shoot, I bet my momma woulda been better to me if she'd read a book 'bout how to do it."

"Well shore, but she'd have to put down her bottle of Thunderbird and learn to read first."

Johnny ignored Dick's comment as he continued rummaging through the basket. "Let's see what else. There's some o' them three-dollar energy bars, a few bottles of water, a couple o' old CDs no real music fan would listen to..." Suddenly, his eyes lit up. "Oo-wee! She's got food! There's bread and crackers, canned meats, and, um, something called foh-eye-ee grass. That ain't look like any grass I ever smoked. What the fuck is *foie gras*, Dick?"

He looked at the fatty, dark, mushy pile inside a clear container stamped, "Made in France." "I think it's goose livers."

"Livers? Yuck! Just the thought almost makes me want to go vegetarian!"

"Shut your mouth, Johnny. Sides, I bet this ain't come from no goose."

"Ah, I know you're right. I's just kidding anyway – I'd never be no fucking vegetarian. I'd get sick of eatin' nothing but vegetables. And chicken, fish, and turkey. So you ever actually ate any o' them goose livers before?"

---

2 Ba-dum-tch! (Insert cheap joke here)
3 Get it?! It's funny because the kid took a bite of momma instead of... ahh, forget it.

"We had 'em once in the Army during some exchange whena mess of French soldiers came over to learn us how they fight."

"The French? What'd they teach you? How they's so good at surrendering? Or maybe how they curled up in a ball and cried when the Nazi's bitch-slapped 'em? Shit, if there was ever a country that got hit by the Yuppie Virus, it's France. By now I figure they must be practically 100 percent either dead or walking zombies smellin' like their own stinky cheese."

"Yeah, they didn't really teach us much. Them soldiers mostly sat around in jaunty berets smoking unfiltered cigarettes listening to this ol' lady named Edith Piaf warble out some awful songs. Give me Patsy or Tammy Wynette any day."

"Not me, I'd rather have Foghat. Or fuckin' Ram Jam."

Dick took one final look around the car. "Well, cousin, I think we done got everything worth getting.' You grab the jack and extra gas we found in the trunk, and I'll bring this here picnic basket with the food and Enya and Dave Matthews CDs. Come on – let's head back to camp."

Act Two: Whence our protagonists' souls begin a slow descent into Yuppie hell, discordance breaks out between Bubbas, Pabst Blue Ribbon is imbibed, and a gift keeps giving.

Dick and Johnny left the Saab and began hiking their way back towards camp through the forest outside Weaverville. Glancing sideways at Johnny, Dick started to giggle.

"What're you laughin' at?" Johnny asked.

"I can't believe I almost ate baby!" Dick snickered.

"It is pretty un-fucking-believable, I'll give you that." Johnny chuckled.

"I'd be drummed out of this group of fellers if they ever found out."

Johnny guffawed, "That's for sure. Baby: The Other White Meat!"

"But that baby was Asian," Dick howled hysterically.

Johnny stopped and turned to Dick. "Wait just a got-damn minute. No fucking self-respecting man I know would ever say, 'Asian.' We say 'Oriental,' numb-nuts."

"Shit. Yeah, you're right. Now that you mention it, I been feelin' a little funny, Johnny."

Johnny started at him unblinkingly. "You must be. Only

Yuppies use them PC terms. Did you somehow become a Yumbie and not tell me?"

"How could I? You been with me the whole time. Besides, you know we're immune. They can't infect us."

"Yeah, that's true." Johnny scratched his head. "But you know, you did spend a lot more time huffin' that weird baby fart. Maybe it's like what happened to me with Merleen's baby but worse cuz o' that nasty green gas – could be with all them floaty fart mites, you got some Yuppie Virus in you."

"Fuck! You don't seriously think so? Oh shit, oh shit, oh shit." Dick dropped the picnic basket causing CDs and bottled water to tumble out on the ground. Trembling, he began talking into his chest, "Okay, don't panic. I just need to think. We gotta get to a nice, safe Starbucks where I can sit down and figure this out."

"There you go, mutherfucker!" Johnny pointed a finger at Dick. "Did you just hear yourself? You definitely picked up something from that baby fart!"

Dick looked at his cousin without recognition. Then he gazed back down and seemed to see the gun in his holster for the first time. He asked himself, "How did this get here? I always thought what this country needs is more gun control laws!"

"That's it!"

Johnny leaped off his feet and tackled Dick to the ground.

"You've done gone delirious!" He restrained his convulsing cousin, holding him in a bear hug. "It's okay, man, I got you now. We got to get you in that stream over yonder and wash off the baby fart."

Dick muttered, "I'm seein' God...and...he looks...he looks just like a BMW Dealer." Then his eyes rolled into the back of his head.

"Don't you die on me, Dick! I got you!"

Johnny picked up his cousin in a fireman's carry and ran as fast as he could before throwing him into the nearby stream.

SPLASH!

Dick went under the water. 15 seconds passed. 30 seconds. One minute. Johnny watched and waited breathlessly. Then the water started to bubble. Dick popped up! He sputtered and started to swim to the edge.

Shouting out to him, Johnny said, "Hold off, man. You're sick with Yuppie. Wash all the fart off you, Dick, before you pull yourself out."

"It's okay. I came to when I hit the water. I grabbed some moss and scrubbed down under there. I feel pretty clean."

"Then answer me this, Dick: Who's the greatest American to ever live?"

"William F. Buckley."

"You're done for!" Johnny started to back up. "I bet it's worse than we thought. If you can't wash it off, I reckon that Yuppie Virus musta got into your brain when you sniffed the baby fart. It survives by smelling so good you'll want to breathe in the virus and carry it around. Farts is how it spreads!"

Dick pulled himself out of the water with a tight smile on his face. "No, it's all right, I feel much better. I was just kidding about Buckley. You know I meant Hank Williams, Jr."

"You serious?" Johnny, feeling relieved, walked over and gave his wet cousin a one-armed man-hug. "I'm so glad. Damn, boy, I thought we'd lost you for sure. Hey, uh, Dick? You're huggin' me with two arms here, and one o' your hands is on my butt. What, uh..."

Dick squeezed Johnny tightly and spoke into his ear. "You know, Johnny, wouldn't it be fantastic if someone in our little group of scavengers found a television and a VCR that actually worked? I'd love to watch some old reruns of Friends. Man, how I love that crazy Ross – he's hilarious!"

"Uh, say Dick, now you're nibblin' on my ear." Johnny wriggled and pushed against Dick's chest as he struggled to get out of his cousin's clutches. "We, um, should really start, mmph, heading back before it gets dark."

"And I could just die for a low-fat double decaf soy macchiato with a chocolate chip Bubba brain biscotti!"

Cha-chunkt! Johnny snapped out of Dick's grip, cocked and aimed his Persuader. "Don't move, mutherfucker! You've become a Yumbie. Now I'm for sure you musta got fucked up big time when you jammed your face all up in that baby fart."

"Well heckaroonie, you smelled it, too, Johnny. So put that gun down. Let's agree to a time out and discuss this rationally. You know, I'd really like to share my feelings with you. And I'd love to hear what you have to say, too. Because right now, I have to tell you...looking down the barrel of your shotgun is very hurtful to my self-esteem. If we're going to continue as cousins, I think we need couples therapy."

"Couples what..?" Johnny's finger twitched on the shotgun trigger.

"And another thing. I really think we'd be better off if we left that tribe of yahoos. All they do is ride around in their Four-By's shooting and eating animals, drinking beer, and jerking off to that old issue of Unclean Beaver Shots. And on that note, my name is Richard from now on."

"But I thought you liked 'Dick?!'"

"I love dick! And I'm absolutely suffocating in this closet. I'm here, I'm queer, and I'm proud. So get over it because I'm somewhere over the rainbow, girlfriend!"

BLAM!

"Girlfriend?"

Johnny walked over to his cousin lying on the ground. Dick's face had gone as white as a Klansman's coward-sheet as he tried to comprehend the gaping wound in his chest.

"Dick, I'm sorry, man."

"It's... 'Richard.'"

"Um, right...Well, I just couldn't stand to watch you become a Yuppie. Next thing we know you'd have been talking about stock splits, leasing a Mercedes, and getting a President Gates haircut. Plus it'd be kind of awkward with you always trying to eat my brains. You know, since you're a homo now and everything."

"I...I don't blame you, Johnny. But I know...you were probably affected, too." Dick struggled for breath as the blood in his lungs gurgled and bubbled. "I can...still smell that...baby fart. Promise me...you'll kill yourself...so you don't infect anyone else."

"But I don't think it got me, Dick, uh, I mean Richard. I think this happened when you kept deep snortin' them baby fart fumes, and you musta got infected by the virus. But don't you worry about me. I'm like Bubba Clinton; I tried it, but I didn't inhale."

"But what...if it did...get you? You have to...do the right thing. Don't...spread it. Just...ask yourself, "What would...Martha Stewart do?'"

Blam!

"Fuck you, girlfriend."

Johnny shot him a few more times in the head, and Dick was silent.

Laying down his gun, Johnny dolefully picked up his dead

cousin. Scanning around, he carried the body to the base of the most beautiful tree in the grove. And after gently laying down Dick in his final resting-place, a single tear rolled down Johnny's cheek as he carved a farewell eulogy into the trunk of the tree.

"Daid Homo Yupe – Dont Tuch"

Then Johnny picked up his gun in addition to the fallen bottles of water and CDs. And after giving an unusual look of interest to the Dave Matthews song list – especially for a fuckin' Ram Jam fan – he walked back to camp alone.

"Hey, Johnny's back! What'd you find out there, bro? I hope it's something good. Jessie here done caught a few squirrels so we gonna be eatin' stew with real meat tonight! And Wayne found something even better!"

"A nudie mag with white women?"

"Naw, not that good. But he did find us some Pabst and Heineken!"

"Fuck that shit! Pabst Blue Ribbon! Bring it on, man."

Willie, the camp's de facto leader walked over to Johnny. "We was starting to get a little worried about you. My cousin, Earl, went so far as to lay first dibs on all your Elvis tapes." Willie looked around. "Hey, what happened to Dick?"

"Well, it's like this." Johnny got very somber, and the other men in their camp who'd already returned from a day of scavenging circled around him. "He done got zombified. So I had to kill him."

"What? Holy shit! How'd that happen?

"I ain't totally sure. I think it all started when we shot us a zombie with my big gun, and it exploded in Dick's mouth."

Dumbstruck, Earl asked, "Dick got some bad meat in his mouth?"

"And not for the first time."

Willie went on, "So how'd you do him?"

"After I shot him in the chest, I plugged him in the head."

Roy, Willie's second illegitimate child, said, "Yeah, that's right. You gotta shoot 'em in the head. Once the brain is gone, they up and die."

"Not always – you're still alive, ain't you?" Willie quipped.

Everyone in camp laughed.

Johnny waited until the men quieted back down and said, "Yeah, that shot to the head killed him. But I dunno... Before that he was talkin,' and he still seemed mostly like Dick. What I mean is, he hadn't totally become a Yumbie yet. It's like the virus is mutantatin' into something else that can infect even us. Something silent but deadly... So one day you're drivin' your Dodge truck and everything's fine. Then you get a few extra bucks, buy a Volvo, and next thing you know, you peel off your 'Bingo Whore' and 'Guns Don't Kill People – I Do' bumper stickers to make room for one what says 'Free Tibet.'"

"What the fuck is Tibet?"

"But Johnny, maybe we coulda kept him alive for a while longer. Try to fix him up or something?"

Johnny took a deep breath and frowned. "Naw, I been thinkin'...it's horrible, but...well, I had to kill him. He'd eventually become a full-blown Yumbie. One day he'd wake up in our camp and, without being able to control hisself, he'd chew up our eyeballs and suck out our brains while we slept. We coulda all been turned into damn yuppie zombies ourselves."

Willie looked at him sternly. "But darn it, Johnny, he was your cousin!"

Other voices chimed in.

"He was my cousin, too!"

"He was my uncle! And my brother."

"He once let me have sex with his sister. Before she became my cousin."

Willie shook his head and smiled sadly. "Point is, he was kin, Johnny. And you don't never turn yore back on kin." Rare tears began to form in the corners of Willie's eyes as his face took on a beatific glow. He held up his hands in a saintly manner and sniffed, "We'll always love Dick, and we coulda made it work out."

Johnny looked at his feet. "He was a homo."

"Well, you did what you had to do. Who wants a Pabst?"

Later that night around the campfire, the men passed around a well-used copy of Unclean Beaver Shots while Johnny ate the last of the squirrel chili. "I don't know about you guys, but I have an insatiable appetite for meat tonight. Willie, I simply must tell you: you're a genius with a stew over an open fire!"

Willie looked up from a dark vaginal close-up and scratched his head. "Genius?"

"And what the hell's 'insashabul' mean?"

Johnny looked down and secretly rubbed the Dave Matthews CD he'd hidden in his pants. "Aw, it's nothing. I guess I'm just tired from everything that happened today."

The rest of the camp looked at him suspiciously. Johnny continued, "Hey, forget it. I got a chili fart comin' on. Give me a stick from the fire!"

The somber mood quickly passed as Bubbas broke out in cheers. "Whoo-hoo! Johnny's got something brewin'! Earl, grab them grahams and Hershey's cuz it's time to make s'mores!"

Johnny took a thin branch with a flame on one end and bent over the fire. After sucking in a deep breath, he squeezed his face and strained and struggled until he pushed out a mighty and powerful roar! [4]

Bpppprrrrrrrrllllllllaaaatttttt!!!!

Marveling at Johnny's enormous blaze, everyone cheered and patted him on the back. In the dark, they were oblivious to a growing green cloud of gas.

Willie was the first to speak.

"Damn, Johnny, that's the sweetest fart I ever did smell..."

THE END

Matt Howl is the sole proprietor (and reader) of the lowbrow literary humor magazine, Howl Movement. A closet Bubba, Matt has visited Graceland on the anniversary of the King's death, ridden his hog to the Sturgis Motorcycle Rally, and visited a legal Nevada brothel with his father. (Really.) A former writer for the defunct music publication, Thorazine, Matt is currently at work on a novel about Satan in Hollywood. Like almost everyone else in the entertainment industry, the Dark One is still waiting for his big break.

Matt and the lovely Mrs. Howl live in San Diego with their two dogs, two cats, and two motorcycles.

---

4 And a little poop. The drippy kind that makes you itch all day. Man, I hate that.

HAL'S CROSSROADS
Robert Pickering

Pedal to the floor, desperate to get away from Madeline and her yuppie-turned-carnivore brethren, Dale Ermine ran headfirst into the town of Buckton. It wasn't much of a town–just a few gas stations and liquor stores around the intersection of state highway 106 and US 49.

As he tore down the deserted highway toward the center of town, he got the idea that something was different here. Instead of the typical smashed up bubba pickups and yumbie SUVs lining the road, Buckton's side streets were all blocked off by school busses and mobile homes, mostly the old silver Airstreams. It looked like a trailer park had migrated into the middle of town.

Lost in that thought, he didn't see the line of barbed wire stretched across the road until it vanished under the hood of his F-150. The truck bounced, the tires blew out with blasts to do a shotgun proud, and Dale found himself skidding. The wire whipped around in his wheelwells, probably wrapped around his axle. One of those shiny Airstreams loomed in his windshield, getting bigger way too fast.

His truck's fiberglass crunched, the trailer's metal squealed. Something round and white–the airbag–punched Dale in the face. He focused on not pissing himself.

A trio of bucktoothed faces peered in the driver's side window. Even with the cracked glass, Dale could tell they were beyond ugly. "Ass-ugly" might do them justice, but the wreck left him too rattled to find the proper description.

One of the Bubbas–he hoped they were Bubbas, and not plumbers who'd won the lottery just before Yuppie-25 hit–used a rifle butt to smash in the window, reached in, and popped the door open. Meaty hands yanked him out of the truck.

At first, he thought he'd ruptured the Airstream's gray water tank and spilled shit all over the street, but then he realized the rank smell surrounding him was the Bubbas' breath. It reminded him of buckets he'd found in his daddy's deer cleaning shop.

The rifle's business end poked him in the nose. The Bubba holding it said, "We're detainin' you by the authority of the United States of America, one nation under God, and with the blessing of His holy instrument, Hal. You a people-eater?"

Dale raised his hands. "What?"

"He don't know Hal. Shoot him, Mort," one of the other Bubbas said. Judging by their matching bulb noses, extra chins, and chubby, stubbled cheeks, they were brothers. In fact, the only way to tell them apart was their attire: one's hat read "John Deere," another's "Schlitz," and Mort's said "Muffler's Feed & Ammo." They all wore greasy jumpsuits, with name patches. Mort, Eddie, and Gordy.

Growing up in farm country, he'd known their type, the ignorant rednecks, from the farms where cattle weren't produce, they were companionship.

One of Dale's unpleasant urges struck him. His wife used to make a wonderful Alfredo sauce, and though it'd been too upscale for his tastes, maybe it could bring out the grain-fed flavor in these three–

Shutting off that disturbing thought, he tried to remember the old, small-town accent he'd spent years overcoming. "You'd best not do that. My name's Dale Ermine–"

"Ermine? Ain't that a weasel?" Eddie asked.

"Weasel's good eatin'," Gordy said.

Maybe they had full-blown Yup-25, and were sizing him up for a meal. Maybe they just got these weird urges like he did. Hell, maybe they were just very flexible in their diets. "No, it's not a weasel, and I'm not good eating. Ain't good eating. Eatin'. You know. But I'm not one of *them*, I'm trying to get back to my country roots. Only my wife, Madeline, she's chasing me–"

Eddie said, "Married a woman named Madeline? He's a people eater."

Mort jabbed the shotgun barrel up Dale's nose like an oversized medical probe. "He's got a point. We only ain't shot you dead on account of that fine truck you drive."

"Drove," Eddie said. "It's dead now."

"Whatever." Mort got to the point. "You eat people?"

"No," Dale said. "Never."

"Well," Eddie said, "you sound a bit defensive there. Why don't you prove you ain't a people eater?"

The quiet one, Gordy, said, "How's he gonna do that?"

"Shit," Mort said. "Suppose we could show him one of them yuppies we bagged, see if'n he eats it."

Eddie said, "If he don't, that don't prove nothing."

Gordy scratched his head. "We'd best take him to Hal."

Great–a redneck quartet. "Who the fuck is Hal?" Dale said.

"He's the one who saved us, when the yumbies poured outta the city."

Gordy raised his voice. "*And when all was lost, Hal did come, and on a mighty John Deere he rode, with the bagging attachment. And he unleashed the power of his voice, and the reek that rode upon it, and the yumbies knew pain. And so it was that Hal smote the children of Dot-Com.*"

Sweat trickled down Dale's neck. Before that bubble popped, he'd done a short stint at a dot-com. These three had the collective IQ of a dog biscuit, but it was still work to hide his secret. He wasn't about to reveal the bizarre hunger pangs he'd had these past few weeks, ones that intensified when he looked at a hefty, meaty person.

At first, he'd tried blocking these thoughts by thinking of something innocuous, but his mortgage, cell phones, or anything from the Sharper Image catalog started him salivating. He'd only been able to stop the urges by indulging them: if he dreamt of putting a person on the pit, over some good charcoal and mesquite, slathered in barbeque sauce, he'd go back to normal.

Somehow, he knew that he wouldn't be able to keep this secret from Hal.

If he was really some kind of messiah, Dale would've expected Hal to hold court at city hall, or one of the churches, but the brothers took him to the town's physical, spiritual, and culinary heart, which sat at the highway intersection.

The Waffle House.

The sign, black letters on those yellow blocks, sputtered and flickered overhead, like it was some spiritual bug zapper, keeping the yumbies at bay.

The brothers ushered him inside, all staying out of easy biting distance, not that Dale was so inclined. Earlier unnatural craving or no, these three were too gamy. As a rule, Dale tried to avoid eating anything with breath that put his nastiest chili farts to shame.

"You guys want an Altoid?" he offered. The Bubbas looked at him like he'd offered them opera tickets. Gordy crossed himself.

The gun barrel jabbed him towards a booth, where a man was lighting a cigarette, striking his match on a no-smoking sign. If this was Hal, Dale was disappointed. A little part of him had expected some shining figure, perhaps with a halo and a nametag saying "Hal," but no such luck.

Hal was no holy figure. Hal was the Waffle House's cook, even if he was slouched in one of the yellow booths like a customer. Middle aged, big potbelly, two-day stubble, American flag tattooed on his forearm, the works. A rainbow of stains meandered down his once-white shirt from collar to crotch. He was smoking Marlboro reds, and wore a folded paper cook's hat.

Mort prodded Dale in the butt, so he slid into the booth across from Hal. He made the mistake of waving the cigarette smoke away and gagged. The stuff had been masking Hal's breath, which packed more pungent punch than Mort, Eddie and Gordy's combined. It smelled like the septic tank under a trailer full of Bubbas with the shits.

"What do we got here?" By speaking, Hal spread more of his special scent around.

Eddie answered. "This here's Dale Ermine. Cain't tell if he's a people-eater or not."

"Ermine?" Hal said. "Isn't that some kind of gopher?"

While Dale rolled his eyes, Gordy Muffler said, "Gopher's good eatin'."

"Well," Dale said, "if you're some kind of mythic savior, what kind of name is Hal?"

Hal just shrugged and dabbed at a mustard stain on his shirt. "Better'n bein' called Ned, I suppose." After getting part of the stain to flake off, Hal turned his full attention back to the conversation. "So what brings you to Buckton?"

"Passing through."

"Case you hadn't heard, Mr. Ermine, people ain't in the habit of passing through much of anywheres anymore."

He hadn't really given it much thought–all he wanted was to get away from Madeline. His old buddy Jim was a race car mechanic down in Texas, about as far from a yuppie as one could be. "Headin' to see an old friend."

Hal's eyes bored into his. "That's not all."

"Okay, fine, I'm running."

Eddie and Mort started chuckling. "Mr. Gopher's got woman problems."

"Why don't you two," Hal said, "go man the roadblock again. Wouldn't want to let any yuppies through, would we?" When they nodded and backed away, he added, "Take your idiot brother with 'ya."

They led Gordy to the door. "Guess we ain't shootin' him," Eddie was saying as they left.

"You'll have to forgive the Muffler brothers. Ain't all there, but they's good kids. Doin' a fine job keeping the yuppies from getting into the back country."

Dale wasn't placated. "If that's what they were doing, why'd they stop me? I'm not a yuppie, I drive a pickup for Christ's sake!"

Across the chipped table, Hal's eyebrows inched toward his hat. "Pickup don't mean you ain't a yuppie. If that was the case, you wouldn't be thinkin' about adding the other, other white meat to your diet, would ya?"

So he hadn't been able to hide it from Hal. Only question now was why Hal hadn't told Mort to scatter his brains all over the syrup jugs and laminated menus.

"But I shouldn't have it," Dale said. "I mean, I'm not frothing like the rest of them, and I come from out here, in the country."

Stubbing his cigarette out, Hal said, "Ain't where you come from, it's how you been livin'. You got the roots, Dale, but you picked the wrong path."

"I took a job in the city, and now I have to eat people? What kind of bullshit judgment is that?"

"Ain't just the job, Dale, but I'll leave all that for you to figure out. You're a wayward soul, but I think you're worth savin', deep down. Not quite sure if this scourge is sortin' out the righteous or the inbred, but it can't make up it's mind with you. You picked up a whole host of problems lately, and if you don't get over 'em, you're damned. They start at this blasphemy right here." Hal leaned over the table and flicked a finger at Dale's shirt pocket, where it thunked off the tin of Altoids inside.

"Somehow," Dale said, "I don't think anyone in this town has room to talk. Besides, my wife's more of a problem, if she catches up to me."

"Fine, if you say so. What's your problem with her?"

This waffle cook had already become a holy leader, so why shouldn't relationship therapist be on his résumé? "Maddie's got the virus, or whatever it is. She'd never liked our mailman, but I knew it was something more when I came home one day to find her stuffing his head and some other leftovers into his mailbag. She said it was 'For later.' Half an hour later, the radio told me what was going on, but I was already gone. Soon as I saw her coming at me with that butcher's knife and a box of Ziplocs, I ran to my truck and hit the road."

"You didn't just leave her cause she tried to eat you, though."

Perceptive, for a guy who'd lived on minimum wage plus tips. "Nope. Our problems started before all the cannibalism. But they weren't anything worth killing each other over."

"Maybe not to you," Hal said. "What'd you do?"

"Nothing, really." Dale bit his lip. "There was one thing, happened about the time things started going bad. Day of our anniversary, I went and judged a chili-and-ribs cookoff, then didn't have a mint or anything before our night out. Kissed her, she said I couldn't see her again unless I started carrying these." He rattled the mints in his pocket. "Seems kinda pissant when I talk about it."

Before Hal could answer, the door burst open, the bell on top jingling. Eddie skidded in. "There's some yuppie woman out on the highway, just outside shootin' range. Yelled at us. Says she needs to talk to Dale."

Stark terror, conditioned through a hundred of Madeline's screeching rants, ran through Dale's blood like antifreeze. "I need a car, a truck, a four-wheeler. Anything to keep ahead of her."

Hal leaned back and straightened his paper hat. "No, what you need is to go face your personal demon-bitch. Mort, show him the way, but don't you boys get too close yourselves. Let's see what Mr. Ermine's got inside."

Madeline waited down the road, resting against her company car, an off-pink Lexus. A pair of star shaped ricochet marks in the asphalt showed that Mort had tested their theory about her being out of range.

Dale had some trouble reconciling this woman with the cheerleader he'd met at a campground beer-and-moonshine party his junior year. That girl went by Maddie, and had gone skinny-dipping with him that first night because he'd helped her with a plan to steal the head cheerleader title.

Now, Madeline wore a sixty-dollar skirt from Designer Outlet, and a blouse matching in origin, nondescriptness and price. She'd probably calculated the color to contrast her fake tan and match her penciled eyebrows. Dale still smarted over the fight they'd had when she came home with those; he'd muttered something about a fourth-grader needing his map colors back.

The only thing alluring was her perfume, a flowery scent that made his head spin and stomach flutter. A nice meal might calm that down, though.

Annoyance replaced terror at sight of her nametag, something she'd never worn home before. "Madeline Ermine-Sewell," it said, right above the name of her new employer, Mary Ell Cosmetics.

"What's with the name?" he said, pointing at the tag. "Thought we swore before God and the Justice of the Peace to be Dale and Maddie Ermine."

"Christ, Dale, it's unprofessional. Sounds like some kind of skunk."

He must have winced, because her face softened.

"I'm sorry, Dale. Didn't mean that to be mean, but I've got to present an image to my clients."

"Well, why don't you go bother them. Or eat them."

She laid a hand on his arm. "You're more important, Dale. Without me, you'd never get your act together. I know you're confused. So you just come with me, and relax, and everything will be fine."

Maybe he was allergic to her perfume, because the ground was heaving underfoot, colors were starting to swim, and she was starting to make sense. "How's that?" he slurred.

"For one, you need to associate with the proper sorts of people. That's not going to happen with you as unkempt as you are now. Some clean clothes, a good meal, and you'll fit in fine. First, we need to do something about that smell."

She pulled a small spray bottle from her handbag. Cologne, he could tell, because the bottle was one of those artsy glass things. He shook his head, but she was already squirting a mist of the stuff towards his neck.

"It's called *Trendsetter*, the essence of fashionable social climbing. Doesn't it just smell like success?"

The smell wiped the last memories of yesterday's ribs from his mind. The phrases *low gas mileage*, *eat human flesh*, and *keep up with the Joneses* filled his thoughts. Next thing he knew, he was down on the hot asphalt, thrashing like a catfish, right up until he blacked out.

When he woke up, he had a vague, dreamlike memory of another car crash, and the Muffler brothers pulling him from Madeline's Lexus. He also had a much more solid feeling that his ass was numb.

They'd locked him in the fridge, amongst the cartons labeled "Waffle Batter–contains 100% artificial milk and eggs."

He scrambled to his feet, the floor slick underfoot. With no handle on this side of the door, all he could do was pound on the cold metal.

"Mort? Eddie? Gordy? One of you bucktoothed goatfuckers want to let me out of here?"

On the far side, the latch rattled. Warm air blew in when the door opened. Outside, Gordy stood, a bit of drool running into his beard. "Goat's good–"

Dale pushed him aside. "Shut up."

Through the kitchen, its walls painted in grease, he found Hal and Madeline at opposite ends of the Waffle House's counter. To his left, his wife waited with a plate of carefully arranged food. It looked like a California roll–rice wrapped around nearly raw fish, though Dale doubted it was fish. A large, open bag sat on the stool next to her, with a butcher knife inside and the words "US Postal Service" on the outside.

Mort stood behind her, his shotgun leveled at her head. The Bubba was grinning, like he wanted her to try anything.

At the counter's other end, Hal slouched on a stool, smoking another Marlboro. When Dale looked his way, he slid a plate at him and nodded. Something like a hash brown mashed with afterbirth sprawled on the plate.

Hal said, "This is your test, Dale Ermine."

If he ate her mailman sushi, Yuppie-25 would win, and he'd never be happy again, except when dining on human flesh–that was if the brothers didn't kill him outright. If he looked at the omelet again, he'd blow chunks.

If he stayed in between them, one of those smells was going to make him break out in hives.

He sighed, closing his eyes.

"Choose, Dale," Hal said.

"Dale," Madeline said, "this is done up just the way you like it. And it promotes proper gall bladder function."

Narrowing his eyes, trying to keep them off the morsel of mailman, Dale veered left, toward Madeline. Maddie. Ms. Ermine-Sewell. Whatever she wanted to call herself.

She held the plate up toward him. "I knew you'd make the proper choice."

"Nah," Dale said. "Just came down here to tell you that I never could stand sushi any more than you could handle chili. Goodbye." Without another word, he turned his back on her and went to Hal's monstrous omelet.

"So what's in here?"

Hal shrugged. "Eggs, grease, sausage, cheese, more grease, some relish, and the whole thing's fried up in enough barbecue sauce to drown an ox."

Madeline's face crumpled. "You're not going to eat that."

Dale did, and with relish. He threw the napkin across the Waffle House, cut enormous bites, chewed with his mouth open, and belched. Against expectations, the relish set off the sausage's flavor, and the barbeque sauce bound all the tastes together. It could've used a touch of chili pepper, though.

When he was done, he picked up the plate and licked it clean of sauce, making sure he smeared some across his chin for later.

It sat in his gut like a box of fishing weights, but satisfied him like nothing had for months. All thoughts of the other, other white meat vanished.

Knowing his breath could stun livestock, he leaned across the counter and said, "How about a kiss, Maddie?"

While she recoiled, he readied the next salvo. "It's in celebration," he said. "See, I decided I'm goin' to Texas, to meet up with Jim. Going to be a NASCAR mechanic when all this yuppie stuff blows over.

"Motor oil's a big turn-on, right?"

Just when it looked like her skin was going to jump off her skeleton in its mad dash to escape him, Maddie's eyes rolled back, and she died, right there in the Waffle House.

By the power of pestilent breath, and Hal's Omelet of Redemption, he was free.

THE END

Robert Pickering is bit of a self-conflicted bubba himself. While he lives in Texas, and works out in the heat, he doesn't own a gun and occasionally partakes of such yuppie jobs as a web developer and insurance filing clerk. Chances are if the virus gets loose, its cannibalism for him.

This is his first real sale.

HALITOSIS

Ajax

Jed was driving when he noticed the smell
It hung in the air like shit-gas from hell
Jed rolled down the window, reached in his cheek
And pulled out the chaw he dipped in last week
He reached for the Dubba Bubba upon the dash
Popped in three pieces and then in a flash
Jed lit up a Winston, swigged some cold joe
The stench had changed but continued to flow
He spit out the gum, got the bag from the seat
Found gas station burritos and started to eat
Jed bought them last night, they tasted ok
But damn it! That reek would not go away!
He saw an air freshener down on the floor
He bought for when this happed before
Jed smiled at the tree wrapped in plastic as
The odor got worse! Damn this was drastic.
He bit at the wrapper; it ripped apart fine
Soon the truck cab was stiff with the odor of pine.

A ROSE BY ANY OTHER NAME
Melanie Fletcher

If you ask me, I'd have to say that life's been pretty swell, what with that Yuppie 25 plague killin' off most everybody in the world except us Bubbas. Sure, we have to fight off a pack of them flesh-eatin' Yuppie zombies every month or so, and I miss the Jerry Springer show something fierce. But we don't have to pay taxes, I can go huntin' whenever I feel like it, and Oprah can't run her fool mouth no more since she got et up by Yumbies on national TV, so it seems like a pretty fair tradeoff to me.

No, the only problem about it bein' the end of the world as we knew it is the lack of female companionship, if you know what I mean. Most of the womenfolk in Ridgeway are either married and not of a mind to help out a lonely neighbor (even if he does have the biggest trailer hitch in town), or their daddies are too damn happy to put a load of buckshot where the Good Lord split you if you come calling on their daughters. Now that's just bein' plain greedy.

And there's Sheryleen, of course, but I was getting real tired of standing in line in front of her doublewide, and it's a bitch trying to find enough pork rinds for her anyway. So when Sheriff Blackwood said the Bud reserves were getting low and we had to rustle up another scavenging party, I figured I might as well go. You never know who you might meet when you're lootin' a 7-11.

The party wound up being this peckerwood named Beau McGraw, Old Man Hubert and myself. I knew Old Man Hubert was one mean sumbitch, but I didn't trust Beau to be able to piss down his own leg if his boot was on fire. Everyone else was busy, though, so we got into my Ford and headed off towards Lewisville. I didn't like having to head out so far, but we'd pretty much cleared out all the Spam, pork rinds and beer from the towns around Ridgeway. Lewisville had a drive-in, three barbecue stands and a roadhouse, so it seemed like a pretty good place to do some beer huntin'.

Unfortunately, Lewisville also had a Radio Shack, which meant it probably had a bunch of Yumbies staggering around looking for some human flesh to eat. Which is why we came packing – Old Man Hubert had his Army M-1, Beau carried two .22's and a bandolier full of ammo, and I had my Remington 870 pump action. All in all, I wasn't too worried – after getting hit with a couple loads of double aught, those damn Yumbies tend to fold up like a New York City tourist with a bellyful of Stinky Pete's barbecue.

When we got to Lewisville I drove around for awhile, keeping my eyes peeled for any blank-eyed zombies with Armani suits or pocket protectors. None of them came shambling after us, so we decided to park up in the center of town and hunt down some beer. Beau headed off towards the Piggly-Wiggly, looking like the Bubba version of Indiana Jones, while Old Man Hubert shouldered his M-1 and went into the convenience store. I'd seen a gas station on the way in, so I headed over there. The electricity would've been off for some time now, but I knew from experience that beer kept just fine as long as the cans didn't get too hot and explode.

The front of the station was full of useless shit like combs, suntan oil and noseplugs. But in the back – hot damn, I hit the motherload. There were at least ten cases *each* of Bud, Miller and Pabst Blue Ribbon, a couple more of Olympia, and some six packs of that foreign shit, just waiting to be hauled home and enjoyed. My mouth started watering at the thought of a nice cold Bud.

I was fixin' to go get the truck when I noticed someone outlined in the doorway. It was a real sweet outline, too, all curvy and round like that Anna Nicole Smith lady before she heifered up and got old. But I knew they had girl Yumbies that were just as likely to suck your eyeballs out of your head as kiss you, so I brought up the shotgun and cocked it.

"You better tell me you don't eat quiche," I called.

"And you better tell me you don't drive a Beemer," she called back, stepping away from the door and into the sunlight.

I almost swallowed my chaw. By God, she was the prettiest thing I'd ever seen, and that's including the time I saw Miz McGraw taking a whiz behind the smokehouse.

She had curly blonde hair, a real nice face, big tits just burstin' out of her Red Man t-shirt, a loaded ammo belt that showed off an itty bitty waist, and legs that were longer than a NASCAR speedway. And the shotgun she had aimed at my stomach was just as sweet – a Winchester Model 97 and clean as a whistle.

It was the Winchester that decided me. I couldn't think of anything better than having a sweetheart who came with her own shotgun, 'less it was one who could load her own cartridges.

I shouldered the Remington and raised my other hand, trying to look innocent. "Didn't mean to scare you, ma'am. My name's Billy Ray Ledbetter, and I'm from over Ridgeway way," I said, polite as pie.

She rolled her eyes, but came back into the gas station. "You didn't scare me, Billy Ray Ledbetter – I heard you and your friends coming from a mile off," she said. "So what are y'all doin' here in Lewisville?"

I scratched my cap, and decided that honesty was the best policy. "Well, me and my friends are here on a little shopping trip, and I was wonderin' – well, do you mind if we clear out the coolers back there? Thing is, we're running real low on beer, and barbecue just don't taste right without a Bud."

She shrugged, which did some wondrous things to those fine titties. "I figured someone would come for it one of these days," she said, giving me this crooked little grin. "What with you bein' so polite and all, I might be willing to let you have it, if you take me with you."

Which just goes to show that my Uncle Hickory was full of shit and God did like me after all. She walked closer, and I forget all about the Bud as I saw those sweet curves bouncing under that t-shirt. Wishing that I'd taken the time to rinse off my pits, I gave her a big ol' shit eating grin and held out my hand. "It's real nice to meet you, ma'am."

She took my hand and shook it, good and strong. "Nice to meet you, too," she said. "My name is Rose-Ellen Briggs."

I found out I didn't have to worry about my pits. Her breath hit my face, and Lord, I almost puked. Now, I've smelled some nasty-ass things in my life – our trailer after Ma made barbecued beans three days in a row, the outhouse when Uncle Hickory'd been in there with his stomach troubles, and that summer we found out why my dog Goober hadn't been around since last winter. But you could roll all of them into a big, stinky ball and they wouldn't even touch Rose-Ellen's breath. Whooee, it was bad.

The minute she heard me tryin' to hold back my lunch, that little smile of hers disappeared. "I know – it's my breath," she said sadly. "That's why I wasn't scared of you. No man can stand bein' within three feet of me – after the Yumbies came, I never even had to defend my honor."

She hefted her Winchester and sounded a little disappointed. I was kinda busy tryin' to stop my eyes from running like a creek, but I smiled at her anyway. "It ain't all that bad," I choked.

She snorted, and I caught another whiff of that infernal reek. "That's bull hockey and you know it, Billy Ray Ledbetter. I know my breath could knock over a rodeo clown at ten paces, but there ain't nothing I can do about it. I tried changin' what I eat, and I brush and floss all the time – I even gargled with my daddy's moonshine once. Didn't do a lick of good."

I didn't know what she meant by flossing, but if she could gargle with mountain dew and it didn't do a damn thing to that stink, then Rose-Ellen's breath was here to stay. I had to think – pretty as her mouth was, could I get past the fact that the Devil's own farts came out of it?

Just then, we heard yellin' coming from where I left the truck. *Aw, shit*, I thought, *that peckerwood Beau finally found himself some trouble.*

Rose-Ellen's eyes narrowed. "Yumbies," she said.

I turned my head to suck in some clean air, and ran out of the gas station. From the sounds of things, Rose-Ellen was right behind me, panting. Made me damn glad she was downwind, I can tell you. When we reached the truck, I saw Beau backed up against the tailgate, firing away at a pack of the undead critters. They didn't even blink as Beau's bullets smacked into them, tearing right through their tattered shirts and silk ties and leaving little chunks of Yumbie meat on the sidewalk. I told him that a .22 wouldn't do dick on Yumbies, but the pissant never listened to me. He just kept screaming, "Help me, Jesus!" as those mutant zombies closed in on him, ready for lunch.

Rose-Ellen fell in beside me, and we brought up our shotguns together like we'd trained to do it all our lives. Man-eatin' zombies or not, souless flesh was no match for a couple of blasts of double aught, and them Yumbies pretty much disintegrated into twitching heaps.

"Nice shootin', Tex," Rose-Ellen said with a smile.

I gagged, but still managed to say, "You ain't half-bad yourself, ma'am."

But the party wasn't over yet. Old Man Hubert came around the corner limpin' as fast as I ever seen him with another pack of Yumbies on his ass. We started firing at them, when I noticed Beau's eyes gettin' big as anything. "Behind you!" he shouted.

Goddamn it, I got so wrapped up in shooting the Yumbies in front of me that I forgot to watch *my* ass. I turned around and saw a third group, lurching towards us with a hunger for Bubba meat glowing in their dead eyes. I managed to blast another two, but they were replaced by their unholy brethren. Rose-Ellen was trying to reload, so I used my last cartridge to give her time.

They must've known we were temporarily out of ammo, because one of them jumped forward, his rottin' mouth gapin' wide for a bite of my intended. Now, Rose-Ellen was just as brave as any gal I'd ever met, but it's a mite unsettlin' to see a Yumbie lunging for you, and she let out a scream right in its face.

I lunged forward, aimin' to hit the damn thing with the butt of my shotgun, then stopped – mainly because it had, too. The Yumbie got this weird expression on its face, like it was trying to figure whether it wanted to shit, run or go blind. And then, I swear to God, the sumbitch *exploded*, scattering the ground in big ol' slimy chunks.

I wiped a smear of Yumbie gunk from my face and whooped. It had to be Rose-Ellen's breath, no doubt about it. The skank-ass air coming out of her mouth was bad enough to make a Yumbie blow up and die. "Holy shit," I yelled, "you're our secret weapon! *Breathe* on 'em, gal!"

Rose-Ellen wasn't stupid, and she started yelling her head off at the Yumbies. Every time her breath touched one of them, the undead bastard would just go all to pieces. She took out that entire pack in less than 30 seconds.

We turned around, ready to blow up some more mutant zombies, but found out we didn't need to. The rest of the Yumbies had seen what happened to their kin, and took off running like Yankee campers with a pissed-off bear on their tail. Proud as punch of my new darlin', I offered Rose-Ellen my arm and escorted her to my truck. Old Man Hubert and

Beau just looked at her like she was an angel from Heaven, at least until she introduced herself. I had to slap Beau awake after that, of course, but Old Man Hubert – well, let's just say he has stomach troubles that rivaled Uncle Hickory's, so he wasn't quite as smell shocked as we were.

Yep, it was a good day – we killed us some Yumbies, found the golden nectar we'd been looking for, and I finally got me a sweetheart, all in a couple of hours. Before I took Rose-Ellen back to Ridgeway, though, I had to figure out a solution to the roadblock in our future happiness – namely, her breath. I knew that Sheriff Blackwood and the other folks would give her a big Bubba welcome once they found out about her Yumbie-busting powers, but I was the one who'd have to live with my honeybunch's halitosis from Hell on a daily basis.

And then it hit me – I'd already seen just what I needed at the gas station. We headed back there, and while the boys were busy loading the beer into the truck I made a little visit to the aisle where they stocked the swimming junk and grabbed all the pink rubber nose plugs I could find.

A couple of days later, Preacher Moon climbed into his robes and hitched me and Rose-Ellen, and we've been as happy as two Bubbas can be ever since. True, I can't really smell much these days, and we don't have a lot of folks stoppin' by to visit, but Ridgeway is Yumbie-free and by my side is the best damn gal in the world.

And her shotgun.

THE END

Melanie Fletcher is a woman of simple tastes – she likes to write, preferably for money. Her credits include "Star Quality" (*Selling Venus*, Circlet Press), "Heramaphrodite" (*Crossing The Border*, Indigo/Gollancz), "Bartok and the Unicorn" (*Quantum Muse*, July 2002) and "The Female of the Species" (*Quantum Muse*, April 2003). She has also produced the chapbooks *The Stories That Would Not Die!* and *Dark Matter – Erotic Sf And Fantasy* (Belaurient Press), which are available through her website (http://www.io.com/~hoosier/spec_fic.html).

LEFRIC LIGHTS A FART

James K. Burk

Lefric was a four-eyed little runt who never really fit in with the crowd at the Rebel Yell Trailer Park. For one thing, he was kind of a furriner – his daddy had married outside the family. He usually had his nose buried in a book, and even when he farted after supper you got the feeling he was just doin' it to be polite.

So when the plague broke out, some people here in the trailer park started lookin' sidelong at ole Lefric. One of the loudest talkers was Ned Sanders. He pointed out that Lefric was only partly kin and accused him of bein' an ae-theist.

"Y'all know he ain't got even one black velvet paintin' of Elvis," he roared.

Well, Ned was meaner than a turpentined bobcat, so it was hard to get up the nerve to say anything good about the boy. Then Hettie, Ned's wife had her say. Now, in the trailer park of life, Ned and Hettie was both double-wides, but while Ned was meaner than a divorce lawyer, Hettie had a good heart in her – as well as bein' the best cook in Cherrystone County. Hard to believe she and Ned was related.

"Ned," Hettie said, "you know that boy's eaten his barbeque sauce like the rest of us. If I thought somebody here was the walkin' dead, I'd suspect you. If you ain't dead, you sure smell like it. The last time you had a bath was when you fell into the crick when you was six, and your breath 'd knock a buzzard off a shitwagon at fifty paces."

Ned blustered some, but the rest of us pretty much got behind Hettie and Lefric. It was a lot easier gettin' behind Hettie.

Lefric needed to have somebody stand up for him. He was an orphan. About six months before the yuppie plague broke out, a twister hit the north edge of the park. We always call tornadoes "Oklahoma divorces," because somehow, somebody's damn well gonna be out a trailer house. That twister crumpled Lefric's daddy's trailer like the legendary

Hulk Hogan squashin' a beer can, with Lefric's folks still in it. He'd been out coon huntin' that night with me and Duane, or he'd have been wiped out too,

Turns out Hettie was a mighty wise woman, because Lefric made life a lot better in the park. He made the still work a lot better – ain't had a new case of jake-leg here in a couple years – and he got a brewery goin'. I gotta admit all I know about beer is how to drink it.

Also, when we begun runnin' out of the good store-brand barbeque sauce, he showed us how the fancy stuff could be mixed with other ingredients so it was almost as good as what we was used to. Hell, even that stuff from New York City would work, with a little ticklin'.

We missed the worst of the plague. The nearest thing we have around here to a town is Two Forks. Some people say that's because that's all they had in the diner attached to the Jiffy Shop. A couple miles up the track is a little town called Possum Hollow. Mosta the people there was good ole boys too. The nearest city is nigh onto forty miles away, and the yumbies that made it this far weren't too much worse than most city tourists. We killed 'em anyway, but it wasn't nothin' personal.

Life in the Rebel Yell Trailer Park was goin' on like usual, with us sittin' around in the evenings and drinkin' beer, lightin' farts, and tellin' stories about Jethro Orloff, the trailer park vampire with just one fang. Yeah, it was smoother than a dose of croton oil. That is, until Ruthann Simpson, Hettie's niece, moved in. She was blond, had more curves than a mountain highway, and was just prettier than a new speckled pup.

Ruthann was a nice addition to the scenery, but it did sorta stir up the hive. Darrell Walsh's six boys; Duane, Dwain, Dwayne, Dewayne, Duwayne, and Duain liked to killed each other tryin' to get next to her. There was about another dozen fellas who wanted to, but they was afraid of the Walsh clan who, when they weren't whuppin' on each other, got together and whupped just about everybody else.

I even seen Lefric lookin' at her with eyes like a calf dyin' of diarrhea in a windstorm, but he wasn't doin' any better than any of the rest of us.

If she even noticed the ruckus, Ruthann paid it no mind. She had her heart set on a prince. She'd gotten ahold of some of them romance books, the kind with a spunky princess, assorted low-lifes, and a prince to help the girl open a can of kick-ass, and Ruthann wasn't about to buy short.

Life in the park was still pretty good, that is, until the late summer morning when BettySue Mapes come tearin' into the park like her butt was on fire, and yelling and screaming about yumbies. Seems most of the women had taken their washing to the crick. They was makin' the best of a bad job, jokin' and tellin' lies.

The fun had barely started when BettySue had to go behind the bushes, and she saw what happened next. The women were havin' the best time they could washin' up dirty clothes when all of a sudden, about fifty yumbies showed up and started grabbin'. They wasn't very fast, but there was a lot of them. When she saw the yumbies she lit out for the park.

We all grabbed for whatever we had to kill yumbies, but Ned puffed out his chest, which made it almost half as far as his belt buckle. "I ain't goin'. Good riddance, I say. That ole heifer was more trouble than she was worth."

Heber Mapes give Ned a look like he'd give a bug spot or bird shit on the windshield of a brand new pickup. "Ned, you are without a doubt the most worthless piece of trailer trash I ever seen. The only reason we put up with your pissin' and moanin' and general crankiness is because of Hettie. Now, you can do the right thing, or you can die eatin' your own miserable cookin'."

Ned grumbled some, but he went and got his shotgun, a forty-one nuthin'. When we got everything out and loaded, Lefric looked us over and sighed. We had a couple deer rifles, five or six twelve-gauges, and all the rest was piddlin' little stuff, and we didn't have a full box of shells for each gun. Heber turned up a couple-three road flares and Darryl, Darrell's brother, had a handful of M-80s he mostly used for blowin' up mailboxes. We did have a buncha corn knives and machetes. Lefric just shook his head and started toward the crick.

We seen where the yumbies come out of the woods and there was drag marks leadin' away. We could tell Hettie's trail real easy. But there wasn't no blood, although a couple yumbie ears was lyin' beside the dirty laundry.

Wasn't no use settin' a dog to try to follow 'em. Them yumbies stunk so bad even Ned's coon hound just got as far from the trail as he could. Besides, the trail was pretty easy to follow for the first mile or two till we started hittin' the rocks around the hills.

I was beginnin' to worry about losin' the trail, but ever' now and then we'd find a scrap of cloth one of the women had torn off her skirt or blouse. We really didn't need much help. Yumbies, at least this bunch, ain't real bright, and they was goin' pretty much in a straight line.

Some of us had hunted off this way, but not many. Game was scarce here and most of us don't really like our ground diagonal. But Lefric and Dwain said it looked like they was headed for a cave up ahead. Sure enough, in another two miles we found a cave mouth with a couple yumbies standin' around like guards.

We all stayed out of sight while we tried to think of a way to get close in and kill a buncha yumbies in a hurry, before they could chow down on the girls.

Ned wiped his sweaty face with the back of his arm, smearin' mud, then groused, "We ain't gonna get anything done sittin' around lightin' farts."

Lefric got a funny look on his face and I held my breath, afraid Ned had cut one of his silent but deadly farts, but Lefric said, "Yes we will! That's exactly how we'll do it!"

He turned and said, "Duane, Dwain, and Dewayne, I need you for a job." All of the brothers stepped forward. Lefric sighed again, then said, "I need you boys to go back and get some stuff we'll need to do this job right. I need about half a dozen egg timers and about a thousand feet of wire. Also, grab me a buncha flashlight batteries even if they won't really make a good light. And I need at least four or five bags of flour or corn meal. Flour's better. And a roll of duck tape."

Heber grunted and dug in his possibles bag and handed Lefric a couple flashlight batteries and a roll of hundred mile an hour duck tape. "This help?"

"Yeah, but we'll need more batteries, and the wire."

The Walsh boys dog-trotted off and the rest of us studied the cave mouth.

"While Duane and the others are gettin' what we need, you boys," Lefric nodded at me and Cletus, "you go around to come up the hill above the guards. When they get distracted, you jump 'em. Use the corn knives. You need to take off the heads, or they'll just keep coming at you."

"That's bullshit," Heber announced. "They die just as

easy as revenoors."

"Dammitall, Heber," Lefric snapped, "quit pissin' on the parade. I'm tryin' to get these boys to do the job as quiet and efficient as possible."

Cletus followed me as I backed away and circled the hill. It wasn't too tricky – them rocks was rough enough for easy climbin'. We took our time but still got set up awhile before suppertime.

We was probably as surprised as them yumbies was when Ned come stumblin' up to the cave, lookin' awful wobbly and wavin' a bottle of shine. He stopped and stood lookin' at 'em, then waved the bottle again. "If you boys ain't revenoors, you're welcome to a spot of some of the best shine in the state."

I don't think it was the shine that got their attention as much as the fact that ole Ned would probably dress out at better'n two hundred pounds, and even with all the gristle and meanness, he was still a pretty good blue plate special for yumbies. The yumbies looked at each other and started toward Ned.

Somehow, I knew what was comin', so I motioned holdin' my nose to Cletus, held my breath, and snuck up behind 'em.

Ned had cut one of his silent but deadly specials. Now, they say yumbies don't really breathe, and they stink somethin' awful themselves, but Ned outdid himself, and them yumbies turned a different shade of green and got all mottled.

I struck fast, takin' the head clean off the one I was after, and I saw Cletus got his, too, then we both hurried upwind. Even with holdin' my breath, my eyes was waterin' somethin' fierce.

Lefric and the rest of the crowd snuck out of the bushes, and we all trooped into the cave. Onct we was inside, we knew we were in the right wrong place; it smelled worse than the park clubhouse after a beer and chili dinner. Ever so often, Lefric would leave one of Duane's brothers with some tape, a timer, a flashlight battery and either a bag of cornmeal or flour and an M-80, or else a road flare.

It got harder to see, and the smell got worse, and I could hear voices from deeper in the cave. I was afraid I'd have to use a flashlight, then I saw a dull red glow reflected off the walls. The voices got louder as we took a couple of turns and I could see where the tunnel widened out into a big room, with a fire. I snuck closer, findin' a little bitty side-tunnel and waited for the others to catch up.

There was only four of us left: me, Cletus, Lefric, and Ned.

Lefric crept past me and motioned for me to follow, quiet-like.

We could hear the voices clearer now, and it was some fella yellin', and then the rest of the yumbies chantin' back something that sounded like shablee and bree. Past Lefric, I could see all them yumbies gathered in a big circle around a fire and, in the middle, prowlin' around the fire walked this yumbie who looked like he'd been beat to death with an ugly stick. He was wearin' a raggedy three-piece suit, with a briefcase in one hand and a closed umbrella in the other.

"Stock portfolio," roared the guy who had to be a leader or witch doctor or something.

"Shablee and bree," answered the mob.

"Fiduciaries and debentures"

"Shablee and bree!"

Lefric slipped around the corner and, after taking a deep breath, I followed him. Right at the back of the big cavern, lay the girls, tied up like turkeys. All them yumbies was watchin' their top dog, and Lefric started cuttin' the girls loose. They was awful pale and more'n a little green around the gills, and they had some trouble walkin', but Lefric helped 'em around the corner. We managed to get all of them back into the tunnel, then Lefric tapped Ned on the shoulder.

"Ned, we're gonna need someone to slow 'em down. You got another good blast in you?"

Ned grinned like a kid findin' a pony under the Christmas tree. "I can take care of it."

"Good. You let us get outta sight, then cut loose and shag ass."

Cletus led the way, helpin' Hettie, and Lefric and I followed the rest of the women. Ruthann was a real trooper, and she was helpin' Bettyjo.

We got around a turn in the tunnel and even over the chantin', I could hear Ned. This wasn't one of them quiet, sneaky ones, it sounded like this one was tearin' the seat outta his pants. All of a sudden the chantin' changed to screamin', and I could almost see them yumbies clawin' out their own eyes to stop the burnin'. I tried to hurry the girls, afraid the back-blast would get us too.

When we got to Duane, Lefric stopped and set an egg-timer he was carryin' then set the timer attached to wires, one wire taped to the battery, and the other to the M-80 tucked under a bag of flour. Another wire run from the firecracker to the other end of the battery.

Ned come runnin' up, wheezin' and cacklin', and Lefric hollered for everyone else to clear the cave. I stayed with him, partly to make sure the yumbies didn't catch up with him, partly to see what he was doin'.

He stopped at each timer, settin' them to match the one he carried.

"Look," I said, "them things ain't real bombs or napalm. They ain't hardly gonna slow them yumbies down, unless they have trouble seein' through the flour."

"Don't you worry," Lefric said, "just be ready to run like hell."

We finally stopped at the last timer and I saw we only had a couple minutes before things started gettin' interestin'.

When we finally got shut of the cave, I was trying to run and draw big, deep breaths at the same time. Lefric kept everybody else runnin' but Ned was wheezin' like a steam engine goin' up a steep grade and Lefric and I stayed with him, about a hundred fifty yards or so from the mouth of the cave, and at an angle to it.

I heard a bunch of little explosions in the cave, all comin' within a second or so. Some flour dust rolled outta the cave and a couple of yumbies had gotten to the mouth when there was one helluva boom. That hill just sorta seemed to shrug, then loose rocks started fallin, and the hill sorta fell in on itself. The yumbies at the cave mouth was blown clean out.

"What the hell was that?" I asked.

"That, my friend, was what is called a dust explosion. It's the same thing that leveled grain elevators. Figured anything that could rearrange a concrete grain elevator could pretty well mess up a hill. The yumbies inside are gonna be nothin' but grease spots on the walls." He had a smug look like a cat with mouse on his breath.

The two yumbies that had been blown out of the cave was staggerin' around like cockroaches that had been bug-bombed. It wasn't but a couple minutes work to finish them off.

So Lefric was a hero, and he spread the glory around, even makin' sure everybody knew how important Ned's part had been. Ruthann figured a hero was as good as a prince, so she and Lefric got hitched. A couple months later, they decided to go west to see more of the country, although I figured they caught on that the only thing worse than havin' Ned as an enemy was to have him as a friend.

Lefric taught Duane and Dwain how to run the still and to brew beer. He offered to teach me, but I figured on headin' south and west myself, thinkin' maybe I might find a furriner woman.

And that, ladies and gentlemen, is how Lefric saved the Rebel Yell trailer park by lighting a fart.

THE END

James K. Burk is the professional name of Jim Burk (THE james k. burk is his party name, but that's another story.) Unlike Athena, who sprang full-grown from the brow of Zeus, Burk just turned up at a science fiction convention.

He had been a reviewer and critic for *Delap's F&SF Review* and, later, for *Tangent* before he forsook the dark side and became a writer. He's had two chapbooks from Yard Dog Press, *Strange Twists Of Fate* and *Illusions Of Sanity* and has a novel, *High Rage* due out in August from Renaissance Alliance Publishing.

He really doesn't know that much about trailer parks, and he's not his own uncle, but he had a lot of fun writing the story.

THE BUBBAS OF TROY COUNTY

Gloria Oliver

I want to thank you right off for taking me in. I would have died out there without any kin, without a home. And in gratitude, I want to tell you what led me to such a sorry state, so I might save you or your children from trouble.

It's been a while since it all happened – weeks, maybe even days. But I can't forget it. It haunts me late at night. Strikes me plumb full of awful fear, but also makes my mouth water.

So many of us were lost that day – in such grisly ways, too. There was all the running, screaming, biting, choking on foul air. Blood everywhere you looked. But we lost more than just folks that day – we lost something which grows more precious every day.

I'm sure you've heard about the Yuppie 25 fiasco. How all those people just up and died from some strange virus while others turned into monsters or some such? To us in Troy County, none of that meant much. Out there, we never cared much for the going-ons of city slickers. But it sure made for some good conversation and speculation. I personally think it had something to do with computers, or that dang Internet. Anything that can make people talk in something that sounds like another language has got to be bad. The whole mess sounded like one of those science fiction things so many of the young folk are so crazy about. Rots the brain.

Still, the stories coming from those who were able to escape the cities and not catch the damn bug were enough to make your hair stand on end. So the young ones, always in a hurry to boss us old folks around, regardless of the fact most of us are kin, decided on their own that we should build us a fort like in them injun movies. They figured with one of them, we could hole up and be safe from any who might have a sudden craving to meander our way.

So off they went a-building, arguing, and fussing about how tall it ought to be, how wide, and other foolishness like that. I tried to tell them the way it needed to be done, but they were just too stubborn to pay any attention to their betters. But never you mind that part. I think you all are different. And that's why I'm here telling you my story, so it won't happen to you.

Anyway, the young men finally got their big old fort ready. They rounded everybody up, every last cousin, kissing cousin, whatever kind of cousin and put us in there. A lot of squawking and complaining went on for a while as everyone picked their place and brought their trailers and stuff in, but eventually we all got settled in and we slept good, because we knew nothing could happen to us in there. We were safe.

We couldn't have been more wrong.

So time moved along and we all pretty much figured out who should be doing what and so forth. Still, after the boys had stripped every store and house for miles around, there were a few necessities that started getting scarcer than a dog when it's time for its bath.

And these here were important things too, don't you know. Stuff like Ben Gay for the old arthritis. And then there was the chaw. Heck, even the one-gallon jugs of barbeque sauce. You know, things a man's just not supposed to do without. I mean, who'd have ever guessed most of our favorite things came from those big, city slicker factories and what not. With all them city people going crazy or dying, they just weren't being made anymore.

These here things weren't the worst of it. Some, if not all of them, we could recreate on our own, or at least fake them well enough where it didn't matter. Yet there was one thing we had to have, one thing which our souls cried for but no matter how much effort was put into it, we couldn't come close to making a substitute. We couldn't recreate that wonder of wonders, that elixir which made life worth living – *beer*.

Every time Rusty tried one of his new concoctions, it would taste worse than his last batch, and the wailing and weeping of men could be heard late into the night. I mean, how were we supposed to survive without beer? Sure Rusty could make a mean moonshine, but that's for special occasions. You'd die if you drank it day after day, especially at my age. It would eat clean through my intestines.

Anyway, hell had come to earth and no relief was in sight. Heck, we got so desperate, we sent a bunch of our boys out to brave the wilds and go see if they could bamboozle some out of one of those factories where they used to make it at.

You see, we knew there was one down in Flo-ri-da. One where they used to let you take tours of the place and even get free samples. I was planning to take the wife down there myself some year for our anniversary. Sure would have been a ton of fun.

So the boys got themselves armed and took one of the pickups, and with some of Rusty's brew for fuel, they went on their way. We had our hopes and futures pinned on those boys. We surely did. It's a pity none of them ever came back.

So we went on, living in that hell without beer, only memory and Rusty's barely palatable stuff for company—then one day...

I was up on the wall doing my tour of duty as watchman at the beginning of one beautiful morning, the sun coming up like a ripe orange out there in the horizon, when I saw it. I swear it was the most beautiful sight I'd ever seen in my life. And I don't expect anything will ever top it either.

It was so tall. I spotted it shimmering through the trees on the other side of the no man zone. As the sun worked its way up, its rays reflected off the tall shiny surface, the light refracting every which way off the frost still clinging to the rim. The familiar red and white colors were so bright, I could easily see the name after whom I'd named two of my own children—-Budweiser.

Yes, yes, I know, it's hard to believe, but sure as I live and breathe there it was, a fifteen-foot tall can of Bud sitting out in the middle of the wilderness.

Well, before you could hum the first bar of Dixie, I was off that wall waking everybody I could get my hands on.

Ah, you should have seen their faces when I told them. Every last one of them rushed up to the wall to see the beautiful thing for themselves. It was a miracle. God had finally taken pity on our souls and sent us some manna from heaven.

Well, it doesn't take a genius to figure out what we did next. We opened the fort's gates and we rushed out there to go get that can before anyone else might decide to show up and take it.

We were like kids at the candy store with a dollar in their pocket. We pinched each other all the way there to make sure we weren't dreaming.

And we weren't. Every step took us closer to her, every step made her look bigger and bigger, more awesome than before. We were the happiest bunch of folks you ever did see.

When we got there, we rushed around her like it was Christmas morning. She had thirty or so spigots coming out of her, and on each one was hanging a beautiful clean mug for drinking the beer. Our mouths watered right then and there. A couple of the women went into a swoon. I found myself reaching out to grab one of them miraculous mugs.

"Don'tcha do that!" Old Meg, my cousin four times removed, hollered out. "We've no time for it. Whoever left this here is gonna want it back."

Her words stopped us cold. No, we couldn't have that. Finders keepers, dang it! Those were the *rules*. But we decided it'd be best not to take any chances. We set out to get the sucker home right then and there.

Luckily for us, the good Lord had been kind enough to leave the giant can on a trailer. It sure made things a whole lot easier, let me tell you. Like a bunch of them Egyp-tians on one of those big rocks, we surrounded the trailer and started pushing her home.

So lickety-split we got that sucker home. Once it was in the big central yard, we closed the fort's doors and put the beams across it so nobody would be disturbing us as we got down to business.

Everyone was just happy as pie, till it got to be time to start drinking that is. We had us a conundrum you see–thirty spigots, thirty mugs, and a whole lot more folk than that dying to have some beer.

Well, I piped up that us old folks should get the first taste, and I definitely should as I was the first to see it. Heck, it could be our last chance for this piece of heaven and as the elders of the family it was our right to be first. But the young ones were having none of that. Selfish kids. We almost came to blows at that point, mind you. A man can only be pushed so far; even by his own kin, don't you know.

Ah, but that's when the women piped in saying they should be the first to have it because they're ladies, and if we had any manners we'd let 'em. Crazy women. Everyone knows beer is for men more than them! My old lady was watching me though, so I couldn't just out and say so.

So now the old folks, the men, and the women were about

to come to blows. But luckily for us, out of the mouth of babes came the voice of reason.

"Why don't we do one of those contests with paper, scissor, rocks, you all? The top thirty winners get to drink first." This came from Bewler's boy, Johnny 3 (Bewler liked the name so much he used it more than once). He was a strap of a boy, who'd had his first taste of the elixir not long after leaving his mama's tit, so he was hankering for some about as bad as the rest of us–a sign of great intelligence, if you ask me.

So there we went, doing a contest all could be a part of and maybe win–every last one of us looking to be the first to get that first taste of heaven.

Took plum three hours to figure out the winners, it did. First everyone had to split up into groups of two, then everybody had to stand by and watch each group play–only way to make sure there was no cheating.

Well, by the time it was over, everyone had grown mighty thirsty. We eyed the winners with sharp jealousy as they stepped up to the spigots for their prize. Condensation was dripping down the sides of the can, making me feel more parched by the second.

Joe, my second cousin by marriage, opened the tap and the golden liquid poured out to fill up his mug with a head of foam you wouldn't believe. It took all I had not to rush up there and steal it from him. It was almost pure agony to watch the ecstasy shining in his eyes as he took his first gulp, the beer's foam making a ring on his beard and mouth.

Screaming kids cut through the crowd and rushed the spigots with their own cups, which they'd stolen from the kitchen. I was fit to be tied when I saw that. I should have thought of it myself.

In total panic me and everyone else without a glass took off to find one. I got smart, and instead of running to the kitchen like everyone else, I scampered off to my own room and got the glass I use to keep my teeth in. I was praying to the Lord the whole time, asking him to make sure all the beer wasn't gone before I got back.

Pushing and shoving, I got back outside and close to the mighty can. One of the younger boys got his share and then left the spigot running. I could have killed the darn fool right then and there. "That beer's more precious than your hide, boy," I told him. "Sweet Jesus, it's more precious than gold

You don't just let it bleed to the ground like that, fool."

Hearing about this, his mama sought him out and gave him a good whack to the side of the head. I was thinking she went easy on him. Dang fool boy!

Eventually I was able to get a glassful of my own. As I moved to take my first drink, I could feel my knees quivering. It'd been so *long*. Would it still be like I remembered it? Would the magic still be there for me?

I shouldn't have worried. It was everything it ever was and more–pure, pure heaven.

We all went back for seconds, thirds, and fourths. Sometime during the melee, somebody got smart and brought out some instruments. Music broke out all around and dancing followed. We had us a party, an old-fashioned hoedown! The beer never stopped flowing, and we never stopped drinking. We had a lot of catching up to do with this beer, don't you know?

By dark, we were plumb schmuckered.   You couldn't have found a happier bunch of folks the whole world over.

Still, despite our best intentions, one by one the alchi-hol got the better of us. Folks lay down where they stood, cuddling their glasses, dreaming about partying some more once the sun came back up.

Me, I found myself a dark corner against the outer wall, a good spot where I could keep most of the can in view, and stared at it with half open eyes, content as pie.

I fell asleep at some point. I don't rightly remember when, but I don't think it was for too long. The moon was full and dreamily wobbling above me when nature called and woke me up. I got up to take a leak, my eyes swiveling to look at our miracle again. That's when I first noticed it, and I just stood there with my noodle in my hand, as part of the can popped up and over.

As I watched in stunned amazement, some feller came up out of the inside of the can. At first I was thinking what an utterly great idea it was to go swimming in the beer and how I should get my ass up there too, but that was before I realized I didn't know the guys up there. They had suits on, so I knew they weren't from anywhere around here. Besides, who in their right mind would go swimming in beer with their clothes on? It wasn't natural! Blasphemous even! Nobody wants threads or buttons in their beer.

I was just about to tuck the noodle back home and give them what for when one of them just up and jumps from the top of the can like he was Superman. My jaw dropped and then fell even lower when the feller hit the ground and then stepped away not stumbling at all. Obviously he hadn't been drinking the beer. Dang fool.

Some of the others jumped down too, even as more fellers climbed out of the can. The first of the strangers walked on over to Hugh, who was on the ground not far from where the feller landed. The suit belched a big one, then knelt down next to Hugh.

Ladies, you might want to clear the room of the kiddies before I go on to this next part. It's not for them. Thank you kindly.

As I was saying, the feller knelt down next to Hugh, put his arm around him like he was one of them fruity fellows, and then... then... Lordy, this is hard. Then that feller bit Hugh's nose off. Blood started spurting everywhere and the stranger was chewing it like it was the tastiest bit of beef he'd ever had.

Well, even with his nerves deadened by beer; Hugh felt that one. He screamed and kicked and cussed, but couldn't get away from the suit. He was too strong. Two more showed up beside the first, opened their mouths and breathed on him. Hugh stiffened up real quick and went sort of quiet, then they started chewing on his arm and leg. Pretty soon more screaming was tearing the night as the suits went and found more of my kin for supper.

With all the hollering, running, yelling, and them suits eating that old prude Ms. Briggs – skinniest, toughest bag of bones you ever did see – the alcohol just plumb run out of my blood, leaving me as sober as a preacher at a revival.

Heck if that hadn't done it, the reek coming out of their mouths sure would have. The more they breathed on folks, the stronger the stench coating the air, worse than any farts me or my family had ever made, even after a chili eating contest.

The suits didn't care who they ate—men, women, children— all were the same to them. They didn't even cook them, or use barbeque sauce. They just took them raw, like them Japanese fellers eat their fish—they just breathed on 'em and ate 'em. One of the suits kept walking around laughing and calling out for some woman named Helen. Never did figure out who the heck he was looking for. We didn't have no Helen in Troy County. Could he have meant my wife, Heleene? I'd met her at a hoedown in a neighboring county and brought her back with me. Could these suit fellers be her kin? I decided maybe I better go find her so she could explain things to them. Things were getting worse by the second.

It was just plumb awful, like pigs at the slaughterhouse. Billy Joe actually made it to the gate. That boy sure was strong–he got both beams off the doors on his own. He even got one of the sides partially open before one of the fellers came up and bit him on the back of the heel laughing like a loon.

Cletus somehow managed to get his shotgun, and though he couldn't stand straight for long, he got one of the suits with some buckshot. Hardly even slowed the sucker down.

After seeing that, I knew there was nothing that could be done. It was every man and woman for himself, if you know what I mean. So quick as I could, I followed what shadows there was, trying to skidaddle on closer to the open door out of there. Every step of the way I used some of that positive thinking stuff one's always hearing about–old people don't taste good, old people *don't* taste good.

And I guess it worked too, cause I was able to get to where I was going with only a close call or two.

As soon as I was outside, I ran like the devil was on my tail till I couldn't run anymore. I did go back a day or two later, during the day time, once I was able to pump up my courage, and went to see if I could find any survivors. The can was gone, the suits were gone, and the fort empty as a ghost town. There were no bodies, no kin to say goodbye to or bury. The suits had taken every last bit of them with them. It was the creepiest thing you ever did see.

So I said a few prayers, the whole time looking around to make sure none of them were coming back. That sticky smell from their mouths still coated everything. So I got out of there, hoping to find some living folk somewhere. And then I found you.

That's what happened. Swear to God. So please, I'm an old, scared man, but listen to what I tell you. If you ever, ever find a fifteen-foot can of beer at your door, for heaven's sakes, seal the top closed tight and drink all you can, but don't ever, never bring the sucker inside.

Gloria Oliver lives in The Colony, Texas in her own corral round up with her husband, daughter, three cats, and two hyper ferrets. She is the author of the novel *In the Service of Samurai*, and her second novel *Wings of Angels* should be out in early 2004.

When not busy working with numbers at work, she enjoys reading, writing, watching movies, Japanese Anime, trying to learn Japanese, and making her mind mush by translating Japanese comics.

HOME BAKED AIR BISCUITS
Garrett Peck

The world was a much different place after the coming of the Yuppie Madness.

Shortly before CNN became the last network to go off the air, they had broken the story of how most of the citizens of cities and suburbs had either died outright or had been transformed into walking ghouls whose appetite for human flesh was surpassed only by their enthusiasm for frequenting trendy boutiques and cafés. It was all the fault of those peckerheads in Malfunction Junction, of course. The airborne virus "Yuppie-25", responsible for the mass infection, was traced to a secret chemical weapons research laboratory the government kept stashed away underneath Virginia. The resulting carnage had made the bumper sticker slogan "Die Yuppie Scum" a way of life.

Even though the country had gone to hell in a Gucci handbag, very little had changed in Cheyenne County, Kansas. The farming community, located in the extreme northwest tip of the state, was a fair distance from any large cities. The closest major airports were in Denver and Kansas City. Travelers still needed to drive another 300 miles from either location to reach it, and very few had reason to. Tourism was not a part of the county's economic planning.

Though he certainly wished no harm on anybody – except maybe commies, blacks, Jews, slants, towel heads and Democrats – Dean Wilkerson found his circumstances improved under the New World Order.

Dean had worked most of his life as a tenant farmer, growing and harvesting corn, wheat, sorghum and sunflowers on land owned by a "gentleman farmer" named Guy Hughes, who had lived most of his life in Humboldt, Nebraska and then retired to West Palm Beach, Florida. Before the phone lines had gone silent, Dean had managed to contact Hughes to report on the status of the corn crop. "No more corn," Hughes had insisted, "Grow Belgian endive."   The man's slow, dreamy voice, as well as the highly unusual planting request, confirmed that Hughes had become one of them. Dean had hung up the phone and there had been no further contact.

The way Dean saw it, he could lay claim to the Hughes land and receive full payment for the crops he nurtured, rather than the usual percentage. With the fall of the government, however, paper money had become essentially worthless... although it did make a fine substitute for the toilet paper that quickly fell into such short supply. When the cash ran out, they could always switch to corncobs. Lord knew there were plenty of those around.

Dean was quite content in his new situation. Since earning money was no longer a concern, he only needed to farm a small portion of the land he had once slaved over. One section produced more than enough corn to feed himself, Vida and their modest number of livestock, with enough left over to produce alcohol as an alternative fuel source to keep his farming machinery and home generator running. He only needed to expend a fraction of the effort it once required to keep the homestead going, which was fine with him. Despite all his hard work, he had never had a good enough season to put anything away for retirement. As far as he was concerned, the Yuppie Madness had done more to secure his future than any government payment ever had.

Vida, however, was less enthusiastic. Although she was glad her husband didn't need to work his fingers down to the bone anymore, the lightening of Dean's burdens did have its downsides. He didn't get as much exercise as he used to, but still insisted on eating the three square meals a day he was accustomed to. Consequently, he put on weight. He'd always been a big man, but his bulk had been due to the finely tuned muscles he'd developed working the land. Now he was simply fat. He'd gotten so heavy she could no longer perform her wifely duties. In the missionary position his weight crushed the air from her lungs. She wouldn't hear of any other positions, as her religion had taught her that all others were sinful.

With no sex or television to relieve his mounting boredom, Dean took to drinking a great deal of his home-distilled alcohol. Though he certainly wasn't a mean drunk, there was one aspect of his drinking Vida couldn't abide. The corn liquor caused noxious clouds of gas to build up in his digestive system, which he expelled with great gusto and no sense of shame whatsoever.

One fine June evening they were playing a rousing game of canasta in their living room. Dean sipped his 'shine and puffed away on the one pipe-full of tobacco a day he rationed himself. Just as Vida leaned forward to move her pegs on the canasta board, Dean lifted himself up on one butt cheek and blatted out a raucous fart. The shitty stink wafted right towards her, causing her eyes to water and her nose to crinkle up in disgust. She thought his pipe smelled nasty, but this was much, much worse.

"Honestly, Dean!" Vida snapped, waving her hand frantically in front of her face. "Can't you go to the bathroom to do that?"

"What would be the point? Ain't gotta crap or nothing."

"But it ain't polite!"

"Shit, how many years we been married, woman? I didn't think we needed to stand on ceremony. Besides..."—at this he lifted up again and let out a furious fart even louder and smellier than the previous one—"... with all the gas I've got bubbling up, I'd be running to the toilet every thirty seconds. We'd never finish our game at that rate."

She was about to tell him that it was impossible for her to enjoy the game while choking on his fecal aroma when the sound of a vehicle pulling up outside stayed her protest. "Sounds like we have visitors. Wonder who it could be?"

"Don't know," Dean answered, rising to his feet. "But it don't sound like no American car."

Vida understood the significance of Dean's remark. Everyone in the area drove American made vehicles. After all, why would good farm folk send their hard-earned U.S. dollars out of the country? Even though folks stole their vehicles these days and there technically wasn't a country anymore

Dean tamped out his pipe in the ashtray and stuck it in his shirt pocket. He motioned for Vida to join him. The couple walked quietly to the front windows and peered out through either end of the drapes. They were just in time to see the tri-sectioned circular hood ornament on the sporty little convertible sitting in their driveway before the driver turned off the headlights and engine. Though he'd never seen one in person before, Dean recognized the internationally known symbol.

"Vida," he whispered, "I think that's one of them Mercedes Benzes. It's an expensive Kraut car. Lord, what if they're Nazis coming to take our farm?"

The suspicious vehicle's doors opened, causing the overhead light to briefly illuminate the faces of the exiting passengers. One was entirely unfamiliar, but Vida recognized the other instantly, even though it had been years since she'd seen it in the flesh.

"That ain't no Nazi," she gasped. "That's our son!"

"Kermit?" Dean frowned. "Are you sure?"

"Of course I'm sure! Don't you think I'd recognize my own son? It's our Kermit, come back to us at last! Praise God!"

"Shit," Dean replied, punctuating his remark with another prodigious poot. The old wound in his heart gaped open.

Kermit had left home on bad terms. After graduating from High School, Dean had expected his son to stay in St. Francis and continue helping him with the farm. Kermit would have none of it. He'd said living in a nowhere town like this was crushing his spirit and he had to get away. Dean had continued to badger him to change his mind up until the day he packed his bags. "You can have a good life here, son," he'd insisted. "Find yourself a good woman, settle down, and raise a passel of kids to help you work the land like the Good Lord intended."

Kermit had stopped stuffing his suitcase and looked at his father. "I'm not really interested in any of that, dad."

Dean had been flabbergasted. "What you mean you aren't interested in any of that? I mean, what else is there to life?"

"Well, for one thing, I don't want a wife."

"Don't want a wife? Why not?"

"I... don't really like girls."

The words had stunned him. "Don't like girls? That's ridiculous. You're not telling me your some kind of faggot, are you?"

Kermit had drawn himself up to his full height, clinched his jaw defiantly and looked his father straight in the eye. "Yes, dad. That's exactly what I'm telling you. I'm gay. I like guys. Is that plain enough for you?"

"No, that's... just not possible," Dean had stammered in shock. "You can't be gay; I raised you up right!"

"It's got nothing to do with how you raised me, dad. It's just who I am. Don't you see? I could never be my true self here. People wouldn't accept it. I've got to go to the big city and find others of my kind."

"That's the last thing you need, boy! What you need is a good beating to knock this foolishness out of your head!"

Kermit's eyes had darkened with rage, his lips curling into a cruel smirk. He had raised a limp wrist and said in an outrageous falsetto, "Oooo... you wanna spank my bare bottom, daddy? Go ahead. I always thought I got this from your side of the family."

So infuriated he could barely restrain himself from smacking the shit out of the mincing stranger before him, Dean had ordered Kermit to leave his home, advising him not to return until he had repented from his wicked ways.

"Please don't make him leave like this," Vida had begged. "He's still our son. We have to love him, no matter what. We can work this out."

"No, we can't," Dean had insisted. "I won't have no goddamn sodomites living under my roof. This is a Christian home, Vida. What he's doing is against God. I won't tolerate it!"

That had been that. Kermit had left and they hadn't received so much as a postcard since – even before the coming of the virus. Vida sometimes wondered aloud what might have become of him, but whenever she did Dean would demand she not mention that name in his presence. She had learned to keep her thoughts about their son to herself.

But now, the name came unbidden to her tongue.

"Kermit! My long lost boy!"

"Hush, Vida!" Dean hissed. "Can't you see they're walking funny? They might be dangerous."

"Dangerous? How could he be dangerous? He's our son!"

"You know he was moving to some big city... probably San Francisco, or one of them other towns homos like. He could be one of them yumbie things!"

Now it was Vida's turn to put her foot down. Her anguish at being separated from her only child for so many years could be kept silent no longer. "You're a paranoid old man, Dean. That's your son out there. He's probably walking like that because he's stiff from driving so far to come see us."

"I don't think so, Vida. Didn't you see the color of their skin? All green and sick looking? I'm telling you, they're those yuppie things that was eatin' folks in the cities! We've got to go hide in the basement. Maybe they'll go away if they think we're not here."

Vida eyes burned with resolve. "I'm not hiding from my own son, who I haven't seen in ages. If you're not man enough to face him, you go down in the basement. I'm letting him in and I don't care what you have to say about it!"

A knock, followed by the slow dragging of knuckles, sounded on the front door. Vida marched deliberately over to it.

"Vida, don't you open that door! You'll get us both killed!"

Vida began turning the doorknob. She clearly had no intention of heeding her husband's warning. He cursed softly and ran for the basement, his giggling buttocks releasing another slow, hot burner in his wake. It was as though he was using jet propulsion to aid his escape.

Vida pulled the door open exuberantly and stepped back to allow the two slow-moving figures to enter.

"Kermit? Dear God, is it really you?"

"Mom..." the slack-faced figure wearing her son's face drawled.

"I knew it! I knew my boy would come back to me! Who's your friend?"

"Not friend. Boyfriend."

"Oh... I see. What's his name?"

"Garth" said the stranger.

"Brought him over... for dinner."

"Of course! You two must be starving after your long ride."

"Yes," Garth agreed. "Starving..."

"Well, come on in the kitchen and let me fix you all something to eat. But first, come here and give your mother a hug."

Kermit stepped forward and Vida wrapped her arms around him. He raised his arms stiffly, not returning the hug. Vida stepped back, getting a closer look at the odd tint of his skin. "Are you all right, Kermit? Your skin looks awful."

"It ain't easy being green," Kermit said.

Not knowing what to make of the comment, which seemed strangely familiar somehow, Vida asked her prodigal son what she should fix for supper.

He didn't reply. Instead, he finally tightened his arms around her and leaned down towards her face. Vida thought he meant to kiss her, but when their mouths made contact he sank his teeth into her bottom lip. She shrieked in agony as he worried it like a dog, finally ripping it free along with a good portion of the meat off her chin. Blood ran down what was left of her face and drizzled down her son's chin as he sucked the chunk of flesh into his mouth and chewed thoughtfully She beat at his chest in an effort to free herself, but the blows had no effect. She continued to scream as he swallowed, then turned toward his gruesome lover.

"Taste momma's home cooking," he suggested, then threw Vida into Garth's awaiting arms. The zombie proceeded to chomp off the middle of the old woman's face. The sound of cartilage crunching was audible above her renewed screams of pain and betrayal.

"Nose candy," Garth said with approval, swallowing the delectable organ.

Mercifully, shock overwhelmed Vida's system and Garth allowed her to slide to the floor, unconscious.

"Told you mom would make us a good dinner," Kermit said.

"She has good taste," Garth agreed.

They dropped to their knees and began to dig into Vida's chest. The trauma reawakened her and she screamed as her ribs were ripped loose. The screams became gurgles as her son's hand wrapped around the pulsing organ he sought and yanked it free of her body. She shuddered her last as he brought the muscle up to his face.

"Home," he opined sagely, "is where the heart is."

A sound like Rush Limbaugh sitting on an oversized whoopee cushion drew the diners' attention toward the entranceway leading to the kitchen. Dean, unable to bear the guilt of hearing his wife's death-cries, had belatedly found the courage to emerge from his hiding place. He stood framed in the doorway before the unimaginable tableau of horror.

"My God," Dean groaned in anguish. "What are you doing?"

"Having mom for dinner," Kermit said quite reasonably as he stood up.

Garth followed suit, adding, "Dinner was good. How about dessert?"

Nodding in eerie synchronicity, the zombies began approaching Dean. In his shock and burgeoning grief, Dean remained rooted to the spot, utterly unable to move. His paralysis finally broke when two pairs of cold, clammy hands took hold of his arms, but by then it was far too late. He struggled and cursed, but was unable to break free from their unnaturally strong grip. They dragged him out of the doorway and into a clear area of the living room, maddeningly close to Vida's cooling corpse. Kermit held his father from behind as Garth knelt down to unbuckle the farmer's belt. He then unbuttoned and unzipped the farmer's jeans, drawing them and the gray boxer shorts beneath them down to Dean's ankles. Garth took the fear-shrunken meat he'd revealed in his hand.

"Cream horn," he declared, opening his mouth in preparation to devour the tasty morsel.

"No," Kermit disagreed. "Cocktail weenie. Nuts. Snack food, not dessert."

Dean's emasculation was delayed as Garth considered his dead lover's words. "Then what we eat?"

Kermit grinned with bloody teeth. "Bum cake!"

With that, he bent his father over, feasting his eyes on the blubbery buttocks before him. "Hold on," he instructed Garth. "Bum cake needs icing."

"White icing," Garth agreed.

Dean had a good idea of exactly what kind of "white icing" the ghouls had in mind. His fear was confirmed by the sound of a zipper being drawn down behind him. He struggled vainly against Garth's iron-like grip, clenching his vulnerable sphincter in dread of its pending violation. "Get your filthy hands off me, you goddamn yuppies!" he protested savagely.

"Not yuppies," Kermit said. "Guppies."

Dean abandoned his last desperate hopes for deliverance. He lowered his head and closed his eyes in reluctant resignation to the inevitable.

Just then, he felt two objects slip from his shirt pocket. He opened his eyes and saw his pipe and lighter lying on the ground before him. His inspiration was instantaneous.

"You want a hot ass? You've got it!"

Dean snatched up the lighter, holding it between his legs. He bore down on his gut muscles with all his strength and flicked his Bic. Flaming flatulence shot from his bunghole with the force of a flamethrower.

Emitting a hideous high-pitched squeal, Kermit stumbled backwards, his incestuous intent forgotten as the fiery fart seared his sausage. His pubes continued to crisp and curl as he beat at his groin, shrieking: "Brushfire!"

The sudden burst of fire had also startled Garth, who drew back instinctively. Pressing his surprise attack, Dean grabbed his pipe, stabbing it upwards into Garth's face. The mouthpiece struck pay dirt, sinking into the zombie's eye. Garth fell backwards and Dean, tripping over the jeans around his ankles, fell on top of him. Dean held the pipe stem steady and pounded it deep into Garth's eye socket. It pierced the zombie's reanimated brain, shutting it down permanently. Garth's corpse shook spasmodically, then stilled.

Hearing a bestial roar behind him, Dean flipped onto his back. His slavering son was trying to advance on him, but had forgotten his pants were also down. Kermit fell forwards and landed on his hapless father.

Straining to keep his throat out of the range of Kermit's gnashing teeth, Dean reached behind himself. His fingers scrabbled over Garth's dead face, desperately searching for the pipe Vida had always said would be the death of him. The back of his hand brushed the bowl, but before he could curl his fingers around it, Kermit lurched further up his body, the rotten mouth opening wide as it descended toward his jugular.

"Still hungry, fairy boy?" Dean growled. "Then maybe you'd like some beef jerky!"

With that, he closed his other hand around his son's fried phallus and yanked, stripping off the flash-cooked flesh. Kermit's howl was inhuman. He scrambled away from the source of his pain, futilely attempting to protect his decimated dick.

Dean wasted no time. He glanced away from his whimpering son just long enough to snatch the pipe out of his butt buddy's face. Kermit was so concerned with trying to spare his manhood further mutilation that he didn't even try to protect his face. Dean drove the pipe through his eye, puncturing all the way through to the back of his son's skull, sending him to that never-ending pride parade in the sky.

When it was over, he crawled to Vida's body. With her bottom lip torn off, her exposed teeth appeared to be grinning in approval of his victory. And dear Jesus, they had torn out her heart and bitten off her nose!

His body heaved with a huge sob, forcing another fart from his rectum. The sobs mutated into mad chuckles when he realized that without her nose she'd never be able to complain about the stink again.

THE END

Garrett Peck is a two-time nominee for the Bram Stoker Award in Nonfiction, first for the anthology *Personal Demons* co-edited with Brian A. Hopkins (Lone Wolf Publications), a collection of essays on CD-ROM by 42 horror authors on their personal experiences with terror, then for editing and publishing *Hellnotes Newsletter*, along with founders David B. Silva and Paul F. Olsen. He also co-edited the two-volume anthology of creature fiction *Tooth and Claw* with J. F. Gonzalez, also from Lone Wolf. His short fiction can be found in the anthologies *Stories That Won't Make Your Parents Hurl, More Stories That Won't Make Your Parents Hurl, Bubbas of the Apocalypse, Brainbox: The Real Horror, Stones, Raging Horrormones, The Parasitorium: Terrors Within* and *The Red, Red Robin Project.* He reviews horror fiction for *Gauntlet Magazine, Cemetery Dance Magazine, Flesh & Blood, Hellnotes Newsletter* and the forthcoming *The Horror Within.* He directed the U. S. premiere of Clive Barker's *Crazyface* and the world premiere of F. Paul Wilson and Matthew J. Costello's *Syzygy* for the stage. He has narrated audio books for WyrdSisterS ProductionS, including the Bram Stoker Award finalist *F. Paul Wilson's Conspiracies* and *David B. Silva's Sudden in a Shaft of Shadow.* He is serving his third term as chairman of the Bram Stoker Award Additions Jury for the Horror Writers Association. He lives in America's oldest city, St. Augustine, Florida, where he has worked as a Ghost Tour guide, and enjoys writing about himself in third person because he thinks it makes him sound more objective. His home on the web is http://www.authorsden.com/garrettpeck. He welcomes correspondence at garrettp@aug.com.

RAVEN'S BACK IN TOWN

Bradley H. Sinor

"So what do you think of my new hat, Ed?" asked Charlie Clark as he sat down at the Lucky Lady Bar & Grill's lunch counter.

Ed Roberts set down his beer after taking one last swallow, reached over into a bowl of pickled eggs and snagged one. He popped it into his mouth, purple juice running out the sides of his lips, as he chewed.

"First off, Charlie," he said. "That is one piss poor hunting cap. It's thinner than shit and wouldn't do diddly towards keeping your head and ears warm. Secondly, in case you haven't noticed, you've got the thing on sideways. The flaps are supposed to go over your ears, not hang down in your eyes."

No one was paying that much attention to Ed and Charlie; the noonday crowd was pretty much used to their arguments, and usually ignored them.

"If this isn't a good huntin' hat," said Charlie. "Why else would it be called a deerstalker? It's one of them English hats, the kind that ole Sherlock Holmes wore in all his detective movies when he went huntin' criminals."

"Detective movies? If that hat is supposed to be so damn special, Mr. Detective, sir, then why don't you solve the mystery of what's been happening to those gals who've been dying around here so weird like," said Ed.

"They was just movies!" said Charlie.

"They ain't showing around here, are they?" asked Ed.

"Naw, I ain't seen any since we used to go over to visit my Aunt Lynn in Coffin's Corner, Arkansas. On weekends we'd go out to the Canyon Wall Drive-In Movie and Holy Tabernacle. Watch movies all night and be there for Sunday morning services," said Charlie.

The mention of the Canyon Wall Drive-in Theatre was enough to cause Raven Harkness, sitting at the far end of the counter, to pay closer attention to Charlie and Ed's conversation.

It had been four months since Raven had left Coffin's Corner behind, along with her reputation as "that woman". The people of Coffin's Corner had known her as a hooker, plying her trade with the locals and passing truckers. Which suited Raven just fine, since she was really an undercover field agent for United Pharmaceuticals, working with her partner, Penn Mulroney, to find some clue to the plague immunity that some people had.

Unfortunately, most of the data they had gathered was destroyed during a zombie outbreak at the self same Canyon Wall Drive-in. The two of them had left town quickly after that. After filing her report Raven had told Penn and her bosses that she was taking a few weeks off to visit her hometown, Lawton, Oklahoma, the scene of her 'misspent youth'.

"It's been more than a few years since we went to Coffin's Corner for a visit, not since Aunt Lynn died," said Charlie.

Hearing that was a relief. Raven had taken pains to change her appearance: red hair three shades darker, different glasses, and a complete change of wardrobe. But you never knew who you might run into.

"Raven? What the hell are you doing back in this town?" Raven smiled as she looked around to see an old friend. Madison Cromwell was the same age as Raven, but because of her diminutive size, (she stood barely five feet tall) she had always been mistaken for her younger sister. Wearing dark glasses and a sleeveless jean jacket, her short dark hair pulled back under a baseball cap, Madison looked hardly any different than when Raven had left town five years before.

"I'm here to raise hell, just like I always have!"

"Then let's get out of here and find some trouble to get into, girlfriend," said Madison.

Madison reached into the cooler that sat on the backseat of Raven's Barracuda and pulled out a can of beer. She popped the top and took a swallow, spewing the contents out of her mouth a couple of seconds later.

"Damn it," yelled Raven. "If I've told you once, I've told you a hundred times. Don't spill food in the car! Or I'll make you clean it up!" She'd been fanatical about the appearance of her car since the first day she had slid behind the wheel.

"Ye gods, what is this stuff?" demanded Madison. She

held the beer can up and squinted at it. "Hobb Nail Brewery? Whoever made it should be taken out and beaten within an inch of their lives with a pair of their own hob nails."

"Hey, you take what you can get sometimes," said Raven. "It wasn't as if I could wait to get back here and get the good stuff."

Back when the plague hit there had only been a thousand or so people left in Lawton; too stubborn to leave, Raven's father had said. One of the local industries that had been a priority to keep going had been the beer bottling plant; in fact, it had become one of the major exports for the town. As Raven's father had said "It was amazing how people heard about it and moved to Lawton. This town doubled its population in just a couple of years. You just got to have your priorities, and beer is definitely one of them."

Raven steered the car onto the street and headed toward Cache Road, one of the central streets in Lawton, literally running from one end of the town to the other. On more than one occasion the Barracuda, with Raven and Madison in it, had spent the night cruising up and down the avenue.

"So what the hell are you doing back here, Raven?" asked Madison after riding several blocks in silence.

"I don't know, just got an odd feather up my ass, an urge to see the old stomping grounds. Maybe it was just an urge to see my best friend; it has been a few years. What's a matter, not glad to see me?" said Raven.

"Of course I am. I been tempted to write to you and get you to meet me down in Dallas. We could do some serious partying and then stay over for services at the Tabernacle of the Sportatorium."

Madison had long ago become a convert to the religious wrestling circuit. Raven had been to a few matches herself. Even blood-covered, some of those wrestlers were good preachers.

"Mad, you never were good at hiding things. Something's going on, so talk. What's the deal?" said Raven.

Madison sighed. "All right, then. I take it you remember Peggy, Mary Anne and Jodeana?"

Raven remembered them all right. They had been friends, not as close as she and Madison, but still friends. At times they had been the best of friends and at times they had been the worst of enemies; typical teenagers, in other words

"Of course. And?" asked Raven.

"They're dead. All three in the past six weeks." Madison told her.

"Was it a zombie attack? Or did they come down with the plague and just go over themselves?" Raven hoped that if it were the latter, none of their families had been the ones to put the girls down. That was the sort of thing that could ruin a relative's whole day

Raven used both her knees to hold the barracuda's steering sheel steady, as she twisted around to grab a beer from the cooler.

"Nope, it was hit and run, all three of them, late at night and no witnesses. Peggy was killed near the Baptist church, Mary Anne on the access road near the water slide and Jodeana out there near Big Bob's Lumber," she said.

"This is that thing that Charlie and Ed were talking about?"

"Yeah, there's a whole lot of talk floating around about it. Fact is nobody knows a whole lot."

"I think I know somebody who would," said Raven.

Raven wasn't sure that she even wanted to go and talk to her grandma, Wanda Davis. Ever since she had been a little girl there had been something about the older woman that made Raven uncomfortable. Problem was, Raven didn't feel like she had a lot of choice in the matter. If anyone in Lawton knew what was going on with the three girls dying, it would be her grandmother. It wasn't that Grandma Davis was a gossip (that was a word you never used in her presence) information just seemed to make it to her doorstep naturally.

Wanda Davis lived in the abandoned air traffic control tower on the south side of Lawton, two miles from the dirt track speedway. Raven's grandmother had once explained that she liked the tower for the privacy it gave her, not to mention the clear field of fire on any strangers.

Standing at one of a dozen rose bushes spread around the tower was a man, a pair of pruning shears in one hand, carefully trimming several branches. He was big; hitting 300 pounds, if not more, and looked like there was hardly a muscle anywhere in his frame. If he noticed Raven, the man gave no reaction, just kept right on working.

"Excuse me, is Mrs. Davis at home?" she asked him.

The man looked up, and then pointed toward the building.

It was only when she was well past him that he spoke. "Nice to see you, Miss Raven. I'm Ned."

Raven wondered how he knew her. To the best of her knowledge she had never laid eyes on the man before. More than likely, her grandmother had shown some pictures of her to him, though that didn't really seem like the sort of thing that Grandma Davis would have done.

The door was open just a crack. It only took a touch to make it swing inwards, without a sound.

"Well, don't just stand there like an idiot, girl. Get yourself inside!"

Wanda Davis was in her seventies, at least that had always been the conventional family wisdom. When asked what her birth year was, all you would get out of the woman was an icy stare that definitely suggested it would *not* be a good idea to ask a second time.

Raven spotted her grandmother sitting behind a large wooden table that was covered with a number of paint palettes, display stands and open guidebooks. In one hand she held a brush, in the other a china plate. She moved the brush across its surface.

"Don't get in my light," she snapped, holding the plate up. "So tell me what you think of it?"

"Well," Raven said, deliberately stretching her words out as she studied it. The picture showed a man and a woman in camo, armed of course, standing over the body of a man in a suit with his briefcase open and papers flying around "It's interesting."

"I told you when you were a little girl it isn't nice to fib to your grandmother. This is a piece of shit and I've just wasted the last day and a half on it."

With that she sent the plate flying across the room. It clipped the edge of the couch, bounced and slammed against the wall, shattering into several dozen pieces.

The pewter-colored cat lying on the couch opened one eye, yawned and went back to sleep.

"Now, what'n hell do you want here? And don't tell me it's a family call. You know what I said about fibbing to me," said the older woman, pushing herself away from the table, reaching for the coffee cup that sat on top of a pile of old newspapers.

Raven dropped onto the arm of an overstuffed chair and stared at her grandmother. "Look, the only reason I'm back was a bit of morbid curiosity to see if this town had changed. Hell, fifteen minutes after I sat down at the Lucky Lady I could tell it hadn't. But then I started hearing some weird shit, that three girls I grew up with all were killed in hit and runs in less than six weeks," said Raven. "That's just a bit too much of a coincidence, even for me to believe."

Grandma Davis picked up her cup and took a sip. She seemed to be mulling over things.

"That is a wee bit odd, I'll admit," nodded her grandmother. "So I'd be looking both ways, anytime I crossed the street while you're back here, if I were you, Raven. But I'm about to make it odder. I know about those three girls being killed. I also know that their bodies are missing."

""I beg your pardon."

"No need, I was quite clear. All three of those girls bodies were stolen out of their graves within four days of their funerals," she said.

"Why?" asked Raven.

"Pardon me, Miss Harkness." Raven looked over to see the big gardener standing near the window. How he had moved so quietly was a mystery. "There are some things that it might be better if'n we just left 'em alone."

"Look my friend, there are questions that need to be answered," she said turning toward the window.

"Raven," said her grandmother. "I expect you to look at me when you're talking!"

"I was just talking to him," said Raven and gestured toward the window, only there was no one there.

"What are you talking about?" asked the older woman.

Raven was about to say something about Ned, but thought better of it. "So why haven't people gotten up in arms about this whole thing, even if it does sound like something out of a bad drive-in movie."

"There's a lot that can be learned from bad drive in movies, girl. The sheriff might not be the brightest bulb in the package but he's right. With only two deputy's he's got to keep this thing quiet."

"I guess I should tell you that it isn't three girls you know who are dead, it's four. A truck hit Kelly Golden a few days ago. The family kept it quiet, didn't even have a real funeral. They buried her three days ago. I'm not even sure if the sheriff knows about it, yet."

Another face, another set of memories ran through Raven's mind. She hadn't been that close to Kelly, not like the others. But they had been friends.

"So you think that if someone is going to dig her up, maybe it'll happen tonight?"

Wanda Davis picked up a ceramic mug and began to dab at it with a thick bristle brush. Raven knew when she had been dismissed, and the futility of trying to get her grandmother to talk when she didn't want to.

"You owe me big for being out here tonight, real big." Madison told Raven.

"What, did you maybe have a really hot date?" Sitting in a cemetery for three hours was definitely not the way that Raven had planned to spend a Saturday night. Instead of heading for the dance that was going on over at the bingo hall, she and Madison were parked behind the maintenance shed at the Sweet Heaven Cemetery watching the grave of an old friend.

"So, are you going to tell me about this big date that you're missing?" asked Raven.

"I suppose so," giggled Madison, "since you asked so nice and polite. His name is Eric Dawson. He is seriously fine, to the point that I could very easily come in my pants just thinking about him. He works over at the bottling plant, drives a Mustang that he's reconditioned. I met him at the dirt track races three Saturday nights ago. He's smart, intelligent, and I made sure he's falling for *moi*."

"So, have you given him the acid test?" asked Raven,

"What do you mean?"

"Have you screwed his brains out, yet? I'd make sure you were way out in the country. As I recall from more than one or two of our double dates, you do tend to get vocal," said Raven.

Before either could say anything more, a van turned into the cemetery. It took several wrong turns on the unlit roads but eventually came to a halt near the new grave that bore the name Kelly Golden. The vehicle was in fairly good shape but there was a discolored area on the side, as if marking a place where a sign had been removed.

"Bingo," said Raven. She watched two figures climb out of the van: one tall and gangly, the other smaller, both dressed in army fatigues. It was too far to make out their faces, but there was something familiar about the bigger one. Raven just couldn't put her finger on what it was.

An annoying scratching sound from the back window of the car got Raven's attention. Twisting around, she saw a figure standing next to the car, slowly moving its fingers up and down on the glass. There was more than enough light to see the pale skin and eye hanging out of its socket to recognize it as a zombie.

Before she could gun the engine to life and roar away from the undead thing, Madison was out of the car, a two-by-four with a half dozen nails protruding from one end in her hand.

"Shit," muttered Raven, grabbing up her pistol and following her friend.

Madison slammed her club into the creature's head twice in quick succession, then hit it in the back of the legs. That was enough to put the thing on the ground. The sound of wood striking bone, driving nails into it, was very satisfying as she pounded at it, blood and bits of broken bone flying everywhere.

Once the thing stopped moving, Madison turned back to Raven.

"You could have helped," she said.

"Far be it from me to interfere in your fun. Any particular reason why you tore into this one so vehemently?" asked Raven.

Madison leaned against the car, dropping the club at her feet. "Yes. That thing used to be Eric. The guy I was telling you about!"

"Whoops," Raven grinned, but the grin vanished when she saw the look on Madison's face. "So were you going to let him? Get in your pants, I mean. There's a mighty good chance that he might have gone over while you two were doing the mattress shuffle."

"That's gross!" said Madison.

"Well, you don't have to worry about it now."

The sound of the van's engine got Raven's attention as she watched it pull away. The grave was open, and she could just make out a coffin lid peaking out of the hole.

"Let's go." She wasn't sure if the bad feeling in the pit of her stomach was from what was happening or because the chili they had for dinner wasn't sitting well.

The van headed north, onto the old Ft. Sill military

reservation, disappearing into the rat's maze of roads that criss-crossed the area. Nearly two hours later there was still no sign of the missing vehicle. Much as she hated to, Raven had reached the point where she was ready to give it up as a lost cause.

Founded at the tail end of the days of the Wild West, Ft. Sill had been intended to help keep settlers safe and Indians under control. After the plague, the army had attempted to hold out at the base for a few years, but had eventually abandoned the site.

"It may be time to fall back to Plan B," muttered Raven.

"What, pray tell, is Plan B?" asked Madison.

"I'll let you know after I think of one."

They were passing a small cinder block church in the center of the base. It occurred to her suddenly that just beyond the church was the large bowling alley, another favorite hangout for teenagers who were trying to see who could scare the others the most.

"There," she whispered to Madison. Parked in the area just behind the bowling alley was the van. "Feel in the mood for some bowling tonight?"

Raven slid her colt 45 into her belt, and then touched her boots to assure herself that the two knives hidden there were ready and waiting. Madison had her own gun, a nine-millimeter with silver grips. She also picked up the same club she had used earlier, the wood and nails now many shades darker because of the bloodstains.

"If you got any blood on the upholstery, you are going to be the one to clean it off, with a toothbrush," said Raven.

"Yes, mommy," Madison laughed. "So, we going to stand out here all night flapping our jaws or are we going to go see what's going on in there?"

After the two women had gone through the back door, a lone figure came ambling around the side of the church building and looked over at the bowling alley. Ned was wishing that the sign was on; he'd always liked the way the neon pins would fall over and then be picked up, to fall over again across the front of the building.

There was no light inside, beyond what leaked in through broken windows on either side of the entrance. If it hadn't been for the flashlights they had brought along, the depths of the place would have been pitch black.

Raven caught a glimpse of her own reflection in the cracked mirror that hung behind the shoe rental area. Here and there in the small cubicles, between rat's nests and trash, she noticed a few unmatched pairs of bowling shoes.

At the far end of the alley, pushed up against the east wall, was a raised stage with a complete drum set in the center and three microphones at equal intervals around it. Shining her flashlight on the drums, one thing struck Raven right away. There was a fine layer of dust on almost everything else in the bowling ally, but the drums and microphones looked shiny new, like they had just come from the music store.

"Is there maybe a concert around here that no one told me about?" asked Raven.

"I suppose you could say that," said a voice from behind one of the alleys. The words were punctuated by the very distinct sound of a machine gun being cocked.

"Dexter? Is that you?" asked Madison.

That name and that voice brought back a memory to Raven: a gangly scarecrow-like figure with an unruly thatch of red hair that looked like it had never been within ten miles of a comb.

"I'm touched that you remember me, Madison. Though a bit surprised, since you, just like the rest, barely acknowledged I was alive, unless you needed me to do something," said the man, as he ducked low and came in below the machinery in one of the lanes. It was the same fatigue-dressed figure Raven had seen earlier.

"Drop you weapons, please," he said gesturing with the barrel of the machine gun.

"Dexter? Dexter McPherson?" asked Raven.

"The same. Now, the guns."

"Are you that good a shot?" Asked Raven. "It seems like there are two of us and we have the advantage of numbers and weapons."

"If he's not, I am" From the shoe rental area came the other figure from the graveyard. Only now Raven could see that he was considerably younger, the fatigues hanging loose from him. He was no more than twelve or thirteen at the most; the shotgun cradled in his arms seemed almost bigger than he was.

Behind him came a third man, three times the boy's size at least. It took Raven a moment to realize that it was her grandmother's gardener, Ned.

The two came up behind the two women and began to pull their guns from them, but missed Raven's knives. Ned threw Madison's club against the far wall, hard enough for its points to sink into the plaster.

Once they were disarmed, the boy produced a cord and tied both women's hands behind their backs. Raven found herself forced to sit on one of the curved plastic benches at the end of one of the lanes. Dexter said something to the boy and Ned, and then sat down next to Raven, as the other two disappeared into the darkness.

"Now," said Dexter. "I suppose you are wondering why I called you all here."

"Oh come on, Dexter, get to the point," said Raven. She had already managed to work one hand free of the knots. The kid had been more interested in copping a feel than in making sure the knots were tight.

"Oh, all right," laughed the man. "The truth is, I am putting together the greatest rock and roll band that the world has ever seen. This is our rehearsal hall."

"That's ambitious, Dexter," said Madison. "We all knew you had talent."

The gangly boy had a genius for machines of any sort. He had been the one a lot of people called on to fix machines of every size from a mixer to a bulldozer. The only trouble was, he had always wanted to go further, working with computers and things like that. Those sorts of ideas scared a lot of the people.

"So what's a band have to do with your digging up bodies? Trying to make a band from parts?" Raven asked him.

"Close. I tried to recruit Peggy, Mary Anne & Jodeana, to share my vision with them, but they all laughed in my face, the same way you all did when we were growing up. So I had to get them into the group another way," he said. "Just watch," Dexter pulled a small walkie-talkie from his pocket and spoke a few words that Raven couldn't hear.

The door that Ned and the boy had left through opened. Even in the dark, Raven could see several people coming through. They moved up onto the stage, each movement seeming mechanical and exaggerated. The boy was the one guiding them into place behind two of the microphone stands and the drums. Over his back he carried guitars that he fitted into the hands of the two figures behind the mikes.

"It's show time, folks!" laughed Dexter. He held his hand up, the walkie-talkie held like a magic wand, and made a gesture with it. Spotlights came on, focused on the stage.

Raven stared in disbelief.

Behind the two mikes were Peggy and Mary Anne, and just peeking over the drum set was Jodeana. At first she thought they might be plague zombies, but no plague victims she had seen had ever looked like that. Their eyes were rolled back in their heads and their skin was fish belly white; every movement was stiff and jerky.

"Play it, girls," yelled Dexter, a smile on his face.

Peggy and Mary Anne began to drag their fingers across the strings of their guitars, but in no coherent way that even resembled music. Behind them, the only sound that emerged from the drum set resembled the sound of a motor that had thrown a rod.

"You sick bastard, what have you done to them?" demanded Raven.

"Oh, just made some improvements. When they turned me down I knew there was no way they would be willing to be my ticket to fame and fortune. So I had to "draft" them. Some arranged accidents, ones that didn't damage their bodies too bad, along with a special preservative I developed and my computer, make them move. Now I have myself a band. I'm thinking of marketing that preservative; it does a great job with fruit and pickles, as well."

Raven stared, incredulous, at the animated corpses of the three women. Her eyes kept returning to the silver necklace Mary Anne wore.

"I had thought about trying to develop a variant of the plague, but this way works much, much better. I can make them into the ultimate rock band. We don't even have to have a bus; the girls can just sit in the closet of my camper. The only thing they need now is practice, and then we can go on the road. Every zombie in the world will be lining up to hear them.," said Dexter.

"Dexter, I may have thought you were weird before, but now I know you are one sick fuck," said Raven. "The only thing you should be doing on the road is being run over by a semi. I know a truck driver who would be more than happy to oblige."

"Now," continued Dexter, ignoring Raven, "I've got Kelly downstairs. She needs some work before I can get her ready for the stage. Then I can start on you two; you'll add just the right sound as backup singers."

"Not on your life, little boy." Raven spat in his face, pulling her hands free from the last of the knots and brought her knee up to slam into his crotch. Dexter bent almost double in pain, the air rushing out of his chest in a wave of bad breath and mentos.

On the stage there was a sudden crashing. One of the spotlights had come loose from the ceiling and fallen, sparks flying everywhere, setting the cheap carpet on fire. The other lights in the alley sputtered and faded out. The "girls" continued to make noise with their instruments, oblivious to everything.

Raven grabbed Dexter's machine gun, ran toward the stage and sprayed the whole place with bullets, concentrating on the girls. Their flesh flew apart, an odd bluish-green liquid spurting out from their wounds. The kid came running out of the door behind the stage, shotgun in hand. Raven gave him his own blast with the machine gun.

She looked around for Ned, but the big man was gone.

Dexter was struggling to his feet. Raven launched a kick at the side of his head and that was enough to put him back on the floor. She pulled Madison, who still hadn't worked her way free from the ropes, to her feet and the two of them sprinted for the door. Already the fire was spreading, acrid smoke filling the place.

"I think its time to blow this party," Raven shouted, as she grabbed the other girl's arm and headed them toward the door.

"Yeah, this place blows," her friend answered. "Let's find something exciting to do."

The lights had gone out quickly, so they had to feel their way along the wall toward the door. As they passed the concession stand, Raven looked up into the big mirror. She could barely make out Ned, standing and just looking around like a fascinated child, a yellow circus balloon in one hand and cotton candy cone in the other.

When she glanced back into the alley, no one was there.

"I was tempted to just not untie you and drop you off at your place like that," laughed Raven.

"I'm sure that my neighbors would have loved to see me walking around like that," Madison said.

Raven picked up the coffee cup that sat in front of her. "Hey, I think it would have done wonders for your reputation," she said.

"Gee, thanks. That's just the kind of reputation that I need around this town," she said, rubbing her wrists. "I still have to explain the rope burns."

"What are friends for, if we can't help each other out? Now, pass me the barbeque sauce," Raven told her.

It was nearly noon, but The Lucky Lady was still serving breakfast. Scrambled eggs, grits and black coffee seemed the order of the day. For the past few minutes, besides Alex, who was cooking and working the register, Madison and Raven had had the place to themselves. That suited the two women just fine; there were some things that no one else needed to hear.

By the time they had gotten to the car the whole bowling ally had been totally engulfed in flames. That the fire had spread so quickly was weird, but right then the only thing Raven wanted to do was put as much distance between herself and the place as she could.

In the hours since, she had heard a half-dozen different explanations for the fire; everything from kids starting it to some kind of zombie orgy. Charlie and Ed had suggested that maybe some little green men had come down and set the fire, since they couldn't find a cornfield to leave designs in.

"So how did your grandmother react when you told her about Ned being dead?' asked Madison.

"Now, that is getting really strange, though after last night I'm not sure what that word really means. I went over to see Grandma this morning, but when I mentioned Ned, she asked who was I talking about. She claimed that not only did she not have a gardener, but the only person she had ever known named Ned had died more than twenty years ago. Not to mention the fact that she would be damned if anybody but her was going to touch her roses bushes," said Raven as she poured some sauce over her eggs, not that it helped the taste.

Madison furrowed her brow. "Next thing you're going to tell me is that we hallucinated him," muttered Raven's friend.

Alex appeared with a fresh pot of coffee in his hand and refilled both women's cups. "By the way, Miss Harkness, ma'am. When I opened up this morning I found a big manila envelope stuck in the door. It had your name on it."

"My name?"

"Yeah, its up here by the register. I forgot about it until just now."

Raven's name was indeed right in the center of the envelope, written in crude block letters with an orange crayon. She tore open the envelope and poured the contents on the counter.

It was a necklace, her necklace, the very same one she had last seen hanging around Mary Anne's neck last night, just moments before she had blown her face off.

The necklace wasn't the only thing. Lying next to it was a length of string tied around the stem of what remained of a yellow circus balloon.

THE END

While researching a new recipe for BBQ sauce in the secret Bubba archives, **Bradley H. Sinor** discovered that the heroine of his BoA story (written in collaboration with Lee "He dragged me into this!" Martindale) also came from the same SW Oklahoma town that he had. He's not a bad influence, in spite of shat certain people say.

Brad's stories have been collected in two chapbooks, *In The Shadows* and *Dark And Stormy Nights* (Yard Dog Press). He will also have new stories appearing in the near future in anthologies such as *Haunted Holidays*, *Rotten Relations* (a collaboration with his wife Sue), *The Magic Shop*, and *Men Writing Sf As Women*.

SWEET MEAT

Glenn R. Sixbury

Friday night.

Leastways, folks around the Deer Hollow trailer park called it Friday night, and more important, our last poker game had been seven nights ago, meaning it was time for another.

Like usual, I was the first to arrive at Ned's. Didn't have anything better to do. Besides, I wanted to get a better lock at that new gal Ned had found up north of the creek three weeks ago. She had a hell of a set of jugs and liked to strut around his yard wearing nothing but a faded-orange tube top and cut-off jeans, but something about her wasn't right. What girl in her right mind would put up with Ned for more than five minutes? That belchin', fartin' bastard was three bricks shy of a full load and had a dick the size of a caterpillar. Not that I particularly wanted to know, but Ned had a habit of whipping it out and letting it spray whenever the urge struck, and that included in the middle of a poker hand. Most important thing when he did that was to keep the cards from getting wet. And the pork rinds.

Ned had a terrible aim.

I stepped over one of Ned's rusty engine blocks and tripped on a hubcap laying just the other side. Damned near fell flat on my face. Worse, I damned near dropped my jar of moonshine. I was still cursing when the metal screen door slammed and Lulu's sweet voice carried through the twilight.

"Won't your mother be proud? You got a worse potty mouth than Ned with a hangover."

I looked up at Lulu and gasped. How the hell did Ned get so lucky? I'm almost 61, an old geezer in these times, but Lulu made even my wrinkly old Willy sit up and take notice.

After sipping a bit of white lightning for courage, I grinned with what was left of my teeth and tried hard not to stare at a set of nipples that seemed to be staring back. "It's alright, Lulu," I said, "my mama died before you were born. She was an accountant. Plague took her first thing."

Her bottom lip jutted out a bit. "I'm sorry," she said, her voice coating my ears like aged whiskey, just one of many pleasures I thought I'd learned to live without.

Lulu had a knack for sounding genuine, but a short attention span. Two seconds later, she bounced over to the picnic table and spread a red- and white-checkered tablecloth across the gray, cracked wood. I was so busy looking at her boobs, I hadn't noticed all the stuff she was carrying. Like a fool, I stumbled forward.

"Want some help?"

Lulu dumped over an old coffee can, and dirty, plastic chips bounced across the table. She looked over her shoulder, her thick eyelashes fluttering over her luscious brown eyes. "What kind of help?"

I swallowed, my throat dry. "Whatever," I mumbled.

Get a grip, old man. Even with her looking at me, I couldn't help stealing a glance at her ass and wondering how she got denim pulled that tight without splitting the seams.

"James, you're so sweet."

Lulu was the only one who called me James. Not that I particularly liked the name – I always thought it was a bit on the sissy side, that Bond guy not included – but when it came from Lulu's lips, it sounded different, the way Ned's farts did in the middle of winter. Artistic, sort of.

Suddenly her hand reached out to caress my stubbly cheek. "You don't belong here. You know that, don't you?"

I soaked up her touch like a cat laying in a patch of sunshine. Why not? Lulu's fingers on my cheek was the closest I'd come to getting laid since a rattlesnake took out old Miz Nelson two winters ago. Then Lulu's touch was gone, and her words sunk through my thick skull to what was left of my brain. "Uh, why don't I belong here?"

"You're smart. Too smart for these parts. You could make something of yourself. Go somewhere. Be someone."

"Go where? Be what? There ain't nothing left, is there?"

"A bit," she said, thoughtfully, displaying that pouty look again. "There could be more, if folks like you tried to make something of it."

Just then, Bo pulled into the yard in his old '78 pickup. The pickup was two years older than I was, and the only thing holding it together was rust, but at least it didn't have that computerized crap to keep it from running on my moonshine.

Bo popped out of the cab like a hound hopping off the porch. He was a big bastard who never took off his dirty cowboy hat and could have scalped people with his belt buckle. Still, he was a decent shit, unless you pissed him off.

"Hey, Doc," he said, "you still droolin' over what you can't have."

"Damn you, Bo, you son-of-a-bitch!" I said.

I was afraid he'd upset Lulu, but she just smiled and put her arm around me. "You're just jealous, Bo. I'll bet old James here is hung like a mule."

Mule was right, whether she meant it or not. Didn't matter, though. Bo was too stupid to know the difference.

"Doc?" Bo jerked his thumb in my direction. "Everything he's got is spoiled. Now if you want some fresh meat, all you need to do is sneak down to my place after Ned passes out. I'll show you a real good time."

"Sure you will," Lulu said, heading back toward the house. "At least your goat ain't complained yet."

"What? Who told you?"

The screen door slammed, leaving us alone. Bo grinned and hunched up his pants by pulling on his buckle. "She's sure got some fire. What the hell's she doing with Ned?"

"Fuck if I know. I'm going to drain my weasel."

I went behind the house. My dick had been hard when I headed back there, and I'd half been thinking I might pull on it a while, but by the time I unzipped my fly, it was soft as jelly.

I looked down and spoke aloud. "What the hell are you good for?"

I tried to conjure an image of Lulu's tube top, the way I'd done several times the last few weeks, but all I could think about was what she had said. *You could make something of yourself.*

Ya, and yumbies were nice once you got to know them.

When the weeds were good and wet, I headed back for the party.

The five of us usually ate barbecue before we started playing poker, but Lulu said she didn't like the stuff, so we skipped supper and went straight to the cards. We always played seven-card stud: Ned, Bo, me, Tater and Ear Wax. I almost always won. It wasn't that Ned, Bo and the others were all that brainless – well, maybe they were – but mainly I was old enough to be patient. I'd bet low until they were all shit-faced, then take them for everything they could spare, but tonight, as I watched Lulu pass around bottles of home-made beer, I thought I'd be willing to give up a bit of patience for something warmer.

As usual, Ned was the first one to drink himself stupid.

He bet three blues without so much as a pair to back them up.

"Raise!" Bo crowed, and plopped down a couple golds.

"How much is that?" Ear Wax asked, looking at his meager pile of chips. A second later, his finger went to his ear. After digging around a bit, he pulled out a gob of dark, brown goo that he flicked toward the bushes.

"Same as it's been every week since you learned how to pee," Tater growled. He and I had already folded.

"Don't matter, anyway," Bo said to Ear Wax. "You ain't got it."

"I got it," Ned said and farted.

Each week, the big loser from the week before had to sit downwind. Fortunately, Ned was almost always the big loser. If not, none of us would have lived this long.

Bo fanned his face, shadows from the Coleman lantern dancing across his forehead. "Hell, I know you got that!" Bo growled at Ned. "What about the chips."

Ned picked up his last two gold chips, about all he had left, then burped so loud and so long, four mosquitoes dropped from the fumes and landed in the bowl of pork rinds. Either Ned didn't see or didn't care, because the next second he took a whole handful of those golden nuggets and shoved them in his mouth.

I watched Lulu, but her only reaction was to hitch up her tube top—her boobs were always fighting gravity—then pick up the empty beer bottles and carry them into the house. I picked up the remaining empties and followed her inside, not caring who won between Ned and Bo.

"Ned's drunk," I said, stating the obvious.

Lulu worked the hand pump by Ned's sink, wiggling too much for my comfort. "That ain't drunk. He's still talking."

I helped her rinse out the bottles. The beer was Ear Wax's form of money, but he got the bottles back. My payola was moonshine. Bo's was food, mainly goat cheese, venison, and pretty much anything he could kill. Tater's was, of course, potatoes, along with carrots, squash, okra, cucumbers, tomatoes, and whatever else he could grow in the red dirt around here.

But Ned, who usually couldn't tell his ass from a hole in the ground, controlled the mother load. He could afford to lose at poker every week because his chips were backed by bullets: Remington's, Winchester's, all calibers along with a dozen or so types of shotgun shells. Since bullets were the only thing standing between us and being eaten by yumbies, they were a new form of gold. Every man, woman, and child in our dingy trailer park always carried enough weapons with them to start a small war, but Ned was our only source of ammo, and he kept his stash hoarded in some secret place no one had ever found.

Maybe that's why Lulu was with him. While the rest of us got by in leaky, old trailer houses, Ned lived in a real house and had plenty of people willing to help him fix it up.

"I ain't never slept with him," Lulu suddenly said.

I snorted before I could catch myself.

"I ain't," Lulu said, with more conviction.

She was still washing bottles, still wiggling that behind, but her voice held a ring of truth.

"Why not?" I asked.

"'cause he snores," she said, and giggled.

She ran her finger across my cheek on her way to the yard with another round of brew.

Ned was completely shit-faced by the time I started winning. He'd lost almost all his money to Bo and I would have a harder time weaseling it out of him than if I'd taken it off Ned in the first place. Worse, Ned was getting nasty.

"I been watching you," Ned said as I raked in another pot.

"Learnin' anything?" I asked.

"Ya, I'm learning you wanna fuck my woman."

I laughed. Didn't matter if it was true. Lulu would never run off with an old geezer like me.

"Shit, you dumb redneck mother-fucker," Bo said. "Everybody wants to fuck your woman. We'd fuck you if we were drunk enough."

Lulu stood behind Ned, sipping on a beer and swaying back and forth to music that existed only inside her head.

She sensed all of us looking at her. Smiling at the table, she leaned over Ned's shoulder, exposing plenty of cleavage, and kissed him on the neck.

"You're the only one for me," she said. Ned smiled through his drunken haze, but when Lulu pulled back, she quietly spit, then wiped her mouth with the back of her hand.

"Shit, Doc," Ned said. "Everybody knows you're too old to get it up, anyway." He looked at me and grinned.

At that moment, I could have killed the son-of-a-bitch.

The yumbies attacked when the only people left in the game were Bo, Taters, and me. Ned and Ear Wax had both passed out; Ned in the bowl of pork rinds.

What pissed me off the most, I suppose, was that I had four queens, my best hand of the night, when twenty of those rotting, stinking sons-of-bitches stumbled out of the trees and headed right for the picnic table.

I pulled out my .38 Special and put two bullets straight through the brain of the nearest yumbie. That was a week's worth of moonshine, but I wasn't taking any chances. I'd seen enough yuppies turned zombies to last until the day I died, which would be tonight if I didn't hustle.

Taters carried a sawed-off shotgun that he could load quicker than I could sneeze, but he was more cowardly than a rabbit. After blowing a couple yumbies in half, he disappeared into the trees, high-tailing it for home.

Bo, as usual, started with his .357 Magnum. He was a deadly shot and hit all six times before he needed to switch weapons.

The booming shots roused Ned and Ear Wax. Ned ran for the house, pushing Lulu in front of him. Lulu easily made it inside, but Ned was too toasted to walk straight and he tripped going up his own front steps. While Ned carried three pistols at all times, he tended to be the last one to shoot. We always gave him shit afterwards about being a cheap-ass, but truth was, we didn't mind his not firing because he was a lousy shot and had just as much chance of hitting us as hitting the yumbies.

Ear Wax came up swinging. He must have been having a dream because everybody knows a fist in the face of a yumbie don't do nothing but make him mad.

I fired another two shots and dropped one of the yumbies

as it lunged for Ear Wax, but a second shredded his throat with a clean sweep of its carefully manicured nails.

"You bastard!" I jumped on top of the picnic table and put two bullets into the head of the yumbie that had killed Ear Wax. Unfortunately, that was it for my .38 Special, and my other gun was a .22 pistol. The ammo for it was a lot cheaper and it could hold ten bullets at a time, but with that wimpy caliber, it didn't have enough stopping power in a close fight.

I fired all ten shots anyway, hoping I could distract the yumbies long enough for Bo to get to his truck and retrieve his shotgun.

Two of the yumbies were chanting, "Meat, meat," and closing in around Ear Wax, but six went after Bo as he opened the door to his truck and the other three came straight at me.

I was desperately trying to re-load the .38 special, but I'd drank too much and dropped half my shells.

"Help me out!" I called to Ned. "Take a few of these bastards down before they tear me a new asshole."

Ned raised his .44, but didn't fire. "No," he said, putting the weapon back down. "You wanted to fuck my woman How about fucking one of those yumbies instead?"

"I'm going to die, you bastard!"

"Good. Die!" Then Ned laughed so hard, he farted. That was his mistake. Nothing attracts one of those yumbies so much as someone who stinks worse than they do. All three of them turned and headed straight for Ned.

"You stupid sons-a-bitches!" Ned yelled at them, his nasty breath exciting them that much more. "Kill him! Not me!"

I don't know whether it was Ned's stench or whether these yumbies were a bit livelier than normal, but I swear two of the three broke into what I could only call a clumsy run Ned killed the first one with two quick shots, but the numb-nuts was so terrified, he sent four bullets over the head of the other one before he ran out of ammo and was clicking on empty chambers. Ned tried to scramble up his front steps, but the yumbie's putrid hands closed around his throat as it tried to drag him down from behind.

Bo, being the Good Samaritan he was, pulled his shotgun from his truck and ran toward Ned swinging it left and right like Babe Ruth on steroids. As soon as he broke into the clear, he raised the gun and blew out the back of the yumbie that had caught Ned. Unfortunately, smatterings of shot ripped right through the corpse and struck Ned in the ass.

Feeling Ned had earned his due, I pulled the buck knife out of my boot and cut the head off the third yumbie, then turned to help Bo finish off the others.

By the time all the yumbies were dead, we were out of shells and the stench in the yard was so thick, even Ned could have ripped a big one and none of us would have noticed.

I pulled the shot out of Ned's ass using needle-nosed pliers and liberal doses of moonshine. Most of the moonshine went down my throat rather than across Ned's hairy ass.

As for Lulu, she watched me work, her hands rubbing my shoulders, her lips wet against my ear. Bo, meanwhile, secured the area, then buried Ear Wax. Nothing brought yumbies back like the promise of fresh meat. Taters, we were certain, would be hiding out in the closet of his trailer, ready to shoot anything that came near.

Ned, at least, had the decency not to fart while I was sewing him up. Then again, maybe it just hurt too bad. Either way, I was grateful. It was the only bright spot in an otherwise crappy evening. Not only had I lost a poker buddy when the yumbie got Ear Wax, but it'd take a month's worth of moonshine to replace the shells I'd shot up, and my back couldn't take the work like it used to. I longed for the days when I could walk into K-mart and buy enough ammo to impress my cousin-aunt of a sister-in-law. Not that it mattered much anymore. She was dead, along with every other member of my family. Even so, Deer Hollow had fared better than the other trailer parks around here, the last of which had been completely overrun by yumbies a few months ago.

Outside of Tater, none of us went home that night. Bo slept on the couch and I took the floor, my re-loaded .38 Special for company. Even with the yumbie attack and losing Ear Wax, I probably could have slept – I'd been through a lot in my life – but Ned, the cheap-assed bastard, wouldn't even lend me a blanket, and his green indoor-outdoor carpeting was so thread-bare the floor-nails dug into my back.

Instead, I lay there thinking, wishing I were younger, wishing my pecker was good for more than pissing, but most of all, wishing Bo would stop the hell snoring. Every few seconds, his breath would catch and his snore would stick in his throat like a lawn mower about to die.

Even so, I was almost asleep when she knelt beside me. I felt her hand on my shoulder, then her heavy breast as it fell into my hand. She took away the .38 and lay it aside, then settled on top of me.

At first, I was afraid that I wouldn't be able to do anything, but with her hair across my face and her warm skin all over mine, I was as frisky as a puppy. To hell with Ned—and to hell with the yumbies. Lulu smelled a lot better than them, anyway.

When we were finished and dressed, Lulu took me by the hand and led me outside. "I know where it is," she whispered.

"What?" I asked, my loins still tingling from Lulu's touch.

"His stash," Lulu said. "Get Bo's truck, and I'll take you to it."

I stared at her, not knowing what to say. She put her hands on my shoulders, her tube top pressing against my chest as she pulled herself close. "It's the stuff dreams are made of."

As she gently bit my ear, I came to full attention for the third time in one evening, a stunt I hadn't pulled off since I was in my thirties. In a hoarse whisper, I said, "I'll get the truck."

Bo always left the keys in the ignition. None of the locals would ever dream of crossing him, and yumbies wouldn't be caught dead in a pickup. Normally I'd worry about the engine noise waking Bo, but after burying Ear Wax, he'd finished all that was left of my moonshine. He'd sleep like the dead until morning.

I started the truck and we made our way down the road, past the trailer park where most of the locals lived, and out onto the old highway, now overgrown with weeds and lined with trees. About a mile outside of town, Lulu took her hand off my crotch long enough to point me toward the river, then down toward the old boat ramp. As the truck turned, just before I was in line with the ramp, the headlights flashed across what looked like several pairs of eyes.

I slammed on the brakes, thinking Lulu had led me directly into a yumbie ambush, but as I focused past the headlights, I saw shadows that were just too darned big to be yumbies.

Lulu giggled as I got out and carefully made my way forward.

Pulling aside some short Cedars, I found an old, broken-down building. Shards of glass in the rusty window frames sparkled in the truck's headlights. "The old bait shop?" It had been closed even before Yuppie 25 killed 90 percent of the city folk and made the rest into bigger pains than they had been when they were alive.

I turned back to Lulu, who had stepped out of the pickup. "You brought me out here for this?"

She walked to me and kissed me gently on the cheek. "It's a gold mine," she said, then led me inside.

Lulu was right. The whole bait shop was filled with ammo, carefully wrapped in black plastic garbage bags to keep them dry and out of sight from any snoops. Shortly after the virus hit, Ned, for all his stupidity, must have raided every store in the county for shells and hidden them here. "We're rich," I said as I ripped open bag after bag.

"Rich," Lulu repeated, and licked her lips.

It took the rest of the night to load the truck with shells. As the first light of dawn shot pink rays above the trees, Lulu and I turned onto the old highway and headed north, away from Deer Hollow, away from Ned, and away from the past.

After an hour on the road, I looked at Lulu in the morning light. Her face was ashy white, probably from lack of sleep. Not that I would know. I wasn't sure I'd ever really looked at her face before. "So how did you know where the stash was?"

"I followed Ned."

I bit my lip, not sure I believed her. People had been trying to follow Ned for years. They assumed he had the shells hidden somewhere, but no one had ever been able to trail him – until Lulu.

"What now?" I asked.

"Now we get some sleep."

I pulled off the road and parked the truck behind some trees. Not that I had to worry about Ned coming after us. Bo had the only working pickup in the whole trailer park and besides, no one in their right mind ever got far from Deer Hollow in case yumbies attacked.

I made Lulu and I a bed out of tree branches, then settled down. It wasn't a feather mattress, but it was a hell of a lot softer than Ned's floor. Besides, I was plumb pooped.

Lulu didn't sit down beside me. Instead, she looked at

me, then slowly, seductively, licked her lips.

I groaned. I was starting to get sore. Then I noticed her look was just a bit different. She wasn't horny. She was hungry.

"You played right into my hands," she said. "You always thought you were smarter than what you were. I admit, I stroked that a bit, in more ways than one, but you were easy, old man. Too easy."

"What are you talking about, Lulu?" Not that I didn't know. Her too-white face. The hungry look in her eyes. The way she'd been able to follow Ned when nobody else could. It all made sense, but I wanted to hear her say it just the same.

"Why do you think I came to Deer Hollow? To sleep with Ned?" She spit. "That pig couldn't have someone like me in a million years. On the other hand, you, James, were sweet. Stupid, but sweet. So I let you try me. Now I'm going to try you."

She walked toward me, not with her normal sensual gate, but with a shuffling kind of urgency, a need that drove her forward. "Meat," she said, and licked her lips again.

I'd heard the stories, about the yumbies that weren't slow and clumsy, that still had their full wits, but this was too much to believe. "You can't be a yumbie."

"Why? Because I'm little ol' sweet Lulu who don't know no better?" She rolled her eyes, then gave me a dimply smile and a flutter of her eyelashes. "I grew up around trailer-trash like you, but at fifteen, I ran away to the city. I was an actress before the plague hit – or at least I was going to be. I went to all those fancy parties with their fancy food and their fancy ways. By the end, I'd slept with some of the best producers in the country. One was going to give me the lead in a big budget movie. I was going to be somebody. I still will be. Nothing's changed, except the smell of the people I have to sleep with."

"What good is being somebody?" I asked. "There's nobody left to watch your movie."

"Ah, James, sweet James," she said. Only now, James didn't sound artistic; it sounded menacing. "It was never about acting. It was always about power, and I've got more power now than I'd have ever had in the old world. All I have to do is keep my fans well fed."

She knelt onto her knees, straddling me, still licking her

lips.

Instinctively I reached for my .38, then remembered it was lying on the floor of Ned's house. I had to hand it to Lulu – or maybe I should say, I did hand it to her.

"You're helpless, James, just as the people of Deer Hollow are helpless. We've been trying to eat you out of house and home for years, but it seemed you always had an infinite supply of ammo. It took a long time to figure out who was responsible, but once we did, it was easy. Fortunately, I have folks who still understand electronics. We attached a tracking device to Ned's underwear – and he never changes it."

"That explains the smell," I said, pulling my knees up in a feeble attempt to keep her away from me.

"Hardly," Lulu said, leaning over me, her hot breath on my face. Was it just my imagination? Or did I detect the faint aroma of rotting meat? Amazing what an awesome pair of knockers can cover up.

"Now, James, sweet James, it's time for breakfast. You, I'm afraid, are the main course."

She straddled my bent legs, lowering herself, her sensual thighs pressing against my waist, her heavy breasts grazing my chest. For a moment, as her round lips parted, I wanted her; I wanted to let go and forget the struggle to survive. But then I would never be more than I had been. And suddenly I wanted more.

"Sweet," I said slowly, "but not stupid."

I shoved my buck knife up beneath Lulu's ribs and deep into her chest, black blood flowing down my wrists as I twisted the blade, tearing her heart apart. The stunned look on her face told me that she might be more clever than I was, but she hadn't lived around the sneaky sons-a-bitches that I had all my life.

Her breasts heaved a final breath, then I pushed her off into the branches I'd used for our bed. After making sure she was dead, I cleaned the black blood off my buck knife using her tube top, then tucked the blade back into my boot. I took one last look at her mostly naked body. Damned waste of flesh.

After stretching my back, I climbed into Bo's truck and drove slowly back to Deer Hollow, watching for yumbies along the way. Lulu was right about one thing. I could be someone. I could be the person who freed my neighbors by giving them all the ammo they could ever use.

Then again, even I need laid once in a while.

THE END

Glenn R. Sixbury is the author of *Legacy*, an Earth: Final Conflict novel that can be enjoyed by anyone. You can find his stories in several Marion Zimmer Bradley anthologies and Yard Dog's own *Stories That Won't Make Your Parents Hurl*.

Although Glenn was born and raised too far north to be a true Bubba, he gets along quite well in his native Redneck environment of far Western Kansas. Not only can he survive on cheap beer, beef jerky, and pork rinds for weeks at a time, but he owns more guns than he can count, a rusty pickup, and an overly hyper hunting dog. His wife and kids put up with him anyway – at least most of the time.

INCEST

Ajax

Delbert was watching her hang out the clothes
Dew clung to her legs like spot on a rose
Her behind in stretch shorts, so firm and so round
Made Delbert swallow like a horny young Hound
She reached in her basket and pulled out a bra
Her breasts drooped in her tube top, and not one flaw
Did Delbert see as he peeked through the blind
And chewed a fruit roll-up, with love on his mind
He sighed a big sigh He knew he was smitten
And he longed to possess his soft little kitten
Delbert was anxious; what to do what to say
The sun caught her mullet; it shone like dry hay
She was a vision in flip-flops that came from Walmart
Delbert knew she loved him; he knew in his heart
She had conquered his spirit with her fire and sass
Del was happy his sister was a fine piece of ass.

A CRAZY TASTY LUV STORY
Mark Shepherd

Preacher Hickey, a holy man of unknown denomination, paced back and forth before his wayward son, Pudwacker.

"And I saw in the right hand of him that sat on the throne, the Sacred seven-pack of beer," the preacher roared, thumping his Bible enthusiastically. It was a Special Edition Bible of Last Chance, Oklahoma, and contained all the truths of the universe, no more, no less. The portion of Revelation concerning the Apocalypse was his favorite passage, and he had most of it memorized... which only made sense, since he had written it. "And an angel in a Hooters T-shirt came forth and shouted in a sassy way, 'Who be worthy to loosen the plastic rings and drink the seven beers therof?' And no one in Last Chance had the gumption to take her up on that."

Pudwacker squirmed under his daddy's heated gaze, wishing he were anywhere else, even at the bottom of a cesspit. That would have been downright *pleasant* compared to this. But he'd sinned and he knowed it, and with his head hung low, he'd resigned himself to the sermon. The doublewide was hot, but it was hotter outside; he sat at the baby-shit-green Formica kitchen table and tried to look attentive as his father fumed and fussed back and forth in the kitchen-dining room, waving the Bible around in a meaty fist.

He heard his sister's plaintive crying in the back bedroom, and with a heart heavy with guilt and remorse he ignored it as best he could. The walls of the doublewide were thin and he knew she was hearing the whole darned discussion. Pudwacker's ears burned with the memory. *Why in God's name,* he thought, with the clarity of 20-20 hindsight, *did we do it where we could get caught?*

Hickey continued, his voice rising, "And lo, in the middle of the trailer park were the Four Critters, including the goat with seven horns and seven eyes. And four *and* twenty Important Fellers of the trailer park fell down on the gravel drive before the goat, who offered gifts: jars and bottles and such, and a big can of Glade. And the critters said, 'thou art worthy to drink the Sacred Beer, for the Holy Bubba has a sense of humor, and gave you the seven horns and seven eyes, jus' what the fuck was up with *that*? But thou hast redeemed yourself to the almighty. And we all shall reign supreme on the earth.

"The Important Fellers got kind of excited, but who among them would be worthy to pop the first Sacred Beer and drinketh of it?

"When no one volunteered the goat said, 'screw it,' and opened the first beer. And the Important Fellers heard, as if a noise of thunder, a tremendous ripping fart as it spewed from the heavens. It was loud enough to make your back teeth hurt. Then came the stench of all stenches, and lo it was the foulest kind, worse than even the septic tank of Leroy's motor home. It made paint peel, it made rope unravel and made Styrofoam cups shrink into quivering little marshmallows. Even Leroy couldn't top *that*, even after a vat o' chili and a keg o' beer.

"Then one of the Four Critters said, 'holy shit, check this out,' and a great big white '76 Delta Eighty-Eight with a green fender and a rag hanging out of the gas tank, all pretty like, dropped out of the heavens, and a Feller came out in a greasy Rapid Muffler uniform brandishing a wrist rocket and a bag of peanut M & M's. He said 'Behold! For I am the Bubba of Flat-ulence. Look upon me and weep.'

"Then the seven horned goat opened the second Sacred Beer, then said, 'Why, looky here,' and a big fat bubba driving a red Ford pickup fell from the heavens and landed next to the Delta Eighty-Eight. 'Behold the Bubba of Bad Breath, archenemy of Listerine and fastidious dental care. Blessed be those who shirk regular flossing."

Then there was a long spell of silence. Pudwacker squirmed with a vengeance, enough to give himself a half boner, which reminded him why he was in this fix in the first place. Preacher Hickey drew himself up and looked real serious like, as if gathering up great heaps of spiritual mojo to pile upon his young son. Pudwacker gulped. He'd seen that look before. He was in the deepest of doodoo now.

"And *then* the seven horned goat, who was feeling pretty buzzed by now from the two Sacred Beers, stumbled forward and opened the third Beer. And lo, there came a black bull, kind of mangy but with a full set of horns that would make anyone think twice, ridden by an old man that reminded everyone of their favorite lecherous uncle. 'I am the Bubba of Incest,' said the Bubba of Incest, 'and I will trade even, a penny for a rubber, and three pennies for a tube of KY, long as no one's stepped on it." Hickey closed the Bible with a sharp snap, and eyed his son evenly. "I know, you jus' become a man, being eighteen an' all, but you gotta know, you jus' *gotta know*, the Bible spells it all out in black and white. The Holy Bubba gave you the gear to go forth an' multiply."

Hickey leaned forward. The boy could reach up and touch the blood vessel on Hickey's forehead that was about to burst, he was that close. "But not multiply with your *sister!*"

As if on cue, sister Sally wailed even louder.

"Why caint you jus' leave your little thang *alone?*" daddy roared.

His big ears burned with even more shame, and he could not look his daddy in the face. The adjective "little" didn't help either. Yet he felt strangely compelled to escalate the situa-tion. "But I thought 'incest' meant we had too many roaches!"

Preacher Hickey rolled his eyes expressively. "That's *in-fest*, you idgit! Now you leave Sally alone from now on. Leave your thang be until you're ready to marry! It's enough to make me want to wrap you up in Saran Wrap until you're twenty one!"

More than anything, Pudwacker wanted to ask his daddy that if he was supposed to leave his thang alone, why in tarnation did they named him *Pudwacker.* But even he had the presence of mind to know this jus' was *not* the right time for such inquiries.

With a sickening hiss, Preacher Hickey whipped his belt out of his jeans with a single fluid motion and said, "You're getting thirty licks for this one. Drop your drawers and grab the back o' that chair!"

After the punishment had been administered, Pudwacker came limping out of the doublewide. His butt was seriously on fire now, and he looked around for a watering trough to sit in, but as he walked the burning on his cheeks diminished to a dull simmer. Now he could go do what he *really* wanted to do, and that was hide from the whole stinkin' world. He was crying and didn't want no one to see him in this miserable state.

Well, he'd finally done it, got good and laid an' all, even though it was with Sally. For years now his body had awakened with a new hunger, one he didn't seem to be able to control. All he'd wanted was one girlfriend, *jus' one,* though preferably one with a different last name, someone with whom he could share his most intimate secret (as well as screw on a regular basis), someone who would be there for him, someone he could call a friend. But Pudwacker was not exactly a looker, being a homey lad with buckteeth and ears that were just too big an' all, and all the girls of Last Chance had scorned him, an' that only made it worse.

He was generally alone, bein' a preacher's son. No one would hang out with him for fear of getting into some unspecified trouble. His daddy was the only preacher of Last Chance, Oklaho-ma, a gated community of mobile homes and Airstreams founded shortly after the virus hit. Hickey scrutinized everyone who came near his son, looking for some sign of the devil. And since every teenage boy had the word "devil" stamped on their pimply foreheads in neon red letters, Pudwacker ended up without any friends at all. Hickey didn't take kindly to outsiders, never knowing if they were one of the Yumbies or not, and anyway daddy didn't like interference from heathens; and in Hickey's mind, a heathen was anyone who didn't live in Last Chance. They scav-enged abandoned Wal-Mart's of distant lands, and stored the booty, which could be literally any ole' damn thing, in a giant warehouse in the middle of town.

Pudwacker walked by that warehouse now, a monstrosity of mix n'match siding and rusty steel roofing. It didn't look like much but it was weather proof, and private, and that suited Pudwacker jus' fine. Inside were meticulous rows of boxes piled high on wooden pallets. In the corner was a set of heavy-duty halogen work lights on an aluminum tree, which ran off a bank of batteries connected to the wind farm up the hill. Then behind it he saw something new and different, a store mannequin striking a stylish pose. It must have come in on the last run. Pudwacker gaped, his jaw dropped, and his tongue fell out on the ground. It was a woman! And what's more, she was... *nekkid!*

Before he could fully process what he was seeing he sprung

a three quarter boner, and immediately felt dirty. In his mind's eye he reviewed his daddy's sermon, but that didn't do diddly about his stiffy.

"Oh, Lordy, what am I going to do?" Pudwacker said to no one at all.

The mannequin was a real pretty lady, but when he tapped on her right tit he discovered that she was hollow plastic. Must have been a real fancy store they found her in. She was slender and sexy with big, hard boobies, but oddly, no nipples. Yet this deficiency did not detract from her beauty. Delicate lips formed a sultry pout, and when he imagined those arms wrapped around him and those fingers trailing down his spine, he got a chill.

When he saw the pallet of Spam next to her, the boxes embla-zoned with the catchy phrase, "Crazy Tasty!" he got an idea, and his huge ears began to wiggle. He didn't have to look in the Bible to be certain that Spam was not mentioned. Even <u>he</u> knew Spam wasn't invented until much later, like during the medieval times an' such. So, if it ain't in the Bible, it can't be sin. Right?

So. Pudwacker had a ton of Spam and a plastic woman with a sultry pout. But how to put the two together? Despite his goofy appearance, he wasn't an ignoramus. He had some smarts. And a leatherman in his pocket. He took it out, turned on the work lights, and got to work.

The seam in the plastic molding was easy to separate, and in no time at all he had the two halves of Peggy, as he'd already named her, laid out on the ground. The Spam was not as squish-able as modeling clay, but with a little kneading became sufficiently malleable for his purposes. Soon he discovered Spam Lite worked best in the small areas like Peggy's finger's and toes, and Turkey Spam made a good solid foundation for the torso. Spam Hot n' Spicy . . . well, that went to the naughty bits. He filled both halves of Peggy with Spam, squooshing and squeezing it between his fingers and filling out the mold just so. By the time he was through he was an exhausted mess, covered in Spam debris. Amid a mountain of empty Spam cans he fit the two halves together, stepped on them to squeeze Peggy together real good. A little bit of the pink paste oozed out from the seams, but otherwise she seemed to go together just fine.

Well, now what? He hadn't really thought this through,

eager as he was to get his project underway. He tried to lift
the mold off his creation, but there was some sort of suction
thing going on that kept it from separating. It never occurred
to him that he might need some sort of mold release. Perhaps
if he drilled holes in strategic locations (on the boobies it
would have to be the nipples) it would separate. Only way to
find out would be to try it.

As he stepped back to go in search of a drill he tripped
over a cord, then cartwheeled backwards into a tall stack of
toilet paper boxes. The topmost box teetered, then fell over
on the work light. Pudwacker watched in mute panic as the
whole rig fell on Peggy and shorted out in a fountain of sparks.
Flames shot out from the seams as the mold twitched and
quivered like a salted slug. Then as soon as it began it was all
over; the sparks quit sparkin', and the smell of ozone was
replaced with the rich odor of freshly cooked Spam. He ran to
examine Peggy, who was sizzling like frying bacon inside the
plastic halves.

In spite of the calamity, he found her new scent strangely
arousing.

But other issues needed to be dealt with first. "Oh lordy,
I'm in deep shit now," he said as he righted the work light. "If
that popped a main breaker... "

But before he could investigate the breaker box, something
moved in the mold. Granted, Pudwacker knew this whole
thing was a tad on the kinky side, but his creation was not
supposed to *move!* Another waft of cooked Spam came over
him, followed by a feminine sigh from within the mold.

Pudwacker froze. His crazy tasty Spam creation was alive
and breathing. How the fuck did that happen?

The top half of the mold opened like a coffin lid, and Peggy
sat up from her plastic cocoon, and looked around.

"Um... Ub... Ub... Um... Um... " he stammered intelli-gently
as Peggy stood up on her two Spam Lite feet with her hands
on her hips. Rivulets of hot grease ran down her slender
form, and she looked like she had just stepped out of a shower,
and was looking for a towel. Her movements were a little
wobbly, but she showed no signs of toppling over.

Oh Lordy, she was a sight to behold! Peggy was a luscious
apparition of animated pink luncheon meat, with the same
sultry pout on the mannequin, with even a little bit of grease
dripping off her nose. And even though she looked like a

severe burn victim Peggy didn't appear to be in any pain, for which Pudwacker was grateful. He wouldn't want his creation to suffer on his behalf. And of course she had no hair where women were supposed to have hair, but that made no never mind to Pudwacker as he stood there with full 100% boner.

Peggy swiveled her head around on her Spam neck and said, "Did someone summon the Bubba of Incest?"

"Huh?" Pudwacker mumbled.

She eyed him impatiently. "Revelations. The Seven Sacred Beers. Ring any bells? Or have I appeared to the wrong Important Fella?"

Comprehension dawned on him he replied brightly, "It was my daddy. He jus' tole me about the evils of incest."

She smiled a greasy smile and took a step forward. Her eyes were a bit of a distraction, mostly because she didn't really have any, but obviously she saw him somehow. She towered over him, but Pudwacker didn't feel threatened. He scrambled to his feet and knocked the dust off his britches, then slowly looked up at Peggy, who stood a whole head taller. She was smiling.

"You're a lonely lad," she said, with a voice like vanilla frosting. "I can see it in your face. Your heart aches, and all you want is a girlfriend, is that right?"

Pudwacker nodded. "An' I want a *friend,* too. Someone I can talk to." He didn't know where the words were coming from, but they just kept piling up in his mouth, and he had no choice but to let them out. "My body is on fire all the time. Cold showers don't do nuthin anymore. I wake up at night, all hot and sweaty, thinkin' about *watermelons.* An' the girls all laugh at me, even when I jus' try to talk to them, no funny business." He met her eyes, and saw her looking deep into him, with a face creased with concern and caring. His heart made a little dance. "And no one understands me."

Her face melted into an easy, comfortable smile, and there was nothing awkward 'bout it, despite the raw material she was made from. "I understand you. Honey, you're bursting with so much love its about to spill out of your ears!" she exclaimed, and reached over and took his chin in her hand. He didn't even flinch. It was warm and slippery, and made his whole body shudder. As she looked into his face he knew that Peggy could see everything about him, that she could see into his very soul. At one time he might have found that threatening, but now he did not. He felt safe and secure for the first time in he didn't know how long.

He didn't know he was about to cry. A single tear dribbled down his cheek. If somethin' didn't happen soon he was going to start bawlin' like a baby.

"Come here, sweetie," she said, and he let her reach around and hold him, and he held her. With his face against her warm Spam titties all the pain went away, and felt like he'd just found the other half of himself. "Don't cry, honey. It's gonna be all right. I'm the Bubba of Incest, and I'm here for you, and you alone."

He looked up at her. "Really?"

She winked at him wickedly. "You're not a virgin, are you?"

He wasn't even going to try to guess how she knew that.

"'twas your sister, wasn't it?"

He nodded dumbly, no long ashamed of anything. He knew Peggy would understand, and not judge him, like his father had. "But you ain't my sister," Pudwacker observed.

She gave him look that made his knees go weak. "You're right, sweet pea. I ain't."

Later, much later (actually, much, much later) Pudwacker came ambling out of the warehouse, covered from head to toe in Spam grease. To his astonishment it made a marvelous hair gel. And he had Spam grease in places Hormel had never meant it to be. But he didn't care. Good gosh awmighty, he didn't care!

Oh, this is luv! It's luv! Pudwacker thought in a daze, as little hearts, stars and moons swirled about his head in a heady, frenzied orbit. He whistled a happy tune. Pudwacker didn't know he could whistle.

He should have been exhausted, but he wasn't, though certain bits of his person were a little on the raw side. His step was light, and he felt like any moment now he would fly away like a bird. They'd made love five times (or was it six?), and in between they'd laid back and talked, about everything, about the world, about him, about her. Turns out Peggy was sent by the Holy Bubba to see to his needs, *all* of them, like she was an *angel* of some kind, because the Holy Bubba was good and kind and didn't like to see his children in pain. They finished each other's sentences. They laughed because laughing felt good. They held each other, and he didn't want to let go, ever.

Then she asked him what he had always dreamed of doing with a girl, very *specific* things, some of which he had doubted were anatomically possible, but he told her anyway. And she did them.

But the day had gotten away from them, and time for parting had come. She made him promise to hurry back as soon as he could. Amid a flurry of kisses and hugs he tore himself away from her to go deal with the rest of the world.

It was already suppertime, and he had to move quick. He snuck back into the family's doublewide through the back door and crept into the bathroom. Thankfully, it was empty, and he took a long, hot shower to rid himself of the evidence of his carnal activities, an operation that required heaping gobs of orange hand cleaner to cut through the grease.

He went to the babyshit-green Formica table smelling like a giant orange, but no one paid no never mind. Sally was already sitting there, staring at her plate and playing with her peas. Momma was fussin' and bangin' about in the kitchen gettin' the rest of supper ready, and Daddy was as his usual place at the head of the table, ruler of all he surveyed.

"So how did your day go, son?" Hickey asked, giving no indication that he had whipped the living shit out of him earlier.

Pudwacker couldn't keep from smiling. He was in wonderfully good mood, and didn't care who knew it.

Hickey's eyes narrowed. "I know that goofy grin. You're in love. Or you just got laid." He eyed Sally suspiciously.

"Wadn't me," she said as she chased a pea around on her plate.

"Naw, daddy, I learned my lesson," he said. "I just..."

A suicidal part of him wanted to blurt out the whole, weird story, convinced as he was that there was no sin involved in fornicating like a dog with an wanton Spam nymphomaniac. But another part of his mind, the survival part, reminded him that he had only one ass, and it was still very sore from the earlier whoopin'. The fact that Peggy was a manifestation from the Bible itself was a nice bonus, but he feared his daddy might be jealous that the Bubba of Incest had chosen to appear before Pudwacker instead. So he said nothing.

Then Momma came to the table, and he could not suppress the look of utter horror. On a serving plate, cut into thin slices, was a circular arrangement of pink, freshly microwaved pineapple slices... and Spam!

Oh no! he thought, suddenly sickened at the thought of actually *eating* the raw material his new girlfriend was made from.

"Honey bun, what's wrong?" Momma asked as she set the plate down. "You love Spam!"

If only she knew how much *I love it*, he thought morosely. He hid his emotions deep down, lest his secret get out right then and there.

"Uh, nothin', Momma," Pudwacker said with a forced smile. "Is there enough of it to go around? I'm mighty hungry tonight for some reason."

Despite his brave facade he could only manage to eat the Spam by surreptitiously shaping it into something resembling a taco.

Sometime during supper they became aware of a ruckus out-side, which was punctuated by the ratta-tat-tat of AR15 fire.

Preacher Hickey dropped his fork. "What in God's name is going on?"

But Pudwacker was getting a sick feeling. Somehow he knew that it involved Peggy, that she was in danger. Then his brother-in-law, Clem, opened the door and stuck his big fat head inside, a belt of ammo slung across his chest.

"Yumbie attack!" Clem shouted, and he was gone.

The preacher seized control of the situation. "Now every-one, just relax, now. Just lock all the doors and windows, and stay inside. The Militia can handle it..."

But Pudwacker didn't hear a thing. Before his daddy could get the words out of his mouth he had grabbed a Glock and an extra clip, and was out the door, running for the warehouse.

His worse fears were confirmed by the crowd assembled at the warehouse. Militia, dressed in various shades of camouflaged gear, had surrounded the east end of the ramshackle building, where two Yumbies in ragged dress shirts and ties were making a run for the entrance. Someone's machine gun cut one down, but the other got into the warehouse without a scratch.

"Peggieeeeee!" Pudwacker wailed, chambering a round in the Glock as he ran headlong into the warehouse.

It took a moment for his eyes to adjust to the darkness,

but only a moment, before he saw the shifting shadows off in the corner. Heedless of his own safety he ran to where the motion was and beheld a sight that would traumatize him for life.

Five Yumbies were devouring Peggy like vultures on a dead cow. One had seized an arm and was knawing on it like a corncob. Two others were fighting over a leg, and the torso, or what was left of it, was scattered all over the place. There was no sign of her head, or her face with the sultry pout.

He stared in shock at the carnage, and felt his heart break-ing up into little pieces. The he shook off the stupor and screamed *"You bastards!"* and started shooting.

The first round caught the first Yumbie in the chest, spinning him around, and the second blew the hand off another. He kept firing until the clip was empty, slammed the spare in, and resumed the slaughter. Yumbie bits flew all over place, flesh, shreds of ties, mutilated dress shirts, and designer eyewear. When it was over and done with a pile of five well-ventilated Yumbies lay motionless on the ground amid the half-eaten scraps of Spam.

The militia came upon a most curious sight. Pudwacker was on the ground amid piles of empty Spam cans, bawling his eyes out as he gathered up the scraps of Spam, trying to piece them back into some semblance of... well, whatever it had been.

"Peggy, Peggy, Oh, Peggy," he cried, blubbering as the Spam bits dribbled through his fingers. "Please, don't die! You mean everything to me! You were the first! I love you! I love you so much, pleeeeease don't leave me."

The sight might have been heart-wrenching to the hardened militia warriors, had it not been so utterly bizarre.

"It was his first love. Must have been," a militiaman wearing a Ford Trucks ball cap muttered knowingly.

"Whatever the fuck *it* had been," another said, confused, and a tad disgusted.

"I have an idea," said yet another. "He's a brave a warrior. He killed these five Yumbies single-handedly. He deserves a reward."

They gently lifted the grieving lad to his feet, and led him weeping from the remains of his first love, congealing on the floor in little pools.

"Come on, boy, it'll be Ok," the soldier said. "We have

something to show you."

They led him to another part of the warehouse, and showed him something that stopped his crying. A goofy grin spread across his face, and he beamed at the others with a look of gratitude.

The pallet was piled high with shrink-wrapped cases of Armour Treet.

THE END

Mark Shepherd writes fantasy and science fiction, and has published the Baen novels *Wheels of Fire* ('92), *Prison of Souls* ('94) (both with Mercedes Lackey), and the sequel *Escape from Roksamur* ('97); The urban fantasies *Elvendude* (94), *Spiritride* ('97), *Lazerwarz* ('99); and with Yard Dog Press, *Blackrose Avenue* ('01). He has also appeared in the anthologies *Bending the Landscape* (White Wolf), *Swords of the Rainbow* (Alyson), *Lammas Night* and *Sword of Ice* (Baen), *Magic: the Gathering,* and *Bubbas of the Apocalypse.* He has also produced five electronica albums under his own homebrew label, *Elvendude Productions.*

He is currently developing an unsold epic fantasy, *The Isles of Pendalon*, and a post-apocalyptic science fiction novel for Yard Dog Press, *Madlander.*

GAS

JOHN M. LANCE

It is hard to be certain exactly why the first sentient fart emanated from Clem's ass that warm July day. Perhaps the barbecue sauce that he had been so suspicious of earlier really had turned and, through some sort of alchemical miracle, had reacted just so when mixed with the warm Bud he had been drinking. Or maybe farts had always been living organisms and this was simply a natural leap up the evolutionary ladder. Or maybe the story about Clem's great great grandfather-uncle actually being a Wall street refugee before coming to the county to marry Clem's great great grandmother-aunt was true after all and the Yuppie virus, rather than changing Clem into a zombie, had instead taken up residence in his innards until it could work some other malignant mischief.

It is unlikely the world will ever know for certain. But what we do know, or at least, what Clem knew, was that the fart ripped into the world with more rolling, rippling thunder than any other fart Clem had ever cut. The sides of the outhouse shook and for a moment Clem was afraid he would blow himself off the seat. The stink was equally impressive.

"Damn!" Clem hollered. "Holy Shiiiit," he added for emphasis. "That there was a record breaker. Hey, did anyone else hear that? Zeke? Jeb? Erlene?" When there was no reply he added, "Linus?"

But all was quiet outside.

Clem shook his head and muttered to himself. It was an old habit that allowed him to periodically have a conversation with an intellectual equal. "Ya know, it never fails. Try and catch a moment's peace on the shitter to flip through *Guns and Ammo* and they're banging at the door, telling you to hurry on up, but blast out a record setting fart and there's no one around to hear."

"I heard," said a smooth, oily voice that reminded Clem of one of those lawyers that used to have commercials on TV, the ones that had all turned into zombies.

"Jeb, is that you?" Clem asked.

"Nope, it was me." A strange fog rose up before Clem. It was a lemony yellow, the same color as Clem's teeth, with bands of black smoke floating through the center.

"What the hell?"

"Ahhh," said the fart, "eloquent to the end. So unfortunate that this is our first, and final, conversation."

"What do you mean?"

"I'm going to kill you."

"But, why?"

The fart shrugged, or at least, it did what a fart's version of a shrug would be. "Why not?"

It was a difficult argument for Clem to counter. "Well, you don't scare me. After all, everyone's farts smell sweet to themselves, so you can't do nothing to me."

The fart laughed. "Idiot, I learned how to talk, don't you think I can change my own odor."

Clem was suddenly struck by the most heinous stench he had ever smelled. It was as if dog shit had been dropped into a blender with a generous amount of puke, horse manure, and high priced yuppie cologne, and then set on fire. Clem tried to get up, but his knees buckled under the overpowering assault and he collapsed back onto the seat. The one consolation he had as he gasped his last gasp was that he was going out just like the King himself, with his head held high and his pants around his ankles.

Zeke and Jeb piled out of the pickup truck's cab, laughing and joking back and forth. Trips into town always put them in a good mood, particularly when they found four cases of Bud and Zeke got to blow away a zombie or two with the shotgun that hung in the truck's gun rack.

"Jeb, go get Linus and unload the beer from the back. I'm gonna unstrap the carcass." Zeke patted the skull of the zombie tied across the hood of the truck, "Never realized a yuppie could grow so big. I may have this one stuffed and put it in the livin' room."

Jeb shook his head, "Can't unload the beer right now, Zeke, I gotta see a man about a horse." Jeb headed off toward the outhouse without waiting for a reply.

"Told you not to eat that can of Spam. Everything has an expiration date, whether they admit it or not." Zeke yelled after his brother. Turning back toward the shack, Zeke hollered, "Erlene, Linus, we're back. Come on out here and give me a hand."

There were several muffled exclamations from inside the shack, followed by frantic scrabbling.

"Erlene? Linus?" Zeke called again to his cousins.

Erlene's head appeared in the doorway. Her blonde hair was tousled and, while certainly not a fashion guru, Zeke had the distinct impression that her tank top was on backward. "Be out in a second hon. I was just, we was just . . ."

"We were scaling catfish for the barbecue," Linus finished as he appeared beside his sister. Once again Zeke was struck by how the twins resembled each other, aside from one being a man and one being a woman, that was. The shape of their faces, their thin, willowy frames, they were like two sides of the same coin. Except for their eyes. Where Erlene's eyes were a cheerful green that reflected her own good nature, Linus's eyes were ice blue and always looked like he was thinking about something. And it wasn't like the gentle, dumbfounded look that Clem had when he tried to tie his shoes, no, when Linus was thinking he reminded Zeke of a cold-eyed gator eyeing a big, juicy, muskrat. Zeke would be happy when they finished fixing the boy's trailer so Clem, Jeb, and Linus could move back out. Not only was he looking forward to getting away from Linus's piercing stare, but he also couldn't wait to get a little "private time" with Erlene. Ever since the boys had moved in, she had claimed to be "too tired" to perform her wifely duties. Zeke suspected she was just being shy, what with the boys in the next room and all.

"Erlene can finish scaling the fish herself. Come out here and help me unload the beer."

"Did you find any Bud Lite?" Linus asked.

"No," Zeke rolled his eyes. Linus and Erlene were like that sometimes, putting on airs and acting all high and mighty, asking for a Bud Lite and all. They had even eaten tofu once. Zeke blamed the genes that had come down from that crazy Wall Street great granduncle-father. While he and his brothers Jeb and Clem had turned out fine, Erlene and Linus could be downright strange. It didn't help that their well-read momma had gone and named Linus after a literary character, making a big to-do about how he was just as smart as the boy in the Peanut's comic. She would have named Erlene after a character, too, if she could've remembered the name of the girl. As it was, Erlene had very nearly been named Woodstock.

As Zeke handed Linus a case, he said, "Once we get the beer inside, why don't we get Jeb and Clem and see if we can't finish fixing your roof." Zeke shook his had and snorted, "Ya know, I still can't believe you boys fell for that."

"It was Clem, something about they promised him he could see Viva Las Vegas whenever he wanted."

"But even Clem should have been able to spot two Yumbies dressed as satellite installers. I mean, did they even have tools with them? All you'd have to do is see a Yuppie try to use a hammer to know somethin' ain't right."

Linus shrugged. "Hard to be sure. That dish pretty well squashed 'em flat."

"Well, we should have that hole all fixed sometime today, and then you boys can move back this afternoon." And I can finally get the lovin' I deserve, Zeke added to himself.

"That'd be great," Linus said, but when he glanced back toward the shack, Zeke thought he saw a tear at the corner of his cousin's eye.

"You'll still be welcome back for barbecue, of course," Zeke quickly reassured him. "No need to get all choked up or anything."

Linus waved his hand. "Oh it's not that, it's just, you know what they say, 'Parting is such sweet sorrow,' and all."

"Sure." Zeke nodded slowly, not understanding at all and desperately hoping for some sort of distraction before Linus got off on one of his long rambling tangents.

Fortunately, Zeke was rescued by a high-pitched scream. "Erlene?" Zeke called.

"That wasn't Erlene," Linus replied. "Erlene's never screamed in her life. That came from over there." Linus pointed off in the direction of the outhouse just as Jeb came running into view.

"Zeke, Clem's dead!"

"Jeb, was that you that screamed like a little girl?" Zeke asked.

Jeb grabbed Zeke by the front of his overalls. "Damn it Zeke, didn't you hear me? Clem's dead!"

"I heard you, and it's a shame, but it's still no reason to cry. Died on the shitter, huh? Well, at least he went the way he always wanted to, like the King."

"I don't know Zeke, this don't look natural. It's not like he was straining and burst a blood vessel. He's all purple and puffy, like he drowned."

"He fell in?"

Linus interrupted. "He means Clem suffocated. If you've ever tried to use the outhouse after him, it really comes as no surprise. The man could've made a dung beetle gag."

"Yeah, Clem and those crazy records of his." Jeb snuffled nostalgically.

Zeke eyed Jeb suspiciously. "Well," he said uncomfortably, "Let's get the beer into the fridge before it gets warm, and then we can bury old Clem."

Erlene had fixed her tank top and cleared out a space in the fridge. As they loaded the cans in, she said, "Zeke, I think I heard another possum scrabbling around in the bedroom. You want me to take care of it or do you want to do it?"

"Don't be silly, sugar, you know I love thumpin' the ugly varmints." Zeke picked up the Louisville slugger he kept beside the fridge for such emergencies.

"But Zeke, we've gotta bury Clem," Jeb said.

"This won't take but a minute." Zeke replied as he headed into the rear of the shack.

"Clem's dead?" Erlene asked.

"Yep, died on the shitter," replied Jeb.

"Like the king," Erlene observed. "He'd be happy about that."

"Jeeeze," Zeke shouted, "It stinks back here. It must be a skunk rather than a... holy shit!"

Zeke backed out of the bedroom. Behind him emerged a smoky, undulating cloud.

"What is it?" Erlene asked.

"Who wants to know?" the fart giggled.

"It talks?" Jeb asked.

"Why not? You do, or at least, you did," the fart replied. A hazy tendril shot out and enveloped Jeb's head, cutting his high-pitched shriek short.

As his brother gasped and flailed, Zeke cried, "Hang on Jeb, I'm coming." Wildly swinging his bat, Zeke charged into the middle of the cloud.

The fart giggled, "And here I had been afraid that I had killed the king of the idiots. I hadn't realized there were so many others waiting in the wings." Zeke dropped his baseball bat and clutched at his throat.

"Hang on Zeke." Erlene yanked open a drawer and pulled out a lighter. "I ain't yet heard of a fart that could stand up to a lighter."

"No, you'll kill us all." Linus knocked the lighter from Erlene's hand, then grabbed her arm and dragged her outside.

"But Zeke, and Jeb," Erlene cried.

"They're dead," Linus said. "It's just us now." He held Erlene close, enjoying the scent of her hair that reminded him of their younger, more carefree days, before Zeke. "I'll take care of you." he assured her.

"I know, momma always said you would."

"We can go live in my house; fixing the roof won't be too hard. Now that Clem and Jeb are gone, there'll be lots of room."

Erlene shook her head. "I can't leave my home. All my curlers, and hair spray, and tank tops are here. Not to mention my color T.V. We've got to get rid of that fart."

"Alright, let me think."

There was one last case of beer left in the truck. Linus popped open a Bud, and despite the extra calories, sucked it down as he eyed the shack. When he was finished, he tossed the can to one side, belched, and reached for a second, then stopped. "Of course!" he cried.

"Of course what?" asked Erlene.

"Well, we can't hurt the fart, right? We can't shoot it or hit it or do anything else of the like, and while we might be able to light it on fire, the resulting explosion would kill us and destroy the shack, along with all your valuables. The only way we can stop the fart is to mitigate it."

"Mita-what-it?"

"Mitigate, means that we make it go away."

"Don't you mean fumigate?" Erlene asked. She had heard of fumigation, though only in vague terms. It wasn't something she had ever experienced first hand.

"Nope, I mean we've got to find the exact opposite of a fart and bring it in contact with it. Then the fart will just implode and cease to exist, like when matter and anti-matter are brought together. I saw it on a sci-fi movie once."

Erlene looked at Linus as if he had three heads. "Umm, Linus, you're scarin' me, hon. The last person who talked like this was Ms. Jenkins, that yoga teacher from town, right before she got all zombified and Zeke had to put her down."

Linus waved his hand dismissively. "Don't worry about me, I had my barbecue for breakfast. And this plan'll work for sure. All we have to do is find the opposite of a fart."

"Which is?"

"A belch, of course. After all, a fart is just a belch that came out the wrong end. Heck, Clem even called 'em ass belches."

"But how do we find a belch that will combat that?" Erlene gestured toward the shack.

"I think there's enough beer here to do the trick."

Linus downed the rest of the case in the next five minutes. He refused to allow even a single burp to escape, and by the time he was finished he was so filled with burbling gas that he didn't dare open his mouth. Kissing Erlene once on the cheek for luck, Linus strode, or more accurately staggered, into the shack.

Zeke and Jeb were lying on the floor of what was laughingly referred to as the sitting room. Jeb was cold and still, his face frozen in the anguished expression of someone that had just stepped in dog shit with his bare feet. To Linus's surprise, Zeke was still breathing. He carefully rolled his cousin over.

Zeke's eyes fluttered, and he reached a dirty hand up to touch Linus's face. His lips quivered, as he struggled to speak, but all that emerged was a whispered, "The horror. The horror." Then he was gone.

"Who would have thought he was a student of the classics?" the fart asked as it drifted out of a corner toward Linus. "I thought you and the bimbo would have fled by now. I wasn't even planning to come after you. I've discovered that I really like it here, particularly the couch; there are so many other stinks to keep me company." Long gaseous tendrils began reaching out to Linus. "I must say, you are being awful quiet, so unlike your friends. Rather disappointing, actually. I rather enjoyed the fish-out-of-water flopping and choking they did."

Linus took one last huge gulp of air.

"Oh please, do you think holding your breath is going to save you? How can you resist this?" A thin tentacle of odor tickled Linus's nose with the smell of Clem's underwear. Linus nearly puked.

"That's more like it. Shall we finish this?"

Linus nodded, then opened his mouth and belched.

Normally, he would have attempted to say the entire alphabet or repeat the opening soliloquy from Richard III, but this time he didn't want anything to interfere with the raw power of the belch. The belch rolled forward like a wall of sound and stink, blowing out the shanty's windows and making it rock like a B-grade porn video was being shot inside.

"Eeeeek!" squeaked the fart, but the onrushing belch was so fast and powerful that it couldn't escape. Trapped, the fart contracted into a tighter and tighter ball until it disappeared with a small pop.

Linus staggered outside into Erlene's waiting arms. They kissed long and hard, comfortable in the knowledge that a whole new world awaited them, and that Erlene's curlers were safe.

Inside the shack, the first sentient belch looked out one of the shattered windows and sighed, "I love romantic endings."

THE END

John M. Lance lives in New England with his lovely wife, Debra, and their beautiful daughter, Morgan. John is renowned for his scholarly studies of the rare Northern Maine Bubba and was the subject of the critically acclaimed, but commercially disastrous, documentary, *Rednecks in the Mist*. When not observing these fine, beer swilling specimens in their natural habitats, John spends time playing with his dogs, Hershey and Cadbury, and writing short stories, including "The Thing in the Cabinet" which appeared in the anthology *More Stories that Won't Make Your Parents Hurl.*

MR. NED AND DR. TED

Andrew Zimmerman Jones

Evil nested in the heart of the To-Fun Tofu Factory. Jimmy Lyle crouched behind one of the large vats, shotgun gripped tightly, one hand on the trigger while the other supported the barrel. He was the leader of the group, by circumstance more than anything else. His degree in animal husbandry made him one of the most educated people in Lylesville, Tennessee. As such, the town looked to him for guidance when the mayor, sheriff, and the rest had been eaten by the Yombies.

Yombies that were holed up in this factory, continuing their production of low calorie, low fat soy products, with protein supplements. Namely human flesh, along with some pork fat. Right now the bastards were circled around the corpse of their latest victim. Jimmy wondered what poor fool they'd caught.

Ned Lyle, Jimmy's cousin on both sides, sat next to him, hunched over low. He had a baseball bat slung across his lap lazily. He leaned closer. "Jimmy, when we gonna move?"

"Quiet, dammit. When Beau gives th' signal."

Jimmy watched Ned's face twist in intense concentration. Trying to be quiet, he leaned in close to ask, barely audibly, "What's the signal?" The effort of leaning, however, triggered unexpected consequences.

Ned let rip with a roaring gust of flatulence.

"Shit, Ned!" Jimmy slapped him upside the head, almost gagging from the stench. "Move!" he shouted to the rest of his crew as he stood and stepped out, gun raised.

The Yombies looked up from their kill. "Tofu. To-Fun," they muttered in unison. Jimmy recognized their dinner. It was Ho Sing, the owner of the local Chinese buffet restaurant. He'd been spared in the plague because he'd been using a local generic barbecue sauce in his General Tzo's Chicken recipe. Jimmy was sorry to see him go. He was a decent enough guy, for a foreigner and all.

Beau Riley jumped from behind some boxes, gun blazing in each hand. He wore his standard issue combat fatigues, from back when he was in the army. Two bullets nailed one of the Yombies, sending the creature stumbling over Ho's body.

"Spread out. Stay mobile. Use your speed!" Jimmy yelled.

He didn't have to tell Beau twice. Beau dropped to the ground, like he was sliding into home plate, and came to rest under a large metal table.

Explosions began going off throughout the factory. Mike Carlisle had rigged up fireworks as a distraction–made mostly useless by Ned's monstrous fart.

Ned was trying to make up for it, swinging his baseball bat at anything that moved. What he lacked in common sense and strategy he made up for with sheer determination. Jimmy knew that so long as Ned didn't use his brain, they were fine. "Rev, how many we got?" he yelled.

The Reverend shouted, from near the door, "I count me seven."

"We got four down here. Where are the others?"

"Up on that catwalk. They're goin' for Mike."

Jimmy turned, pumping his shotgun. He fired one blast square into the chest of the Yombie nearest the stairs. The force of the shotgun lifted the animated corpse off the ground, flying back into a pile of Evian waters.

Another one of the Yombies took off running awkwardly up the stairwell. Ned ran after it. When they reached the top, Ned brought the bat around in a fast swing. The Yombie's head lifted clear off its shoulders, flying through the air. Ned began to move toward the other three Yombies on the catwalk.

Mike was on the catwalk, fighting with a sword–the best weapon against Yombies, but requiring more discipline and skill than most of Jimmy's crew could handle.

That left three for Jimmy and Beau to take out.

They cornered the three, then the Reverend came out. He walked slowly, since he was sixty-three years old and had a gimp leg, but he had his uses.

He carried the Molotov cocktails.

The undead went up in an instant, screaming, as the Reverend flung the weapons. Ho Sing's body went up in flames, as well.

Beau shook his head. "Damn shame. He made good

shrimp fried rice."

The Reverend nodded sagely. "He will be welcomed into the arms of the Lord."

There was a scream from above. Jimmy, the Reverend, and Beau looked up at the catwalk just in time to see Ned flung over the railing by one of the Yombies. An instant later, Mike's sword hacked off an arm.

There was a loud splash as Ned landed in one of the large Tofu vats.

"Shit. Get him out of there," Jimmy said.

Beau asked, "How?"

Jimmy raised his gun, firing into the vat. It was a flimsy aluminum structure, giving easily under his bullet.

Beau knelt quickly, unsheathing the Bowie knife strapped to his calf. He drove the point into the hole made by Jimmy's bullet. His muscles flexed as he cut through the aluminum. Thick, milky white fluid, not yet congealed, flowed through the growing hole.

Jimmy grabbed one of the flaps of metal, yanking and twisting. Blood flowed from his fingers, but he didn't let go.

A body came slamming through the hole, knocking both Beau and Jimmy back. Covered in tofu, they slipped around on the ground, stumbling over themselves.

"Shit, Ned, you had me scared." Jimmy reached down, grabbing his gun. He hoped the tofu could be cleaned out.

Mike ran down the stairs. "They're all dead. Is Ned okay?"

Jimmy turned toward his cousin, covered in pasty tofu. He tried to keep from laughing, but couldn't resist. "You look like them guys at the end of *Ghostbusters*."

Ned stumbled over to a nearby table. He reached down and grabbed an Evian. He stood up tall, better posture than ever causing his back to crack, and downed the whole bottle of yuppie water.

Slack jawed, the other four watched as Ned wiped his face with his hand. He glanced between them and said, "Sorry for the mess. I'll pay for the janitorial service. Now, I don't suppose any of you would know a good chiropractor, would you?"

The silence lasted at least a minute before the Reverend shouted, "He's got the devil in him!"

Beau brought a gun up, aimed square at Ned's forehead.

"Hold up!" Jimmy shook his head. "Let's not get crazy

here. Ned, what the hell is going on?"

Ned blinked. "Excuse me, are you talking to me?"

"Yes, I'm talking to you, dumbass."

"Vulgarity isn't necessary. And my name isn't Ned. I'm Ted Day, doctor of homeopathic medicine."

"Doctor?" Mike and the Reverend said.

"Ted?" Jimmy and Beau said.

He nodded slightly. "Yes to both. Now, could we return to my condo? I could really use a bubble bath."

Beau whispered to Jimmy, "Sure I shouldn't shoot him?"

"Doctor Ted" was duct-taped to a chair in the bowling alley. He wiggled against the confinement, while the other four gathered in the concession area. "Please? Untie me. I don't have any money. I don't know what I'm doing here. I think my BMW must have broke down."

"Shut up!" Beau yelled. He leaned into the others in the booth near the refreshment stand. "What the hell are we going to do? If anyone in town sees him like this, they'll want to lynch him."

"Don't you think I know that?" Jimmy sighed. "He ain't our Ned no more, that's for damn sure. Mike, what do you think?"

If there was one person in Lylesville that was smarter than Jimmy, it was Mike Carlisle. The worldly type, he'd gone up to Vincennes University, in Indiana, to study bowling lanes management before returning to buy the bowling alley five years ago. Most in town thought that he was a little uppity. This mostly started when an ex-girlfriend said that she'd caught him reading the articles in Playboy after jerking off to it. Jimmy didn't believe stories like that, but he knew Mike was a smart guy. He trusted him.

Mike stroked his chin, in that thoughtful way intellectuals do. "Well, I been reckoning on that. Seems to me like Ned can't be a Yombie. He never had the sickness and he ain't tried to eat none of us."

"Thank the Lord for small favors," Reverend said.

"Amen," muttered Beau.

"So if he ain't infected, there's gotta be another explanation. Seems likely that it's psychosomatic, then."

"Pscyho-so-what-sic?" Beau asked.

Mike rolled his eyes. "Psychosomatic. Means his brain's

got all mixed up with his body."

"Ned's got a brain?" Jimmy smirked, trying to lighten the mood.

"This is serious. They got a name for it. Post-traumatic stress disorder. I think his brain done split, gone all dissociative," Mike said.

"How do you know this stuff?" Beau asked.

"I read about it in a mystery book once."

Jimmy gave a thoughtful nod. "Them mystery writers are smart. Okay, then, let's say this is what happened. How do we fix him?"

Mike glanced over at the man duct taped to the chair. "We got to find a way to traumatize doctor homeopathic over there back into good old Ned."

They sat quietly for several minutes, thinking.

"Please untie me," Ted yelled. "If you do, I'll give you a free session. Have you ever had your chakra revitalized?"

Beau threw an empty beer bottle, smashing it into a nearby chair. "Dammit, Doc Ted, I don't care where you come from, we don't talk like that to men out here. Now shut up, or I'll cut your chakra *off*."

Ted whimpered, then went silent.

"What about pouring barbecue sauce down his throat?" Beau asked.

"We could have him make out with Jimmy's sister," Mike said, "like he did in high school."

"Nah, that's just nasty," Jimmy said. When studying animal husbandry, he'd learned that animals shouldn't mate with their relatives. He figured if it wasn't good enough for a goat, it wasn't good enough for him.

The Reverend leaned forward, eyebrows bouncing in anticipation. "I could perform an exorcism."

"Jeez, Rev, he ain't possessed." Beau took a long swig of his beer.

The Reverend sighed. "I reckon not. But in that movie, the girl shit and puked on herself. Bet that'd snap him out of it."

A slow smile flowed over Jimmy's lips. "You're right, Rev. I bet it would." He stood up, grabbing his jacket. "Beau, head back over to the factory. Grab a bucket and fill it up with tofu."

Beau frowned. "Why do you have a hankering for tofu?

You sure Ned ain't contagious?"

Jimmy shook his head. "It's for Teddy over there, not me. I gotta run down to the storage warehouse."

"What for?"

"Gotta get me some drugs."

Ted called out, as he noticed people leaving, "If you're going to the store, could you get me some Lavender Paradise bubble bath?"

They sat around the table. Ted looked among the others nervously, but continued to eat the tofu.

It was unnerving watching him eat with a fork.

"Thank you so much for the food. And the bath."

Jimmy nodded. "Well, we're tryin' to be hospitable to our new Doc. Been so long without one and all." Jimmy was impressed with the amount of food he was packing away. The new personality still had Ned's appetite.

Ted sniffed. "I think that I'll begin with implementing a hygiene education program in the community."

"You callin' us smelly there, Doc?" Beau asked, hand reaching into his jacket.

"No, he's callin' us dirty," Mike answered.

Beau took his hand out of his jacket, apparently appeased by the response.

Jimmy waved a cold beer in front of Ted. "Care for a brew?"

"No. Any white wine spritzers?"

Mike nodded. "I got all the booze in town here. We've got some fruity drinks." He stood up and walked into the back.

Rev began laughing. "How's that tofu," he asked.

"Wonderful. Would you like some?"

"No. Eat up."

Mike came back out, tossing a bottle through the air. Doctor Ted had better reflexes than Ned and was actually able to catch it. "The seal's broken," he said.

"Yeah, but it's fresh. I always pop the cap for my customers."

Ted smiled. "You know, I don't know why you rural folks get such a bad rap. You're good chaps." He sipped on the drink.

"Want any more tofu?" Jimmy asked.

"No, thanks. I couldn't eat another bite." He drank some

more of the beverage.

Jimmy glanced at his watch. "Wonder how long it'll take."

"Take?" Ted glanced at the other four men. He reached down to touch his stomach.

"Nothing," Jimmy said.

Ted stood up. "If you gentlemen will excuse me."

Beau's hand whipped up, holding a gun aimed at Ted's head. "You'll stay where you are, smart guy. We're gettin' our friend back."

His hands beginning to shake, Ted muttered, "Really, I need to go to the lavatory."

"Tough shit," Beau said. He chuckled. "Or not so tough, in your case."

"What do you mean?" As the words were leaving his lips, though, he winced, pain stabbing through his abdomen "Uh-oh."

"This ain't gonna be pretty," Mike warned.

It wasn't. Ned had eaten chitlins for breakfast, before the raid. And beans. And spare ribs.

And over the last hour he'd eaten a good two pounds of tofu.

Laced with laxatives.

Rolling on the ground in pain, stinking of his own shit, Dr. Ted's mind snapped. His scream was all the fury and remorse of hell unleashed.

Then he went silent and blinked. He looked down at himself and then began laughing. "Shit, how many beers did I have? I don't remember a damn thing."

"Believe me," Jimmy said. "You don't want to know, Ned."

On some level, Ned did remember. From that point on, when he fought Yombies, it was personal. Every indignity – the Evian, the tofu, the bubble bath, shitting himself – had left its mark, and he wanted revenge.

He understood the Yombies intuitively. Their weaknesses and patterns. He racked up as many kills as the rest of the crew together. When his instinct took over, he was unstoppable.

One thing never changed, though: when Ned used his brains, things went to hell.

THE END

Andrew Zimmerman Jones lives in his own mind, but is in the process of relocating his physical presence from Detroit to Louisville. He spends his days teaching algebra to elementary and middle school students. He is originally from Vincennes, Indiana, where the local university is reputed to have the only degree program in "bowling lane management" in the country. He is proud to have attended a different university, where he studied physics, mathematics and philosophy. Other mildly intriguing things about him are that he is an Eagle Scout, a member of Mensa, and twenty-six years old. This is his first published story and his friends describe him as "giddy" about it.

He maintains a web presence at http://www.azjones.info/

.

BUBBA IN A BLUE DRESS

Gary Jonas

I was shocked to see a white boy stroll into Leon's Bar. It ain't that he was white, though. Hell, my friend Ned is white, too and he was sitting right beside me. Everyone got past all that racial crap when the world came to an end. Turned out that the white folks and black folks who survived had plenty in common. We all hated rich white folks, we all loved beer and let's be honest, it was our barbecue recipes that saved us all. So anyway, in walked this white boy with singed hair and no eyebrows. And the kicker? He was buck-naked.

He grabbed a dirty dishrag off a table and covered his pecker. The bar was smoky and it served barbecue sandwiches, corn nuts and cold beer, which was something of a rarity. White Boy spotted me and came right over. "You're Sam Washington," he said. "Right?"

"What's it to ya?"

"I want to hire you." He sat on a stool and let rip with a nasty ass fart that could wake the dead.

"God damn!" I said.

"I have gas," he said. "Pretty much all the time."

"Something crawled up your ass and died," Ned said.

People cleared out of the bar, waving their hands in front of their faces. The owner burst out of the back office and stared at White Boy. "What the hell do you think you're doing? Get your naked ass out of my bar!"

"Sorry," the man said.

"You better not leave a stain on that stool, boy."

"He ain't sure you wiped proper," I said. "From the smell of it, I'd say he's right."

"I said I was sorry. I need your help."

"Near as I can tell, you're just a crazy naked white guy."

"I can make it worth your while," he said.

"All right, let's move this outside so I can stand upwind."

"Don't come back, you hear" the owner said.

As soon as we were out in the fresh air, I asked, "You a

nudist?"

"Naw, the wife's boyfriend blew up my trailer."

"And?"

"I was inside the trailer when it happened."

"You couldn't have grabbed some skivvies?"

"I was in the bathtub. Fucker must have tossed a grenade through the door. I managed to crawl out through the bathroom window."

"If we're gonna talk, we gotta get you something to wear. What's your name?"

"Thomas Baxter."

"Okay, Thomas, Ned here stays just down the road. He might have something you can wear. Right, Ned?"

"If you say so," Ned said with a shrug.

We walked toward Ned's place. "So why'd you look me up? Did you hear I was the best PI in Mississippi?"

"No. I heard that Cletus Newton owes you a favor. I want to kill Myron, but I gotta get past Cletus to do it. I thought you might be able to help me out."

I stopped and stared at him. "Hold up," I said thinking about who Cletus worked for. "Your wife's boyfriend is the Corn Nut King?"

"Yep," he said.

"Hmm. So what's in this for me and Ned?"

"Well, if I kill Myron, my wife will inherit the corn nut factory. I can hook you both up with an unlimited lifetime supply."

"I do like corn nuts. How'd your wife meet the King and why would she inherit?"

"They grew up together. Tammy Lynn's maiden name was King. In other words, he's her brother. You might say they've always been friendly." He gave me a knowing look and added, "*Real* friendly."

"That don't bother you?"

"Not until today. Thanks to my gastrointestinal disorder, I figure if I want some pussy, I can't be too particular. Especially these days with the pussy shortage and all. Tammy Lynn ain't much to look at, but we get all the free corn nuts we can eat. To top it off, once a week she'll put on a gas mask and let me fuck her so I wasn't gonna complain. But the bastard blew up my home with me in it. A man's gotta draw the line somewhere."

We reached Ned's house and I told Thomas to wait outside while Ned fetched him some clothes. No one paid much attention to a naked white guy in these parts. After all, we'd seen stranger things before we built a wall around the Hood to keep the yumbies out.

Ned came out with some clothes. He didn't want to part with them, but when I shot him a look, he handed them to Thomas. "You'll bring these back, right?"

"Sure," Thomas said. He got dressed and let another rip. "Do farts have lumps?" he asked.

"Uh, maybe you can just keep those pants," Ned said.

"Thanks. Any chance you can help me with my problem?"

"I can handle Cletus, but you might need some firepower anyway. The King has folks working for him who might not take too kindly to you killing him."

"They don't take too kindly to me being on the property at all, now that you mention it. I've got the firepower covered, but we'll have to make a stop."

"I didn't figure you had a gun shoved up your ass," I said. "Ned, you're driving."

Ned's truck was parked in the yard. As he opened the door, he pointed at Thomas. "You're riding in the back."

Thomas climbed over the tailgate, then moved a tackle box, fishing poles, a tarp and who knows what else to clear a space to sit down. Ned and I jumped in the cab.

Ned looked up at the afternoon sky. "Might be dark before we get home. Yumbies'll be out."

"Run 'em over like usual," I said.

Ned sighed. "You know how hard it is to clean them sumbitches out of the grill?"

"Beats gettin' ate up."

Ned scratched his head. "I guess that's a fair trade," he said and started the truck.

After a quick pit stop so Thomas could fetch a weapon, we drove to the outskirts of Jackson. We passed the corn nut factory, which was still in operation.

Parked at the top of a hill another mile down the road was the huge doublewide trailer where the Corn Nut King stayed. The place was tricked out to the max with vinyl siding and skirting. I slid open the back window and heard Thomas moving around in the bed of the truck. "We're going to the front gate," I said. "Hide under the tarp back there and keep quiet."

When we pulled up to the gate, the guard motioned for us to stop. Ned rolled down the window.

"You lost?" the guard asked.

"No," I said. "I'm here to see Cletus Newton."

"You Sam?" the man asked.

I nodded. "Is Cletus here?"

"Yeah, old 'Zilla's up at the house."

"Thanks," I said.

We were just about to pull away when Thomas farted. The guard looked at the back of the truck. "What was that?" he asked.

"What was what?" I said.

"I heard something. Sounded like a fart."

"That was me," Ned said with a grin. "Sorry."

"Sounded like it came from back there."

"You know them old boys who throw their voices?"

"Yeah."

"I'm working on throwing farts. It's a big hit at parties."

"Sounds like you got it down," the man said. "Smells like you threw it back there, too."

"That's the best part," Ned said. "The smell goes where the sound goes. Means I can pin the blame on anyone I want."

"I'll bet that comes in handy. Y'all can go on up to the house." He opened the gate and let us through.

"That was close," I said. "Good thinking on the fart throwing."

"I've actually been practicing that. Got a ways to go, though."

We parked around the side of the house and hopped out of the truck. "You can come out now, Thomas."

Thomas flung the tarp off and sat up. "I think there's a fish hook in my ass."

"Serves you right," Ned said.

Thomas clambered over the side of the truck and brushed himself off. "Let's do this. Get me past Cletus. Then I'll just go inside and shoot Myron." He pulled out a nickel-plated pistol.

"Cool," Ned said. "Can I see the gun?"

"Sure," Thomas said and handed him the pistol

"That's really not a good idea," I said.

"Nice gun," Ned said. "Check this out."

"Don't do it," I said.

"It's okay, Sam. I've been practicing." Ned twirled the gun around on his finger. He smiled and nodded. "See?" He went for a fancy move to switch hands and the gun spun around and dropped to the ground. The pistol went off.

Ned squealed and grabbed his balls. He dropped to the ground screaming. I hoped the gunshot and screams wouldn't bring out the guards.

"You okay?" Thomas asked.

"I blew my fucking nuts off!"

I sighed and knelt by Ned. "Let me see."

Ned moved his hands. There wasn't much blood, but there was a hole in his jeans. "Is it bad?" Ned cried.

"I think it's just a flesh wound."

He sat up and gingerly checked his balls. He sighed with relief. "They're both still there. The bullet just grazed my bag."

"You okay to wait in the truck?" I asked.

"Since my nuts ain't over in the field there, I guess I'll be all right. Be fast about it, though."

Thomas and I left Ned at the truck. "Let's get this over with," I said.

I knocked on the door and Cletus opened it. He loomed over us, big as a mountain. He wore a blue dress and one of those doctor's masks. Cletus looked pissed when he opened the door, but when he saw me, he brightened. "Yo, Sam. What's up?"

"Thomas here needs to have a chat with your boss. I was hoping you could sneak him through."

"Boss ain't here right now. I thought I heard a gunshot out there. A yumbie get into the compound?"

"Naw, Ned just shot himself in the nuts."

"Again?"

I shrugged. "You know Ned."

Cletus looked at Thomas. "You look familiar."

"I'm Myron's brother-in-law," Thomas said. "What's with the dress and the mask?"

Cletus growled. "It ain't a dress, it's a muumuu."

"Yes sir."

He touched the mask. "The boss makes me wear this in the house. Beats popping Altoids every five seconds."

"His nickname is Godzilla," I said. "My friend here has the strongest breath this side of the Mississippi."

Cletus beamed. "Damn right. I can knock a man unconscious with one breath."

"Oh yeah? Well, I can knock a man out with one fart," Thomas said.

"That sounds like challenge," Cletus said, puffing out his chest.

"Oh no, let's not go there," I said.

"You're on," Thomas said.

Cletus pulled his mask off and stepped forward. "Now you'll know why they call me Godzilla."

Thomas turned around. "Take your best shot."

"Guys, let's not do this," I said.

They ignored me. Cletus let out a horrible belch and at the same time, Thomas cut the raunchiest fart I've ever heard.

Next thing I knew, they were slapping me awake.

"You okay?" Cletus asked. His mask was back in place.

Even though the wind was blowing, I could still smell leftovers. That smell had crawled up my nose and would stick around for days.

"God damn!" I said and shook my head. "Who won?"

"It was a draw," Cletus said. "We done went and knocked each other out."

"I think you won, 'Zilla," Thomas said. "After all, I was facing away from you when you belched."

"Yeah, but your fart stained the porch brown. It would have knocked me out at ten paces."

About that time, a pickup truck pulled into view and parked in front of the house. The Corn Nut King himself stepped out dressed in overalls. His fly was open. The sleeve of his white T-shirt was turned up over a pack of Lucky Strikes. Tammy Lynn climbed out of the truck wiping her mouth with the back of her hand.

"Myron, you son of a bitch!" Thomas yelled and pulled his gun. "You tried to kill me!"

The Corn Nut King zipped his fly. "Calm down, Thomas, nobody tried to kill you. Hell, I'm glad to see you alive. Put the gun down. This is just one big misunderstanding."

"You want Tammy Lynn for yourself!"

"That's not true. My sister loves you," said the King. "I wouldn't do anything to mess that up. I thought we had a pretty nice routine going."

Thomas held the gun steady. "You blew up my trailer!"

"That was an accident."

"How do you figure?"

The King sighed. "I stopped by to pick up Tammy Lynn just like always. I was waiting for her on the front porch. Problem is, she opened the door right as I was lighting a cigarette. I guess you'd been farting all day and there was a lot of methane in the air. I'll be goddamned if my match didn't ignite those fumes. Next thing I knew, the whole place exploded."

"We thought you was dead," Tammy Lynn said, "but as we was leaving, I saw you running naked down the street. We drove around the block, but you disappeared. We've been trying to find you for hours!"

"I went into Leon's Bar." He lowered the gun. "I guess I overreacted."

"It's all right," Myron said.

"What about our trailer?"

Tammy Lynn smiled. "I've been working on a down payment for a brand new one," she said.

Ned limped over. "Ain't you gonna shoot him? Don't tell me I'm the only one gettin' shot today."

The Corn Nut King looked at Ned. "We can fix that. I can turn on the bug light over by the fence. The light attracts yumbies. When they get zapped, it stuns them for a second. Makes for great target practice."

"Cool," Ned said.

"But first, let's have dinner. We have chicken and beer inside." The King looked at Thomas and Cletus. "On second thought, with these guys around, maybe we should eat outside."

I shrugged. At least I'd get a free meal for my troubles. That's a damn sight better than a bullet in the balls. Even so, I made sure not to sit anywhere near Cletus or Thomas. A belch or a fart from them and my beer might go flat.

THE END

Gary Jonas gets paid for telling lies. The longest lie so far is his novel *One Way Ticket To Midnight* (a Yard Dog Press title, so buy extra copies). His shorter lies are buried in anthologies like *Robert Bloch's Psychos, It Came From the Drive-In, Prom Night, Sword and Sorceress VII, Horrors! 365 Scary Stories, Crime Spree* and others. He's also in a few of the other Yard Dog anthologies (*Stories That Won't Make Your Parents Hurl* and *Bubbas of the Apocalypse*). If you want more information, or you're just really bored, check out his website at www.garyjonas.net

BUBBA-RAP

Bennie Grezlik

"John-Boy, get down offin' that pipe rack. You an' me are wanted at the front office."

John-Boy looked down at his paw. He didn't think of himself as John-Boy. He wanted everyone to call him Tex, but no one would do it, especially paw.

"I done hear'd ya callin', Paw, but gimme a minute, I gotta crawl."

John-Boy inched his way down the pipe rack scaffolding. When he stepped onto the concrete apron of the ethylene production unit, he danced around a puddle. Those puddles held God-knows-what chemical brews. They would eat up a good pair of Red Wing work boots in three months if you weren't careful. John-Boy faced his father.

"Just for me, John-Boy, can you cut the rap-crap when we get to the office? I think Jim-Bob got somethin' important in mind fer ya."

John-Boy shrugged. Now that his feet were on solid ground, he felt them move to the beat that bounced around in his head every waking moment.

"Paw, you know I tried, an' I ain't lied,
to make my lines without no rhymes.
But my black soul makes ma tongue roll
in measured beat that moves ma feet.
You most of all should dig my call."

When John-Boy's feet stopped moving, he cut a fart that complemented the last two beats of the rap.

Paw-Boy shook his head. "Shit, John-Boy, you don't have to tell me we're black. But I raised you with these white folks here at the plant. They good folks, too. They treat us fair, ya gotta admit. We likes everything they like, right down to barbequed ribs smothered in Texas Red. Yeah, an' yer barbequed beans, too, which I wish you'd eat a smidgen less before ya gas me outa our trailer. I'm not askin' ya to be somethin' yer not. Jis make me proud, okay?"

John-Boy smiled and nodded.

"You're my Paw
an' that's the law.
My attention I'll pay
to what The Man has to say."

"Another thing," said Paw-Boy. "You got a shirt to put on over that little leather vest? Some of the men kind of take you showin' off your muscles the wrong way, if you get my drift."

"Ain't got no shirt to wear, but I got opinions to spare
'bout why my bicepts bother their precepts."

"Yeah, I guess you do. Okay, you my boy, an' I love ya the way you is, so let's go."

They climbed into Paw-Boy's company pickup with the yellow and black Yokum Oil logo and drove the half-mile between the cracking units of Refinery number three to the front office.

When John-Boy and Paw-Boy walked into the office, they noticed that every foreman in the plant was there, plus a bunch of men that neither of them recognized. The strangers wore hardhats with different logos and colors than the yellow and black stripes of Yokum Oil.

Jim-Bob, a big man with wide shoulders, rose from where he'd been sitting on the corner of the manager's desk.

"We been waitin' fer ya, Paw-Boy and John-Boy. We got foremen here representin' every refinery up and down the Houston ship channel. These boys agreed that I would represent their interests because Yokum number three is the biggest refinery on the channel."

Everybody waited while Jim-Bob paused to stuff his cheek with a fresh pinch of Beechnut.

"Everybody knows things ain't been the same ever since that Yuppy 25 virus hit a few months ago. None of us seem to have been affected much, except that limp-wristed manager we had. I had to shoot him myself when he went for my throat, the little prick. Yes sir, we been doin' about normal refinery business, if you don't count havin' to patrol the fence for those yuppie zombies."

"They make good target practice, Jim-Bob," said one of the foremen from another plant. Everyone laughed, including John-Boy. He got to shoot one himself a few nights ago.

"That they do," said Jim-Bob. "But here's the problem. We're goin' to be runnin' outa feed stock for the crackin' units pretty soon cause the world is screwed up with the virus. That means no more gasoline distribution, which is tough shit for the rest of America, but good news for us. We're goin' to have plenty of gas in those storage tanks for a lotta years to run our pickups and generators for Houston's East side."

"So what's the problem?" asked one of his foremen.

"The problem is that Yokum Oil headquarters downtown says the gasoline is theirs and we shouldn't touch it."

Someone snorted a laugh and the dam broke. Everyone in the room guffawed until Jim-Bob had to quiet them down.

"I know that sounds a little funny, those white-collar, headquarter yuppies tryin' to tell a bunch of gun-totin', cigar puffin', Beechnut chewin', all-American good ol' boys what to do. Hell, the way the world is shapin' up, we got as much right to the gas as anybody."

They waited.

"The real problem is they got what's left of the Houston Police Department on their side."

"You mean they got the yuppie sissy cops from the West side," said Sam, the foreman who'd spoke up before "Hell, them pretty boy cops whine more than my dear granma."

"They do that," said Jim-Bob. "But they quit cryin' long enough to shoot pretty good, I hear."

Paw-Boy stepped forward. "If'n it comes to war, I guess we'd do ya proud, Jim-Bob."

"I don't doubt it. But what I think about is they got grenade launchers from the National Guard Armory. These tanks would go up like the Fourth of July."

"Two can play that game," said Sam. "If we booby trap the tanks, just in case, mind you, then they cain't win no war. We could blow 'em if they looked like they was a winnin'."

The men murmured approval as Jim-Bob held up his hand. "That's a good idea. Kim-Boy, git over here."

Kim-Boy, a Korean who had immigrated to the U.S. as a young man, was Jim-Bob's oldest and smallest foremen. He stepped forward looking like his head was lost within the yellow Yokum hardhat.

"What you want me to do, boss?"

"Get some o' yer men an' rig up the tanks so we can explode 'em if'n we have to. Can ya do that?"

"You betcha, boss. What color explosions you want?"

"Ha, ha. That's what I like about you, Kim-Boy. Ya gimme

choices. No special colors, just rig 'em to blow. The other plants can do the same thing."

The multi-colored hardhats from the other refineries nodded assent.

"Still, I don't want no war where no one gets the gas."

"Then what can we do?" Paw-Boy asked.

"We can explain the situation to them, how splittin' up the gas is the best way to go, an' maybe they'll listen to reason. I've already agreed that I'd send a delegation downtown to talk about this."

"You gonna talk to them personally?" asked Sam.

"Nope. They're tricky yuppies after all, an' I know who they'd pick to do their talkin'. My old girlfriend, Ashley. She's their Marketin' Manager. She used to be a good ol' red-neck girl when we was both pups, but she grew up to be upwardly mobile while I grew up to live in a mobile home. I think it was that name that ruined her. I still get a little misty when I'm around her, so I can't do it."

"So who's gonna talk for us?" asked Paw-Boy.

Jim-Bob looked at him then shifted his glance to John-Boy. "I reckon I want your son to do our talkin'."

Three of Jim-Bob's foremen jumped up at once. "What?" said Husky, the youngest foreman and even bigger than Jim-Bob. "Look at the boy. He's... he's... "

"Black?" supplied Paw-Boy.

John-Boy's feet began to slip and slide.

> "Yep, boys, black I yam,
> but ya shouldn't give a damn.
> I can shoot an' I can barbeque,
> an I knows how to hold a pool cue.
> But lookee here, Jim-Bob,
> I ain't the man for the job.
> Diplomacy ain't my gig;
> rappin's where I'm big."

Husky took off his hard hat and scratched his head. "Damned if he don't look like one o' them New Village People."

Paw-Boy stepped between his son and Husky. "Well, he ain't. I didn't raise no gay-Boy."

"No offense intended," said Husky. "I just meant he looks kind of... pretty-like. But now that we're talkin' about things, I'm not so sure John-Boy is really one of us."

"What do you mean by that?" said Paw-Boy.

"Well," said Husky, "I can smell by his farts that he been eatin' barbeque beans fer lunch, which is good. I can cut gas with the best of 'em. But there's some other things."

"Like?" said Paw-Boy.

"Like that little vest," said Husky. "Some guys take off their shirt when they're a-workin', but I ain't seen nobody wear a little leather vest like that before."

John-Boy's feet moved.

"I like the vest.
Tell the rest."

"Well, you don't chew Beechnut or Red Man. I seen you dippin' Copenhagen. That's foreign, ain't it?"

One of the men in the back held up a hand. "Uh, I like Copenhagen. I thought it was American. Ain't it the capital of North Dakota?"

"Well, who knows what Yankee capital it is?" said Husky. "Sounds foreign to me. Another thing, John-Boy, you don't drive a Ford pickup like any red blooded redneck, you drive a Chevy pickup, which everyone knows is a Mexican brand. An' on top of that, it's not even full size, it's one o' them little sissy trucks."

"I'm tellin' you to watch what yer sayin'," said Paw-Boy."

Jim-Bob held up his hand. "This line o' prejudice is gettin' us nowhere, Husky. John-Boy's just as much one of us as you an' me."

"He don't even know who he is," persisted Husky. "Lookit that, he's wearin' a belt buckle that says 'Tex'. He ain't Tex!"

"If Tex I ain't, then
Husky you ain't," shot John-Boy.
"Cause you don't like my name,
don't mean that's my game."

"Let me ask," said Sam, "why you picked John-Boy out of all these men?"

"As I was getting' around to sayin'," said Jim-Bob, "I think they're goin' to use Ashley to negotiate 'cause they're guessin' I'll be negotiatin' for our side. And like I said, I can't talk to her without gettin' kinda sentimental. I picked John-Boy because he's black."

There was dead silence in the room for ten seconds.

"It's a little late for the affirmative action thing, Jim-Bob," offered Paw-Boy.

"That's right," shouted several men, "we don't want no big

gov'munt crap on the ship channel."

Jim-Bob jumped onto the desk in frustration. "It's not that. It's 'cause the yuppies is always full o' guilt about disadvantaged minorities – not that yer one of those, John-Boy but, they'll be ashamed of their own position an' they'll cave in."

There was a murmur of discussion from the men. One of them piped up, "That's pretty smart. Fool 'em at their own game."

John-Boy jumped onto the desk with Jim-Bob, who edged over as far as was decently possible.

"I get ya now, Jim-Bob,
an' I'll do a hob-nob
with a Yokum exec
who's yer old ex.
But here's the trick:
Do ya think I'll click,
cause they wear suits
an' I wears boots."

Jim-Bob jumped off the desk to give John-Boy room to rap his feet. "We'll get ya fixed up-"

"I won't wear a tux."

"No, I'm thinkin' of zombie clothes-"

"That's the way I likes ta pose."

"Are you rappin' with him?" asked Husky.

"No, no, I'm just tryin' to talk, is all."

"No, no, he's just tryin' to talk, is all." Repeated John-Boy, his feet shuffling backwards.

"Say, is that what they call the moonwalk?" said Sam.

Paw-Boy shook his head. "I'm afraid it is. There ain't a dance move that he's not ashamed to copy. But he ain't no gay-Boy!"

"Riiight," said Husky.

"All right, that's enough!" Jim-Bob yelled. The room slowly settled down. "Sam, you an' Paw-Boy go find a dead zombie's clothes for John-Boy. Or shoot one dead, I don't give a shit. Husky, I want you to get some men and round up four or five company trucks. We're goin' to the Yokum Tower in downtown Houston in a convoy. Natur'ly, pack yer guns, boys. They're goin' ta think I'll be negotiatin'. At the last second, I push John-Boy forward as my spokesboy, an' they're stuck. Whatta ya say, boys, is everbody in?"

They were in.

The streets of downtown Houston were nearly empty. Every once in a while a yuppie would dart across the street to the nearest Starbucks, and also every once in a while a slow-moving zombie would trail a yuppie, but the yuppie simply evaded the zombie. Certainly, no yuppie ever shot a zombie, sure that they could maybe be reformed no doubt. Everyone knew there wouldn't be any yuppies left soon. They'd die of the plague or stupidity, and either way it wasn't necessarily a bad thing.

The men of Yokum Oil Refinery number three handled the zombie situation differently. By the time the convoy had reached the Yokum Tower, the good ol' boys had blown the heads off five zombies. Husky, driving pickup number two, wanted to circle the block a few more times for a little hunting, but Jim-Bob, in pickup number one with John-Boy and Paw-Boy, nixed that idea. Jim-Bob radioed his men to park on the sidewalk behind him at the base of Yokum Tower.

Fifteen men piled out of the trucks. All of them wore their work clothes and hard hats except John-Boy, who was dressed in a pin-striped blue suit, a power-yellow bow tie, and his brown leather vest, which he showed off periodically by flipping back his suit lapels. Sam and Paw-Boy had tried to make him wear a shirt, but John-Boy would have none of that.

He did agree to wear black loafers (no socks) with tassels that bounced saucily when he walked. When his feet moved to a rap beat, those tassels stayed airborne.

"Ya look a might yuppified," said Jim-Bob.

"Don't make fun o' me, boss
I gotta talk with no loss."

"I'm not funnin' ya, John-Boy. Ya look kinda sharp, like a yuppie that's seen the light."

"Is it safe to leave the trucks right here?" asked Sam.

"I reckon," said Jim-Bob. "Think about it. The yuppies might steal money by jigglin' the company books, but they'd never steal a pickup. An' the zombies don't care about nothin' that ain't walkin' on two legs. Am I right?"

"As usual, you right, boss," said Paw-Boy.

They crowded aboard one elevator for the ride to the sixty-seventh floor conference room where the negotiation was to take place. Half way up, John-Boy ripped a fart that kind of whistled and belched its tortuous way into the world.

"Sweet Jesus!" moaned Husky. "That don't smell like no barbequed beans."

"Beans it is, slightly used,
no apology, no excuse."

The men left the elevator fanning the air with their hands. Waiting at the conference room was Ashley, Darrel Yokum himself, five other executives, and eight heavily armed cops.

Darrel Yokum inspected the refinery workers with their rifles and strapped-on Glocks. "This is supposed to be a friendly negotiation, boys. Why all the weapons?"

"I reckon you got your army behind you," said Jim-Bob, "so we doin' the same."

"The police are impartial. They just want to see everyone obey the law."

Their wrists resting limply on their .44 automatics, the cops stared at the refinery men.

"Either no one packs heat, or we all pack heat," said Jim-Bob.

"Point taken, Mr. Porter."

"Jim-Bob will do just fine."

"Fine, fine, Jim-Bob it is. And please, call me Mr. Yokum."

Jim-Bob nodded. "As we agreed earlier, one negotiator from each side will get together an' talk, while the rest stand back somewheres, preferably in another room."

"That is correct. If it meets with your approval, the negotiators will talk in this conference room while the rest of us retire to the conference room next door. See, there's a glass wall and a glass door between the two rooms. We can see the negotiations, but we are not to signal the negotiators in any way."

"Okey-dokey."

"Our negotiator is Ashley Goodbody."

Ashley stood up and bowed. Until that moment, Jim-Bob had managed to block her presence from his thoughts. Now he looked at her and his knees felt wobbly. He wanted to sit down, but that would be a bad signal.

"I hope you two reach an amicable agreement," said Yokum. He and his group started moving towards the glass door.

"Our negotiator is John-Boy Brown," said Jim-Bob.

John-Boy stepped forward and bowed just like Ashley had done.

"Miss Goodbody do I call,
or Ashley is all?"

Ashley looked startled. "You may call me Ashley. But I thought... "

"If'n it's all the same,
then Tex is my name."

"What is the meaning of this?" said Yokum. "Jim-Bob, you are supposed to be the negotiator."

"No sir, Mr. Yokum. As we agreed, we pick our own negotiator. I picked John-Boy."

Yokum sputtered.

"Let's let them jaw," said Jim-Bob.

Reluctantly, Yokum's group moved through the glass door with the refinery men following. They gathered along the glass wall as a Hispanic woman passed out Perrier.

"This is the weakest beer I ever tasted," Paw-Boy whispered to Jim-Bob.

"It's yuppie water," said Jim-Bob.

"No wonder they're all dyin'", said Paw-Boy.

"Shh. Let's see if we can hear what's goin' on in there."

But they didn't really have to listen through the glass wall. Yokum turned on a speaker so that John-Boy and Ashley seemed to be right there in the room with them.

"Yokum Oil is not heartless," Ashley began. "We are prepared to offer your men a portion of the gasoline."

"That's mighty nice o' Yokum,
but it sounds like hokum."

For the life of him, John-Boy could not sit still while he rapped. He rose, gripping the thick conference table while his feet moved. That would have to do for the moment.

"We prepared to do what's best;
eighty percent fer us, you get the rest."

Ashley's dismissive laugh didn't quite come off. "There is no way- uh, why are you talking in rhymes and dancing?"

"Rappin's what I do.
Does it bother you?"

"Of course, urp, not." Ashley covered her mouth daintily. "Sorry."

"Purty ladies 'r not exempt
from lettin' gas get some vent.
Mine has got a dif'rent route:
Saves wear an' tear on my mouth."

Ashley blushed. "Really, Tex, that is not a topic of polite conversation. Let's get back to business. Yokum Oil is prepared to offer your men twenty five percent of the gasoline."

John-Boy-Tex had to move. He let go of the table and danced around her as he replied.

"Comin' down to seventy fer us,
    you get thirty with no fuss.
See, we kin talk big numbers,
    but it makes us both dumber.
Let's keep movin' that line
Until we gets away from 'mine'.
If you thinks I'm a fool,
    then you ain't so cool.
But if'n ya wanna talk straight,
    then, Ashley, we gots a date."

John-Boy-Tex stopped moving and cut such a vicious fart that it vibrated the glass wall. He heard the refinery boys hoop and holler. It made him proud.

"Oh, my urp God," said Ashley, indignant and embarrassed at once.

John-Boy-Tex twirled in glee.

"I knowed it right away:
Beans fer lunch act that way.
Don't ya worry, ya ain't depraved;
'cause o' beans, we's both slaves.
I likes 'em barbequed with ribs.
You like beans, cum' on, admit."

"Okay, I admit it, I had barbequed beans for lunch. Dammit, what does that matter? Okay, Yokum will go sixty-forty. Sixty for us, of course."

"Sixty-forty yer favor?
Let's try a dif'rent flavor."

Darrel Yokum pushed through the glass door. "Hold everything right there. Miss Goodbody, you are relieved of duty as negotiator."

Jim-Bob and his men came through, quickly followed by Yokum's executives and the cops. "Ya can't do that, Mr. Yokum. Ya already picked yer negotiator."

"We didn't say we couldn't change negotiators, did we?"

"Well... no, I reckon we didn't. But we also didn't say we could."

John-Boy-Tex danced over to them.

"Boss, he can bring more to talk,
but Ashley stays or I walk."

"It's not up to him," protested Yokum. "I can call whoever I want."

"Whomever," corrected Ashley.

"Me too," said Jim-Bob. "John-Boy – I mean Tex – is my negotiator. If'n he walks, we're finished negotiatin'."

Yokum gritted his teeth. "Alright. Miss Goodbody stays. But she will have a co-negotiator. Randall, call Latisha Groovy. Maybe she can talk this jive language."

One of the executives jumped into action. "Yes sir, Mr. Yokum."

A few minutes later, a black woman walked into the room, her shapely hips swinging, her head bobbing from side to side as she studied Tex.

"What's the problem here, Bro?"

"I ain't Bro an' you ain't Sis,
Call me Tex, I call you Latish."

Latisha watched Tex's flashing feet.

"That's cool. We can talk."

"May I say-" began Ashley.

"No you can't," said Latisha. "Randall already give me the scoop. You offered him sixty-forty for us. So we gotta go from there."

Tex held up his hands.

"We been goin' double-time,
Now it's close to suppertime.
No more competin'
Until we be eatin'."

"Maria!" snapped Yokum. "Order some Havarti and Brie. And for our guests, some whiskey from Tennessee."

"Are you rappin' with him?" asked Husky.

"Of course not," said Yokum, "I'm just talkin', I mean talking."

"O' course not," repeated Tex, as he danced around Yokum,

"he's jis' talking, I mean talkin'."

"An' Mr. Yokum, if'n you please,
We don't want no French cheese.
Bring us black ribs an' white bread,
an' buckets o' beans with Texas Red;
'cause barbeque sauce is jis' piss,
unless Texas Red is on the list."

"What the hell is he talkin', I mean talking, about," demanded Yokum.

"That's my boy," said Paw-Boy. "He wants ribs an' barbequed beans with plenty of Texas Red barbeque sauce. I think we could all eat a little o' that, huh, boys?"

The refinery men whooped.

"An' jis' to make us cheer,
We need some Shiner beer."

The men seconded that idea with whistles.

"Well," said Yokum, "that's not what my people want. We're gonna, I mean *going*, to have brie and merlot. Right men?"

Several of Yokum's people made a noise that sounded suspiciously like a moan.

"Look," said Jim-Bob, "You all need to try the barbeque. Jis' taste it, an' if'n you don't like it, go back to sippin' wine and suckin' cheese. Paw-Boy, you an' Sam get some o' the boys an' get a load o' barbeque at Smokey Joe's. I saw one on the corner a block away. Watch out fer them zombies."

"I wanna go, too," said Husky. "Maybe I can plug me a coupla them dead-heads."

"Mr. Husky, get me some of my special barbeque, okay?" said Kim-Boy.

Husky snorted. "Dammit, Kim-Boy, we goin' ta Smokey Joe's, not the Korean House o' Bow-Wow." He turned to Jim-Bob. "Why am I the only one he calls Mister?"

"It's a sign o' respect," said Jim-Bob.

Kim-Boy had been thinking about his barbeque choices. "Okay, no more Mr. Doggy. I eat Mr. Piggy."

They waited uneasily while the barbeque detail went out. Maria tried to pass out more Perrier, but no one wanted any, even Yokum's people.

Husky burst through the door first. "Yaa-hoo! I got me two zombies. It's kinda fun, but they're too damn easy. Say, Maria, I been meanin' ta ask ya. What kinda truck you drive?"

"Cheby."

Husky nudged Jim-Bob. "What'd I tell ya?"

Paw-Boy, Sam, and the rest of the men trooped in carrying grease-stained cardboard boxes and a couple of Styrofoam coolers. They laid out ribs, chicken, pork chops, jalapeno coleslaw, several buckets of beans, a bag of white bread (Texas-toast size), a bucket of Texas Red, paper plates, and six rolls of paper towels on the conference table. Sam set up the

Styrofoam coolers filled with iced Shiners.

"Dig in," said Jim-Bob, "before we throw it to the hogs."

Ashley and Tex went for the ribs and plenty of beans with everything smothered in Texas Red.

Latisha grabbed some drumsticks and dipped them in the Texas Red.

"Say, these ribs ain't, I mean, aren't bad," said Yokum.

"They're de-licious," said Jim-Bob. "But they want a little more sauce. Here let me fix you up." He poured more sauce for both of them.

"Thanks. Say, Jim-Bob, why don't you call me Darrell."

"Okey-dokey. Darrel's a good ol' boy name, ya know."

"True enough. I was raised along the ship channel in Pasadener, where the air is greener."

"Ya don't say. I got a second cousin named Yokum. Ya ain't related to Abner Yokum, by any chance?"

Yokum stopped chewing. "Abner's my brother. My God, that makes us second cousins."

"Well, doggie. Nice ta meet ya, cousin."

They shook sticky hands, laughing.

Tex jumped onto the table.

> "Listen up, friends old an' new.
> We done had a breakthrough.
> Ashley, Latish, git up here with me,
> 'cause we made a deal b'tween us three."

Ashley and Latisha stepped on a chair, then onto the table. With Tex between them, they faced the men. They stepped back once, then forward twice. Tex raised his hands and pointed both index fingers into the air. The women followed suit.

"I gotta hand it to these girls," said Tex.

"He's handin' it to us girls," sang the girls.

"We's past the point where things is iffy."

The girls looked at each other, then belted out, "We get fifty, an' you get fifty." They put their hands low, stepped left, then right, and they sang:

> "We got a deal, that's no crap,
> an' it's all because of Bubba-rap,
> an' it's all because of Bubba-rap."

Most of the men were now bobbing and weaving to the beat.

"Say, that sorta feels like a Texas two-step," said Paw-

Boy.

"That it does," said Jim-Bob. "Come on, let's do a line dance."

"Maria," said Husky, "let's show these folks how ta dance."

Husky and Maria spun out a two-step. She was so good, Husky began wondering if she lied about driving a Chevy.

The rest of the men formed two rows across the conference room. Someone broke out a harmonica and squawked out the Cotton Eyed Joe to a rap beat. Someone else began to drum the two-step rap beat against a mahogany cabinet. One of the cops and one of the hardhats jumped onto the table to join Tex and the women. The cop began:

> "Supper is 'et, a deal is set,
> Everythin's alright, you bet."

Jim-Bob winked at Darrel. "Scratch a yuppie, an' out pops a bubba."

Darrel laughed with his cousin.

The troupe on the table moved back and forth, side to side as if they'd rehearsed all day.

Jim-Bob felt Sam and Paw-Boy pushing him towards the table.

"Naw, I don't want to get up there," protested Jim-Bob.

Then the troupe on the table pushed Ashley off and towards Jim-Bob.

They were face to face looking hard at each other. One more little push and they squashed together real close.

"Ashley... "

"Jim-Bob... "

The men whistled and cat-called.

"Shucks," said Jim-Bob, "ya always been the apple o' my eye."

"An' I always loved you, that's no lie," replied Ashley.

They dipped and swayed into the Texas two-step as the men hollered and stomped. They all sang:

> "We got a deal, that's no crap,
> an' it's all because of Bubba-rap,
> an' it's all because of Bubba-rap."

THE END

Bennie Grezlik lives in Houston with his wife Judy and three yuppies disguised as cats. He first came to Houston in 1956 to work in the space program, so he's seen the city in boom and bust. He like's boom better, when bubbas are kings. He began his writing career in 1978 with a story in *Men's Action.* The story was so good that the publication expired in a paroxysm of ecstatic readership and wafted up to magazine heaven, from where they found it impossible to pay the earthly dollars they promised their budding Hemingway. But their prayers were with Bennie. He eventually found his way to Yard Dog Press, where the checks are small, but do not bounce. He may be found in *More Stories That Won't Make Your Parents Hurl* and, of course, here.

THE ULTIMATE WEAPON
M.H. Bonham

Fuckin' Yumbies.

That's right, I detest them. And now it looked like they were coming for me.

I stretched and yawned, delicately scratching my flea-bitten ears with my hind foot. Ned was passed out on the bed, his snoring loud enough to shake the timbers of the shack he called home and I called sanctuary. I needed a flea dip or at least a new flea collar – assuming they carried those things anymore in Road Apple, Arkansas. Since the Yumbies had taken over the world, Road Apple hadn't gotten a shipment from Hartz in weeks.

Yo! Blue!

I looked up into the rafters. My eyes aren't bad for a Bluetick Coonhound, but I'm a tad on the nearsighted side. I could see Ms. Tibbs, a calico cat holding something daintily between her paws. Probably a mouse. Ugh. She doesn't really like them, but since Ned doesn't feed her much, she's had to hunt. She's used to far better fare like vichyssoise, caviar, and stuff I would normally roll in, that's, of course, if you can believe her.

Hiya Tibbs! How's the mice hunting? I sneered.

Tibbs made a face and drew herself to full height, accidentally dropping the half-eaten mouse into Ned's open mouth. It muffled the roar considerably. Ned continued to snore.

My NAME is Angelica Chelsea Hildebrandt, heir to the...

Yeah, yeah, whatever, Tibbs. You hear the news from Billy?

Ned began coughing and spat out the mouse. He opened one brown eye and wiped the mouse guts off his face. "You say somethin', Blue?"

I can't talk, remember? I'm a dog, I replied. *Go back to sleep.*

"Yup, that's right." He started to close his eyes, but opened them again. "Then why do I hear you?"

Telepathy, I sighed. *We're going to go through THIS again. What news from Billy?*

Billy's seen some Yumbies over near the apple patch. By the description, they might be former scientists.

With Hector Von Trap?

Nah, probably the chumps who tested those IQ enhancing drugs on us.

You think they might make me into a normal cat again? Tibbs asked.

Fat chance, I said. *They're zombies now. Anyway, I wouldn't change you back.*

"Tel-what?" Ned's eyes blinked open. "Telly-what?"

Television, I said firmly. *I'm talking to you through the TV.*

"Like the movies?" Ned said brightly. Ok, maybe I'm exaggerating. Not so brightly. He eyed the TV suspiciously. "Goll darnn thing hasn't worked fer weeks! Now I'm hearin' dang talkin' dawgs!"

Yeah, like the movies, I agreed. *Remember those Disney movies I used to take you to? The ones with the talking dogs and cats?*

Ned gurgled in joy. He thinks he understands. That is, if he thinks. I have my doubts. We still go to drive-in movies together. Ned brings along a date – usually a jug of moonshine – and passes out halfway through the first movie. Tibbs and I share the popcorn. There's not much on anymore – just some reruns of the latest Disney movie and some cartoons. The Apocalypse has put a severe strain on Friday nights. Personally, I think a Yumbie is operating the projector.

So, they're coming back for us? Tibbs asked. *Why? They're zombies now.*

Damned if I know. Maybe they want to make some of their kind more super intelligent. Not that that's a blessing... I suppose I should be grateful, after all how many Bluetick Coonhounds do you know with an IQ of 240? But I was a happy little puppy before they did this to me. Unfortunately, before the experiment completed, everyone in the biotech labs in Little Rock turned to Yumbies, died, or got eaten. Tibbs and I escaped down to Road Apple, Arkansas.

Tibbs coughed up a hairball and lobbed it at Ned, who didn't notice as it clung to his hair. Ned scratched himself, belched, farted – I ran like hell out the door – and took another swig of moonshine. I looked up in the sky – it's a beautiful spring Arkansas day with humidity thick enough to cut with a knife. I scratched the fleas again as Ned followed me to the front porch and unzipped his pants to pee.

"I reckon you couldn't ask for a purtier day," Ned said to me with a near-toothless grin. "Got a date with Ellie tonight at the drive-in." He chuckled.

Your cousin, eh? Looking for an outcross? I remarked.

"She thinks I'm cute," Ned says. He finished, zipped his pants and trundled inside.

Well, beggars can't be choosers, I suppose, I replied staring off into the forest. I thought I saw a flash of light. A loud boom rocked the woods and the porch nearly collapsed on top of me.

Fuckin' Yumbies.

"Ned! Ned!"

People were swarming around Ned's collapsed shack. OK. Only Billy was there. And Billy was worried because he thought the still blew up again. "Ned! You OK?"

Tibbs and I watched from the sidelines as Billy tried to pull Ned from the debris. Tibbs had managed to slide out on her own.

"I'm OK!" Ned shouted. "Jist got hit in the head."

No damage there, Tibbs remarked.

Billy looked at us. "Didya have any other critters?"

Ned looked at me. "Well, there's fleas and such."

"No, no! I mean CRITTERS Ned! Like Blue."

"Nah – I ain't no redneck – Blue's my only dawg," Ned replied.

"I saws the zombie fellers in Thistledown – they plum blown up the town!" Billy said. "Ya don't suppose...?"

"Nah," Ned said. "Road Apple's at least..." He paused and thought. "At least a mile or better..."

Actually, Thistledown is about five miles away, but Ned can't count. The news was more alarming than I expected. I could see Tibb's eyes wide with fear.

Ned dusted his shirt off as he stepped over the splinters of his front porch. He turned around with his hands on his hips. "Well, shoot. It'll take the whole afternoon to fix it and I gots a date with Ellie t'night."

"I'll get Bo and Jake. We'll fix it right up. But we'll need somethin' to wet our whistle with. Was the still blown up?"

"Nah – got it down by the crick," Ned said. "Put it there after it blew up inside twice." And who says Ned can't learn?

"Whoa, Ned! Yah think it blew up?"

"Dunno." Ned looked at me. "What'dya think happened, Blue?"

I think the Yumbies have taken over the moonshine still, I replied.

"You nuts, Ned? Dawgs don't talk," Billy laughed.

"Blue talks through the TV," Ned said proudly.

"Wow! No shit?" said Billy, looking at me and seeing money signs.

No, not really, I replied and looked hard at Ned. You have your gun?

"Why ain't'cha talkin' with your mouth?" Billy asked.

Because I don't have the elongated palate—oh, never mind! I said. I've been captured by space aliens, that's why. I wasn't going to try to explain the biological experiments or the mnemonic transplants.

"Wooowhee, Ned!" Billy exclaimed. "Never said nuthin' about your dawg bein' captured by space aliens! That'd make the Enquirer!"

Shit! I wondered if the idiots knew there wasn't an Enquirer any more.

Wrong move, Tibbs catcalled. I glared at her. She catcalls a lot.

You can see the space aliens, yourself, I said. *They're probably stealing Ned's moonshine.*

Now, there are two things that make Bubbas move fast. One is a sheep tangled in barbed wire (love at first sight); the other is someone stealing his moonshine. Ned tore through what was left of the shack to pull out his shotgun while Billy got his rifle off the gun rack in his 2005 Ford F150 with mismatched fenders. No space aliens were going to steal their moonshine, no sir!

They hopped into Billy's truck and Tibbs and I leapt in the truck bed just in time for Billy to hit the wrong gear and nearly throw us into the cab through the broken back window.

We could walk faster, Tibbs said unhelpfully.

Billy got the right gear and we barreled down the little one lane rutted path that doesn't have enough width to be called a road. Ned and Billy were hootin' and hollerin' in the truck with each bounce. Tibbs hurled her mouse breakfast.

They hit a rut with enough mud to swallow a Honda and stopped. This time, both Tibbs and I hit the back of the truck bed and I was seeing stars.

"Let's winch it!" I heard Billy chortle. Tibbs and I jumped out and headed down the path while Billy and Ned tried to figure out how to operate the winch. As we turned the corner, I heard Billy screaming.

"Oww! Oww! My fingers! Sonofabitch! My friggin' fingers!"

The road went down the hill towards the creek. Already, I could smell rotting flesh and a fire, even though I couldn't see it: Yumbies. The hair on Tibb's back bristled and she looked at me in worry.

What do you think they'll do to us now?

I didn't respond. I didn't know. Yumbies were bad and Yumbies with the intellects of scientists were positively frightening.

"Blue – there you are!" I heard a familiar voice.

I tried to keep my loathing contained, but it was no use. Dr. Kaufmann, a scientist I knew from the labs, stood there. I recognized all of them, despite the rotting teeth and the vacant stares. If it hadn't been for their clothing, I might have mistaken them for the denizens of Road Apple. Another explosion rocked the ground. I could see one of the neighbor shacks blow up in a burst of flames.

Dr. Kaufmann stood armed with a AAA map and wearing an Izod shirt and Dockers. He had tied his blue cotton LL Bean sweater stylishly around his neck and his loafers were caked with black Arkansas mud.

What should I call you now – Biff? I sneered.

"Biff?" Dr. Kaufmann mused over the name. "Yes, I like that name." At that moment, Dr. Jurga stumbled through the woods. I thought Tibbs was going to choke from laughter.

"I sprayed three families with Yuppie 75 – they've taken to it well. They've blown up their miserable excuse for homes and they're going to set up a Cappuccino stand, a Lexus Dealership, and..." Dr. Jurga began and then looked at me. "What's so funny, Blue?"

Preppy gone bad. Dr. Jurga was a blonde woman, forties-ish who wore thick glasses. She had been a no-nonsense doctor in flats and a lab coat. She was now a pert blonde with a hip hairdo and wore a short Black Watch skirt and white blouse. She was also carrying a tank on her back and what looked like a bug sprayer. I began howling – I couldn't stop myself. Biff and Buffy – oh my!

"It doesn't matter," Dr. Jurga said. "We've got enough Yuppie 75 to change the whole town."

Yuppie 75? I paused. I looked at Tibbs, whose expression was as confused as mine. *What's that?*

"Gawddammit, Ned! I said FORWARD!" I heard Billy bellow at the top of his lungs. "Sweet Jesus H. Christ! You'll screw up my OTHER hand!"

"I'll show you," said Biff. "Come on Buffy."

You had to put that in their minds, didn't you? Tibbs said in accusation. I gave her the innocent puppy dog look that I'm so famous for. Biff and Buffy led us back to Billy and Ned. Both men were sitting on the hood drinking cans of Lone Star beer that Billy kept in the cab for just such emergencies. Billy had wrapped his mangled hand in some red utility cloth and Ned was talking about the last fish he caught not far from here.

"Hey, look at that!" Billy said, straightening up as he saw Buffy the Yumbie approach. It was the first time I've ever seen two rednecks try to suck their beer bellies into their chests.

Ned gave a wolf-whistle in appreciation. "You ain't from around here, are ya?" he asked.

Isn't that a line from Deliverance? Tibbs asked hopefully.

Shhhh! I said. *Ned, shoot 'em. They're Yumbies.*

"Nah, they look like a coupla city folk," Billy said. "Got lost from Little Rock, maybe?"

Ned looked confused. "Yumbies? They ain't Space Aliens?"

Space Aliens—Yumbies, whatever! This is your big chance for the Enquirer, I said.

Ned needed no further urging. He reached in and pulled out his shotgun and aimed it at Biff.

Click!

Nothing. Ned racked the shotgun. *Click!* Nothing. Rack. Click. Nothing.

You moron! Tibbs snapped. *You forgot to load your shotgun!*

Billy pushed aside the gun. "He's just foolin' around, folks. Were you lookin' fer sumthin? Got a purty trailer park right in downtown Road Apple."

Buffy raised the bug sprayer wand. "We won't be staying

terribly long. We just need to run a few experiments..." With that, she pumped a noxious gas at Billy.

Billy and Ned screamed simultaneously. Suddenly, Billy was tanned, manicured, and had a full set of teeth. His flannel shirt and jeans were gone; replaced by an Izod shirt and Dockers.

I stared in horror. *What have you done to him?*

"He's a Yumbie now," Biff replied.

With better teeth? Tibbs asked.

"That is a problem," Buffy admitted. "But it's only a prototype. Our later revs will improve things substantially. Watch..."

Billy walked up to Ned. "I'd like a mocha soy latte with a double shot of espresso, please."

No! No! Tibbs screamed. She turned to flee, but I barred the way.

Ned belched in Billy's face and Billy passed out. So much for the hardiness of Yumbies.

So, you turn everyone into a Yumbie, I said, trying to bide us some time. *Then what?*

Biff smiled evilly. "We tried to turn dogs and cats into Yumbies, but dogs don't care about fashion and cats don't listen to anyone."

I could've told you that, I replied snidely.

"So, we're back to Plan D," Biff said.

Plan A, I said absentmindedly. I was watching as Ned was looking through the barrel of the shotgun. *Run like hell when I give the signal,* I tell Tibbs.

I turned to Biff. *So, what will you do with us?*

"We'll need something else to eat once all the humans are Yumbies." Biff's tone had become decidedly nasty.

Tibbs was backing up in sheer terror. The cat would kill herself first before being cat flambé. Not that I wanted to be the main course in the Yumbie cookbook, 101 Ways to Wok Your Dog. There was, however, a tiny chance...

Buffy aimed the bug sprayer at Ned. She squeezed the trigger.

Fart, Ned! Fart! It's our only chance! I shouted and ran like hell. Right on cue, Ned farted. A huge miasma of green gas filled the entire area. It blocked out the sun and spread outward like a fireball. I could hear Biff, Buffy, and Billy screaming loudly.

"I'm melting! I'm melting! Oh cruel world!" I heard Buffy wail.

We're not in Kansas anymore, Tibbs remarked.

And I'm not Toto. I knew there'd be an off chance that the gasses within Ned would counteract that Yuppie 75 concoction. I just didn't know how well...

We waited for a few moments and the gas dissipated.   Ned stood there looking down at the quivering blobs that were once the three Yumbies. The tires on the truck had melted and were still smoking. Everything plastic on the truck had melted to goo. Ned looked as though he had been struck by lightning: his hair stood on end and his clothing reeked of smoke.

Ned, you ok? I asked.

"Shit!" Ned exclaimed. He began chuckling in that gurgling sort of way. "Guess they all got blowed up!" Ned forgot about the still and decided to walk back home. "You see that! They durn near blowed me up! Wait til I tell Ellie about this. She ain't goin' believe this shit!" Tibbs and I followed him back to his shack.

Well, great, just great, Tibbs remarked.   *What do we do now?*

I looked up. Wasn't it obvious?

We help Ned rebuild his shack.

How's that going to help us? The Yumbies are still coming for us.

I smiled a doggy smile. I wasn't worried. I had the ultimate weapon in the universe: Ned.

THE END

M. H. Bonham – a.k.a. Maggie is a professional freelance writer living somewhere in the mountains of Colorado with enough dogs and other redneck accoutrements to be considered a Bubba. (Yes, she eats generic BBQ sauce and likes it). She's the author of six nonfiction books published by Penguin-Putnam, Barron's Educational Series, and TFH, the latest being *The Complete Idiot's Guide to Dog Health and Nutrition.* (Fitting, isn't it?) She has two forthcoming books,

The Complete Guide to Mutts (Wiley) and *The Everything Guide to Rottweilers* (Adam's Media). Some fancy folks in NYC gave her the Maxwell Award not once, but twice, for writing excellence, but Maggie swears it's because they don't know her.

She's been published in various national and trade magazines more times than she can count because she's already taken off her shoes to do so. Watch it though, she may be a yuppie in disguise having been a software engineer (she was a rocket scientist!) and a UNIX guru in a previous life and actually likes Starbucks' Frappucinos and knows what "chai" is.

NED

Ajax

Big Ned awoke with knots on his head
His flesh blue with bruises; he'd been left for dead
Bright morning sunlight was splashing around
Ned spit out some rocks and made a grunt sound
Face down in the lot by the roadhouse again
He craned his neck and saw three men
Splayed and beaten and smellin' of pee
"So them is the assholes who was fuckin' with me"
He tried to remember the night before, then
He tried to sit up, but his gut was too sore
Ned rolled on his back to look to the skies
As he heard a gaggin' from one of the guys
Against better judgment he sat up, then stood
He knew Margie would be pissed, but good
Out all night – there was no deception
It was then he remembered his wedding reception
He hadn't realized how drunk he had got
He remembered it was groomsman, beat up in the lot
That explained the tuxes they all wore
But thinking of Margie chilled him to his core
His sweetie, his wife, his three hundred pound dove
Had his antics finally cost him her love?
Ned sighed; hot damn, I'm a ree-tarded fuck
Then he heard the horn wail from his truck
A horn that played Dixie, man it was cool
He looked at his truck and felt like a fool
There in his truck cab, a vision in white
His chubby angel had spent the whole night
Margie drove up beside him, Ned's heart leapt in joy
She hollered at him, "Get your ass in here boy,
The groomsman is up and ooh is they pissed!"
Bottles crashed on the hood; Ned got the gist.
He jumped in the cab; Margie hit the gas
Gravel rained through he air as they sped away fast

Ned smiled at their first day as husband and wife
They drove toward the sunrise to begin their life.

Ajax lives in Kansas City, where his favorite things, fried food and anonymity, can be found in abundance.

ATTACK OF THE GODLESS UNDEAD ZOMBIES

Tracy S. Morris

Things've settled down in Baymerry since the incident with the bake-off. Of course, we made Ned clean up the whole of Main Street, so that kept him out of trouble.

It's his own fault, of course. You just can't dump a semi full of barbecue on a church social and expect to get away with it, even if you are protecting the town from zombies.

Well, I can see by that expression on your face that you don't know what in the Sam hill I'm talking about, so I reckon that I'd better start from the beginning.

Baymerry used to be a small town; back before the big cities fell to those zombies and all the decent folk that survived ran off to the country for clean living. Even now we try to hold to those ways that kept us upright and on the narrow path, and not the dens of iniquity that places like Raleigh had been.

So every Sunday morning, we all dress up for services to this very day.

"Stanley, you'd best get a move on, before we miss church!" Aunt Martha's stern voice called up the stairs.

"Coming Aunt Martha!" I knotted the noose around my neck, and tucked it into my sport coat.

"You call that a tie?" She stuck her head in the door this time.

"Aunt Martha?" Whining like a twelve-year-old, I put my hands on my hips. "Privacy?"

In response, she rolled her eyes, and bustled through the door. "Town sheriff and you can't even tie a decent tie. What'll the cooks over at the commune think?"

"That you were too busy with the boy to worry about your widowed nephew." I deadpanned my response.

"That this isn't a decent town!" She corrected me. "Why would they want to sell their barbecue to a town where the sheriff can't even tie his own tie? Now get down stairs and tell the boy to quit playing with his toys and eat."

"Yes ma'am." I followed her down stairs without arguing. What my tie has to do with the price of barbecue is beyond me. I don't understand women. My own wife was a complete mystery to me. My aunt is even worse. But it ain't worth complaining about. The boy and I are lucky to have Aunt Martha. Especially after my wife got et by a zombie.

That was before we started the socials. Back then anyone was liable to wake up a godless liberal flesh-eating zombie. Now, once a month the Baptists and Methodists meet for a social. We figure it's the best way to get everyone to eat their barbecue and not turn on us. It's really something to see. The commune up the road brings us a tanker truck full of the spicy, red sauce. In exchange, we give them the right ear from every zombie we can find and kill. Pretty fair exchange, if you ask me.

Other than the barbecue pay-off, there's a square dance. Seems like all the pretty girls get dressed up to try and catch them a fella. If you're not interested in sparkin', then there's watching Betty Sue Crickinbush and Mary Lou Jones throw down at the bake-off. One of them wins it every time, and it's gotten downright nasty between the both of them.

The boy had his mind on the bake off that morning, too. As I entered the kitchen he looked up from his GI-Zombie Killer action figures – made out of old GI Joes – with a question already on his lips.

"Paw, are you going to pick Betty Sue or Mary Lou this time?"

As town Sheriff, it's my privilege to judge the bake-off.

"I'll rely on my taste buds to tell me who the winner is, boy. Now get your toys off the table, afore Aunt Martha grounds us both."

"Yes, Paw." He sounded disappointed, like he always does. "Has Ned said anything yet?"

"Only every day," I sighed in exasperation. "And he'll probably ask again after church." Ned was my wife's brother, and there's more sense in two pennies than there is in his head. I must have made him my deputy out of pity, 'cause he's sure not worth the aggravation that he gives me. Both Betty Sue and Mary Lou have dated Ned over the years. That's where their real source of competition lies; the bake-off is just the chosen field of battle.

The three of us downed our breakfast, cleared the table,

and quickly headed off to the First Baptist Church. As predicted, just when we were getting up from the service, Ned slid up to me like he always does before the contest with the same look on his face.

He likes to think he's being secretive... tiptoeing up with this constipated look on his face. Once, I even think I heard him whistling his own theme music.

"Pst," he said in falsetto, as if no one else could hear. Across the pew, I could see Spanky the barber smile. On Monday when I went in for a haircut, I just knew that all the boys would be laughing over Baymerry's own self-styled Romeo, and wanting to know all the details.

"What do you want, Ned?"

Ned looked at me funny. "What's wrong with you?"

I rolled my eyes. "Nothing."

He nodded, and then went back to looking constipated as we walked out the door. "Don't you think that Betty Sue's egg custard look's awful good today?"

I glanced across the street to the town square, where the two competitors were staring walleyed at each other as they set up the table.

"I thought that you were dating Mary Lou this week?"

His face fell. "She saw me carrying Betty Sue's groceries home Thursday, now she's not speaking to me."

"So you've moved on."

"Aw, she'll come around again."

"You're playing with fire Ned." One of these days, Ned was going to pick one girl and settled down. Then in six or seven months he'd be a daddy. He'd probably spend the rest of his life wishing he'd married the other girl, while the one he did marry turned into a shrew, and made his life a living hell.

At least my wife had the decency to get eaten and spare me that fate.

While the boy ran off to play with his zombie-killer GI Jacks, Aunt Martha got our own barbecue chicken lunch ready, and I set down at the gazebo with my napkin up under my bib, ready for some good ole-fashioned bake-off eats. Betty Sue's egg custard was every bit as good as Ned promised. But before I could try Mary Lou's Blackberry cobbler, Betty Sue tripped, spilling the rest of her dish into Mary Lou's.

Instantly, the band stopped playing. Conversations ground to a halt. Children froze in their steps. All eyes turned to

Mary Lou, whose face was turning purple.

"You did that on purpose!" She shouted in visceral rage.

"I'm sure I don't know what you're talking about." Betty Sue stuck her nose in the air. "Everyone can see that this was an accident."

"You cow!" Mary Lou threw herself at Betty Sue. They tumbled across the table, knocking over drinks and food.

"Fight!" The cry went up across the social, echoed dozens of times, and faded into a dull roar as townsfolk ran to see. Meanwhile, I ripped off my napkin, threw down my fork, and tried to get between those two. All I got for my trouble was scratched, clawed, and bit.

It seemed like things might've gone on like this for a while, except suddenly the screams of excitement from the back of the crowd melted into cries of terror.

"Zombie!" I heard someone yell, then another.

I stepped over the fighting girls, and ran up the church steps to where I could see. Sure enough, there were several zombies in the crowd, busily chewing on townspeople. I drew my gun, but there were too many decent folk in the way to fire on the godless.

I am proud to say that even though most town folk ran away in fear, a few rallied to fight the zombies with the only weapons that they had available: The food. Pies flew. Body parts flew. Zombies flew.

"Darn it!" I shouted over the confusion. "Who's on watch?" We keep sentries posted at the edge of town to alert people. It's Ned's responsibility to assign folk, and keep the schedule.

My answer came from the blank stares of the few townspeople who weren't either running or fighting. Apparently Ned forgot.

"Where's Ned?" My next question.

"I think I saw him running for the barbecue truck." Aunt Martha said as she shoved a lemon meringue into the face of an evil undead. "Right after Betty Sue and Mary Lou started fighting."

"This is no time for the munchies." I cocked back the hammer on my ole revolver. Before I could draw down on one of them undead flesh wagons, I heard the long, deep honk of a semi. I looked up in time to see the tanker pulling down the street at full-speed. Citizen and Zombie alike saw it too, and ran away, proving that even godless zombies aren't damn fool idiots.

As the truck drew near, I could see good ole, stupid Ned behind the wheel. He swerved at the last second, tipping the semi on its side. The tanker of precious barbecue burst open like an overripe egg on the side of a house – Not that I ever did any egging in my life, mind.

The barbecue didn't just spill out of the truck; it broke free in a tidal wave and rolled up the street. It was pandelerium! People, zombies and food were sucked in. Nothing was safe. By the time that wave ran out of steam, there was red stuff coating the buildings on Main Street plumb up to the second story. And there was Ned in the middle of it all, grinning like a possum.

"Ned," I sighed as I walked up to him, gun still drawn. "If I didn't need all my bullets for Zombies, I'd just shoot you right now."

Things settled down after that. The barbecue killed all the zombies, and neither Mary Lou nor Betty Sue are speaking with Ned. It's really for the best. We don't need no Romeo in Baymerry anyhow.

The commune even said that they'd deliver barbecue to us again, just as soon as we replace their tanker truck. We'll find one sooner or later, we ain't in no hurry. Ned still has a lot of barbecue to clean up on Main Street, and the smell keeps the Zombies away.

THE END

Tracy S. Morris lives with her fiancée and three ferrets in Fort Smith, Arkansas. Her hobbies include writing, fencing, gardening, martial arts, and thwarting the ferrets' escape attempts.

She has two short stories already in print, and a chapbook forthcoming from Yard Dog Press entitled *Medieval Misfits*.

As of this writing, she must go rescue a ferret from inside the couch (how in the world did it get in there?).

THE SIEGE AND INVESTITURE OF THE ATHENS BILMART

Mark W. Tiedemann

It began and ended with hygiene. This is not a tale of heroic gestures and profound moments, but of the saving of a small pocket of civilization. You have to keep that in mind.

The Academy stank, but in a different way from the rest of Athens, which had merely smelled bad for a long time.

Soccertease stood over the pot watching the sludge within cool and congeal into a paste the color of rice pudding. The odor of baking soda hung in the air, having nowhere else to go. The rest of us wore little paper masks, held in place by elastic bands and a little strip of aluminum that molded to your nose, but it didn't help much. Soccertease frowned into the pot, with a look of forthcoming disappointment.

She dipped a pinky finger into it, then held it up to the window to inspect the drop of goo by a shaft of sunlight. She nodded and turned to us.

"Al," she said.

"I did the last batch," I said at once. "It's Clint's turn."

She sighed. "Where is he?"

"I'll get him," I volunteered.

It's a trade off with Soccertease. It was largely a pleasure to be around her, but sometimes you had to do things for her that under ordinary circumstances you wouldn't do under threat of eternal discomfort. I used to want to hang around her because she's by far the nicest thing to look at in the whole of McMinn County. But that wears off in time and you have to have other reasons to want to be in a person's company.

I left reluctantly and eagerly. It's enough to make you trip over yourself, that combination. But I'd be damned if I'd try another one of her experiments in making toothpaste.

On my way I passed through the distribution hall, where folks came to deliver or obtain products of Academy manufacture or salvage. Three young women who by their clothes I guessed to be from the Revivalists across town were talking intently with a couple of our volunteers, Molly and Iris, jar of hand cream, several bars of soap, and a box of tampons between them. I continued on through.

Clint was in the main living room with the McNamin Twins, Pete and Repete, Stew Oxletter, who had one of his H & K's stripped down for cleaning, and Boyd Esterhouse, who was telling the story of when he got waylaid by a pair of female truckers.

"–a frickin' .357, I swear," Boyd was saying. "She drew the hammer back and said 'Now how 'bout you just drop them pants and show us what you got.' So–"

"Ah," Pete said, "I heard this before. I still say ain't no way I'd've gone along with it."

Boyd leaned toward him. "Come on, man, a woman holds a pistol in your face and says she wants you to screw her, you're tellin' me you'd resist?"

"Not a very friendly way to be," Repete said. "Was you inclined to say no before she pulled the gun?"

"Hadn't occurred to me one way or the other. After, though, it wouldn't have occurred to me to say no. I imagine most women feel that way when a man threatens 'em."

"Hell," Pete said. "Clint. What do you think? If a woman pulled a gun on you and ordered you to have sex with her, would you?"

Clint blinked large, owlish eyes and looked around at the others. He didn't seem to want to answer. "Well," he said finally, "I'm a-scared of guns."

"Clint," I said.

He looked relieved. "Al."

"Soccertease wants you."

He nodded and stood. "'Scuse me."

Clint was about six foot six and skinny as a mop handle. He covered the living room in four long strides and walked past me.

"Al–" Boyd began.

"Gotta go," I said quickly. Between Boyd's tall tales and Soccertease's experiments, the choice was clear. I followed Clint into the kitchen.

Soccertease had a slab of the new mixture on a cake pan, smoothing it out with a knife. She smiled at Clint. I thought he'd float off the floor at that. No question she had a willing volunteer.

"Batch number thirty-nine," she said and picked up a bright blue toothbrush from the counter. She dunked it in a glass of water and brushed a dollop of the paste onto the bristles. She held it out, handle-first, to Clint.

Clint heaved a significant sigh and accepted the brush. With a reverent look at Soccertease, he inserted the brush into his mouth and began scrubbing.

For more than a minute the only sound in the kitchen was the rasp of the toothbrush over Clint's mouthful of tarnished teeth. His eyes slowly drifted from one side to the next, then up. For a few seconds his head bobbed, as if he were listening to a tune in his head.

Then he pulled the brush out. The end was hidden in a thick mass of bubbly yellow froth. He stared at it, a thin line of milky spittle running over his lower lip.

"That's awful," he said awkwardly, trying not to spit. He handed the brush back to Soccertease. "I'm sorry."

Soccertease handed him a glass of water and pointed to the sink. Clint dutifully took the glass and crossed the kitchen. He swished water in his mouth noisily and spat.

"Uck," he said.

Soccertease stared at the sludge. "Shit."

I sighed. "I'm telling you, it's the baking soda. Stuff's old, it's absorbed god knows how many different odors...how many tubes we got left from the last scavenge?"

"Thirty," she said. "Give or take." She scratched her chin thoughtfully. "Maybe some more ginger..."

What can you say about a person like that, who never gives up? Thirty-nine attempts, thirty-nine failures, and what does she say? Maybe some more ginger. We tried mint, but we didn't have much of it, so we moved from flavor to flavor. The curry one wasn't as bad as it sounds, but it still didn't work. But that's all right, we'll try more ginger. We can do this. This can work.

Sure.

And maybe one of these days one of us is going to fall over dead from one of her experiments. But what the hell. It's not like there's much choice. In fact, there's three choices: Soccertease, oblivion, or the Reverend. Most of us see oblivion and the Reverend as pretty much the same thing, so we only got two choices.

But who am I kidding? No one's going to fall over dead

from experimental toothpaste–anymore than a female might actually waste even the threat of a bullet on Boyd Esterhouse for his body. The risk is minimal. But most of us would take it anyway.

As I watched her scrape the layer of sludge from the cake pan back into the pot, I wondered that anybody could hate Soccertease. She works her butt off for Athens. I wonder why sometimes, but I don't question it too closely. Centipede's legs and all that.

She put the lid on the pot, grabbed the handle, and headed for the back door. I followed her outside.

She went out to the incinerator and emptied the pot into the pan at the base. It already contained the sludge of five previous attempts and I wondered how much she intended to load into it before she lit the fire and burned it off.

Not this time, at least. She pushed the pan back into the barrel innards of the incinerator and came plodding back to the steps. She dropped the pot and sat down.

"Toothpaste, Al."

"Uh huh."

"Imagine," she said. "Since the Disaster, all the things we've managed to accomplish. Right off the bat, we kept people fed."

"Food's important."

"We organized a fire department, assembled a clothing manufacturing group, and learned how to make soap."

"Vast improvements," I agreed.

"Our salvage operations have secured most of the essentials of a civilized life." She nodded toward the row of trailers and sheds stretching along the back of the property. "Athens is shaping up into a town again. A village, at least. People aren't as worried, they're healthier, and the smell is down."

"All in all quite a record of success."

"But toothpaste has me stumped. It shouldn't be that damn hard!"

"Did you ever do it before?"

"No."

"Well."

She glared at me.

I looked away. From the back porch you could look across an expanse of slightly rippled field to a row of dogwoods lined up along the creek that runs through this part of Athens. It didn't used to be a creek, but a sewer line. It fell in a couple years back. For a while it smelled worse than the toothpaste experiments. Several heavy rains and lots of pesky drizzles had pretty well flushed out the worst of it and now it just had a kind of humid musky smell.

To the left was a row of trailers, mostly singles, but three or four doublewides, all the way up to the old highway. Most of them were storage, but some were residences for staff and visitors. The Academy had come a long way from the first days of the Disaster.

Soccertease has owned the place for a long time, since before the so-called feces hit the turbulator. Back then she was Helen Knox—well, she still is, but nobody calls her that anymore, except the Reverend, and he only calls her that when he isn't calling her something else. For my money, worthless as it may be, Helen is about the smartest person in McMinn County. She went to a university back East. Doesn't matter which one—after everything went to hell, nobody around here really believed there'd ever been more than one—only that she went. Why she came back to Athens is anybody's guess—she claims it was for the barbeque. She didn't finish her degree. "Just paper," she says when we talk about it. "I got the important part," she adds, tapping the side of her head, "up here."

Things got controversial when she bought this old B & B and converted it into a daycare. That's when the Reverend got involved.

It's kind of vague these days what exactly a daycare was, since the only folks who ever used one are either dead or absent. The gist of it was that she ran a place where people who didn't have time for them could drop their kids off to be watched over by someone who did have time. Soccertease didn't have any kids, so she had time. Always struck me odd, that. The folks who only had one or two, three at the most, all their own, didn't have the time for them, but Soccertease who didn't have any, had time for about thirty or forty. With a little help, of course, but still.

This brought the Reverend out in full voice.

The Reverend. Yeah. Reverend Ira MacInaw Rychess. The Reverend was an institution around McMinn County before the Disaster. He's the last of the marrow faithful, muscle and nerve, utterly committed, fire-breathing, tongue-talking sawdust-in-a-renovated-theater preachers, and for years he held forth damnation and revelation in the old Astoria Movie House in downtown Athens, where he still is, leading the Revivalists that flocked around his voice the way dust and small rocks flock around the sun. The comparison is apt–get too close to either one, you'll get fried. One time he had a second place in Etowah, but after the Disaster and the decrease in population, he didn't need two anymore.

There were other preachers, certainly, but the Reverend had them all beat for showmanship and box office draw. At one time he sold personalized Bibles over the radio, complete with a pamphlet explaining how to read it (if you must) and offering his interpretation of the Final Days, and a membership in his ministry that came with a discount on tuition to his correspondence course in the ministry, all for the reasonable price of $98.99, unless you wished to have at minimal extra charge a pocket Psalms, a subscription to his Newsletter, and offer a contribution to his ministry's support of the Natural Law Party candidate for Congress (his brother, I believe), plus First-Class Postal Delivery and Handling, adding about seventy dollars to the base price, bringing it up to $168.99, or, as he was proud to point out, fifty dollars less than a similar package offered out of Oklahoma. He'd just managed to get a television spot when all hell broke loose and Civilization threatened to collapse right in our own front yard.

It was tragic for the Reverend. His wife had been handling all the office work for the ministry and spent a good ten hours a day in front of a computer, so she went and turned into a Yumbie right off and had to be put down.

Everyone thought the Reverend was going to end his own life, but he pulled through. Sometimes it seems like things would've been simpler if he had followed Bernice, but at the time we thought we needed every sound thinker, level head, and functioning organizer we could find. The Reverend was certainly the last one, but since has come to seem a bit lacking in the other two.

But that's a matter of opinion. Depends who you support.

When it comes right down to it, the Reverend and Soccertease just didn't hit it off. Their mutual animosity survived the Disaster, but it had been a while since I heard from him. Last time was when Helen Knox acquired her nickname.

The Reverend was against the daycare. He was against it on general principle. He was against it on moral grounds. He was against it because the people who never paid him a seconds' attention were for it. He was against it because the people who hung on his every word liked being against things they didn't understand. But mainly he was against it because Soccertease was running it.

Helen Knox was a single woman who'd been to a university Back East, didn't have any children, attended no church, and voted Democratic in the last election before the Disaster. Any one of those was enough to make her suspect in the eyes of the Reverend, but all of them taken together, she became a minion of the Beast, an agent of Satan, the walking talking breathing exemplar of All That Is Wrong With The World.

Quite a burden, and Soccertease was quite capable of shouldering it.

But the last straw was those jerseys.

Right before the Disaster she tried to get up a junior soccer league. She ordered a bunch of jerseys from this company in Chicago, but they sent the wrong sizes. Best I can tell, they went the wrong way on the chart, and instead jerseys for four-year-olds they sent her jerseys for fourteen-year-olds. A couple of them were large enough for a running back. Before she could return them, the Disaster struck and the daycare failed.

She adapted. A week later, she reopened the place as a first-aid/soup kitchen/town meeting hall (on account of the civic auditorium burned down and the mayor had turned Yumbie and was hole up in his offices with his staff) so on and so forth. The way she figured it, getting people organized and centered was the quickest way to avoid the worst parts of the chaos. She got everybody involved through one of the time-honored institutions of the warm and friendly South–a bake sale.

She had a dozen women volunteer to cook. A big affair. Some folks wanted to be staff and Soccertease handed out those jerseys as a kind of uniform.

Helen's was kind of tight.

She's got the kind of body that looks, well, damn good in tight clothes.

And she chose number 69.

The Reverend had a fit. Called her a succubus, a seductress, a tease.

Thus are timeless labels applied. Within a week Helen was Soccertease.

Turned out not to be such a bad title, though. She had us organized in no time and the B&B/nursery–which is now the Academy–became the locus of the Athens Recovery Committee. Us. And little by little she's been seeing us back to a semblance of civilization.

Things smell a hell of a lot better around here, I'll tell you that.

We make soap here. We use six of the trailers as storage for all the salvage. She concocted a pretty good antiseptic and we got every roll of toilet paper we could find in all the WalMarts, K-Marts, Tar-jays, QuickieStops, and so on, and she's been working on a way of making more. The kitchen runs 24 hours a day and she organized hunting parties that act as part time police and she's been helping a few eager souls in figuring out how to do agriculture for a whole village. My word, there's nothing Soccertease hasn't been able to do.

Till now.

"There's only about thirty tubes of toothpaste left in the stores," I said.

"And about fifty boxes of baking soda," she said.

"Is that important?"

"Every formula I ever saw to make toothpaste is baking soda and something else."

"It's the something else that's got you stumped."

"I've been trying to come up with a baking soda and soap formula, but nobody wants it."

"It tastes terrible."

She looked off in the distance. "Maybe a little ginger..."

"Or peppermint. I always liked the peppermint flavor."

"Where are we going to get peppermint?"

"Well, mint grows hereabouts."

"Mm."

"Charlie Pelberry has a stock of peppermint schnapps."

She laughed. "I doubt he could be persuaded to give it up in the name of oral hygiene." Then she shook her head again and got all sad. "I don't understand what's so damn hard about... toothpaste."

"I still say it's the baking soda. We used to use it to absorb bad odors in the refrigerator. Long as those boxes been around, they probably absorbed all the bad tastes, too."

"That doesn't make any sense. I think I'm still missing a key ingredient." She shook her head. "If I only had access to the internet! You could find everything on the web."

I kept silent for a time. Nobody likes talking about what we don't have anymore, and nobody especially likes talking about anything to do with computers. Far as we know, they caused all our problems.

"Well," I said finally, "one way or the other, we're gonna need a new supply."

She nodded like she was only half listening. I went down to one of the storage trailers to check on what exactly we had left. It's amazing to me sometimes what gets forgotten. Out of all the survivors we've gathered together, we have a talent pool capable of miraculous things. It's incredible what these people know how make. But not a-one knows how to make toothpaste.

It's not like the disappearance of toothpaste was a minor inconvenience. Part of the troubles following the Disaster bore directly on fresh breath. Cleanliness in general, really, but breath became a mission. Yumbies, it turned out, have very distinctive breath. But it takes a while and several exposures to recognize it just right. By then, you might be dead. Problem was, all of us smelled about as bad only different. I mean, it ain't like we all loved brushing after we ate, and when civilization fell in the cess pit, well, it seemed like other things were more important than oral hygiene. Shutting down our own bad smells proved to be a survival tactic.

The level of miasmic stench from combined B.O. and halitosis rose from a thin ground cover to a rooftop level fog in a matter of a few months. After that, it seemed like a not bad thing, since it kind of kept certain feuds at a safe low—hard to get close enough to have it out with your neighbor when they smelled worse than you.

But then we got used to it. You do, you know.

It occurred to Soccertease that this was a serious chink in our armor.

After the chaos settled and we took a look around at what we had, it seemed Athens had survived pretty much intact. I mean, we lost a good three quarters of the population, but no one we could really do without except some doctors. But most of us left behind didn't go to the doctor often anyway and what with Old Beulah as midwife and a couple of EMT folks who stuck around with their heads intact, we figured we had it pretty good.

The Yumbies were a problem, though. About two months after the people who had family somewhere else left and the survivalists scattered into the hills and the New Agers headed for New Mexico for the Second Harmonic Convergence and the militia reported for duty and various other folks who thought they could now afford to live in big cities on account of real estate falling through the floor and the criminals who were smart enough to realize that they might not even get to a court room next time–after all those people left and we tried coping with the remnant, some people started turning weird. They weren't manageable. Violent, flesh-hungry, like something out of a bad movie I saw once.

And a lot of them were living right here!

A lot of carnage occurred before we figure it out. But after that, with what population we had left, we set up perimeters and trained people to recognize Yumbies, and sorted out the ones who would shoot from those who wouldn't (that came as a surprise, frankly, to find out how many people just can't pull the trigger), then all we had to worry over was the stray singles or occasional packs of Yumbies infiltrating.

You'd think this would be easy. You see someone lurching down the street in a threadbare Bill Blass suit carrying a briefcase, a laptop, and a liberated Uzi or an axe, eyes that never blink, and drool running down their chins, you ought to think right off: YUMBIE. And you do. If you see them that far away. Trouble is, some of them are actually clever, and they're quiet. I mean, like, they don't seem hardly to breathe. They walk like ninjas, soundless, and can be on your ass before you realize it.

Because they got no presence.

I mean, you can tell more often than not when someone else is nearby. Unless, of course, you're so absorbed in what you're doing that you wouldn't notice the Apocalypse if it started up around the block. But you can tell. You get this kind of idea or something distracts you and you look around and there's this person. Soccertease says it's because everyone has a Self they carry around with them and it kind of broadcasts, like a cold front, and you feel it. They have

Presence.

Not Yumbies. Nothing. It's like whatever life force they had was sucked inside their skin and spread out like butter that just evaporated in the hot sun.

Of course, if Soccertease is right, it ain't a wonder. Whatever life force they had in the first place they gave over to a computer screen in endless hours of worship. Now there ain't no more computers to speak of, so what are they gonna do? Nothing to connect to anymore, the emanations had to go somewhere, and Soccertease figures it just turned on itself and blew their minds.

That doesn't quite explain the cannibalism, though.

Anyway, Soccertease realized pretty quick that Yumbie's did have one thing that gave them away: bad breath. So bad, they didn't even have to breathe for it to knock you off your feet. Assuming, that is, that you weren't already dead in the nose from your own odors.

Therefore, she said, the best way to defend ourselves from Yumbie invasion was to get cleaned up. Especially our teeth.

But who the hell ever grew up knowing how to make toothpaste? Not even Soccertease actually knew what it was made of. It wasn't one of the basic questions you ask when you get old enough to ask basic questions. The ingredients on the boxes didn't help—we didn't have any of those polysyllabic, lab designed, quasi-organic substances. There had to've been simpler ingredients, since people have been making toothpaste for a long time, long before the argon changed. Anybody who might have known had left. We had a couple of former paramedics who acted as the local doctors, but they didn't know how to make it. I mean, toothpaste!

And even if we could make it, how in hell do you get it into the tubes?

I was about to suggest something when the back door slammed open.

"Bill Stimson's here!"

I craned my neck to look behind me and there was Clint, leaning way over, so far that if he let go of the railing he'd fall on top of us.

"Bill Stimson," I said. "I thought he'd left."

"No, he's here," Clint said. "I mean, maybe he left before, but he's back now. I don't know from where."

"Okay," Soccertease said, standing. "What does he want?"

"His life saved, I figure," Clint said. "He's got a bullet hole right through him." Clint blinked and looked at me. "I'm a-scared of guns."

Soccertease passed right through Clint–that's what it looked like anyway–and into the house. I pushed Clint back through the door until there was room to get around him–of course, with Clint there's never quite enough room to get around him–and hurried after her.

Pete and Repete were leaning over the utterly filthy, beat-to-bloody-pulp form of Bill Stimson, lying on the living room floor. They had his shirt ripped open and peeled back from an ugly wound just below his right collarbone, and were nodding and frowning, looking very sagacious.

"Thirty-aught-six," Pete said.

"Bullshit," Repete said. "Thirty-thirty."

Pete scowled. "Lookit the entry wound! No thirty-thirty makes a hole that petite, you–"

Soccertease straddled Bill between the two brothers and pushed them away. She studied the wound carefully, pushing on the skin around it. A little blood trickled out. She looked at me.

"Cole and Della around?" she asked. They were our best paramedics.

"Crissy Dunhurley's in labor," I said. "They're way the hell and gone over to her farm."

"Leo?"

"Went fishing."

She gave me a look.

"I'm not kidding," I said. "And Bobby Ann and Malcolm are with the search party looking for the Tyree's little boy in the north wood. We're it."

Stew Oxletter let out a curse under his breath, picked up his M-1 carbine, and began breaking it down to clean.

"Kit," Soccertease said.

"Right," I said and ran into the infirmary.

I brought the first aid kit, then went into the kitchen to boil some water. Soccertease worked on Bill Stimson for a good half an hour.

When she walked away from him, there was blood on her arms and splattered on her shirt. She told Boyd Esterhouse and Clint to carry him upstairs to one of the rooms and put him to bed.

"Not as bad as it looks," she said. "Not even a day old. Infection hasn't set it. He'll live." She looked around at the gathered group–me, the McNamin Twins, Molly Stackbridge and Iris Suter, the dayshift cooks, and a couple others. "Anybody have any idea where he's been? None of the patrols reported shooting at anybody, did they?"

We all exchanged looks, as if to verify that we hadn't seen or known anything we already said we hadn't or didn't.

"Far as anybody knows," Iris said, "Bill took off for parts unknown after his brother got eaten by a gang of Yumbies. That was what? About a year ago?"

Soccertease sighed. "Who found him?"

Pete and Repete raised their hands. "Didn't," Pete said.

"He crawled up on the front porch," Repete said.

"Heard him groaning," Pete finished.

"Well," Soccertease said, "there's likely a blood trail, then. Let's see if we can track it."

About half a mile away it got easier. Bill Stimson had left a patch of blood on the fence post at the street and we spotted some recent footprints in the dried mud a short distance south. We figured he'd come north, then, so we just kept going till we found more signs.

Pete picked up the trail of blood spatters. They weren't much bigger than pennies for about a mile, then they came closer together, and then got a little bigger.

But then they led off into an overgrown patch of ground around the old railroad line.

"What's over there?" Soccertease asked, pointing at the twisted remains of an old barbed-wire fence.

"Railroad property," Pete said.

"Private," Repete said.

"No trespassing," Pete said.

Soccertease gave them both a withering look and strode across the track, through armpit high stands of grass and weeds. She reached the wire and peered into the thicket of trees on the other side, then looked back at us.

"Well?"

We plowed through the bug-laden growth till we got to her, whereupon she stepped over a section of the fence that had obviously been knocked flat.

About thirty yards past the line of trees was a stretch of road lined with old conveniences–a couple of gas stations, a burned out QuickieStop, and a Mexican restaurant called La Haciendita. A strip mall ran down the other side of the street, but all the stores had long ago been stripped bare, and not even a legible sign was left.

The blood trail ran across to the restaurant around back.

Behind La Haciendita was more parking lot, edged by a couple of big trash bins and a delivery truck with no tires from Shelby's Floral Shop. Behind the truck, the ground sloped down to an anemic creek bed choked with garbage and discarded appliances that meandered off into fairly thick new growth. A good hundred yards east we could see the old highway above. A storm sewer ran underneath.

We lost the trail then, but it seemed to me to be heading off south. But it wouldn't make sense, Bill Stimson coming from there. Nothing in that direction but a couple of recluses, a private farm or two, and Rog Jaycox. The storm sewer seemed easier to check out anyway.

When we emerged out the other side, the creek widened, though it was still pretty dry. Maybe thirty yards further along, Soccertease gestured up the slope.

We came to the edge of a big parking lot. On the far side was a sprawling building supporting a burned-out neon sign: BILMART!

"What the hell's a BilMart?" I asked.

Then we saw the people. Just a few, drifting out of the multi-door entrance, and ducking back inside.

I pulled out my binoculars.

"Well, I'll be–"

Soccertease snatched them and looked.

"The Reverend," she said.

She handed me the binoculars and through eight-power magnification I recognized Trudy Semple standing just in the shade of the doors. Trudy was the Reverend's new secretary– well, new since Bernice had to be put down.

There'd been rumors about Trudy and the Reverend from before the Disaster, but somehow none of them ever stuck around long enough to become a scandal. Looking at her now, I had to wonder. Trudy was what you'd call Solid. Through and through. Like a brick. Maybe that's a good way to think of her. Without Trudy, I'm sure the Reverend would have melted down into a slag pool of unrecoverable self-pity after Bernice died. Some folks think Trudy runs the whole show anyway, except for writing the sermons. She doesn't talk much.

"BilMart," I said. "You don't suppose...?"

"Let's get back to the Academy and find out," Soccertease said.

Boyd met us on the front porch. "He woke up for a minute," he said, "then passed out again."

Word had gotten out and a few more staff regulars lounged in the living room. Stew Oxletter was cleaning his glock on the coffee table. Clint watched him with large eyes, gnawing gingerly on his lower lip.

"Al," Soccertease said, "bring the kit."

I grabbed the first aid box and bounded up the stairs after her.

Bill Stimson lay under a sheet on the bed in the pink room, looking a bit gray, his shoulder bandaged up as pretty as if it were in a movie. Soccertease stared at him a while, then gestured for the kit. She rummaged around in it till she found the smelling salts.

It took two whiffs for Bill to come around.

"Sorry to bother you," Soccertease said. "But we'd like to know how you got shot."

He moaned. "I feel like hell."

"No, that's how you look. How you feel is grateful."

"For what?"

"Me. Saving your life."

"Is that what you did?" His eyes drifted from side to side, taking in the room. "I wondered."

"Who shot you?"

"I don't know."

"Okay," she said, sitting on the edge of the bed. "Tell me this, then. What's a BilMart?"

About a thousand things must've gone through his mind. You could see them, flickering over his face, like a kid caught in a fib, stealing and trying to get out of it. Then he closed his eyes and let out a long, mournful sigh.

"Shit," he said.

"That's an attitude, not an answer."

"Where you been, Bill?" I asked. "We thought you were dead."

"No, I wasn't dead."

"Almost, though."

He nodded slowly. "That's a fact."

"So who shot you?"

He narrowed his eyes at us. "Specifically, or in a general sense?"

Soccertease rolled her eyes. "Do you know why you were shot?"

Bill shifted and winced. "Well, I suppose. They took my business away."

"'They'?"

"The Reverend and all them sanctimonious morons he's got thinking the final days are upon us."

"Reverend Rychess?" Soccertease pressed.

"Is there another Reverend?"

"Probably, but he's the one we're concerned with, right?" Bill nodded.

"Excuse me," I said, "but what do you mean, your business?"

Again, he narrowed his eyes, as if weighing the choices he had. There weren't many, since we already saw the BilMart, and it didn't take a vast intellect to figure this was the Bill part lying before us.

"You saw it?" he asked finally. We nodded and he nodded. "My business. The Athens BilMart. Been working on it since the Disaster."

"Working on it how?"

He gave a cocky grin. "Same as you," he said to Soccertease. "Scavenging and scrounging. Stealing."

"Hey–" I began.

"Well, it was, wasn't it?" he demanded. "Not that I particularly have a problem with it, mind you. I mean, who were any of us gonna buy anything from? It was all just gonna rot. Might as well help ourselves. But then you crossed the line."

Soccertease appeared to be trying hard not to smile. She folded her arms across her chest and tilted her head to one side. "What line?"

"You stopped being an American."

I got to say, she didn't laugh. "How do you figure that?" she asked.

"You're a goddamn communist."

Then she laughed.

"You think it's funny," Bill said, a bit too strenuously. He screwed up his face from pain and we had to wait till he could breathe right before he continued. "You're just giving shit away."

"So?" I asked.

"Come on, Al, use your head! This country was made great because of what?" When I shook me head and shrugged, thinking perhaps about people and reasonable laws and libraries and things like that, he turned all red in the face. "Idiot! Free enterprise! That's what made America great!" He shot Soccertease a furious look. "And it won't be great again till we reestablish it. Free enterprise."

Silence prolonged. Bill looked pale.

Finally Soccertease sighed. "Bill, there's no money."

"And why is that?"

"Because all the systems that made money viable are gone. All we have is barter."

"There you got it wrong! Money is just a medium of exchange, and its value is based on the availability of stuff."

"Stuff."

"Stuff! Goods and such."

"Sure, but–"

"But if you make everything freely available for no return, then you continually subvert any basis for value. Money can't become worth anything because everything is worth nothing."

"So," Soccertease began.

"You see–"

She held up a hand and Bill stopped. "My turn," she said. "So you've been gathering up stuff for the last year or so to keep it unavailable until there was evident and acute shortages."

Bill nodded.

"Then what?"

"I found an old mimeograph machine, with a hand crank. I made up a couple thousand hand bills I planned to distribute announcing the grand opening of the new Athens BilMart."

"You were going to open a store."

"That's right."

"And sell what you'd stockpiled."

"That's right."

"For what?"

"You know, I gave that a lot of thought."

"Like everything else," I said.

Bill just nodded again. "I suppose you mean, what did I intend to charge people? Well, in a free enterprise system, the market should set the price, don't you think? So I figured the first month or so, I'd let people bid."

"With what?" Soccertease asked, her patience fraying just a bit.

"Why, dollars, of course. Whatever they may have."

"And if they don't have any? I mean, maybe a few folks have some cash laying around as a keepsake, but–"

"No problem." He tapped the side of his head and winked. "I got four hundred and seventy-eight thousand dollars stocked up. You ain't got the cash, I'll loan it to you."

"Loan."

"At two percent interest."

"Interest. Where are folks supposed to get the extra cash to pay the interest?"

"Same way I did."

"Steal it."

Bill held up his hand as if to say, "Of course." He looked right pleased with himself.

"Just why would anybody bother to pay you back?" Soccertease asked. "I mean, they 'borrow' your money, use it to buy your goods, and then walk off with whatever they need and not come back."

"I'm limiting what each person can buy. I ain't financing a competitor."

"Isn't competition the backbone and liver of free enterprise?" I asked. "Sounds fascist, to me."

Soccertease flashed me a grin.

"I ain't stopping nobody else from doing exactly what I done. I just don't have to help them."

"Even so," Soccertease said, "they can always come back and borrow more and buy more."

"Well, there's a time limit."

"And when you tell them no, what happens if they come back with a gun and just take it?"

Bill scowled, looking embarrassed. His eyes fluttered.

"Or," Soccertease continued, "is that what happened first? I'll bet you went to the Reverend with your announcement first, didn't you?"

"Well, his folks ain't been dealing with you! Reverend

Rychess forbids them to. They'd be an ideal market."

"Except they marched in and tossed you out and took it."

"Well...yeah. Look, I ain't feelin' so good..."

I sighed. "You know, Bill, I thought I'd met all the stupid people in the world, but..."

"We got to stop this inexorable slide into socialism!"

Neither of us could help it. We laughed. Sometimes it's all you can do.

"No offense, Bill," I said finally, "but I really don't think many people would bother to come to your store. Not when they can do their own scrounging and not when they can get what they need through Academy programs."

Bill looked annoyed. "There's always going to be things people can't get on their own. There's always going to be stuff you can't provide 'em."

"Yeah? Like what?"

"Well...I hear you're in a bit of a bind over toothpaste."

The temperature in the pink room dropped noticeably.

"What do you know about that?" Soccertease asked quietly.

"Just that supplies are running low." He looked toward the window, puckering his lips. "I got about four thousand tubes of Colgate in my store."

"We'll be making our own before we run out," I said

"Huh," he grunted.

That grunt was a mistake. Later on it came back to haunt him.

I followed Soccertease back downstairs. She stood at the entrance to the kitchen, hands on hips, a deep-thought kind of look on her face. Then she walked out the back door and headed for the trailers.

I hurried to catch up. She opened the door into one of the doublewide storage trailers and stepped in. Near the front end we kept the baking soda stored. She grabbed a couple of boxes and brought them out into daylight. She sat down and began studying the boxes carefully.

"Ah. There."

She pointed and I looked at the box. Just below the top lid was a tiny puncture. She picked up the other one and studied it. "This one isn't so obvious," she said, "but the flap is slightly raised along here." She dropped the box and looked at me. "He's been sabotaging us."

"Bill Stimson?"

"We don't post guards here," she said. "Not anymore. Not enough patrols to go around. Besides, who the hell would conceive a plan to sneak into our supplies and poison the well? Who would do something to our baking soda supply that would render it useless for making toothpaste?"

"A capitalist?"

"Shit."

"What do you think he's been putting in it?"

Soccertease picked a box up. "I don't know. You just have to add something that'd make it taste terrible. Quinine, maybe. Turpentine. Epicac? Wouldn't discolor it."

"So he corners the market on toothpaste and guarantees we don't make our own."

"The man's a born CEO."

I blew out a breath. "So now what?"

"We need to get that toothpaste. Or a new supply of baking soda. Frankly, I wouldn't be surprised if he's got all the baking soda we didn't find stockpiled in that building." She grunted. "I used to wonder why we'd find so many bare shelves in so many stores. I always figured it was people who got there before us, stocking up to ride out the trouble or leave. I would never have thought..."

She stood.

"He said the Reverend forbids his people from dealing with us," she said.

"Yeah, but they do. I seen some Revivalists here this morning."

"Get ahold of Rog Jaycox," she said. "I have a mission for him and his boys."

I went back inside and asked around. Stew Oxletter blinked at me a few times, then started working on a Ruger .44. Pete and Repete said they knew where Rog was, and went off to find him. When I went back outside, Soccertease was talking to Clint. He nodded slowly and plodded off to the trailer where all the sabotaged baking soda was stored.

I told her I'd sent the twins to get Rog, then asked her what she had in mind.

"I'm still thinking," she said. "You know, that's an impressive piece of work Bill Stimson pulled off. He's been hauling salvage back here for a year without anybody seeing him. How do you think he managed that?"

"Lot's of parts around here kind of went all wild again. We

ain't got but a tenth of our old population."

"Mmm."

"You think it's something else?"

"What was that building originally? Do you remember?"

I pondered that for a bit. "Hey, wasn't that the old Prep Shop auto parts and repair place? The one that never seemed to have anybody in it?"

She blinked at me. "The one nobody could figure out how it stayed in business. Yeah."

"There were rumors I heard before the Disaster that it was a chop shop."

"I heard those, too, but nothing was ever proven. No one ever saw any stolen vehicles go in or leave..."

"And it was right by the rail line."

She got a far off look in her eyes, then, and the conversation ended. I wandered back to the trailer.

Clint was bringing out armloads of baking soda boxes.

"She told me to put 'em all in a cart," he said.

"How much is left?"

"Oh, looks like maybe fifty, sixty boxes. What's she gonna do with it all?"

"Ask her."

"I did. She just smiled."

"I hate it when she does that."

Clint got a goofy look. "I don't."

Half hour later, Pete and Repete came into the yard with Rog Jaycox and his three sons. No one knew the boys' names. Rog only ever introduced them as "My sons" and left it at that. The boys never spoke to anyone but their father, and he generally spoke to no one that didn't have business with him. At times I suspected him of being a Yumbie, but I never caught word of him eating anybody. He was just a loner, pure and simple, and a disturbing one at that.

Rog cradled a camouflaged 30-30 in the crook of his left arm. Dangling in a somehow elegant assemblage from his lanky frame were various pouches, belts, and form fitted cases containing a wide array of tools essential for engaging a well-armed mechanized force in any terrain with some degree of certainty for victory. Rog was a walking arsenal. Binoculars, night vision goggles, field rations, a gps (those damn satellites were still there and if you could find a gps locator with a working battery, you could still use them), three or four knives, two .10mm Barettas, ammunition, smoke bombs, walkie-talkie, and other devices of which I have only the merest understanding and a lack of sufficient vocabulary. His boys were similarly arrayed and every time I saw any of them I suffered profound embarrassment and paranoia for my own unequipped, near naked, and distinctly unprepared self.

Fortunately they weren't around often.

Rog lived somewhere well outside town and had three or four generators and a reservoir of gasoline with which he kept batteries charged and radios working and I've heard he is in contact with others of his sort over the entire world. This may be what the UN has come to in these limited days.

Soccertease walked off with him a bit and they spoke intently for several minutes. As I watched, Rog nodded and handed Soccertease a walkie-talkie. Much to my amazement–Rog never loans out any of his equipment. Finally, he waved to his boys, and they all left.

Soccertease paced up and down for a time. I went back inside the Academy, not sure what to do.

Boyd was telling Clint another story. Clint look scared to death. Finding no chance of less confusion, I wandered back outside.

After an hour, Soccertease waved at me.

"Al," she called.

"Where are we going?"

"To talk to Reverend Rychess," she said, walking toward the Academy.

"Well, he won't talk to you."

"I know."

I started after her. "Then what are you going to do?"

"Talk to him."

"But he won't."

"Trudy will."

"No she won't."

"Yes, she will."

Soccertease hit the street and started heading back toward the BilMart. I could do nothing but tag along.

We came out of the creek bed and up onto the tarmac without slowing down and before we got halfway to the front door of the BilMart, a crowd of the Reverend's followers had come out to watch.

Trudy Semple pushed her way to the head of the crowd

and I saw right off that she was in no mood.

Of course, she never was. I can't recall ever seeing Trudy Semple in a mood–for anything. I saw her at a picnic once and you'd have thought she was the chief bull in charge of a prison exercise yard.

Soccertease stopped and waited for Trudy to approach.

Trudy had a .44 strapped onto her utilitarian hips. I counted a solid fifteen hunting rifles of various calibers behind her in the hands of committedly self-righteous followers. Was I worried? Does a squirrel hide his nuts?

"Trudy," Soccertease said.

"Whore of Babylon," Trudy snapped back.

I guess she couldn't help it. Soccertease laughed. I felt a chuckle tickling me just behind the throat, but I held onto it, eyeballing all those guns to remind myself of the serious nature of this meeting.

Soccertease wound down, shaking her head. "Trudy, if you knew how long it's been..." She cleared her throat. "That's beside the point. We have a problem to discuss."

"I have no problem," Trudy said.

"Ah, but you do. You're occupying stolen property."

This time Trudy laughed. An ugly sound, like a sore throat in a thunderstorm, as if she hadn't done it in so long the particular section of her anatomy that would normally laugh had rusted up. I half expected to see brown dust puff out of her mouth and nose.

"That's rich!" she said finally. She jerked a thumb back over her shoulder, toward the BilMart. "You know where that came from?"

Soccertease shrugged. "Does it matter? You shot Bill Stimson and took it from him."

Trudy's mood shifted again. Her face started to darken. "I did what?"

"We've got him all patched up at the Academy. I want to speak to the Reverend, Trudy."

"He ain't receiving."

"When did that change? He's been receiving something ever since I can remember."

"Just tell me what you want. I'll see he gets the message."

"We came for the toothpaste."

Trudy blinked. Slowly, as if stunned. "Toothpaste "

"We'll accept baking soda as well."

Trudy stabbed the air with a finger. "You want toothpaste, you have to come to services."

Now Soccertease blinked, slowly. But the effect was totally different–she didn't look stunned, she looked thoughtful. She looked past Trudy toward the BilMart.

"You've moved the mission?" she asked.

"The Astoria's roof is shot," Trudy said. "This is the only place we found acceptable."

"I see. So if we want anything from here–"

"You must repent!"

"We still have this little problem of who shot Bill Stimson. If you were willing to do that, what's to say you won't kill the lot of us when we show up to pray?"

Trudy looked at me and back at Soccertease. "We didn't shoot you when you came in here just now, did we?"

"No. But then I guess I'm safe enough. Who'd be your new Whore of Babylon if I died?" Soccertease shook her head. "Let's try something else. Trade?"

"What would you have that we'd want?"

"I'm sure we've got something."

Trudy sucked in a couple stout lungfuls of air, drew herself up to her full five feet and four inches of height, and glared profoundly at Soccertease.

"All we want from you," she intoned, with a trembling voice that the Reverend himself would have coveted on a packed Sunday morning, "is repentance! All we want from you is submission! All we want from you is that you acknowledge the word and abase yourself to the truth!"

Soccertease didn't flinch. She waited till Trudy was done. Everyone on the parking lot was quiet.

The walkie-talkie in her hand crackled.

"Excuse me, Trudy," Soccertease said, "I have a call."

The look on Trudy's face was almost worth the worry. Her eyes widened and she stared at Soccertease as if all her clothes had suddenly and inexplicably vanished. Soccertease walked off several feet and you could hear her speak, but not what she said.

She turned then and came back.

"I think we do have something you want," she said. She leaned close to Trudy's ear and whispered.

Trudy went pale.

"I'll need to consult," Trudy said.

"Go right ahead."

Trudy turned around and headed through the gathered crowd. She got nearly to the door of the BilMart, then stopped. Her head bowed and her shoulders slumped. She did an about-face and came right back.

"He'd never understand," she said. "You have a deal."

Soccertease extended a hand. Reluctantly, Trudy took it and they shook.

"Okay," I said on the way back. "What was it?"

"Hm?"

"What made her cave in?"

"Common sense." Soccertease grinned. "I had Rog Jaycox sneak into the BilMart and do a quick look around. I told him explicitly what I wanted to know. He managed it quicker than I thought. Seems Bill Stimson made a couple of mistakes. One serious one."

I thought about it for a minute. "He wouldn't understand?" I struggled. It's hard sometimes. But then I remembered the two Revivalist women that morning–

"Shit," I said. "You're kidding."

"Nope. Trudy will trade. And the Reverend won't understand. Some things supersede ideology."

I started laughing. Bill Stimson was going to be furious. He lost everything in his gambit, but the problem was not intractable for us. Soccertease had worked hard to make sure Athens was a good place to live. She had a practical mind, which drove a lot of folks to distraction, if you take my meaning – especially the Reverend.

In the end though it was her grasp of the essentials of civilization that prevailed. Books were important, sure, as is technology and agriculture and housing and all that. But hygiene is probably the one thing that binds all the disparate faction of a civilization together. No matter what our differences, once we achieve a level of cleanliness and comfort, ideology doesn't offer much of an alternative.

Civilization is not grand works of engineering so much as a matter of hygiene. Soccertease and Trudy Semple bridged the gap of fundamental distrust and suspicion with essentials. They had what we needed, we had something they needed, and it turned out both were things we all needed, whether we wanted to admit it or not. The building bricks of amicable cohabitation and acceptable culture – toothpaste and tampons.

Rog Jaycox was waiting at the Academy when we got back. Soccertease went up to him. His three boys stood nearby, watching.

Soccertease scowled once, really deep, staring at Rog. Then she shook her head and sighed. She shook Rog's hand. But as he was turning away, he leaned over and whispered in Soccertease's ear. She looked utterly stunned.

She stared after Rog Jaycox and his boys till they were out of sight. I came up beside her.

"What?" I asked.

"Hm? Oh. Rog shot Bill Stimson. Seems that the Reverend wanted Bill to steal a generator from Rog as part of the fee to remain partners in the BilMart."

"Bill? Tried to steal something from Rog Jaycox? I thought CEOs were smart." I grunted. "Then Rog let him off easy. I can't imagine that he missed."

"That's how I see it."

"What about that last thing, though? What did he tell you?"

"Um...salt. He said salt."

"Salt."

"Salt. My missing ingredient. Three parts baking soda, one part salt, and some flavoring."

I blinked at her. "Then..."

"Go find Clint and see where he put those boxes."

"I thought you said they were tainted."

"Maybe they are. But we didn't try salt."

No, we hadn't. We looked at the list of ingredients on the tubes. No salt. Stuff like tetrasodium pysophosphate, sodium hydroxide, sodium lauryl sulfate, sodium sacharin. No salt. Didn't say salt. We didn't have any of the other stuff. Just sodium bicarbonate. Plenty of that.

Anyway, so ended the second battle of Athens, Tennessee. Stew Oxletter finally got all his weapons cleaned and adjusted and was ready to go right when it was all over. And hardly a shot was fired–unless you count the bullet in Bill Stimson. Which I don't. Call me shallow.

And Trudy started normalizing relations with us. I wonder sometimes what she says to the Reverend. But basically, the young women who'd been coming around surreptitiously came more regularly now. Openly. Bringing boxes of toothpaste and baking soda and receiving...

Well, receiving a damn sight more than sanitary products. Some of them are even attending classes. Must have confused them at first, you know? I'm sure somewhere along the way they heard that cleanliness was next to godliness. Hell, the Academy's the cleanest place in Athens.

I told you it began and ended with hygiene. What did you expect? Armageddon?

THE END

In his spare time, **Mark W. Tiedemann** indulges cloud sculpture and raises daydreams from bulbs. Having been brought up without the luxury of certainty, he early developed a reliance on books and deductive reasoning, which put a crimp in his social life for a long time, but resulted in a career that has produced seven novels to date, as well as 46 short stories, and a barrel-full of opinion, published and otherwise. The first book of his Secantis Sequence, *Compass Reach*, was nominated for a Philip K. Dick Award. The third book in the sequence, *Peace And Memory*, was released in July, 2003, by Meisha Merlin Publishing. 2004 will see the publication of his eighth novel, *Remains*, from BenBella Publishing. There will, of course, be more. Stayed tuned.

THE BOYS FROM BROWNSVILLE
Jeff Turner

Highway 6 was gloomy on Friday night. My '98 Ranger bumped over endless potholes between widely-spaced pools of pale light. Kinda like a roadmap of my life, I thought, then slapped myself mentally for slippin' back into what Bobbie-Jean called "edgy-cated thinkin'." That's what my semester at the big school had gotten me: random philosophy and exile from my rightful homestead in the Fletcher's Arms Trailer Park just a possum's hop east of Lufkin, not quite dry land, not quite swamp, but perfect for growin' mosquitoes and happy weed.

And it was on account of the second that I'd gone up to College Station in the first place. The folks back at Fletcher's Arms had taken up a collection to send one lucky fella to school in hopes of learning how we could maximize the rate of happy weed growth, and I was the chosen one based 'pon my advanced knowledge of spellin' and countin'. Wouldn't you know while I was in just my third month of studies the damned Yuppie-25 virus broke out, and I was rollin' back to Fletcher's Arms with half of Texas already in the hands of the Yumbies.

And before I knew it, I was run right back outta my rightful homestead. Betwixt my lack of new happy weed knowledge and the little "influences" I'd picked up from my city-folk roommates, my former neighbors looked at me like something one snort shy of a full-fledged Yumbie. Though I could still fart and belch with the best of 'em, they treated me like some kinda social reject. Bobbie-Jean herself put the final nail in my coffin, pointing out my new fondness for "unwholesome" music.

"Johnny Wayne Tucker," said Bobbie-Jean, "you done got weird. You ain't the man I loved–he listened to good wholesome stuff, like Waylon Jennings. Next thing I know you're gonna be eatin' stuff cooked on a stove!"

And with that I was back on Highway 6 with half my kinfolk thinkin' I'd become a Yumbie and the other half sayin' I was close enough to deserve killin'.

Maybe an hour out from College Station I was passing
through one of those dark stretches between streetlights when
a glowing white blur stepped into the pavement. Whatever it
was, it flickered like a bug zapper in the height of July. I
slammed on the brakes and the Ranger fishtailed off the road.
Though I spun the wheel and swore mightily, the front bumper
smacked straight into a tree. Lucky for me, the tree weren't
nothing but a sapling, and it snapped off like a Slim Jim betwixt
a starvin' man's teeth. I jumped out of the cab to face the fella
who'd sent me off the highway.

"Jesus H. Tap-danc–" I began, then stopped and stared.
Crossing the road was none other than the King himself. His
ghost, I mean. He wore the white sequined suit, the black
pompadour, and glowed with a holy paleness about his whole
body.

"Hey," he said. "Thank ya very much for stoppin'."

I squinted. Now, I'll admit to a certain failin' in my Elvis
history, but I was fairly certain the King hadn't died in the
middle of Texas. Why was his ghost a-hauntin' Highway 6?

"Are you–" I started.

His smile disappeared and he seemed to glow a little less
bright. "Well, no, I'm not. Name's George Johnston." I reached
for his hand slowly, but mine passed right through his and
we couldn't shake. "I was on my way up to the Central Texas
Elvis Remembrance Weekend when some damned fool farmer
cut me off in his tractor."

It figured. I didn't rate a spectral visit from the King
himself–I was stuck with the ghost of an Elvis impersonator.

"Well, sorry to hear your troubles," I said.

"That ain't the half of it. I'm doomed to haunt this world
'til I complete one major task."

"What's that?" I asked as I checked the Ranger's bumper.
It was dented a bit, but no major damage.

"I've got to help a woman fall in love. Think you could give
me a ride?"

"Uh, yeah," I said. "I suppose. Hop in."

"Thanks. Oh, yeah–BRING THE TREE!"

I jumped at the sound of that voice from beyond. "Hot
damn," I said when I could breath again. "What was that for?"

"Sorry," said George. "It just seemed appropriate. Throw

the tree in the back."

"What?"

"The tree. We'll need it."

I sighed, but picked up the broken tree and tossed it in the bed of the Ranger. I just wanted to get to College Station, and if accommodating a crazy ghost would get me there quicker, so be it. When I finally got back behind the wheel George was floating in a sitting position just above the passenger seat and looking at the tapes scattered over the floor.

"Hey!" he said, pointing, "could we listen to Waylon Jennings?"

About thirty minutes down the road George disappeared. I breathed a sigh of pure relief; he'd asked me to rewind the theme from the Dukes of Hazzard four times already. I thought maybe I'd just imagined him 'til my headlights showed another truck pulled off the side of the road. Standing next to it was the flickerin' figure of George and another person.

It was a woman, and she was gorgeous. The moonlight made a halo of her long hair, like the glow of lightning bugs through the late-evening fog. Clad in tight jeans and a man's flannel shirt, her body curved like the Brazos River, silhouetted in my high beams. She turned to me and the most supple lips I'd ever seen outside the Harris County Fair kissin' booth parted to say, "Turn those goddamned headlights off you friggin' redneck!"

How she knew I was a redneck, I don't know. I figured she was just one smart woman, and time would prove me right. I flipped off the high beams and got out of the Ranger.

"Johnny," said George, "meet Sue."

"Just 'Sue?'" I asked.

"What the hell's wrong with that?" Sue demanded.

"Um, nothin'. It just sounds kinda, I dunno, short. So, what happened to you, anyway?"

"I was just driving along when all the sudden this asshole–" she pointed to George "–appeared in front of me. I swerved, thinking it was someone who wasn't already dead, and ran right into that ditch."

Her truck was pretty much totaled, which was a shame, since it was a damned fine Ford. While she glared at me George gestured wildly at first her, then my Ranger.

"Well, can we – I mean, can I offer you a ride, Miss Sue?"

"It's Sue, for Christ's sake. Yeah, you can take me to Brownsville."

Behind her, George nodded so hard his head blurred.

"I'm not going to Brownsville," I said. "I'm going to College Station to help with the fight against the Yumbies at Texas A&M–"

"We're goin' to Brownsville," said Sue, and pulled out the biggest damn gun I'd even seen without pump or lever action. It was no match for the sawed-off double barrel I kept stashed behind the seat in the Ranger, 'cept that this one was in her hand and ready to use. I wondered where the hell she'd hidden it.

"This is it!" said George. "My mission accomplished! Oh, sweet afterlife!"

"She don't look much like a woman in love," I said. I tried logic with Sue, as sometimes women respond well to such talk. "I don't have time for a trip to Brownsville. I've gotta–"

"College Station is gone. Overrun by Yumbies."

"What?" I couldn't believe it. Texas A&M was one of the greatest bastions of backwoods rednecks in all the south. Taken over by Yumbies? Impossible.

"Just get in and drive." She waved the gun toward the Ranger. "I'll explain on the way."

George still looked like he was waiting for the hand o' God to reach down and snatch him up. I climbed into the Ranger next to Sue, praying he'd stay put long enough for me to run down his ghostly ass.

"It's like this," said Sue. She kept the gun on me while I drove. "I'm part of the Southern Partisan Anti-Zombie task force, Fort Worth chapter. I was on a courier run through College Station to Houston. Turns out there is no more College Station."

George had appeared between us, turning to me every once in a while to wink and grin. I wished I could hit him.

"What happened?" I asked. "And you mind putting the gun away?"

She didn't put it away, but at least pointed it down at the floorboards. "According to the survivors, a new wave of zombies. A new evolution of some sort – according to the stories they've got breath that'll destroy a man at the molecular level."

I whistled. "Some sort of super Yuppies?"

She stared at me. "No. These zombies are Bubbas."

I slammed on the brakes. "Bubba-Yumbies? Get outta my truck, bitch!"

The gun came back up to stare me in the face. "Keep driving, hick!"

George raised his arms. "Oh Lord, let there be love in the midst of strife, thank ya very much!"

"Drive!"

I drove. For the next forty miles I tried to think of a way to get back at the lying sack of crap in the passenger's seat, but the best I could come up with was to let loose with a silent but noticeable shot from my own internal arsenal. Sue just rolled down the window.

"All right," I said. "Suppose it's true. Suppose there's actually Bubba-Yumbies out there. Where the hell'd they come from?"

"There's more," said Sue. George turned back and forth between us, like he was watching a chip chuckin' contest. "'Bout half these Bubba-Yumbies were the same guy. The survivors said it was like being attacked by identical twins – hundreds of 'em."

"Hundreds" of twins just didn't ring true in the countin' side of my mind, so I let that point drop. "But where from?"

"From Brownsville, or thereabouts. We ran some of their four-wheeler licenses through the DMV, and they're all registered to folk from the Brownsville area."

"Um, not to interfere with the affairs of mortals–" began George.

"You shut up," said Sue. "I'm still pissed at you."

"Okay, but if these zombies come from Brownsville, why are we going there?"

"Because Brownsville is also the home of Dr. Siegfried Roy," said Sue. "He's the south's leading expert on the Yuppie virus, and he was back visiting his family when this last wave appeared. We've got to know if he's still alive–if anyone can figure out where these creatures are coming from, it's him."

We rode along in silence for a while. I kept glancing at the pistol.

"You know," I finally said, "I would'a helped you without the gun."

"Yeah, right," Sue said. "I know men even better than I

know Yumbies. You guys don't do anything you ain't forced to."

I disagreed, but she didn't appear to be in any mood to hear it, so I concentrated glumly on the road. She was a pretty woman, and it rankled me some that she thought so low of me. I glanced once at George, wondering if the ghost realized his mission was no closer to being accomplished than it had been two hours earlier, but he simply smiled.

We rolled up to Dr. Roy's family home, the like of which I never seen before or again. Six doublewides could've fit in the main house alone, and there was another building on either side. The first was a guesthouse, according to Sue, and the second was Dr. Roy's private lab. Thick woods surrounded the estate on three sides and the fog rollin' out of the trees made me nostalgic for Fletcher's Arms. I thought about skippin' off to the trees for a quick possum hunt, but Sue was already out of the Ranger and looking 'round anxiously.

The place was pretty quiet.

"Think I'll go stretch my legs," whispered George, and he floated on off toward the guesthouse. I shrugged and followed Sue to the front door of the main house.

It was a downright fancy place, complete with a mat on the floor that read, "Welcome To Our Home." Sue appeared ready to kick in the door, but I put a hand on her shoulder and pushed the doorbell. I gave what I thought was a reassuring squeeze and she glared at me like I'd done grabbed a tit instead, so I took my hand away while it was still attached to my wrist.

The door opened after a minute and a bent old fella with a shock of pure white hair appeared. When he saw Sue his big, bushy eyebrows shot up like someone'd goosed his boney ass.

"Sue!" he said.

"Ziggy!"

They hugged each other like long-lost kin and I was beginnin' to feel a mite awkward before they finally broke off.

"We were so worried about you," said Sue. "College Station's been overrun–"

"I know." The doctor glanced at me, then looked around nervously. "Come inside – it's not safe out here."

"Johnny, would you get my bag out of your truck?" Sue asked.

"Hurry," said Dr. Roy. They disappeared inside while I ran to the Ranger. Truth was I didn't mind so much being made into an errand boy – it'd give me a chance to grab the double barrel from the back.

I'd hid it cleverly in a hollowed out spot behind some cases of Red Dog, and I was just pulling it out when George's voice boomed, "THERE IS GREAT EVIL HERE!"

I damn near jumped out of my skin 'fore I realized who it was. "Jesus H – George, what in the hell are you doin'?"

"Johnny," whispered the ghost, "I went behind that there laboratory to take a leak and you won't believe what I found!"

I wondered how a ghost might take a leak, but somethin' about his voice convinced me there was more important questions. "What?" I asked.

"Four wheelers! A whole fleet of 'em!"

I started to answer when suddenly I was spun about by the hairiest, smelliest arms I seen this side of my grandma's. I let loose with a shout and my nose was suddenly clogged with the most horrible stench I'd ever experienced. It smelled like my dawg had done rolled in something he normally left behind, then tangled with a skunk, then rolled in somethin' the skunk left behind just for good measure. And the whole noxious mixture was blasting straight from the mouth of the plug-ugliest–

Bubba?

For a second the sight repulsed me even more than the horrible breath. I couldn't deny it: this thing had the dead eyes of a zombie, but the crooked teeth, hair lip, and bowl-cut hair of a bona fide Bubba. I was staring into the face of a Bubba-Yumbie, and it was like starin' into the eyes o' damnation.

I let loose with a wild swing but another blast of that breath made my knees buckle. Spots danced before my eyes and I felt myself slammed against the Ranger's tailgate.

"The tree!" shouted George. "USE THE TREE!"

I groped about blindly and my hand closed on a leafy branch. Tearing it away from the tree, I shoved desperately at the Bubba-Yumbie and felt my fingers poke the leaves into its mouth.

It let me loose faster than you can say, "Gimme another, Ma." Blinkin' and gaggin', I righted myself to see the zombie staggering backward. It shaked and shook like Ole Reverend

Joseph havin' himself a fit, then I'll be damned if its head didn't explode right off its shoulders. The ground 'round us was suddenly drenched with blood, bone, and bits of hair. And suddenly, my last doubts 'bout this bein' a Bubba zombie were gone. There weren't a brain cell to be seen.

"How–" I asked, and George sniffed.

"Eucalyptus," he said, nodding toward the tree I'd thrown in the back of the Ranger. "Must've counteracted that supernatural breath."

"Who the hell plants eucalyptus trees in Texas?" I asked.

"Never mind that," said George. "Get some leaves and the gun. You've gotta save Sue!"

He was right. Somewhere in that grand house there were zombies for killin' and a woman for savin'. I grabbed my tree and my double barrel and ran like the Devil himself was close behind.

Dr. Roy had locked the front door, but I opened it quick enough with one barrel of my universal tool. The boom of the shotgun was music to my ears after havin' snuck all the way 'cross the driveway. I broke it open and had a new shell in place before kicking in the door, eucalyptus sapling tucked under one arm.

I ran inside and let loose with both barrels, one after another, each nearly cutting in half the two Bubba-Yumbies flanking a tall staircase. Their rotted breath filled the room, but I popped a eucalyptus leaf in my mouth and the stench disappeared.

"Holy shit," said George, and I had to agree. Wart for wart, these two Bubbas were the spittin' image of each other. They might've been the same man, if they weren't both lyin' on the floor in front of me.

I started up the stairs but George ran for another door. "Where you headed?" I asked.

"Basement," said George. "Bad guys always hide in the basement."

I couldn't argue that logic, so I followed the ghost through the door and into Dr. Roy's kitchen. Another zombie, a dead ringer for the two in the front room, rose up from behind one of them fancy detached counters in the center of the kitchen. It knocked the shotgun clean outta my hands, but I shoved the whole sapling forward. It thrust into that Yumbie's mouth like a holy lance in the hands of a knight or a centaur or somethin'. Just like the one out in the driveway, its head popped all over the fancy tile.

George pointed to another door, beyond which stairs led down to the bowels of the house. I retrieved the double barrel and near tumbled down the steps. At the bottom of the stairs, though, I skidded to a stop and stared like a young'n catchin' his first glimpse of deer in the matin' season.

The basement was a huge, open space. It must've reached clear under the lab building, and it was full of these tall, round tanks. There weren't a single fish swimmin' in 'em, though. Each tank held the nekkid, hairy body of a man just like those I'd left splattered upstairs. Some were no more than kids and some was full grown, but there was no mistakin' that face.

"God be praised," said George. "The boys from Brownsville are all little Bubbas!"

No sooner had he spoke than a door at the far end of the room swung open and Dr. Siegfried Roy himself walked through. He was scribblin' on a clipboard, and he looked up just in time to see me levelin' both barrels of God's gift to mankind at him.

"Scheiss–" he said, just before I decorated the walls with all his guts and most of his brains. No Bubba there.

Sue screamed from beyond that door. "Reload!" I shouted, tossing the shotgun to George. In my haste I forget about his insubstan-tiatal nature. The shotgun passed right through him and clattered to the floor.

Sue screamed again and I wasted no time. I charged through the door like the last bag of pork rinds in the world waited on the other side. There were two more Bubba-Yumbies inside, closin' in from either side of a table 'pon which Sue was strapped down tight. Her head whipped from side to side, trying to escape the ghastly stench from their twin mouths, but she was fadin' fast. Even as I burst 'pon the scene her eyes rolled back in her head and it dropped back on the table.

One of the Bubba-Yumbies looked up and I jammed that eucalyptus sapling so deep in his mouth I swear it bulged out the back of his neck. His head went the same way as the others, that is to say, all over the place. Unfortunately, the explosion was so violent it blew most of my eucalyptus leaves into nothin' more than tiny green shreds.

The other Bubba roared and turned on me. Even from across the table the stench made me stagger. I ducked a swing of his hammy, hairy fist, then butted my shoulder into his chest. That last was a mistake, pure and simple. Suddenly, those huge hands were poundin' on my back and pullin' my hair–Yumbie or not, this was a true Bubba warrior. I tried risin' up for an Atomic Elbow or maybe even a Double-Snake Neck Lock, but I'd forgot 'bout that killer breath. Next thing I knew I was lyin' flat on my back and that Bubba-Yumbie was leanin' down to finish me off.

"Hey, hey," said George, "who wants a peanut butter and nanner sandwich?"

The Bubba-Yumbie yanked upright and turned to George, just as my hand closed on the last branch of my eucalyptus tree. I leaped to my feet and grabbed his greasy neck with one hand, shoved those leaves into his snaggle-toothed maw with the other. Suddenly, my watery eyes were spattered with red zombie goo and the headless neck slipped from my grip.

But the breath was still caught dead in my throat, clogged tight by that Bubba-Yumbie's dying gasp.

I doubled over and found myself starin' into Sue's deep blue eyes. She was in similar straits, chokin' and coughing 'round a lungful of pure filth.

And I had only one leaf left.

I knew what I had to do. I popped that leaf into my mouth, chewed it to pulp, then bent down to lock my lips to hers.

Eucalyptus filled both our mouths and my lungs dried up in a heartbeat. We stared each other straight in the eye while our tongues worked that leaf dry, then I finally pulled away.

"It was Dr. Roy," she whispered. Her voice was hoarse, but strong. "Genetic incest – he was crossbreeding Yumbies and Bubbas to make his own army. He even developed the killer breath."

"Let me get these off here," I said. I pulled at the straps, wishin' I had my skinnin' knife.

"Johnny, wait," said Sue. I looked at her.

"Kiss me again."

I did as she asked, bendin' down once more to taste the sweetest lips in all the south. When we finally looked up, we found George standin' alongside the table, beamin' like a preacher at a no-shotgun wedding.

"Praise be and hallelujah," he said. "Oh sweet afterlife, take your child home!"

"Goodbye, George," said Sue, and our ghostly friend bent his knee, twisted his hips, and vanished like a bug zapper fadin' out afore the mornin' sun.

"Let me up," said Sue. "We've got zombies to kill."

I couldn't agree with her more.

THE END

Jeffrey Turner is the author of *The Garden In Bloom* and *The Hundredth Magic*. His stories have appeared in *MarsDust*, *The Leading Edge*, and *NFG*. Though his fiction contains a few polysyllabic words, Jeff is a diehard Bubba-in-training and owns a fine assortment of flannel shirts. He can be found in Fort Worth with his wife, daughter, and two dawgs, or online at JeffTurnerFiction.com.

WHY A GOOD MAN NOWADAYS IS HARD TO FIND
Laura J. Underwood

Dear Diary,

In a couple of minutes, I am going to be walking down the aisle and getting hitched, for better or worse, to Ned E. Campbell. The last couple of weeks have been enough to start a girl thinking suicide. Ever since Yuppie-25 turned the world upside down, writing in this diary has been my only solace.

I know I wasn't even born when it hit, so I didn't live through what my grandma calls the Days of Terror when the virus turned a lot of folks into flesh-eating Yumbies. God only knows, the old woman has worn my ears off telling me all about it. Some times, I wish a Yumbie had eaten her, and then I wouldn't have to listen to her moan and groan about missing the good old days when Spam was plenty and Twinkies as common as cockroaches in a trailer park.

At any rate, I'm sixteen now, and Paw was telling me a year ago that it was high time I thought about getting married and doing my part to keep the population of decent humanity stable.

Doesn't matter that Paw and I have different ideas about what's decent, stable or humane.

So any way, about a year ago, he tells me I ought to start looking for a man, and there's where all my troubles began, Diary. Since Yuppie-25 killed off most of the nice ones with good jobs and turned the remains of them into flesh-eating Yumbies, I'm sorta limited in my choices. Granted, I don't really care if the man I marry is not really a knight in shining armor. Hell, as long as he has all the right working parts and takes a bath now and again, it'll be just fine.

I just don't want to marry Ned. He may well be about the only man out there in the Holyhokum Trailer Park that I ain't pure kin to, but I don't know that I want to call him kin in any fashion.

I wish Mama was still here. She ran off practically the day

after I was born. Paw would never tell me why, and Grandma used to spew that my mama had no place among our kind.

Sometimes, I wonder.

But back to marriage and Ned. When Paw told me to start looking for a man, naturally I set my sights on a young fellow lived over by the end of the park. His name was Tim, and he was as cute as a June bug. He had dark hair and eyes, a lot like my paw. In fact, he was as handsome as Paw was in his younger years. I know this because Grandma has pictures on the wall of Paw with Mama cut out...which is why I have no idea what she looked like.

Tim used to run about the park on his motorbike. Don't know where he got the fuel, but I remember someone saying he made it, like moonshine, out in the hollow. Tim was a couple of years older than me, but he had aptitude. His folks kept their trailer in good repair so it never leaked. His mama baked the best biscuits in the park. He had a little sister as well, and his daddy was on the "Council."

I really fell hard for Tim the day he let me sit on his motorbike and took me for a spin. If any man was worth marrying, I decided, it was him.

Trouble is, Paw saw me on the bike with Tim, and I thought Paw was gonna chew nails when he stopped us on the back road. He yanked me off the bike then told Tim to stay away from me. And when I tried to ask why, Paw slapped me and told me to get on home as he had to finish business with Tim. I ran home a crying, and Grandma washed my face as I sat sobbing.

"That boy ain't for you, honey-child," she said.

"But why?" I wailed as Paw came in. "Why can't I marry Tim?"

Paw looked like someone had stuck horseradish in his Red Man as he paced back and forth. Finally, he took my hands and brushed the tears from my cheeks and said, "You can't marry Tim, Jilly, on account of he's your brother."

"My what?"

"Tim's mama and I...well, it was back in the days before you were born and I was on the Council, and she and I was working late one night, and she got to telling me all about how badly old Hiram treated her, and well...we done it there in the office of the trailer park, and the next thing we knows, she's having Tim...so you see, Jilly Baby, you can't marry your own blood kin. Now dry your eyes. There's other boys in the park just as good. Like Ned E. Campbell."

"Ned E. Campbell is a Neanderthal!" I cried and ran into my room and slammed the door.

In fact, I cried all night, and the next day, Tim wouldn't even look at me.

Grandma told me I was being silly. And maybe I was. The next day, I went down to the creek to catch crawdads for supper, and that was when I met Bob.

I'd seen Bob before, only in glimpses. He was curly-headed and had a quiet way of talking. His daddy was the minister, and Bob sometimes read the lays at Sunday service. His voice was like an angel.

I decided then and there that being the wife of a preacher's son was probably a good thing. Not that I was all that religious. And admittedly, Reverend Luke was a bit of a hell-fire-damnation sort of preacher who said the Yumbie plague was God's answer to the sins of the corporations, but I figured he wouldn't object to the union so long as I came to church every Sunday.

So at breakfast on Sunday morning–the day I was gonna propose to Bob–I told Paw what I was thinking. He spewed coffee across half the table. Grandma started fussing like an old hen while Paw looked at me with his dark eyes and said, "Jilly, sweetie, you can't marry Bob. He's your brother."

I have to say that hit me like a ton of bricks, and I sat in silence while I heard Grandma mutter, "The sins of the fathers..."

"But how...?"

"Well, back when I was on the Council, I was also one of the elders of the church," Paw said wearily. "And I used to help the preacher's wife Mary with the books, and one night...well, it just happened, and I'm sorry to say it resulted in the birth of her son Bob, so you'll just have to forget about him and maybe think about Ned..."

"Ned's got a head like a boiled turnip and he smells about as nasty!" I shrieked and once more threw myself into my room to weep.

Well, as you can see, Diary, I was starting to have my doubts. No sooner than I got Bob out of my system, I set my sights on a lad named Jim. Only it was no different. Jim's mama lived in the lower end of the park...and she was a whore.

And I figured she did enough business among the men of Holyhokum that surely Jim was someone else's son. But no. As soon as I suggested his name to Paw, he told me that Jim was my kin too. And so were Brad and Willie and Joe Bob and Tommy...

I was starting to see why Mama left. If Paw was out there spreading his seed among the women of Holyhokum, she probably left him in disgust. It was starting to look pretty hopeless for me. Weren't for the chance of running into a Yumbie on the road, I'd have taken off too.

Next thing I know, Ned started coming over to call, though he pretended to be looking for work. He was short and stocky and wore his hair butch-cut. His eyes were a sort of glassy blue and didn't focus in the same direction. And he had these tits that lay flat on his chest like a couple of half-filled water balloons. Paw kept inviting Ned in for a meal or to help with the chores. I guess he thought if I saw Ned enough, he would grow on me...

Like fungus.

The more I saw Ned, the less I liked him. For one thing, he always wears his tool belt, and he scratches his crotch as though there was something nibbling at his privates. One day, he was helping Paw with the bathroom plumbing, and I swear, when he thought I wasn't looking, he pulled a booger out of his nose and stuck it on the wall behind the toilet.

He didn't have any kin to speak of, except he said his mother lived over Wartburg way. He depended on the kindness of strangers and the skill of his own two hands. Naturally, I was not happy when Paw started being so kind. Especially when Paw kept finding reasons for me and Ned to be in the same room. To keep me there, he would use the threat of leaving wide stripes on my bare behind with a belt. I was forced to sit there and bite my tongue while Paw extolled my womanly virtues. He was doing his best to make me attractive, which even I will admit was not easy. I was a bit of a hunky girl myself. In fact, there were times I looked in the mirror and saw a faint bit of Ned looking back.

Didn't stop Paw. There came the day when he left the room, and Ned finally stammered a proposal to me that I didn't like in the least. Certainly wasn't a decent proposal. It was more like a case of Paw stepped out on the porch to take a piss after downing half a dozen bottles of home brew. He was hardly out the door when Ned pounced on me like a leech and proceeded to ravage me with sweaty hands. Paw came back just as Ned was pushing me down on the couch and trying to smother me with a fleshy kiss. Here I thought Paw was gonna be mad and I'd never have to deal with Ned again, but Paw grinned before he shouted, "Ned, you better be ready to do the right thing by my daughter!"

Boy, did I feel like a patsy then. Next thing I know, Paw's telling everyone that Ned and I are getting hitched next week, and I can tell you that about a dozen other girls around the Holyhokum Trailer Park breathed sighs of relief.

So there you have it, Diary. Gotta go now. Paw's banging on the bedroom door, on account of I locked it. Of course I can hear him fetching his tools to remove the hinges.

Guess he plans to make sure I get to the church on time...

Dear Diary,

Will wonders ever cease? I'm feeling much better now. I don't have to marry Ned.

That's right, Diary. You see, Paw decided to send Mrs. Campbell a note to tell her that her son was getting hitched to me, and inviting her to the wedding. Ned had once told us that his mama owned two trailers, so Paw was determined to have her there to make it look good. He just didn't bother to tell Ned.

And she did come, Diary. Like a fury, I might add. We were half way to the altar, me digging my heels into the floor as much as I could, Paw pushing me from behind, when the church doors burst open and in stalks this woman who is nearly six feet tall and hitting 260 on the scale. But she wasn't fat. Oh, no, she was built like a construction worker and had muscles that any man would have envied. In fact, she looked an awful lot like a larger, stronger version of Ned, and seeing her, I knew where he got his shape from.

She thundered up the aisle, carrying what looked like clothes in a dry cleaning bag, and I can tell you that the floorboards shook. I had to grab a corner of the pew just to keep from tumbling off my high heels.

Well, she walked right up to me, and at first, I thought I was about to be trampled into the floorboards. But then she froze, took one look at Paw and whispered, "Jesse?"

Paw gulped. "J...June Anne?" he said. "You're..."

"Mama?" Ned blurted. "You didn't come to spoil things, did you?"

"You get your ass over here, Neddie!" June Anne retorted. "Now!"

Ned slunk over like a fox. June Anne thrust the dry cleaning into his hands.

"Now, go change!" she barked, "Or I'll take a switch to your legs!"

You'd have thought Ned was the biggest three-year-old in the county. He ducked his head, took the clothes and headed back for the bathroom.

"No, no, no," Paw said. "It can't be you..."

"Hell yes it is, Jesse. Just what in tar-nation do you think you're doing trying to marry my Neddie to..." She looked down at me for the first time. Really looked down at me. "Jilly?" she said. "Jillian Mae? Is that really my baby girl?"

I looked at her hard, and realized it too. The face was an older version of my own. "M....Mama?" I said and grinned.

Well, that was that, Diary. Paw keeled over in a faint, and I was tempted to join him, but I couldn't. June Anne crushed me to her ample chest and cried over and over, "My Jilly, my sweet Jilly." Then she started to yammer on about how she wished she'd taken me with her. That she ran away that day because she got tired of finding out how my Paw couldn't keep his pecker in his pants for more than a minute and that she had known marrying such a handsome man would have a price. But she had left him because she was determined to find her a man who would be faithful.

And she did. Over in the town of Wartburg, she met a hunter named Bart. He took her in and made her his common-law wife. Taught her woodcraft and survival, and never let his eyes rove even though there were plenty of other women in the town. Eventually, they had Ned. But then one day, while Bart was out trapping squirrels for supper, a bunch of Yumbies fell on him, roasted him and served him at their company picnic. Meanwhile, Neddie had run away for getting in trouble with someone's daughter, and June Anne thought Ned had been eaten by Yumbies...

Well, you know Diary. All this filled my heart with joy. "Does this mean I can't marry Ned cos he's my brother?" I asked hopefully.

I was suddenly aware that all the murmuring in the church

had stopped. That all eyes had turned towards the back end. Cautiously, I peered around June Anne.

Ned stood at the end of the first row of pews...wearing a dress. I stared at him, working my jaw. He looked good in a dress...well, except for the tool belt around his waist.

"Sorry, Jilly," Ned said and pushed at his butch-cropped hair. "Guess I should have told you before now..."

I looked up at June Anne again. "Is Ned a...transvestite?"

She shook her head. "No pumpkin. Neddie's your little sister..."

THE END

Laura J. Underwood has been a freelance writer for over thirty years. Born and raised in the Bubbalands of East Tennessee, she sold her first work of fiction in 1987 when Marion Zimmer Bradley bought "Sword Singer" for *Sword And Sorceress V*. Since then, she has produced a wealth of short fiction and novels set in her fantasy worlds of Ard-Taeth and Lamboria, including *Ard Magister*, *Magic's Song: Tales Of The Harper Mage*, and the forthcoming *Dragon's Tongue* and *Wandering Lark* from Meisha Merlin and *Chronicles Of The Last War* forthcoming from Yard Dog Press. Having appeared in *Bubbas Of The Apocalypse*, she now finds herself strangely addicted to writing about Yumbies and Bubbas and Barbecue on a regular basis (though she has not convinced herself to put a hound dog under the porch yet).

1001 ALABAMA NIGHTS

Billy Vincent

Bubba Ray Cyrus considered himself an intelligent man. He knew a great many things and understood the ways of the world. For example, he knew that Oswald didn't kill JFK. He also knew that Elvis had squealed on the mob and was in a witness protection program disguised as an Elvis impersonator in Las Vegas up until his untimely demise in 2007. It was hard to believe that the King was gone, a victim of food poisoning. Damn buffets. But that was twenty years ago.

The Yuppie 25 Virus on the other hand he didn't understand at all. It caused people to mutate into flesh eating zombies and others to die outright. Only a few had survived.

Emma Jean, Bubba's wife had been an early casualty. He loved her dearly and thought of her every day. He had hated to see her go, but you have to play the cards you're dealt. Lately he wondered if he should fold or cash out.

His supplies had run dangerously low and he had taken to scavenging. He had learned early on how to bust locks kick in doors, and all manner of things, but he had finally run into an unusual roadblock.

Bubba had found a 2010 model truck in decent condition. It was relatively intact even though it had no glass. His problem lay in that he couldn't open the 'Yuppie bed cover'. Ice pick, crowbar, sledgehammer, he had tried them all but all he had managed to do was dent it up and scratch some of the paint.

Only one option was left open for him. Bubba walked back to his old rust bucket of a truck and retrieved his battery operated reciprocating chainsaw.

With a few quick pulls of the pull cord, the chainsaw growled to life. As Bubba began to cut with its metal blade he grumbled, "Damn Yuppie Bed Covers!! Truck ain't no status symbol. Ya should buy a truck to haul stuff. Get yerself a car if you haul stuff and gonna worry about thieves. If ya want both get an El Camino. Anythin' but a Damn Yuppie Bed Cover!!"

With a few quick swipes, the saw ripped through the steel

bed cover and the locking mechanism dropped to the ground. Bubba grinned a three toothed smile.

"Yeee Haaaa!!!" he shouted. Bubba pumped his arms in the air in victory. He hopped about on one leg and did a celebratory jig lap around the truck. His wife had always laughed hysterically at his childish attempts to dance. He wished she could see him now.

He cut off the chainsaw and placed it on the ground. Eager with anticipation, he grabbed the trunk lid and lifted it. Much to his dismay, the contents were less than grand. "Just friggin' lovely." Bubba grumbled. "I musta found a friggin' Yuppie survival kit." He tossed a pair of brown loafers onto the ground. Useless. A temporary spare tire, barely worth keeping. A small playmate ice chest that contained two bottles of spring water with a brand name he couldn't pronounce.

Up near the cab rested a leather case and an old wooden crate. Bubba popped open the case to reveal a slightly used polo mallet. Bubba tossed it to the ground in disappointment and slid the crate toward himself. Picking up his crowbar, he easily pried the lid off.

"Let me guess, Aunt Louise's tea set or a mahogeny shuffle board set." To his surprise it was neither. Inside were rows upon rows of caviar. Bubba shook his head in disbelief. "Stuff barely makes good dip for pork rinds."

As Bubba was about to close the lid, something caught his eye. Tucked away in one corner of the crate was another bottle. "Now we're talkin'" he said as he plucked the bottle from its resting place and closed the crate. Upon closer examination of the bottle, he realized that it wasn't alchol. "Looks like it says...Per..." he began. Bubba wiped his forehead with his shirtsleeve and then rubbed his sweaty sleeve on the bottle label.

"Perrier?" he announced. "Great. More phoo-phoo water."

As Bubba was about to discard the bottle, it began to shake in his hand. Unsure what to do, Bubba tossed it to the ground and ran to his truck. He threw open the truck door, glanced at the picture of his wife on the dashboard and said a quick prayer. He then retrieved his shotgun from his gun rack, checked to make sure it was loaded, clicked off the safety and aimed it at the bottle.

As if under great pressure, the lid shot off the bottle and into the air. A thick gray smoke began to billow out and solidify into a form. Then, there before Bubba stood a middle-aged man. Bubba watched as he dusted off his straw hat and then patted his clothes down. His clothes resembled a farmer's. but his bright red suspenders reminded him of Justin Wilson.

"Howdy." he said with a wave.

"Howdy." Bubba said. "Were did ya come from?"

"The bottle my friend." he announced. "I'm D'Jinn."

"Yer what?" Bubba asked.

"I'm called D'Jinn," he repeated.

"Gin? I thought it was phoo-phoo water." Bubba replied.

"No. Da Jinn." he said slowly. "Actually it's short fer Darrel Jinn Nederlander. Everybody has problems with it. Most folks just call me Ned."

"Uh, Ned." Bubba began. "Ya say ya came from the bottle."

"Yeh." Ned stated. "I'm a genuwine bona fide wish granter."

"What?" Bubba asked scratching his head.

"A wish granter." Ned restated. "You know. Make three wishes and all that stuff."

"Oh now bull butter." Bubba said. "Ain't no sucha thing."

"I am, too. Jest wish fur somethin,'" Ned said.

"Hell no!" Bubba shouted.

"Come on," Ned said. "I'll prove it to ya."

"Ya can't prove it." Bubba said. "I bet ya can't even make it cooler out here."

"Is that so! Well, jest watch this." Ned said, closing his eyes. He then tucked his thumbs up underneath his suspenders and then pulled them out about six inches. Ned opened his eyes and said in a slow monotone voice "HEE HAW". Upon speaking those words, he released the suspenders and they sprang back into place with a loud snap.

The white puffy clouds overhead began to turn gray and get bigger. Soon the sun was blotted out and the wind did an about face and began blowing in from the north. Bubba looked around, expecting rain to pour down like a cow pissin' on a flat rock but it didn't.

"As the song says, 'Since we got no place to go'" said Ned.

From the sky came some of the hugest snowflakes Bubba had ever seen. Course it was July so any snowflakes tend to be big.

"I have to say that I'm impressed." Bubba smiled.

"I told ya so." Ned reassured him.

"So ya did." Bubba said. "Now can ya stop it."

"Stop it?" Ned asked. "Uh, stopping it is the hard part. I mean starting it is simple as pie."

"So can ya or cain't ya." Bubba asked.

"How's about ya make a wish and I'll work on it," Ned said with a smile.

Bubba closed his eyes and thought about it. The Yuppie Virus had destroyed everything. His wife, his friends, and great vittles.

"How's about I wish for a real lunch that I don't have to scavenge for." Bubba said.

"Lunch it is." Ned smiled. He closed his eyes and snapped his suspenders with a mighty "HEE HAW".

Bubba's ears became filled with a rumbling sound. He looked to his right just as a Fed-Up truck barreled past him. It slammed on its brakes and screeched to a halt. It then backed up until it was even with Ned and Bubba.

A man in a brown shirt and shorts jumped out and slid on the snowy ground. He regained his footing and handed Bubba a picinic basket.

"Bubba Ray Cyrus?" he asked.

"Yeh." Bubba answered.

"This is yours. Please sign." He handed him a clipboard and Bubba scrawled out his name. "Weird weather we been having."

"Yeh." Bubba said handing back the clipboard.

The Fed-Up man returned to his truck and sped off.

Bubba's mouth salivated as he looked at the basket. Finally, a meal he didn't have to scavenge, loot, plunder, or steal. He sat down on the tailgate and opened the basket. Bubba reach in and instinctively pulled his hand out. He peered inside and saw what his hand had brushed against. Bubba carefully extracted it so he could examine it in the light. Between two fingers he held a fuzzy piece of fruit.

"Ned, I think yer magic is gettin' old. This here lime done spoiled on ya." Bubba stated as he placed it on the tailgate.

"Spoiled? Ya numb nut that's a kiwee." Ned replied.

"A kiwee." Bubba said shaking his head. He reach again into the basket and retrieved a plastic wrapped sandwich. "Now that's a little more like it."

He unwrapped the plastic and noticed that the crust was cut off it. Bubba rarely ate the crust anyway so it wasn't a bad thing as far as he was concerned. He sunk his teeth deeply into the sandwich and bit off a huge mouth full. Chewing vigorously, Bubba's taste buds were assaulted by a wretched taste. He spat the half chewed sandwich onto the ground.

Looking for something to wash the taste from his mouth, Bubba grabbed the bottle resting in the bottom of the basket. He smacked the cap down on the corner of the truck bed and popped it off. A white froffy foam burst from its neck and Bubba caught most of it in his mouth.

Bubba swished it about in his mouth then spat the contents out. Bubba angrily threw the half sandwich and partial bottle at Ned.

"What the hell kinda operation are ya runnin'!" Bubba shouted. "What kinda lunch is this? Spoiled food and hot beer!"

"One ya didn't have to scavenge." Ned answered. "I apologize that yer beer was hot. Ya didn't like the rest?"

"Hell no!!" Bubba shouted. "What made ya think this was somethin' I'd like?"

"Look around ya. I figgered ya liked this sorta stuff so I made ya a lunch of kiwee, water crest sandwich, and beer." Ned replied.

"One outa three ain't bad." Bubba grumbled.

"At least I got the snow to stop." Ned said.

"Great. Ya think ya can grant me my next wish without screwin' it up?" Bubba asked.

"Hey, I'm still a little rusty, buddy. Gimme a break " Ned said.

Bubba closed his eyes and thought hard. Two wishes left. The food was a bust. He knew what he wanted. He knew what he needed. He was gonna put Ned to the test.

"Okay." Bubba said. "Now please listen real careful to what I'm about to wish for. This is extremely important. Don't screw it up. Ya got me?"

"Yep." Ned answered with a nod.

"I wish for my wife to be returned to me." Bubba said as he wiped a tear from his eye.

"Okey dokie." Ned said, closing his eyes. He then snapped his suspenders again and yelled "HEE HAW!"

Bubba was terrified to look around. He was almost afraid the Fed-Up guy would pull up and deliver her in a box with a bow on it. Bubba took a deep breathe and then turned around.

What Bubba saw took his breath away.

Standing there before him in all her glory was his wife Emma Jean Cyrus. The sun had come back out and glistened off her bright yellow sun dress. She was exactly as he remembered her though her hair was a little different. She stretched out her arms toward Bubba. He walked toward her, longing to embrace her.

As Bubba drew closer to hold her, he reached up and brushed the hair back that covered her face. Bubba drew back his hand in revulsion. Where a beautiful woman's face once was, the torn bone remains of a shattered skull now resided, she was a Yombie.

The memories of that fateful day came flooding back to Bubba. Emma had been in the garden picking corn fer dinner when a zombie sprang up and attached her. Bubba killed it, but it was too late fer Emma.

"Damn you!" Bubba shouted, shaking a clenched fist at Ned.

"I brought her back," Ned said. "Jest like ya wished fer."

"Not like this!" Bubba said, pointing to the monstrosity behind him.

Emma lunged at Bubba. Instinctively, he smacked the remains of Emma's face with the butt of his shotgun. She staggered backward and Bubba backed away.

"Make her go away," he demanded of Ned.

"I'm sorry, Bubba, but rules is rules," Ned said.

Bubba gritted his teeth as Emma continued her pursuit of him. He raised his shotgun, then pointed it at Emma Jean. Bubba's finger rested on the trigger and lingered there for a few seconds. "Baby..." he said, "please forgive me." Bubba took a deep breath, exhaled, and then squeezed off the hardest shot he'd ever have to make. The Emma yombie tumbled backward and crumbled to the ground. Bubba spun around and aimed his shotgun at Ned.

"Hold on partner," he said. "That weren't my fault. Any way guns don't work on D'Jinns."

"I don't care if yer malt liquor." Bubba announced as he fired on Ned. Hot lead burst from the gun and passed harmlessly through Ned's body.

"Ya see? I told ya it wouldn't work. Ya think yer the first to try that sorta thing?" Ned asked.

Bubba tossed his shotgun in frustration at Ned but it also

passed through Ned's body.

"I'm real sorry." Ned said. "Ya seem like a nice enough feller. I know yer mad, but I'm sure we can git yer last wish right on the money."

"My last wish?" Bubba asked. "Ya know what I wish for?" Bubba moved up close and stood eyeball to eyeball with Ned. Bubba grabbed Ned's hands, stuck each thumb under Ned's suspenders and pulled back as hard as he could. Ned tried to protest but it did no good.

"Now get this real clear, Ned." Bubba said. "Ya screwed up my dinner. Ya screwed up givin' my wife back to me. I got me one wish left." As Bubba released the suspenders in anger he said, "I wish ya...."

Bubba sat on the tailgate looking at the ruin his life had become. Yuppie food everywhere. The decaying carcass of his late wife. An empty shotgun. His life was truly horrible.

Yet Bubba started to snicker. That moved into a giggle and cascaded into a doubled over belly laugh. Still laughing, Bubba rolled off the tailgate and onto the ground. Soon he was almost light headed and his face almost hurt. But he couldn't get the picture out of his head of Ned grumbling and sulking away.

As Bubba released Ned's suspenders in anger he said, "I wish ya had that Perrier bottle shoved up yer ass!!" And Ned finally got the wish done right.

THE END

About himself, **Billy Vincent** says, "I've lived in Oklahoma my entire life.

"I've been married to my beautiful supportive wife Michele for six wonderful years. Our only child is Sally the cat.

"My publishing credits include "Taking It For Granite" in *More Stories That Won't Make Your Parents Hurl* by Yard Dog Press and the story you are now holding in your hands."

NED AND THE COOKIE GIRLS
Julia Blackshear Kosatka

"Order! Order!" Bob banged the Craftsman hammer down so hard the table creaked. "I'm gonna have order in this here courtroom, or some o'you sumbitches gonna wished you'd never been born." He glared at the noisemakers and waited impatiently for them to settle down some. This was *his* hardware store and by gum, if the rest of the town wanted to be in it, they'd best behave. "OTIS!" Half the crowd jumped like a toad on a hot rock, the front window rattled and for the rest of her days, Mary Lou Schermermyer swore she saw a bird fall dead out of the sky. Nobody in Stiller wanted to make Bob mad. Right nasty temper, that one. "Otis, stop pawing that girl and go git Ned in here so we can git started."

"I ain't pawin' her, Bob."

"*Don't* call me Bob! I'm Y'r Honor right now."

"I'm sorry... Y'r Honor. But after all, Mary Sue and me, we's engaged."

"No you AIN'T!" Mary Sue's husband grabbed her by the arm and started dragging her away from Otis. She didn't seem to want to go. "She's MY wife!"

"Well, shore she is, Tom, but we wuz engaged afore you got married. That makes us *almost* family."

"OTIS! I *ain't* gonna tell you again. Go stand there by your Aunt Minnie and leave Mary Sue alone for now!" The crowd parted long enough for Otis to slouch to his assigned spot just as Bob added, "And lets not have you two makin' cow eyes at each other. This here's an important meetin' and I expect you to behave while it's goin' on. Tom, *you* go get Ned."

A quick elbow to the ribs from Aunt Minnie shut off any protest Otis had planned. Probably cut off most of the oxygen to his brain, too, given that his lips were turning blue and he looked like the first bass caught at a fishin' tournament. Nobody messed with Aunt Minnie. Besides her rig was the only one left that could make the trip up to the brewery in

Lawton, OK. At least she just used her elbow. Last time Otis did something she didn't like, she put her cigar out in the middle of his forehead.

"Comin' though! Comin' through!" The crowd parted and Tom led Ned to the front of Bob's table. "Here ya go, Bob, I mean, Y'r Honor." He stepped out of the way and shoved Ned up to the table, giving the other man a friendly slap on the back.

Bob looked Ned up and down. Ned grinned at him and Bob found himself grinning back. How could you not like Ned? A kinder, more generous soul never walked the Earth. Why, without even askin', he'd show up when you needed somebody to have a beer with. Who wants to drink alone? When you needed somebody to hold the ladder while you tacked new tar paper on the roof of your trailer, there was Ned. Course he did have a habit of wandering off to help your brother with a messed up fishing reel, but that could happen to anyone. Besides, Waymon did need help and Old Lady Simmons was sure he wouldn't lose the end of his little finger after all. Ned would give you the shirt off his back. 'Course Bob remembered when *he* gave Ned the shirt Ned was wearing right now. It had been red once upon a time. Now it was kind of a dirty orange with broad stripe of yellow on one side. "Ned, where'd that yeller paint come from?"

"Well, Bob, it's like this here. I was walkin' over here from Tom and Mary Sue's place and I seen that Missus Jensen done started paintin' that shed door again." Ned twisted halfway around until he spotted Missus Jensen in the crowd. Bob looked over at her, too, and couldn't help but see that she was trying frantically to get to the door. Poor thing, she didn't look good. Gone all kinda white in the face.

"Y'all move over there a little and let the lady out, she's lookin' kinda poorly. You take care, now Martha." Bob turned his attention back to Ned and smiled. "Good job you happened along. I don't think I've seen Martha lookin' so off her feed in donkey's years. She seemed just fine a few minutes ago. Must be havin' a relapse. Guess you just cain't never tell with some folks."

The noise level in the courtroom/hardware store was rising with Martha Jensen taking sick all the sudden and Bob banged his hammer down again. "But let's get down to business." He motioned Ned over to an empty chair at the end of the table.

"Have a seat, Ned and then I need to ask you some questions."

"You wanna know about them little cookie girls, doncha." Bob nodded, smiling a little. He was glad he had Ned to deal with. Here was a man he could trust. Good storyteller, too. Sure he made some mistakes now and again, but who didn't? Like nobody else ever set fire to a barn with a peanut butter and banana sandwich. It could happen to anyone.

"Well see, it's like this. I'd been up t'th'pond catchin' me some breakfast and was on th'way home when I saw 'em. They was just about the cutest little things you ever saw." Bob nodded, smiling, that they were. Heads bobbed throughout the room. Cute as little buttons.

"Hey, mister!"

I nodded and waved to the little girls across the road.

"Wanna buy some cookies?"

I thought a bit and wandered across the road t'see. "You two sellin' cookies? What kind ya got?" I peered into the little wagon they wuz pulling along behind them.

"We've got some vanilla ones and some peanut butter and some chocolate fudge ones." Ooh, chocolate fudge. My mouth watered like a fire hose. Nothin' I like better than some good chocolate fudge with a beer or two.

"How much you sellin' 'em for?"

"They're free samples, mister. If you like 'em, we'll come back and then you can buy the next ones."

"Free? Well, now, ain't that nice." I pondered the situation for a moment. "Y'know, I wouldn't count myself no kinda neighbor if I didn't share this. Why don't you girls come on into town with me and I'll show you around. I bet I know just who'd like your cookies best." The two girls looked at each other, smiling oddly. But they wasn't from around here. That's why they call 'em strangers. Then them sweet little faces turned to me and nodded all eager-like. They was awful cute.

Off we went, stoppin' at every house along the way to share the girls' free samples. Well, almost every house. I didn't mention Old Mr. Foster's place. That old man was right strange. Every time I come near him that there Mr. Foster got all red and puffy in the face and then he starts sputterin' and wavin' his arms around. I just don't think he's quite right in the head, y'know. Sad really. He'd been just fine when I was over helpin' him sort out his plumbin' problems. Poor man, had trouble with his septic tank *and* his well on the same day. Why, if I hadn't shown up, Mr. Foster might never have found that problem with his well. Course, he took real sick right after that. That musta been what made him so strange. If it weren't for bad luck, some folks just wouldn't have no luck a-tall.

By evenin' them little girls' cookies was just about gone. I always get a nice warm glow that comes from helping people. Well, sometimes it comes from standing too close to a gas range, but still. I done good that day and figgered I deserved a little reward. Bob's missus had been cookin' up a right nice smellin' 'possum stew when we stopped at their place. I decided to go back by and have dinner with them.

"We got to go home now, Mister. Thanks for helping us out." The girls whispered to each other for a moment. "Hey, Mister, you got a car? It's getting awful late and we've got a long way to walk home."

"I'm sorry, honey, but I ain't got me no car." Dang. My warm fuzzy feeling just kinda faded out. How could I let them two cute little things walk all that way home in the dark? Their folks' would be worried sick if they didn't get home soon. The girls was whispering to each other again when I got one of the best ideas I ever had. "I ain't got a car, but my buddy Otis does. C'mon, I know he'll let me borry it."

I got to say, I was back to feelin' pretty good about things by the time we got to Otis' house... Otises' house... Otis's... the place where my good buddy Otis lived. The windows was dark and even the yeller dog that'd been hangin' around lately was sleepin' quietly under the porch. Come to think of it, the whole town seemed kinda quiet tonight. Oh, well. Otis musta walked over to see Tom and Mary Sue. There was his new black truck, sittin' in the yard next to his old, not quite black anymore truck. I thought the block under the right front wheel looked like it was sinkin' into the ground some. I coulda fixed it, but decided it could wait until after I ran them little cookie girls home.

"C'mon, girls, hop in." I opened the driver's door and waved the girls up into the cab all gentlemanly-like. "Just slide on over and we'll get going. Wouldn't want your folks to worry none."

"Mister, ain't you gonna ask your friend first?"

"Naaah, don't look like he's home anyway. Otis won't mind.

Look, he even leaves his keys in the truck, just in case." I pulled down the sun visor, but the keys weren't there. "Um." Next I checked under the seat and felt around. Came up with a couple of shotgun shells, an empty snuff tin and a pork rind, but no keys. "Now don't that beat all. Otis done forgot to leave the keys. That boy'd forget his head if'n it weren't glued on just right." But I didn't let that stop me. I knows my way 'round the underside of a dashboard. "Ah-ha! Here we go. If y'know what yer doin', you don't need no keys." Didn't take but a minute with the wires afore the truck's engine turned over just as nice as y'please. Purred like a kitten. I just gave those little cuties a smile and put the truck into gear. Danged if that blamed engine didn't just shudder and die afore it moved an inch. I couldn't believe it. "Otis ain't been takin' very good care of this here truck. It shouldn't oughta do that." How could I take these sweet little things out in a truck that was acting like this? "There's nothing for it, girls, I'm gonna have to have a quick look under the hood. You two just wait right here. I think I know what's wrong and it'll only take a minute."

I just grabbed that there little toolbox out of the back of the cab then climbed out and popped the hood. The engine gleamed in the glow of the front yard's mercury vapor light. It was a real shame. Otis should know better than to let his truck get into this state. Shore, it was clean, but clean don't mean *squat* if the blamed truck dies when you put it into gear. I dug around until I found the right tools.

An hour and thirty minutes later, I was done. I put away the wrenches, screwdrivers, hacksaw and duct tape, closed the hood. I just tossed them silly extra parts they always put in into the back of the old truck. Otis didn't have no rag in his toolbox, so I wiped my greasy hands on the back of my pants, climbed back into the cab and settled into that cushy leather seat. Wouldn't want to muck up that shiny new steering wheel. "That should do 'er, little ladies. Let's give 'er another try." I grabbed them wires once again and afore long the engine turned over with an ear-splitting roar. I knowed I was grinnin' like a fool, but it just felt so good to do somethin' nice for a friend. I shouted over the noise, "Now *that's* what a engine's s'posed to sound like!" I popped it into gear and though the entire one-ton truck shuddered and bucked, the engine kept going. Y'know, I really liked working on stuff with my friends, but sometimes it was nice t'just get the job done all by my ownself.

We roared slowly out of the strangely still town. The truck still wasn't running quite right, so I didn't want to push it any more than I had to. I figured it would get us where we needed to go and bring me back, but no need to go too fast. I decided me and Otis needed to sit down and have a nice long talk about proper care of fine machinery.

Then, just as we turned up the road that led to the pond, I could see what looked like torchlight movin' all jerky-like through the woods off the road. The engine raced even harder as I stopped the truck to see what was going on.

"Don't stop, Mister! We gotta get home! Please don't stop!" Both girls looked plumb terrified and I was right torn between taking them on home and my natural curiosity about what might be going on in the woods. Maybe there was a big 'coon hunt and I was missin' it! Much as I loved a good 'coon hunt, though, I knew I had a responsibility to get these girls home and you know me, I ain't nothin' if not responsible.

"It's just a 'coon hunt, I s'pect, honey. Nothin' to get upset over." I got the truck to shudder into gear and kept going. Damn transmission. The girls turned around and stared wide-eyed out the back window. "Now, where 'bouts do you two live?"

The girls turned back around and crouched in the seat. "We live a long way from here, but our folks' are campin' not far from the pond up there." One of the girls pointed to one of the old roads that went up into what used to be the national forest before the world ended. It was badly overgrown, but I figured the truck could handle it ok.

Just as I started to turn off the pond road, I saw flashes of light in the rearview mirror. That 'coon musta turned this way. That settled it. No way could I count myself no kind o'friend and neighbor if I didn't do my part to help out now. I stopped the truck, but decided not to shut it off. This wouldn't take but a minute and them wires was gettin' kinda brittle-like. I grabbed the shotgun off the gun rack, and loaded it up with the two shells I found under the seat.

"You girls just hang on here. I won't be but a minute and then we'll be on our way again." Two little faces glowed unnaturally in the moonlight as they peered out of black pits where their eyes should be. I shook my head at the things bein' hungry could do to ya. I was surely lookin' forward that 'possum stew at Bob's. I on walked toward them torches feelin' like them girls was watching me through the open driver's door. Didn't blame 'em a bit. This was the best part of a 'coon hunt.

As I moved away from the roar of the truck's engine, I started to hear the hounds. They was on the scent. That there 'coon had them real ticked off, too. Probably one o'them big males. The hunters' voices weren't far behind, but they sounded odd. Almost like they was scared of somethin'. Course, who wouldn't be scared of losin' a prime 'coon. They's damn good eatin'.

I took a look around and picked me a spot. The worst thing that could happen would be if'n that 'coon got across this here road and into the thicker forest on the other side. So, I'd just set up right here and wait. Then, if the hounds didn't tree the critter first, I'd bag it when it broke cover. Seein' as how them torches was movin' pretty damn quick it shouldn't be no more'n a minute or so. 'Coon don't like torchlight. Nosireebob. That's when somethin' crashed through the underbrush at the side of the road. I had me my gun up and fired both barrels before the 'coon cleared the ditch. Damn! That was a big critter! Then, right behind, another broke through and then another. They seemed awful big there in the shadows, but the night sometimes plays tricks on the eyes.

I stood up and waved my arms, trying to scare the live ones back toward the other hunters. Then, they stood up and ran right past me! Damn, they wasn't 'coons! As they came out of the shadows and into the bright moonlight I could see 'em clear as day. They was *yombies*! I brought my gun up again, then remembered I'd already fired both barrels. Before I could shout, they'd jumped into the truck and roared up the track, taking them cute little cookie girls with them.

The lead hounds raced on past me, still in the chase even though the truck's taillights had already disappeared from sight. Tom and crazy old Mr. Foster panted close behind. Before either of 'em could say a word, the fading roar of the truck's engine was replaced by the sickening crunch of metal quickly followed by a deep boom. Fire blazed up into the night sky for a moment and then settled down to a warm glow that marked the end of the yombies and the borrowed truck.

"And that's what happened." Ned sighed. "Them poor little girls." Most of the townspeople in Bob's Hardware and Farm Goods store made sympathetic noises as they, too, thought about the tragic end of those poor little cookie girls. Not to mention Otis' truck... Otises' truck... Otis's... that there truck Otis used to own.

Mr. Foster shoved his way to the front of the crowd, turning bright red and sputtering. "POOR LITTLE GIRLS? Are you people CRAZY? They were YOMBIES! They tried to KILL us! How many of you ate those goddamn cookies? How many of you would be dead by now if some of us hadn't noticed what was going on?" He glared at the crowd and then turned back to Ned sitting next to Y'r Honor Bob's judgin' table. "YOU! You did this! YOU brought them here!" Mr. Foster looked wildly at the faces around him. "Can't you people see what he's *done*? Can't you see this man is a *menace*? He's worse than any yombie! He poisoned my well! He nearly cut Waymon's finger off! Otis! First he *stole* your truck and then he *blew it up*!" Mr. Foster was almost panting now, obviously distraught due to recent events. "You don't see it, do you? None of you see it. He burns down a barn and you just smile, shake your heads and go back to your dinners. He's going to kill us *all*! We've got to stop him!"

Everyone had gotten very quiet during old Mr. Foster's outburst. Bob crooked a finger at Aunt Minnie who shoved her way through to the front of the crowd. "Aunt Minnie, would you mind helping Mr. Foster home? He's right upset over all this and ain't thinkin' straight."

Aunt Minnie took Mr. Foster by the shoulder and nudged him fairly gently toward the door. His face got redder and puffed up. He started his sputtering again and waved his arms around. The crowd parted to let the pair through. Not that it mattered much to the two of them, but at least no one got any broken bones from being in Aunt Minnie's way when she was on a mission.

Ned sat with his head bowed. He sighed and looked up at Bob. "Poor old Mr. Foster. He just ain't been right in t'head since he got sick that time." Bob and most of the rest of the crowd nodded sagely. Truer words they'd never heard. "And Otis? I am right sorry about leaving your truck runnin' for them yombies to steal."

Otis nodded then shrugged his shoulders. "'Sokay, Ned. It could happen to anyone."

THE END

Julia Blackshear Kosatka lived a long time ago in a galaxy far, far away (Houston, Texas, actually). From time to time, she is still called upon to do battle with the forces of darkness (to be honest, she works in Higher Ed, sheeyeah, like there's a *difference*). There being no Bubbas in her Empire (except at family reunions, of course), writing this story was an amazing feat of talent and creativity (c'mon, pull the other one). She's the mother of a nine-year-old daughter (kid's waaaaay smarter than she is, btw – *Hey!* Whose side are you on?) and is forced to share her castle (itty-bitty apartment) with two fierce predators (they stalk the wild cat food like nobody's business). Her Imperial healers (they wear spiffy white coats, doncha know) hope to lift the curse that has plagued her for centuries (the new meds should kick in any time now). In the meantime, she's had to sell her soul to a demon (the editor) in exchange for her life (as in, *Selina won't kill me for being so late turning this in if I feed her kegs and kegs of cheapass beer the next time I see her*).   Her first story, "Bones of the Dead" (no Bubbas and no jokes, sorry folks, but there *is* blood and implied sex) appeared in the Summer 2001 issue of Black Gate Magazine.

THE PSYCHO PIGS MEET THE YUMBIE BITCH FROM HELL

Bill D. Allen

We called ourselves the Psycho Pigs. It looked real good on a T-shirt–pig in sunglasses with blazing tailpipes for tusks. We'd spent weekends riding together for about a year. I had a Road King, Ned rode an old Panhead, Jessy had a Heritage Softtail, and Freebird owned a brand spankin' new Electraglide Ultra Classic–that goddamned thing cost more than my house trailer.

We worked during the week. I had a factory job. Ned (when he was working) was a welder. Jessy cooked meth, and no one knew what the hell Freebird did.

Well, when the world went to shit, we just sorta kept it up. We scrounged oil, spare parts, modified the bikes to burn alcohol. The meetings were still every weekend at Greybeards, what used to be a damn fine little bar. All it has nowdays is moonshine liquor, Spam sandwiches and rat on a stick– mesquite smoked though, and pretty damned tasty.

But what we was missing was a tall cold one. An amber, beads of sweat rolling down the side, liquid piece of heaven. None of us had drunk a beer in two years.

One day, a drifter came through. He was riding a Sportster that had so much shit tied to it, he looked like an Okie from the Dustbowl. He told us he'd been to the Promised Land– Sturgis. The apocalypse didn't slow down Sturgis none. It just scraped off the civilized bullshit that held it back before. The rally of all rallies was still going strong, and best of all they had cold beer.

We got the itch to go. We planned and scoured around for gear. Tried to work out a route to avoid the war between the Bikers for Jesus and the Church of Elvis, and made sure to steer clear of them yumbie ridden big cities.

I planned on packing some firepower too, in case them damn UFO bastards decided to mess with us. Figured some double-aught buck up their green asses would put an end to that abduction shit real quick.

I say "we" planned. All of us, but Freebird that is. He just sorta showed up for the meetings and sat in the corner, nodding "profoundly". But, we figured if there was something he didn't like, he had the opportunity to speak up. If he decided to bitch later, fuck him.

When the day finally arrived, we met in front of Greybeards at the crack of dawn. I had my gear packed and ready to go. When I pulled up, Jessy was already there, and he had a passenger. It was a girl. Or should I say it had once been a girl. It was a yumbie. But she did have some really nice titties.

"What in the hell do you have there?" I asked.

"Her? I call her Lulu. I picked her up last week. What do ya think?"

She looked to have been about 19 when she died. He had her bungee corded to his sissy bar, and she was struggling to get free. If Jessy hadn't been keeping the bike balanced, she would have knocked it plum off the kickstand.

Her long blonde hair was a nasty rat's nest, she wore cut off shorts and go-go boots.

Jessy had a leather muzzle over her mouth—-good idea if you didn't want your brains eaten. She was naked from the waist up, and like I said, she had some impressive and perky tits, although they were a bit blue. The left one was tattooed with a butterfly. Which might have been cute if 9 out of 10 tattooed tits didn't have a damn butterfly on them. Plus, like I said, she was as pale as a Safeway chicken.

"Who you figure she was," I asked.

"I dunno. Maybe a computer porn babe that sucked too many computer rays and got yumbied when the virus came, maybe she was a dancer? Hell, there ain't no way of knowing, but I figure looking like that she weren't no Sunday School teacher. I found her sneaking around the back of the house last week. She damn near got me before I hogtied her."

"I guess you intend to take her along?"

"Yep. I know you won't believe this, but she is the best piece of ass I've ever had."

I was proud of myself cause I kept a straight face. "I believe you–I assume you ain't counting kin. I just think you're fucking crazy."

"Hear me out. I've been working on something." He dug

in the saddle bag, and pulled out a syringe and a bottle of some reddish liquid. He filled the syringe, then grinned. "Check this out."

He injected Lulu with the hypo. Almost immediately, she slowed her struggling, then some pink started coming through the dirty pale blue skin.

"It works pretty good for about an hour. But the more I use it, the longer it seems to last. Usually that's when we get together. She's even warm!" He emphasized the point by grabbing himself a handful of tit. "Here, try for yourself."

"No Jessy, I don't want to feel up your dead ass girlfriend. She's a yumbie! She aint' never gonna be nothing but a brain eating killing machine!"

"What about the cure? If I keep experimenting, I can make her come back full time. I'm smoothing it out with some brake fluid and Red Devil lye—"

"Jessy, running a meth lab don't make you a goddamned scientist! I can't believe you are actually screwing that.. thing. You have got to be the sickest bastard I have ever met."

"Come on, Jimbo. What choice do we got? There ain't no pussy, no where. At least not for the likes of us. Most of the warlords here and there got pussy, but they ain't sharing. Sure, there's the Amazons. You can tamp that ass as much as you want for a day, and then they tear you apart like a bunch of weight watchers at a buffet restaurant—just so's you don't get uppity."

"There's the whores in town," I said.

"Yep, but they cost ever damn thing you own, and to tell the truth I think health wise, you're better off fucking the yumbies."

I shook my head. "I still think your pecker is gonna fall off."

About this time Ned shows up. "Holy sheep shit! Where'd you find that fine piece of ass?"

I knew then that the yumbie bitch was going to be coming with us, because if nothing else, the Psycho Pigs are a democracy, and that always left things two to one. Jessy and Ned versus me. Ned of course, was a dumbass.

Freebird always abstained. Speaking of Freebird, the son of a bitch stood us up so we left without him.

We were on the road to Sturgis. I had a tank bag strapped on the bike that had a clear pocket for my coffee stained old Walmart map. I'd looted the road atlas in the early days after the world went to shit. Right away the looters hit the liquor stores, the Walmarts and bait shops – pretty much in that order, too.

It was the same all over. The city council and the other local politicians that didn't die right off or turn yumbie, had to step in and arrange a rationing system.

That lasted about three hours before they were beaten up, screwed in the ass and shot by the early warlords—not necessarily in that order neither. The biggest, baddest motherfuckers who were around, the ex-cons, general hill apes and banjo picking ogres pretty much took over and it's been that way since. There was a definite pecking order.

Anyway, by the time I had my chance to do some "shopping", about the only thing left was books and most folks were using them for toilet paper or fire starters. The road atlas had been a lucky find.

Poor Ned got his turn right after an 80 year old woman that used snuff. He'd have pushed his way in before her, but the look of that dried shit in the corner of her mouth spooked him. Not that I blame him, she looked pretty damned mean. Anyway, Ned didn't get anything worth a shit.

I heard a roar of pipes behind me and I watched in the mirror as Jessy caught up to me. He was waving with his left hand for me to pull over. I headed over to the shoulder and stopped.

"What's up?" I asked.

"Lulu needs to take a leak," He said.

"What? Yumbies don't piss!"

"See! I told you she was getting cured up."

"How did she tell you?"

"We got a code worked out. She butts me in the back with her muzzle—"

"Whatever! Just get it over with, we're burning daylight."

I watched as he unstrapped her from the bike and led her over to the bushes. Ned was eyeing around to catch him a peek.

"Why don't you just ask Jessy to let you take a look at the goods? Hell, he'd probably even let you take her on a test ride if you cleaned her up when you got done."

Ned blushed. "Shit. I wouldn't feel right about that. Heh,

heh."

"But you wouldn't mind an accidental look, right?"

Ned smiled and nodded.

Ten fucking piss stops later, it was just starting to get dark. That's when we came across Freebird. He had set up a campsite and already had a fire burning. I spotted him sitting by the fire and sipping on a cup of coffee. I raised my hand and signaled and then we all stopped.

"What's up, brother?" Freebird asked.

"How did you beat us here? Where did you find coffee?"

Freebird just smiled and nodded. "The Freebird has skills. I set things up here for y'all. I'm gonna head out and scout the road up yonder. I'll see you tomorrow. Keep the rubber side down and the shiny side up."

"Okay, whatever," I said.

"Live to ride, man" Freebird said, then started his Electraglide and left.

"Yeah, 'it's not the destination, it's the journey'. 'Loud pipes save lives' and all that shit," I mumbled and went to unpack the bike.

I had just got to sleep when I felt someone tap me on the shoulder. I jerked awake and shoved the barrel of my little sawed off .410 shotgun into Jessy's face.

"Jesus!" he screamed.

I put the gun down and sighed. "What do you want?"

"Lulu wants to sleep here."

"What?"

"Lulu is a little cold and she wants to take this spot. You see, you are a little closer to the fire, and the tree and the rock here kinda protect you from the wind."

I stared at him.

"I wouldn't ask for me, but you know how it is."

I didn't have a damned clue "how it was." But I no longer considered Ned the stupidest person I had ever met. "Did she tell you that in code?"

"No, she's started to talk a little. I think she's really getting better. Here, look for yourself."

He brought her closer to the fire, and I could see that he was right. Maybe it was a trick of the campfire light, but she was looking fresh and pink. Cleaned up a little bit and she would be mighty fine! Hell, I maybe even liked her dirty a little bit more.

What in the hell was I thinking?

"Here, you and your yumbie bitch can have my spot. I'll go over there, but don't wake me up again." I waved my gun in his face to make the point, then I drug my wool blanket and the rolled up leather jacket I used for a pillow to the cold side of the camp. "Fucking yumbie bitch," I grumbled as I went back to sleep.

This time I awoke to a blood-curdling scream. I jumped straight up, throwing my blanket and aiming my gun in the direction of the commotion. My eyes were struggling to focus in the dim light of the dying fire.

Ned was rolling around on the ground yelling his head off. Jessy was holding Lulu. Her muzzle was off, and there was blood around her mouth.

"Oh shit! Jessy, get out of the way, I'll blast her!" I screamed and ran toward them.

Jessy turned toward me and stood defensively in front of the yumbie. "No! Jimbo, don't! Wait! It's not what you think!"

Ned screamed, "Shoot her ass! She bit my dick off!"

I froze, my gun aimed in Lulu's direction. Yumbies did not normally go for the crotch. "She did what?"

Ned was crying. "She bit my dick off! The bitch bit it off! Kill her!"

"How did she get to your dick, Ned?"

Jessy pointed down at Ned. "That stupid bastard took her muzzle off and stuck his pecker in her mouth!"

At that moment, Ned resumed his rightful rank as the dumbest son of a bitch I have ever heard of. "You did what?" I asked.

"It don't matter. She still needs to be kilt! Look at my pecker!"

I looked the other way as he tried to show me his bleeding dick.

"She didn't bite it off," Jessy said. "She only bit at it. She was asleep and she just clamped down by reflex. She's not a yumbie no more. She's cured! You can't kill her!"

I risked a peek at Ned, and sure enough, there was a bloody bite mark, but everything seemed to be intact. "You'll be okay, Ned."

"What if it was your dick? You'd kill her then, wouldn't you?"

"I ain't stupid enough to stick my pecker in the mouth of a yumbie!"

"She ain't a yumbie!" Jessy yelled. "Tell them, honey."

I looked at Lulu clearly for the first time. She was wiping the blood from her mouth and making gagging sounds

"Oh my god!" she said. "Does anyone have any mouthwash, this is so gross! You nasty pervert!" she yelled and kicked at Ned.

"Shoot her, Jimbo!" Ned yelled.

"Well, you *are* a nasty pervert," I said.

Ned was silent. He looked at me like a kid whose balloon just popped. He glared at Jessy and Lulu, then stuffed his pecker back in his jeans, got up and started to walk off.

"I didn't mean it personal or nothing," I said, trying to cheer him up.

Ned slowly packed up his gear, then he started his bike and left.

I watched him ride off. I couldn't think of a damn thing to say to him to make him come back.

"About time," Lulu said.

"Hey, Ned's my friend. He might be a dumbass, but he's good people."

"Whatever," she said, rolling her eyes.

"Come on, Lulu, Honey. Let's get back to bed," Jessy said with a grin.

"My name is not Lulu, and what makes you think I would go to bed with you. My name is Ashley, and if you come near me I really will bite your dick off!"

With that she picked up Jessy's blanket, then took my blanket too and made herself a bed next to the fire.

I looked at Jessy. "I liked her better as a yumbie."

"I heard that!" Ashley said.

"*I heard that*," I mocked back at her in a high-pitched whine. "I guess I'm supposed to crawl over there and curl up like a damn dog and sleep with my nose in my ass to keep warm?"

"I don't care what you losers do, as soon as we get to Sturgis I am leaving your sorry butts for the biggest, baddest, meanest biker I can find and I hope he whoops your ass for being so mean to me."

I looked at the gun, and I looked at the bitch. I looked at the gun, I looked at the bitch. "I'm having a hard time here, Jessy."

"Give her a chance, after all, it's..." he mouthed the word "pussy."

"As long as I have hands, I don't need pussy like that," I said.

About that time, Ned came rumbling back to camp. I went up to him to apologize. "Listen, Ned. I'm sorry. Hell, I'm a fucking pervert, too. One time I fucked an old lady when I was collecting for newspaper money. I shouldn't judge you like that."

Ned smiled. "Don't worry about it."

"How's your pecker?"

"Fine...er...well, it *will* be fine. I found something that you guys should see. It's only about a mile down the road."

We left "Ashley the pecker biting bitch" by the fire and followed Ned down the road a piece. There, parked just off the road in some trees was a huge semi tractor-trailer. It looked new. The back door was open a crack and light spilled out from it into the night.

We sneaky peeked up to the door and when I looked in. I about shit a brick at the sight.

The inside of the trailer was customized like a fancy RV. There was Freebird's Electraglide near the door, and beyond it was Freebird himself sitting with four lovely, big titted ladies and it looked like he was drinking beer. Cold beer!

I looked at Ned and Jessy and we all nodded. On the count of three we swung the doors open and charged inside.

"What in the Wide Wide World of Sports is going on here?" I yelled.

Freebird jumped up and dropped his beer in the process.

"No!" I screamed and dropped to my knees. I tried to suck up the remains out of the shag rug. I could only get a taste of beer, actually it tasted more like hair and mud. But there was *some* beer there and it was worth it.

"Hi guys. Uh, Jimbo, I got more beer," Freebird said.

I stood up and looked him in the eye. "What is all this?"

Freebird looked devastated. "I didn't want you guys to find out this way. After all, we have the trip to Sturgis going on, and the journey, that's the thing..."

"What are you talking about? Where did all this stuff come from? Who are these girls?" I smiled and extended my hand. "My name's Jimbo, how are you lovely ladies doing tonight?"

They giggled. I love that shit.

"This is my truck. These are my employees."

"Employees?"

"Yes, you see, my real name is – John Klahrson."

"You're John Klahrson?" The name was a famous one. Before the world ended Klahrson had built a wildly successful chain of topless barbershops. A man would pay a lot of money to have a nipple in his ear while he was getting a trim. "You're the *Shave and A Haircut—Two Tits!* guy!"

"Yes, it's true. I didn't want you guys to know because I've always wanted to be a biker. That's why me and the girls here survived. We ate so much barbeque that the virus couldn't touch us."

"But surely, after the end of the world, you could have let us in on this. After all, you've got food, and beer, and puss – er – lovely ladies."

"But I didn't want to take your lives away from you. I wanted so much to be like you guys, but I couldn't. I could only playact on the weekends. Like this trip. You guys are enjoying the journey. I'm only a bystander really. And now, I've taken that away from you. It's about the journey, not the destination."

I sighed. "Don't worry about it, Freebird. Sometimes, the destination is fine and the journey sucks shit through a straw."

I sat next to one of the girls. "Now, what is your name? I think we should all have a beer and get to know each other."

The next morning, we loaded the bikes in the back of the truck and started on our way. Sturgis was after all still a kick ass destination except now we were traveling in style. The ladies, I could tell had been pretty bored with only Freebird as company, and all of us except Ned got our brains screwed out. Which would have been redundant with Ned anyway.

Ned's dick was kinda crippled. Still, Ned's girl was mighty satisfied with having to settle for what Ned *could* offer – until his tongue cramped up.

I started the truck and we pulled out of the woods onto the roadway. I hit the brakes when I saw that Ashley was there in the middle of the damn highway.

"There you are, you asshole! Where did you guys go? Did you lousy losers think it was funny just leaving me there? When we get to Sturgis, I'm gonna—"

I caught her in mid-bitch. And you know? The suspension on that truck was so good that the others didn't hardly even notice the bump.

Bill D. Allen lives in Owasso, Oklahoma and recently had an epiphany. After he cleaned it up, he realized something that had eluded him for years. It's okay to have fun. Writing for entertainment is a noble and legitimate pursuit. "Those that are too snooty to crack a smile or have a good time can kiss my bubba butt." Bill is a former reviewer for *Tangent*, former editor of Ozark Triangle Press, and has published stories in *BOTA* ("I am the fart guy!"), *Personal Demons, Stories That Won't Make Your Parents Hurl* and was frequent contributor to YARD DOG COMICS.

ABOUT THE COVER ARTIST

Keith Berdak was born at a very young age at Scott Air Force Base, Illinois in 1955, the son of an Air Force rocket scientist who really was a "rocket scientist." Growing up as an Air Force brat on various Strategic Air Command ICBM bases across the U.S. instilled in him an interest in all things scientific, particularly prehistoric plants and animals. He was also artistically inclined from the earliest age. Berdak dedicated four years to the production of Abstract Expressionist art, but gave it up after entering kindergarten. Some years later he attempted to study fine art at Lindenwood College (now a university, so they say) in St. Charles, MO, but was instead pushed toward Abstract Expressionism. He left college and pursued dual careers as both an illustrator and professional musician. Inspired by the people that he met at science fiction conventions, he retired from the rather dull St. Louis music scene in 1983 and focused on doing artwork.

Berdak's artwork is best known in the areas of Science Fiction and Fantasy illustration, with paperback and magazine cover work published in the U.S., Japan and throughout Europe. His most recognizable work is the series of cover paintings for Glen Cook's *Chronicles Of The Black Company*, published by Tor Books, and the first *Bubbas of the Apocalypse*. He has done a program cover painting for the U.S. Navy Blue Angels, and numerous pieces of commercial work. Berdak also won a Darrell Award for his short story in *BOTA*.

Berdak spent a few years in Austin, Texas doing illustrations and computer graphics for Origin Systems, Inc., and did a lot of the artwork for the popular *Ultima* adventure game series. Upon returning to Missouri he started working on various projects with Paleontologist Guy Darrough, including the preparation and restoration of a Triceratops skull and a fossil bone bed at the St. Louis Science Center. He is currently working as project illustrator (and digger) with Darrough and a group of scientists and engineers on the Missouri Ozark

Dinosaur Project, a unique dinosaur excavation currently under way in Southeastern Missouri.

In the real world, Berdak works as a graphic designer/illustrator for R.K. Stratman, Inc., where he produced custom art for silkscreen print garments for the Harley-Davidson Motor Company and its dealers. When time permits, he likes to do presentations and "Draw-along" sessions at area libraries and children's hospitals.

Yard Dog Press Titles as of This Print Date

A Bubba in Time Saves None, Edited by Selina Rosen
A Man, A Plan, (yet lacking) A Canal, Panama, Linda Donahue
Adventures of the Irish Ninja, Selina Rosen
The Alamo and Zombies, Jean Stuntz
All the Marbles, Dusty Rainbolt
Almost Human, Gary Moreau
Ancient Enemy, Lee Killouth
*The Anthology From Hell: Humorous Tales From WAY Down
     Under,* Edited by Julia S. Mandala
Ard Magister, Laura J. Underwood
Assassins Inc., Phillip Drayer Duncan
Bad City, Selina Rosen & Laura J. Underwood
Bad Lands, Selina Rosen & Laura J. Underwood
Black Rage, Selina Rosen
Blackrose Avenue, Mark Shepherd
The Boat Man, Selina Rosen
Bobby's Troll, John Lance
Bride of Tranquility, Tracy S. Morris
Bruce and Roxanne from Start to Finnish, Rie Sheridan Rose
The Bubba Chronicles, Selina Rosen
Bubba Fables, Sue P. Sinor
Bubbas Of the Apocalypse, Edited by Selina Rosen
The Burden of the Crown, Selina Rosen
Chains of Redemption, Selina Rosen
Checking On Culture, Lee Killough
Chronicles of the Last War, Laura J. Underwood
Dadgum Martians Invade the Lucky Nickel Saloon, Ken Rand
Dark and Stormy Nights, Bradley H. Sinor
Deja Doo, Edited by Selina Rosen
Dracula's Lawyer, Julia S. Mandala
Dragon's Tongue, Laura J. Underwood
The Essence of Stone, Beverly A. Hale
Fairy BrewHaHa at the Lucky Nickel Saloon, Ken Rand
The Fantastikon: Tales of Wonder, Robin Wayne Bailey
Fire & Ice, Selina Rosen
Flush Fiction, Volume I: Stories To Be Read In One Sitting, Edited
     by Selina Rosen
Flush Fiction, Volume II: Twenty Years of Letting it Go!, Edited by
     Selina Rosen
*The Four Bubbas of the Apocalypse: Flatulence, Halitosis, Incest,
     and... Ned,* Edited by Selina Rosen
The Four Redheads: Apocalypse Now!, Linda L. Donahue,
     Rhonda Eudaly, Julia S. Mandala, & Dusty Rainbolt
The Four Redheads of the Apocalypse, Linda L. Donahue,
     Rhonda Eudaly, Julia S. Mandala, & Dusty Rainbolt
The Four Redheads: The Wrath of Satan, Linda L. Donahue,

Rhonda Eudaly, Julia S. Mandala, & Dusty Rainbolt
The Garden In Bloom, Jeffrey Turner
The Geometries of Love: Poetry by Robin Wayne Bailey
The Golems Of Laramie County, Ken Rand
The Green Women, Laura J. Underwood
The Guardians, Lynn Abbey
Hammer Town, Selina Rosen
The Happiness Box, Beverly A. Hale
The Host Series: The Host, Fright Eater, Gang Approval, Selina
    Rosen
Houston, We've Got Bubbas!, Edited by Selina Rosen
How I Spent the Apocolypse, Selina Rosen
I Didn't Quite Make It To Oz, Edited by Selina Rosen
I Should Have Stayed In Oz, Edited by Selina Rosen
In the Shadows, Bradley H. Sinor
International House of Bubbas, Edited by Selina Rosen
It's the Great Bumpkin, Cletus Brown!, Katherine A. Turski
The Killswitch Review, Steven-Elliot Altman & Diane DeKelb-
    Rittenhouse
The Leopard's Daughter, Lee Killough
The Lightning Horse, John Moore
The Logic of Departure, Mark W. Tiedemann
The Long, Cold Walk To Mars, Jeffrey Turner
Marking the Signs and Other Tales Of Mischief, Laura J.
    Underwood
Material Things, Selina Rosen
Medieval Misfits: Renaissance Rejects, Tracy S. Morris
Mirror Images, Susan Satterfield
Mirror, Mirror and Other Reflections, James K. Burk
More Stories That Won't Make Your Parents Hurl, Edited by
    Selina Rosen
Music for Four Hands, Louis Antonelli & Edward Morris
My Life with Geeks and Freaks, Claudia Christian
The Necronomicrap: A Guide To Your Horoooscope, Tim Frayser
Playing With Secrets, Bradley H & Sue P. Sinor
Redheads In Love, Linda L. Donahue, Rhonda Eudaly, Julia S.
    Mandala, & Dusty Rainbolt
Reruns, Selina Rosen
Rock 'n' Roll Universe, Ken Rand
Shadows In Green, Richard Dansky
Stories That Won't Make Your Parents Hurl, Edited by Selina
    Rosen
Tales from Keltora, Laura J. Underwood
*Tales Of the Lucky Nickel Saloon, Second Ave., Laramie, Wyo-
    ming, U S of A*, Ken Rand
Tarbox Station, Rhonda Eudaly

Texistani: Indo-Pak Food From A Texas Kitchen, Beverly A. Hale
That's All Folks, J. F. Gonzalez
Through Wyoming Eyes, Ken Rand
Turn Left to Tomorrow, Robin Wayne Bailey
The Twins, Selina Rosen
Wandering Lark, Laura J. Underwood
Wings of Morning, Katharine Eliska Kimbriel
Zombies In Oz and Other Undead Musings, Robin Wayne Bailey

Fantasy Writers Asylum (A YDP Imprint):

Blood Songs
Julia Mandala
Gateway to Corimar
Julia Mandala & Linda L Donahue
Tale of the Black Heart
Linda L. Donahue

Double Dog (A YDP Imprint):

#1:
Of Stars & Shadows,
Mark W. Tiedemann
This Instance Of Me,
Jeffrey Turner

#2:
Gods and Other Children,
Bill D. Allen
Tranquility, Tracy Morris

#3:
Home Is the Hunter,
James K. Burk
Farstep Station,
Lazette Gifford

#4:
Sabre Dance,
Melanie Fletcher
The Lunari Mask,
Laura J. Underwood

#5:
House of Doors,
Julia Mandala
Jaguar Moon,
Linda A Donahue

Just Cause (A YDP Imprint):

The Bitter End
Selina Rosen

Death Under the Crescent Moon
Dusty Rainbolt

The Ghost Writer
Selina Rosen

It's Not Rocket Science: Spirituality for the Working-Class Soul
Selina Rosen

Meditations of a Hoarder
Melinda LaFevers

Not My Life
Selina Rosen

The Pit
Selina Rosen

Plots and Protagonists: A Reference Guide for Writers
Mel. White

Vanishing Fame
Selina Rosen

Non-YDP titles we distribute:

Chains of Freedom
Chains of Destruction
Jabone's Sword
Queen of Denial
Recycled
Strange Robby
Sword Masters
Selina Rosen

Three Ways to Order:

1. Write us a letter telling us what you want, then send it along with your check or money order (made payable to Yard Dog Press) to: Yard Dog Press, 710 W. Redbud Lane, Alma, AR 72921-7247

2. Use selinarosen@cox.net or lynnstran@cox.net to contact us and place your order. Then send your check or money order to the address above. *This has the advantage of allowing you to check on the availability of short-stock items such as T-shirts and back-issues of Yard Dog Comics.*

3. Contact us as in #1 or #2 above and pay with a credit card or by debit from your checking account. Either give us the credit card information in your letter/Email/phone call, or go to our website and use our shopping carts. If you send us your information, please include your name as it appears on the card, your credit card number, the expiration date, and the 3 or 4-digit security code after your signature on the back (CVV). Please remember that we will include media rate (minimum $3.00) S/H for mailing in the lower 48 states.

Watch our website at
www.yarddogpress.com
for news of upcoming projects
and new titles!!

A Note to Our Readers

We at Yard Dog Press understand that many people buy used books because they simply can't afford new ones. That said, and understanding that not everyone is made of money, we'd like you to know something that you may not have realized. Writers only make money on new books that sell. At the big houses a writer's entire future can hinge on the number of books they sell. While this isn't the case at Yard Dog Press, the honest truth is that when you sell or trade your book or let many people read it, the writer and the publishing house aren't making any money.

As much as we'd all like to believe that we can exist on love and sweet potato pie, the truth is we all need money to buy the things essential to our daily lives. Writers and publishers are no different.

We realize that these "freebies" and cheap books often turn people on to new writers and books that they wouldn't otherwise read. However we hope that you will reconsider selling your copy, and that if you trade it or let your friends borrow it, you also pass on the information that if they really like the author's work they should consider buying one of their books at full price sometime so that the writer can afford to continue to write work that entertains you.

We appreciate all our readers and *depend* upon their support.

Thanks,
The Editorial Staff
Yard Dog Press

PS – Please note that "used" books without covers have, in most cases, been stolen. Neither the author nor the publisher has made any money on these books because they were supposed to be pulped for lack of sales.

Please do not purchase books without covers.